TEGAN LAVIER

Shades of Blue

First published by Tegan Lavier 2026

First edition

ISBN (paperback): 978-1-7645834-0-4
ISBN (hardcover): 978-1-7645834-1-1

This book was professionally typeset on Reedsy.
Find out more at reedsy.com

No matter the truth, I will not allow the red destruction.
No matter my youth, I shan't threat the orange of regret.
To my child self. Forever tinted in the yellow of nostalgia and innocence.
Never to be destroyed.
Forever protected, in a bubble of green.
However the threat of blue rain, never to be captured in chains.
For purple fear, shall never destroy the sphere.
And pink desire, will never harm the choir.
Eternally painted in the colours of life.

- Shades of Blue

Contents

Preface

THIS BOOK CONTAINS **CONTENT WARNINGS**.

Growing up in a small town, I learned quite quickly that the things you do and say matters. I was raised by a single mother, along with my older sister, until my mother married when I was 10. I now have four younger siblings.

Throughout my life, I have been introduced to many uncontrollable situations. With reflection, I've been able to pinpoint a lot of things that I'd have done differently If I had the chance to. It took a long time for me to forgive myself for the decisions I've made, and I'm still not completely there.

I have met many people in only 20 years and have been introduced to many different cultures, backgrounds and pasts. I've learned to observe people and to respect that every person is different, because everyone experiences life differently.

My family has been heavily impacted by drugs, alcohol, and domestic violence, and has resulted in a lot of children in my family being split apart.

Many stories come out about those dark years and the things some of those children went through, it'd make any normal human physically sick.

I've also seen a lot of people my age affected by similar issues, and many differing problems. I've seen people my age taking their lives, or taking the lives of others, due to the lack of love and the inability to share their voice.

Children are not safe, and have not been for a long time. I believe it is the way we are raised, that depicts the quality of life we will have.

Generational trauma has been a long cause of excuse for a very long time, and it is becoming undeniably controlling.

I don't want to see anymore children being taken advantage of, or feeling like there is no way out of the cycle.

I don't want young girls to feel inferior to angry men anymore. I don't want young boys to feel invalidated or fearful.

I want people to read this story and to understand that there is always a way out. That no matter how dark it may seem, there will always be a light to help you out.

It should not be so common for people to relate to the topics depicted in this story. That is how you know we have failed as a society.

The actions, and selfishness of others is the reason so many people die so young or live with regret. It is the reason I gained 4 foster cousin/siblings in my teens. Because children have repeatedly been failed and left unprotected.

The actions of someone else can and has destroyed the lives of others. A mere memory is enough.

This book has been inspired via my own relationships- friends, family, previous partners.

CONTENT WARNINGS

THIS BOOK CONTAINS **CONTENT WARNINGS**.

Warnings for Content:

- Drug Addiction
- Alcohol Addiction
- Discussion of Addiction
- Underage drinking & drug use
- Underage Sexual Acts
- Discussion of Sexual Assault
- Discussion of Childhood Sexual Assault
- Suicide
- Attempted Suicide
- Aggravated Violence
- Domestic Violence
- Discussion of Violence Against Animals
- Discussion of Weapons
- Drug Distribution
- Childhood Mutism
- Cheating
- Bullying
- Discussion of Low Financial Income
- Discussion of Accidental Bodily Harm
- Discussion of Mental Health
- Discussion of Death
- Active use of Profanity

- Threatening Language

This book does discuss topics that may be sensitive to some viewers. Please read this book with caution if you are susceptible to the triggers listed.
The purpose of this book is to spread awareness for those who are affected by these topics and to spread the warning signs for certain topics.
The purpose of this book is to allow survivors a voice, and to be able to express themselves openly without judgment or fear of judgment.
Your story matters.
Viewer discretion is advised.

Prologue

Days were brighter then. Denis and Ronald Glass were born to a young Francine and an older Nigel. Francine's family were originally from Provence, France, but migrated to Australia when Francine was thirteen for work.

Nigel- a rugged Australian boy raised by an absent father and a mother who barely made ends meet. Classic tale.

Francine met Nigel at school. Her first and only boyfriend, before falling pregnant at sixteen. Nigel's parents refused caring for their baby. Back then, Nigel's father was around, and the second he heard Nigel got a girl pregnant, he beat Nigel black and blue. Nigel's mother pleaded he rid the problem, because they'd never have enough money to support a baby.

Francine's parents had a much different outlook. Though, Nigel neither had much interest- not until they'd discovered she'd be giving birth to twin boys. Suddenly everyone was excited at the prospect- even Nigel's father.

Francine's parents bought everything- all the clothes, the bassinets, changing mats, swaddles, dummies, nappies, wipes, everything they needed to successfully raise twin babies.

Denis- who would be named after Nigel's father- and Ronald, who would be named after his Grandfather- would be born on December 22nd, 1977. Born into a country still battling the Intergenerational trauma of the Stolen Generation.

Nigel would be in and out of the boys' lives while growing up. He was working a lot, and when he wasn't working he was drinking. Alcohol is a gene that runs through the Glass bloodline like dimples.

Nigel wasn't a bad father, but he wasn't much a father at all. Francine did the best she could. Her father would die of lung cancer soon after the twins'

6th birthday. Her parents were much older then Nigel's, so it was only a matter of time before all the weight would remain on her shoulders.

It was easier once the boys were in school- then she could work and help Nigel provide while her Mother stayed home, nurturing her frail bones and cooking French dinners whenever they had the ingredients.

Regardless of the life that surrounded her, Francine had never sipped a drop of alcohol- she was, though, a smoker. But never around the boys.

Ronald- the older twin by 3 minutes- was always a good student at school. He was smart- not incredible- but smart enough to do well and Ronald always made enough friends to share with Denis. Denis could never make his brain focus- and it seemed he suffered some of his fathers short temper genes. Every time he'd sit in class, all he could surround himself with was the sounds of tapping pencils and chewing gum. His eyes would never center on whatever complication his teacher would speak on.

Once the twins entered High School, Denis became friends with another boy named Carter Truette. One of the few African boys at the school who lived with his Australian cousins. Back then he had a slight accent from his childhood. Denis never really knew what happened to Carter's parents- he never liked to talk about them, and Denis never really asked.

The two weren't best friends- but they both related on how much they struggled with school. Neither of them really attended classes, and when they did, they'd often use the excuse of bathroom breaks and then never return.

Denis started stealing Francine's cigarettes to share with Carter behind the school church. Soon enough their small friendship of two grew to a group. Mostly older boys who had access to alcohol and had enough confidence to steal from petrol stations and the handbags of teachers. Jaxton Ritcher was the worse. He'd managed to steal a teachers purse while engaging in conversation with her, and she didn't notice it was gone until the end of the school day.

Ronald never snitched on his brother- he'd always felt bad for him. Francine and Nigel were always too busy to notice that he needed help. But he was never a terrible kid- Ronald just believed Denis was misunderstood.

He tried to tutor Denis a few times with home projects from school, but Denis would never receive information and could never keep his chair stools on the ground.

Once the two left school, Ronald started working and studying his Diploma toward construction and engineering, while Denis bounced around between jobs- similar to Nigel. He'd never keep a job for longer then a few months, as he'd either spark an argument with a customer, or his boss. That would be a nuisance enough to terminate him.

Denis' first time getting arrested was when he was 21 after his boss had fired him from a packing factory for stealing product on camera. His boss settled to not call the police but Denis refused to leave the building and resorted to violence. Denis was locked up and Ronald had to bail him out. Eventually he'd be let off with a short warning and a fine.

By 24, Ronald was already making a steady income and dating a beautiful lady by the name of Nicole. Opposed sister of Jaxton and Blade Ritcher.

Denis, at the time, was fresh out of a job and kindly, Ronald offered him a small and quiet position under his management.

It was around that year that Nicole would introduce Denis to one of her childhood best friends, Charlotte Mitchell. A tall girl with dark hair and a lawyer for a father. A richer family from Rupert Mitchell and Uma Mitchell- and their three beautiful daughters, Charlotte, Hannah, and Meredith.

Denis and Charlotte went on a few short dates, but it seemed Charlotte was a lot more interested in him, then he her. Charlotte's father was also not the biggest fan of a man like Denis. Rupert knew the Glass family- everyone did. Everyone knew what they were like, and everyone was shocked when Ronald came out the way he did. All perfect and prim and successful.

Of course, the story could end uncomplicated and simple there- but that wouldn't be much of a story, would it?

A year into his relationship with Charlotte, Denis started batting his eyes for a different young lady- one who seemed much closer then anyone expected.

Meredith Mitchell- aged 16 at the time. Charlotte would have no idea about Denis' infidelity with her younger sister. Often describing Meredith as the black sheep of the family. A troubled girl with a taste for attention and adrenaline. Already secretly smoking marijuana and sneaking out of their large house to meet with older boys by age 14. Meredith was also always remembered for her uneven mood. Though, her parents would never admit it.

One minute, she could be the most simple, quiet girl. And at the flick of the switch, she could be crying, or threatening her sisters with a knife. Her parents never wanted to believe that something was wrong. Her mother assuming that maybe she was just spoiled.

Meredith flaunted her pregnancy with Denis like a kid with a new toy. She and Charlotte had gotten into an argument over dinner and Meredith blurted out their secret against Denis' wishes. The look in her eye as menacing and evil as one could imagine. Her laugh echoing as Charlotte looked to Denis for his denial.

But her wishes fell on empty ears. Denis couldn't deny it anymore. Charlotte's eyes welting with the efforts of unsuccessful conceptions replaying in the back of her mind as her little sister laughed a hysterical tune as she successfully shut her older sister up.

Regardless of the betrayal and deceit, Meredith's parents didn't shut her out, and instead bought Denis and Meredith a small, low end house on the river side of the city.

Meredith dropped out of school once she entered her second trimester. Ronald, too, tried to help Denis and Meredith financially.

On the day of their first child's birth, Francine would die in the same hospital from Pneumonia.

Cipher Denis Glass, born October 23rd 2002. A beautiful boy with big green eyes, looking just like his father and uncle did when they were born. His first outing being his Grandmothers funeral, only a week after his birth.

The next few years Denis would describe as an insufferable blur. Meredith and Denis' relationship was never perfect. She could never handle the sound of Cipher's cries. She always tried to breastfeed but he never latched and overtime she grew a deep hatred for motherhood.

Cipher would've never noticed though. All Denis ever allowed his children to see were the happy parts. The only parts that consisted in colours and light.

But Meredith and Denis were always arguing, and Denis was only ever taught to resolve conflict in one way, and that is to get drunk. Denis' friends threw the best house parties, so Denis and Meredith would often attend to resolve their issues. Constantly having to take Cipher to a friends house to be babysat- such as Cooper 'Eyeball' Brown and his missus and kid. Or if Eyeball happened to be at those parties too, Cipher would spend the night at Uncle Ronald's.

Meredith would often reach her breaking points with their arguments and would threaten her life against Denis, and would threaten lying to the police about him abusing her if he ever left her.

They'd have these intense arguments, sometimes so loud neighbors would call police- but then they'd go to bed that night cuddling and reminiscing about their blossoming love. Meredith would often make Denis hand knitted bracelets and rings and the two would suddenly forget they were ever mad.

Soon enough the couple would welcome their second child- Fiona Meredith Glass, born on April 26th 2005. Regardless of the fact that the two could barely last three days without an argument, and the fact that Meredith clearly hated being a mother, the two tried for months to conceive Fiona, and were relieved when the test was finally positive.

Maybe Denis saw another child as a sign. Maybe the family did have a few guardian angels in the sky.

When little Cipher was only three years old, Denis' childhood friend Jaxton Ritcher would die in a house fire. A fire that nearly killed three friends instead of one. Eyeball showed up to the house that night too with Carter- he was the one to call Denis and tell him that Jaxton was dead.

The death of a childhood friend was hard for Denis, but he had a family to look after, so Its apparent that Denis may have never fully received closure for that event.

Nicole, despite her and Jaxton never having a bonding sibling relationship, was distraught when she discovered he was dead. She blamed his lover,

Rose Lavery, for his death. Though, it would be ruled an accident. Someone simply forgot to turn the stove off.

Meredith had always threatened taking off, but Denis never believed she would actually do it.

7 years after the birth of their second child, Meredith would get pregnant again, and would birth their third and final child- Blue Rupert Glass, born August 2nd, 2012.

Cipher and Fiona were infatuated with their beautiful baby brother with big blue eyes and a smile identical to Cipher's.

Though, the happiness couldn't last forever. Three weeks after the birth of Blue, Denis would be driving Ronald late at night, after picking him up from his home with Nicole.

Ronald and Nicole had been trying for a baby for over 10 years and had never been successful, until a month prior when Nicole finally got pregnant. Ronald was over the moon and bought everything they could possibly need and more. But that was until Denis had done the math- Ronald had gone on a business trip two weeks after Blue's birth. Ronald could not be the child's father.

Ronald had called Denis in shaken tears, and Denis didn't hesitate before driving across the city to pick his brother up. Denis begged Ronald to leave Nicole, and Ronald argued in disbelief of the truth.

Unfortunately their conversation was cut short as Denis drove through an intersection and a driver of a small truck who had been on the road for two days, no sleep, ran a red light and plowed into the passenger seat side of Denis' ute.

The entire left side of the ute crushed by the truck, killing Ronald Glass. The driver of the truck suffered a concussion, while Denis suffered the terrors after learning about the death of his twin brother after waking at the hospital.

Eyeball tried his best to tell Denis in the calmest possible way. But nothing with Denis Glass is calm and simple.

During the crash, Denis suffered a spinal injury, resulting in the need of surgeries to fix it. Denis was required to participate in physiotherapy in order for the surgeries to take affect and for his body to grow strength again to be able to one day move and work effectively.

But Denis, who was burdened by survivors guilt and the depression of losing someone he's had by his side supporting him since birth, suffered greatly as he refused treatment, and took up his old habit again of drinking his feelings away.

Denis couldn't stand for long without suffering a pain that would induce a deep rage, often becoming frustrated with his own body as he felt it worsen day by day.

Meredith had never been born with the art of sympathy, empathy and comfort- and maybe that is how she knew what she'd do before Denis and the children returned from the hospital that day.

Meredith had taken off before Cipher and Fiona returned for the night- and along with her invisibility, was the linger of a missing baby Blue.

Denis tried for years to find Blue and Meredith, but he and the polices attempts were failed, and after time, the alcohol and fury overtook him, and soon enough he was nothing but a man on a couch.

Fiona, as a child, spent most of her time supporting Denis- grabbing him more beers when he'd request, or cleaning his hands or helping him to the toilet.

For the first few years after Meredith left, Cipher started getting into trouble a lot at school, and often skipped class to sneak off with friends, or girls. He and Denis would fight a lot, and while Denis could still stand he'd often have Cipher pinned against a wall, instilling a fear his father used so often as a child.

By Cipher's 15th birthday, Denis couldn't stand on his own, let alone pin Cipher against a wall. But by that point, Cipher felt nothing but utter pity for his father, and never did much to make his life neither easier or harder.

Maybe things would've been different if Meredith had stayed. Maybe this entire story would've never happened. Shall it be Meredith's fault? Or Nicole's? Or the truck driver?

Who to blame when a chain of events sparks the butterfly affect of endless blue?

1

Chapter One- Skye

24/May/2018

It's been 2,098 days since my mum left with my little brother. I can't even remember her voice. I can't even remember if I ever loved her or not. I loved my little brother, though- that I know.

I'm thirteen now, my older brother Cipher, who will be 16 in October, gifted me a leather journal a few weeks ago for my birthday. I don't know how he got the money for it, considering he hasn't got a job. Maybe he stole it. I don't know.

I wasn't even going to use it at first, but today when I woke up for school, I thought about my baby brother Blue, and I wondered where in the world he'd be right now. I hope he's okay, and I hope my mum is happy, wherever she is.

I wish she could've taken me with her, then I could've avoided the horror that is my school. I've never really had friends. This year I started Year 7 at Berry High School, and for a few weeks I was actually super excited to make new friends.

I thought it might be different, considering there'd be a lot of different people that I'd never met. But as it turns out, everyone who doesn't know me, knows my brother. And if they know my brother, then they think they know me.

My older brother Cipher has always hated school too. He's never struggled making friends. In fact, a lot of people wish to be his friend- especially girls. People either love him or they hate him. I love my brother, I love the way he defends me, even when sometimes it makes things worse.

But I hate the way he and my dad speak to each other. They're always fighting. Cipher skips classes a lot, and every time he's marked absent for a class, they message my dad. So every time Cipher and I get home, they always get into arguments.

My dad used to smack my brother around, sometimes. Only when their arguments would get super heated. The last time my dad hurt Cipher, he pinned him against the wall and spat in his face after Cipher called my dad a 'virgin'. They used to argue like that all the time.

My dad gets scary when he's angry, but he always regretted hurting Cipher. The last time they really got into it, he'd hurt his back real bad and fell to the floor in pain. Cipher and I had to help him to his chair by the TV. I cried because I was scared he'd made his injury worse.

After the car crash, my dad suffered some kind of injury that paralyzed part of his body. The doctors performed surgeries to fix it and he was supposed to participate in physiotherapy, but he never did.

My dad left the hospital after finding out my mum had taken off with Blue. Ripped everything off of his body and left in the hospital gown to find me and Cipher with our Grandma Uma.

After the car crash, my dad hated Nicole. I never understood why until the day of my Uncle Ronny's funeral. He screamed at her, demanding she leave. She cried and pleaded for my dad to forgive her but he refused. He mentioned a few things during the argument- such as the fact she was pregnant, and the fact the baby wasn't Uncle Ronny's.

In case you were wondering, She had the baby, a little girl. I can't remember her name, but I remember she looks just like Nicole in the photos Cipher showed me. Cipher hated Nicole, called her a lot of mean names and dad always agreed. But I always liked Nicole. I was always jealous of her pretty blonde hair, and her smile.

I miss my Uncle Ronny, and I know dad misses him too, and it makes me sad knowing my dad misses him. I wish he wouldn't have to be sad anymore about Uncle Ronny, or Blue, or mum.

My dad spent years working with the police to find Blue, but the day after the fight with Cipher, my dad could barely find the strength to pick up his own cup, let alone assist in finding a woman who doesn't want to be found.

Eventually people just stopped talking about Blue and my mum, like they never existed. My dad never liked to talk about his pain either. He hates it when I offer to help him. He always wants to get up and grab his own beer, or make his own sandwich. It's hard, because I know he is supposed to have help. I know the doctors are supposed to fix him, but for some reason he refuses to let them. He never goes to the doctors, even when the pain makes him cry.

Cipher always makes me breakfast, every morning before school. He's always up, and making me a bowl of cereal. My dad barely ever eats. He always just drinks. There's a man named Nevel who works at the closest petrol station to our house, who's brother used to work for Uncle Ronny. He always lets Cipher buy my dad beer after school on Fridays. He's the only worker that'll sell to him.

I think I'm going to take my journal to school with me. Then at least, at breaks, I can sit and pretend I'm doing something, instead of staring at the wood on the picnic tables and watching the ants as they crawl past.

My dad was still asleep by the time Cipher and I left for school. We always had to walk, luckily it was only about 10 minutes away. Our house is where people call 'River Side' of the City, its a more rural area where people who don't have much money often live. The school is directly in between River Side and the actual City, so there's a lot of different people that go there.

The High School, Primary School and Senior School are directly across the road from each other, so even when Cipher is old enough to go to Senior School, we'll still be able to walk together.

There's not anyone at school that I specifically hate, I just know there's a lot of people that don't like me. For the first few weeks of school, there was a few older boys that tried to take pictures up my skirt. Cipher found out when one of the boys accidentally laughed about it to him, and he got suspended for a week for making his nose bleed in the boys bathroom.

I don't know why people don't like me. I know a lot of people don't like my older brother, and I guess that means they automatically don't like me. But sometimes, a lot of girls who like my brother, also don't like me.

One time when I was walking down the hallway, I accidentally made eye contact with a boy in the Year above me, and his girlfriend was standing right by him. Later that day she and her friends found me in the bathroom and ripped my skirt and told me to never look at him again.

I had to walk out with my jumper wrapped around my waist, and had to walk all the way home by myself in the middle of the day. I was crying so much and my dad was so angry that I was skipping school.

Until I showed him what those girls did to my skirt. It was the first time in weeks he'd gotten up from his chair, and rushed to his phone to call the school. He screamed at my principle over the phone for hours.

The girls never got suspended though, because their parents said I had no proof that they did it. The next day at school, the girls came up to me again, calling me a snitch.

At the next school assembly, Cipher made sure to sit behind the girl, the one with the boyfriend, and took off the lid of a squeezy paint bottle and squeezed the entire thing into her hair. She screamed so loud, and the entire school laughed at her.

The boyfriend tried to fight Cipher right after that, but Cipher got suspended and by the time he came back everything had fizzled out.

The first three-ish months of school have definitely not been anything like I expected. High school always looked so much funner in movies and TV shows. People just get meaner the older they get. I don't know why though.

30/May/2018

I'd never realized until this year, but I'm actually quite good at English. During Primary School, I'd participated in every end of year school play, so I always knew I loved theater and singing. But I never knew I'd enjoy English class this much.

I've never owned a book, but this week we started learning how to write reading analysis', starting with Pride and Prejudice by Jane Austen. My teacher let a few of the students borrow the second hand books from the library, while some of the students' parents bought the books for them.

A few of the corners of my book are bent, and there's a big green stain on the first page, but I'm absolutely obsessed. We were given three weeks to read the book in our own time, but I read the entire thing in two days. I've started writing my analysis today as my homework, and I'm enjoying every bit of it.

31/May/2018

I had my English class double period again today, and my teacher, Mr Eden, was beyond shocked when I told him before class that I'd already read the whole thing.

For class today he discussed the difference of responsibilities for men and women in past generations. It's quite interesting really. On the outside, it would appear a lot of things have changed since the 19th century. But in truth, many things haven't differed.

After class, I asked Mr Eden if there were any other books he'd suggest that were just as good as Pride and Prejudice. He quickly wrote down on a sticky note a few different books and their authors for me to check out at the school library.

Students are only allowed to check out three at a time, and Pride and Prejudice would already be considered as one, so I just chose the two books I located first. Little Women by Louisa May Alcott, and To Kill A Mockingbird by Harper Lee.

The Librarian Mrs Smuthe, said that they were classics.

3/June/2018

I started Little Women, and so far my favorite character is Beth March. I love how whimsical and innocent she is. I've always wanted to learn an instrument. Piano would be amazing, I'm just not sure how I'll find one.

8/June/2018

My brother made me go with him to the petrol station to grab our dad beers from Nevel. Nevel is quite interesting to me. I think he is Lebanese, and he has a really big scar on his chin.

Nevel once told me that my Uncle Ronny helped Nevel's older brother get sober. He gave him a job at his construction company, and he helped Nevel's brother become a real dad to his kids. He said he gave him his brother back. I'm glad my Uncle left a legacy as prominent as Nevel depicts.

Today, Cipher and Nevel chatted as they always did, and Cipher handed him cash, like he always did. I searched around the store, looking to see if they had any of those sour skittles I love. Of course they didn't. Everyone must visit the store while I'm at school and buy them all before I get there.

Instead, something else caught my eye. At the front door of the store, there's a small shelf of magazines, and this months Vogue Magazine.

Rihanna, Up All Night. Do you think she ever struggled making friends?

16/June/2018

My dad hadn't had a nightmare in a while. He used to wake up screaming on the couch every night, reliving the moment his brother died. As much as my dad put all the guilt onto Nicole, I do think he blames himself more then anything. His nightmares got so bad he started drinking as much as he could before passing out. I wouldn't know, but I guess the drunken nights go by a lot smoother then the sober ones. Maybe his mind is too muddled by inebriation to be reminded of the worst night of his life.

He woke up last night screaming. He'd run out of drinks and Cipher didn't come home yesterday after school. He walked me home, but he didn't step foot in the house. Said he was going to meet with some friends. I asked who but he only named Yana and Brownie. Said they were going to the lake for the weekend. Cipher has been friends with Yana since Primary school. I like Yana, she's super pretty. Her family used to live across the road from us, which was always so fun because she had so many siblings and we used to all play football together on the road. I was so sad when her family moved to a different house.

When I told my dad about Cipher, he was furious. He was angry, but not because Cipher didn't ask first, but because Cipher forgot that he's supposed to visit Nevel on Fridays. It's the only day of the week Nevel is working around 4pm, and nobody else will sell alcohol to someone my age.

It makes me sad knowing my dad can't get up and drive to the lake and demand Cipher to come home. I know it probably sounds bad, to wish my brother would get in trouble. But it isn't about that. It's about the fact that he can't, not until he returns home. Because my dad cannot physically do anything until Cipher is back inside the house. As much as he wants to. As angry as he is. He'd never make it three steps out the door, let alone drive all the way to the waterfalls.

I can't help but cry for my dad, and be angry at Cipher. He's tormenting our dad. He does all of these things because he knows our dad can't do anything until Cipher is ready to deal with it. And even then, Cipher can just walk away to his bedroom and muffle out the sounds of our dads anger through loud music and the drop of heavy weights.

17/June/2018

Cipher finally came home. I'd already cooked a microwave soup, and had sat down with my dad to eat together. He loves the soup with the small noodles in it, says Mamie used to cook it all the time when they were kids.

Mamie died the day Cipher was born, so I never got to meet her. There's a few photos of Cipher and I with Poppy Nigel when we were little, but Cipher said he got diagnosed with Lung Cancer and died way before Blue was even born. I don't remember his funeral, but there's photos of us there. My dad was sort of the last one left, if it weren't for his kids.

My dad was watching the sports channel, he'd always loved footy. Cipher didn't even bother to enter the house quietly, slamming the door as a grand entrance.

My dad shouted at him from the couch, barely able to turn his body toward the front door. Demanding him to stand by the TV. But Cipher didn't listen. I guess he wasn't ready to have that conversation yet.

My dad put his cigarette out on the table beside his chair, and with a shaking fury he stood up and supported his weight on a walking stick and grabbing onto close furniture as he slowly made his way toward Cipher's room, where Cipher had shut himself with loud 'Paint It Black' by the Rolling Stones shouting from his room. A cigarette secretly lit in his mouth and beginning to rep his heavy weights.

The buildup of the song echoing through the house as Cipher is unsuspecting to our dad basically crawling toward his bedroom door.

I tried to stop him, but when my dad is angry, nothing could ever stop him.

My dad was basically huffing with pants as he ripped Ciphers door open, his walking stick wobbling beneath his palm.

"CIPHER!" he shouted. I couldn't see Cipher's face, but I'm sure he was shocked that dad even made it that far.

"WHERE THE HELL HAVE YOU BEEN?" my dad asked.

Cipher ignored him. My dad, who was standing beside Cipher's table holding his stereo speaker, used all his strength to shove it to the ground.

"WHAT THE FUCK?" Cipher shouted, dropping his weights. Cigarette still hanging from his lip as he approached my dad with the same anger.

Their personalities so similar. Not only do they look the same, with Cipher possessing dads youthful curly and messy mullet and green eyes, but they act the same. Both dominating with that familiar intimidating manner.

My dad didn't say anything to Cipher. Nothing but a slap across his face. A slap that snapped Cipher from his exhausted and heated mind, causing him to pick up our dad from the corners of his ripped shirt and slam his frail body into the wall. Just as my dad always did with him growing up.

I could see the fear in my frail fathers eyes.

"CIPHER, STOP!" I shouted, hoping he'd listen. But the sound of the music beating into the floor numbed my words. I couldn't predict what would happen next, I couldn't stop anything and suddenly my body froze. I was useless.

When it felt as if it would never end, Cipher finally snapped out of whatever he was stuck in and let go of our dad. We both watched as he fell to the floor in pain.

"DAD!" I shouted, as I ran to his aid, but he shoved me away.

"GET OFF ME!" he yelled, trying to stand himself up on his own, but he couldn't.

Cipher just stood there and watched as I forced dad to let me help him. The look shared between the two of silence and utter shock.

I wanted to run to my room and cry beneath my sheets, but I couldn't. I couldn't leave my dad, even after I helped him back to his chair.

Cipher shut off his music and slammed the front door shut again as he exited, all while my dad flicked me away and screamed that I stop touching him.

For the next hour I watched through the corner of my eye as my dad choked back his tears. He'd never cried in front of me before, I don't even know what that would look like, or sound like. Even when he was at his hardest with missing Blue, I'd never seen him cry. I couldn't even tell if he was crying from pain, or sadness. The quiver of his chin made me upset. I wish Cipher had never done what he did.

My dad and I hadn't spoken a single word since the fight, and when Cipher finally came back I was basically nodding off on the blue beanbag on the floor of the lounge room.

My dad didn't say anything as Cipher walked back inside, it was night. He knew it was Cipher, he didn't have to ask, he just knew.

Cipher didn't say anything either. Not a single word. All he did was walk through the house slowly, the stomps of his feet creaking against the floor boards as he approached the chair our dad was glued to. I watched as he placed down a 6 pack of Great Northern's on the table beside dads chair, before proceeding to place four more 6 packs from a plastic bag in the fridge.

My dad didn't even ask where Cipher got the beer from. It was Sunday Night, Nevel wouldn't have been working so he couldn't have gone there. I guess maybe my dad didn't want to know.

He didn't waste a second before opening one and beginning to drink his night away. Cipher returned back to his room, my best guess is to fall asleep.

I didn't go to bed until 2am, because that's after my dad had finally fallen asleep. I turned the TV off like I always do, and made sure the remote was within reach of my dad. I made sure he still had cigarettes in his packet and that he had enough beers beside him to last while I'm at school. I hope he sleeps well tonight.

I suppose life could always be worse, Marmee March knows that.

18/June/2018

I wonder what I would look like If I cut off all my hair. Though, I don't have anyone to save with it's loss. If only my hair could be enough to send my dad off into the sun and return one day with my mum and little brother on his arms.

29/June/2018

'Well now, mother, I go, I go. How beautiful everything is tonight.'

I've been crying all night. I have school in a few hours, but I have no idea how I'm supposed to sleep now. Beth March is dead!

12/July/2018

Samantha Crove is the meanest person I've EVER met! She purposely poured glue on my dress in art class and the teacher YELLED AT ME for yelling at her! It's not fair. Every time someone does something to me, somehow I'm always the one getting into trouble.

I didn't even do anything to her. I accidentally bumped her while I was collecting more wood chips for my project and she got back at me by pouring GLUE on my school dress! Now my dad has to buy me a new dress with money that he doesn't have! He's probably going to hate me.

2/September/2018

It's fathers day today. My school always opens stalls for us to buy presents on fathers and mothers day. I hate mothers day. I always find it so hard to find something that doesn't specifically say 'mother' on it, considering I don't have a mother to give it to. And the school always forces us to get something. I always end up just giving it to my dad.

14/September/2018

Cipher got caught smoking behind the church next to the school. Apparently some of the cameras face that way and he got caught smoking cigarettes with Brownie. His real name isn't Brownie. His real name is Cooper, but everyone calls him Brownie because his last name is Brown.

My dad must've been asleep when the school called him, but Cipher got sent home for the weekend, and the principle told him to tell our dad to call back on Monday before sending Cipher to school again.

I think he might be in big trouble this time. I don't even know where he could've gotten the cigarettes from. I don't think Cipher would steal from our dad. Probably from Brownies dad, Eyeball. Or Yana's brother, Dare.

26/April/2019

It's been a while since I'd written in my journal. Honestly, when I started writing in it, I was just hoping that maybe one day I'd get to write that my mum had come back. But it's been a while now and she's still not back. Maybe she wont ever come back.

It's my birthday today, and every year on my birthday I dream that she'll surprise me with a birthday cake and balloons when I wake up, but she never does.

I'm fourteen now, and I'm in Year 8. Cipher is 16, and he started his first year at Senior School. We still walk to school together every morning. But now it's just a little bit more lonely, because sometimes Cipher would let me hang around him and his friends instead of sitting by myself. But now, he's at the school across the road, and I can't find him during lunch anymore.

I spend most of my breaks at the library. It's quiet in there, and only a few people, mostly older kids, go in there. I'm not allowed to eat in there though, so I haven't been eating at school anymore. I get hungry sometimes, but I guess it's okay. I've gotten used to it by now.

My dad saved up enough money to buy me a Phone for my birthday, just like he did when Cipher turned fourteen. I was so excited. I've been begging my dad for a phone for years and he finally actually got me one!

I think my dad gets paid from the government for his disability, I think that's how he saves his money. My Grandparents, my mum's parents, told my dad that they'd visit on the weekend to give me their present. I'm pretty excited about that because they're super rich.

I never get to see them often. Every time my Grandma sees me, all she talks about is how much I look like my mum. To be honest, that doesn't really mean much to me anymore. If it weren't for the pictures displayed on every wall of their house, I'd never remember what she looked like. I try to, but overtime her appearance has slipped from my memory, and all I know for certain is that she has super dark hair like me, and bright blue eyes like my brother. My Grandma always says that I remind her the most of mum. She says we have the same nose. She always looks like she wants to cry when she talks about her.

Her real name is Meredith, but everyone except my Granddad calls her Merry. My dad doesn't call her much anymore. Every time my Grandparents bring her up he pretends he's deaf and doesn't engage in the conversation at all. I don't think he hates her, I just think he misses her too much to talk about it. I guess it would be hard, he probably still loves her.

My first class today was Health. I didn't expect any of the students to wish me a happy birthday, but I kind of wished some of the teachers would've. Not in front of everyone, but privately. Maybe that sounds ridiculous.

My class had barely started, before the principle entered the room with a girl I'd never seen before. She was of similar height to me, with dirty blonde hair and blue eyes. She was super pretty, and I noticed that her dress was hemmed and I sort of loved the look of it. I'd seen a few of the older girls do it, but I never thought of doing it myself until I saw her with it.

The Principle introduced her as Skye Sallow, and he helped her find a spare seat. We didn't have specific seating in any of the classes, but most people chose to sit in the same seats every class. I sort of hoped that in the next class, I'd end up sitting next to her.

My next class was English, and I sort of tried staying back behind Skye. I wanted to see where she'd sit, and see if I could find a spot by her so I could talk to her.

A lot of the other girls were already talking to her on the way. She seemed really nice, from what I could hear.

Unfortunately, the group of girls that followed her to class took up all the seats surrounding Skye, and for the rest of the day, I couldn't help but find myself sitting the furthest away from her.

2/May/2019

Sometimes It kind of makes me sad to think about the fact I have no friends. Cipher is always leaving with his friends to go and do things and all I do is go to school and go home. I never have any fun. It's just the same thing every single day.

3/May/2019

I had English class again today with Mr Eden. We've started poetry assignments, and are required to submit one famous poem that we love, and to write our own poems about something we enjoy.

After English I had Drama class. I don't particularly like my Drama teacher this year. My teacher last year was much more extravagant.

Today we were introduced into a new assignment that would last until the end of term which required us to be in groups of two, and pick a popular children's bedtime story, and make a short live play to be presented to our teacher at the end of term.

I actually prefer it when teachers choose who our groups will be in teamed projects. I hate being the last person standing, especially when there's an odd number of students, and the teacher has to just shove me into a group that doesn't want me.

I was actually super happy with my grouping today, the teacher paired me with Skye Sallow, the new girl in my class. Although, I don't think she much likes Drama class, but maybe I can change her mind with our short play.

10/May/2019

I had drama class again today, and we were instructed to branch off into our pairs to do research in the library on bedtime stories and pick the one we'd like to do.

Skye always seemed so confident when she was talking to everyone else. She was super quiet when we were walking through the library looking for a story. I thought maybe she didn't like me much. She can't just be shy, considering she was new and was already friends with our entire year level.

Finally she asked me for my opinion on what books were my favorite. But I didn't really know what to say, because I'd never really read any bedtime stories. I just told her that I didn't really know any, and she told me that she'd seen me reading books during breaks before. I didn't realise she'd notice me like that.

She told me her parents had never touched a book, let alone read her a bedtime story. She said she'd heard about Goldilocks and seen Disney movies, but she'd never actually read any bedtime stories.

As she told me little things about herself, about her parents. I realized, she and I weren't much different from each other. My parents had never read me any stories either, that I can remember. If it weren't for school and other kids, I'd never know about the three bears, or the very hungry caterpillar.

We combed through a few different books, but none of them seemed too interesting to the both of us, and a lot of the other groups had already picked a few of the stories, and we didn't want to do the same play as anyone else.

Eventually, I found my hand caressing over a green and yellow book. Goodnight Moon by Margret Wise Brown. We sat on the floor between the book isles and I dramatically read out the story to Skye. She actually thought I was funny.

The school day had ended. I walked across the road to meet Cipher by one of his friends, who was sitting in his older brothers red car. Cipher was in the process of lighting a cigarette, and a nearby teacher shouted for him to do it out of school property, so Cipher took one step to the left, to put him just out of property reach, and laughed as the old teacher steamed at his nuisance.

A skinny girl with brown hair and eyes approached Cipher with a big smile. He wrapped his arm around her and offered her his cigarette as I greeted them. She said her name was Victoria Liase.

Suddenly, I heard as someone shouted my name from across the road, as they ran past, narrowly missing a car, flipping them off at the sound of their horn. It was Skye.

She asked me where I was going, If I was going straight home. I explained that Cipher and I had to make a quick stop at a shop nearby, like we did every Friday. She almost begged if she could come too. It was only then, In that moment that I realized Skye had braces, with pink bands.

Cipher cut in and explained that he had somewhere to be after we visited Nevel, and said it would be more convenient to him if he could give me the drinks to deliver back to our dad. I was scared dad would be mad again, but Skye insisted that she wanted to hang out, and that she had more space in her backpack to carry anything we needed. Cipher was convinced.

The four of us walked toward Nevel's station together, Skye and I behind Cipher and Victoria. Skye had asked me if Victoria was Cipher's girlfriend, and I said I didn't know. Cipher was always hanging out with different girls. He was always kissing different girls and going places with different girls. I don't even know if he's ever actually had a real girlfriend- when I was little I always assumed Yana was his girlfriend, but I guess not.

She also told me my brother was hot, which I obviously thought was disgusting. I told her Cipher looks exactly like my dad, and she said that made her even more excited to meet my dad. I think she was joking.

Skye asked me if Cipher had a job, wondering how he afforded buying all those beers and cigarettes. But I explained that my dad gave him money. My dad doesn't know that sometimes Cipher buys a little extra for himself. I don't think my dad cares enough to question where all his money goes, and why it seems more expensive sometimes. Maybe deep down he knows the truth, and he knows that there isn't much he could say or do to make Cipher stop so, why bother?

Skye found me staring at the new Vogue cover of May. Kate Moss.

"I wish I could be a model" I told Skye.

"Are you kidding? You're so much prettier then Kate Moss."

Skye then looked around the store skeptically, before suspiciously pointing to a separate magazine. Playboy.

"Have you ever read a Playboy magazine?" she asked. "I bet Cipher has."

I'd never really taken much notice of the Playboy magazines. A lot of the time I think they're hidden behind other magazine's for important reasons.

Skye told me her dad used to always leave Playboy magazines lying around, and that they're the best magazines. She told me that as she took one of the magazine copies, and rolled it up, placing it in the seam of her skirt, and beneath her school jumper.

I'd always wondered what it would feel like to steal- though, I never expected it to be at Nevel's store.

Cipher and Victoria ended up leaving, I don't know where they went. Skye and I walked back to my house. We talked the whole way about Skye's old school and old friends. She said by the end, no one was really her friend anymore, and she didn't want to make the same mistake at her new school by becoming friends with the wrong people again. She didn't really say anything else about her parents, or if she had any siblings. I didn't want to ask because I didn't want it to seem like I was forcing her to tell me something. I don't know, maybe I'm thinking too much into it. I just don't want to ruin my chance of having a real friend.

When we got back home, my dad didn't say much. I walked over to where he was sitting, watching the Secret of NIMH.

"Dad?" I spoke in a hush, hoping not to disturb him. A mere grunt in return.

"Hi, Mr Glass." Skye responded. Her voice young and light.

My dad was shocked to hear an unfamiliar voice. Looking up, he saw a skinny girl with dirty blonde hair, perfectly straitened. Blue eyes, pink braces and a kind smile.

"Uh.. whats ya name, kid?" My dad responded. His voice awkward and old. He'd always referred to anyone younger then him as 'kid'.

"Skye Sallow. I just moved in with my Aunt and Uncle a few weeks ago. You might know them- Ben and Nancy Sallow?"

A realization of remembrance sparking in my dads eyes. "Ah- you're-you're Vin's kid, or are you Sydney's?" he stutters, cigarette smoke blowing from his mouth.

"Vin." Skye responds with hesitation.

I watch as my dad takes a long inhale of his cigarette, almost increasing uncomfortably with continuing the conversation.

"You, uh- you still see him much?"

Skye shakes her head. A level of understanding circulating between them. Something I couldn't understand.

We left my dad with extra beers and cigarettes and went into my room with the door shut. Skye took out the Playboy magazine from her seam and laid on my bed with a giggle as she begun flipping through the pages. I'd never seen so many naked women, but somehow, they made it classy?

"I bet your brother has way more of these in his room." Skye urged.

"I wouldn't know, I don't go in there."

"Ever?" Skye asked with a smile.

"He'd probably kill me if I did."

"Right, but he's not home, is he?"

I didn't really want to go into Cipher's room. The Playboy magazine was cool, but not cool enough to get caught by my older brother. But Skye was convincing, and I didn't want her to think I was too scared to try.

My dad was way too busy with his movie to even notice we'd left my room. I assume he'd probably be mad if he knew what we were doing. He'd kill me if I ever did half the things Cipher gets up to.

His room circulates with a vicious smell of lynx and male odor. His heavyset weights left to the floor. He'd cleaned up his speaker and table, but his room was still a mess. Skye's smile was beaming as she admired his room. I don't know why. It was messy, smelly and the walls were stained with tobacco.

She immediately got to work searching in his drawers for more magazines. All she found were cigarettes, lighters, and dirty socks.

She held up an old white packet of cigarettes that had been hiding away in one of his drawers, and a red lighter.

"Have you ever smoked?" Skye asked, looking at me with a smirk.

"No."

"Do you want to?" she asked.

I couldn't respond. I knew my dad and brother would kill me if they ever found out. I knew I wasn't supposed to, but something about the situation, the offer, it felt enticing. As she awaited my answer, she continued searching, and eagerly found more magazines underneath Cipher's bed. Raunchy, mysterious and sexy photos printed on every page.

Skye and I rushed back into my bedroom with one of the magazines. We sat on top of my desk in front of my open window. My bedroom door shut. Skye gave me the magazine and I started searching through each of the pages as she lit one of Cipher's cigarettes.

"I wish I looked like that." I told her, pointing to some of the women.

"I bet you do." Skye responded, huffing on the cigarette. "Do you want to try?"

I hesitated, fearful. But If I was going to get in trouble, I would be anyway. Adding a little extra fuel to the fire couldn't hurt, right?

Placing it between my lips, sucking and unknowing about what exactly I'm supposed to do. I had my first taste of the cigarette, I coughed so loud my dad could've heard. luckily he didn't, I don't think.

It doesn't taste very nice, I don't know why people do it. It left a dirty residue in my throat, and it made my eyes water.

"Do you smoke often?" I ask, handing the cigarette back.

"My mama used to let me share with her sometimes."

Her mum? I tried to hide the shock on my face when she told me. My dad would never let me share his beer or his cigarettes.

"So, what do you want to be when you grow up?" Skye asks, out of the blue. Still huffing on the cigarette.

"I don't know. I like reading, and my brother gave me a journal for my birthday last year- and I've really enjoyed writing in it." I explained.

"Do you think you could write a book? A real one?"

"I don't know. Maybe."

"Well, If you do, can you write one about me?" Skye asks, handing me the cigarette.

"But- I don't really know you." I giggle awkwardly.

"But you will." she assures. "We're gonna become best friends, Fiona Glass."

16/May/2019

Skye and I have been spending a lot of time together. She's been sitting with me during lunch breaks and during every class. She slept over all weekend last weekend, and for the past two days we've gone for walks around the city together after school.

Today, though, Skye wanted to visit the big shopping center in the City Central. I'd only ever been to the mall a few times, before my mum left. She used to take me and Cipher with her whenever she needed more clothes. Or when she was pregnant with Blue, she always used to go there to look at baby clothes and toys, but she'd never end up buying anything.

Skye said she used to love visiting the mall after school with her old friends. She said it was fun to pretend to be grown and to have enough money to buy whatever they wanted.

Cipher wanted to go for a drive with some of his friends anyway, so he didn't care that I was going.

Skye always talked about Cipher. She was always asking me questions about him, about the girls he hangs out with, what he does on weekends, who his friends are. She always asks me super personal questions about him. Sometimes I don't even know the answer to them.

I'd forgotten how big the Shopping Center was. A three story building, with underground and above ground parking, as well as an underground floor with shops, a middle ground, and a second floor.

The first place we visited was a little stall on the middle floor by the escalators. Skye said she was craving a juice smoothie, and I'd never had one. I told Skye I didn't have any money, and she offered to pay. She said her Aunt and Uncle were always giving her pocket money. She said they only did it because they felt bad for her, because her parents weren't around to buy her things or take her shopping.

Skye's Aunt and Uncle seemed nice. I met them on Tuesday when we stopped by their house so Skye could pick up some coins so that we could get hot dogs from a corner shop.

Their names are Nancy and Ben. They're super young and have two daughters who are 8 and 6, Delilah and Viola. Nancy was tall with dark hair and blue eyes. She was super sweet and always smiling, and I think Skye said she's a social worker. Ben looked a lot like Skye. They have similar hair colours and both have blue eyes and pale skin. Ben was super tall and strong. Skye said he owned a concreting company, and that he's also a personal trainer on weekends. I thought he was super handsome. Delilah and Viola were really cute too. Delilah loves to draw and Viola is identical to Skye. They're a really nice family, in a really big four bedroom house with two lounge rooms and a big backyard. Sometimes I wish Ben and Nancy could be my parents. Delilah and Viola seem like they're pretty happy. And they get to spend a lot of time with their parents.

I wonder if my family ever looked like that, clean and together. I guess not. Cipher said Mum and Dad used to fight a lot. Ben and Nancy are super strict on never drinking or smoking. And it seemed like they'd never had a fight in their lives.

Skye got a watermelon berry blast, while I got a banana and mango moon. We switched our drinks every 5 minutes, to ensure we'd both got to taste the different flavors.

Skye was eager to visit Supre. I'd never been before, but I'd seen some of their clothes in the magazines I've looked at. I've never really had much of a choice with how I dressed. Sometimes my Grandma Uma gave me hand-me-downs from when my Mum and Aunties were young, but most of the good stuff went to my cousins that I never speak to because they all go to Private Schools. Other then that, Dad makes me wear Cipher's old hoodies and t shirts. Most of the time I'm wearing my school uniform anyway.

Skye loved looking at the different tank tops. She kept pointing out different tops that I should try on, but I'd never worn revealing clothes. It sort of made me feel uncomfortable. I didn't really like looking at my body much. But Skye insisted, demanding we try on some matching clothes and that I'm not allowed to say no until I've at least tried them.

It was actually kind of fun, collecting a bunch of shirts and skirts and trying all of them on. I'd never really looked much into fashion, and the clothes I've worn have never really made me feel pretty or confident. Skye and I were changing in the same stall, and when she saw that I was wearing a sports bra she nearly choked on her gasp.

I admitted to her that my Dad had never bought me real bras, and that I've been wearing the same sports bras since I was 12. Skye immediately convinced me that we needed to go look at some underwear. But first, Skye sneakily slipped a few of the tops and skirts into our backpacks. I pleaded that she didn't, because stealing in a big place like this is daunting. But she convinced me it would be fine, that the shopping center was old and still hadn't added alarm systems and that they'd never know. Skye made sure that we still had enough clothes left to be able to walk out and put them back so the employees wouldn't suspect anything. Luckily, the store was pretty busy so no one even asked to check our bags. I was freaking out the entire way out of the store. The adrenaline, almost made me feel like my heart was flying. It was exciting, nothing like I'd ever felt before.

Skye's laughter at my nervous face as we walked away giggling made it even better. I loved it. I'd never had so much fun in my life.

Next we went to the only underwear shop without security out the front. It was also packed with busy mothers and loud children, which Skye said were a great distraction for the workers.

Skye said she looked best in red. That it worked well with her lighter hair, so she took some red sets into the change rooms. I wasn't sure which ones I'd look good in, so Skye made me hold up a variety of colours against my face so she could see which would compliment my skin, eyes and hair the most. In the end, we landed on black and dark blue.

We hurried into the change stalls together and Skye immediately started undressing. I'd never been naked in front of anyone before. I was sort of worried about her seeing the way I look with nothing on. Especially after she completely undressed and I saw how perfect her body was. She was so skinny. But in the same breath of my thoughts, she blurted out how much she hated her boobs, thought they were too small. When I'd finally taken my own clothes off and started trying on one of the sets, Skye gasped and expressed how jealous she was of my boobs, that they were way bigger then hers, and that my stomach was so tiny. I couldn't believe it. But honestly, after we both put on the first set of underwear, I started to understand how women look the way they do in those magazines. Even though I am no where near as beautiful as they are, the right bra and underwear definitely helps.

Skye told me to pose in the mirror. She wanted to take a photo. An anxiety washed over my body as my stomach knotted, but she promised me she wouldn't share the photo anywhere, that friends never break their promises.

On our way out of the store, a selection of bracelets caught Skye's eye. I didn't realize until we got home, but two of those bracelets came home with us.

Later on we went back to Skye's house. She practically begged me to let her do my hair and makeup. I'd always just kept my hair natural, never straightened or curled. I'd always wanted to but I've never owned anything to do it with. Skye said her Aunt had the best straighteners and curlers, and she immediately got to work.

She straightened my hair to perfection, leaving it silky and shiny. I'd never seen it look so clean. She started doing my makeup exactly how she did hers. A little concealer, contour, blush, mascara. The more and more she piled on, the more I started to a see a different me in her vanity mirror. A girl I'd never seen before. I was sort of nervous at the start that I wouldn't like it or that It wouldn't feel right. But once she'd finished, once we were both pampered and wearing a brand new outfit. After she'd doused me in perfume, I finally felt sexy.

This was when Skye showed me the bracelets she stole. Handmade bracelets on brown strings, one with yellow and green beads. One with pink and blue. Skye gave me the yellow and green one. We had matching bracelets, friendship bracelets. She made me promise to never take it off, and I wouldn't.

I loved the perfume she used, fruity and sweet. She told me to keep it, that she rarely used it and her Aunt was always buying her perfume for special occasions. We took so many photos that evening, photos that she posted. People were finally seeing me for me, not for my brothers little sister. I was finally a human, someone sexy and grown. It felt amazing, the kind of feeling I'd never want to lose.

1/June/2019

Skye got invited to a party, and she told me to come with her. We spent hours getting ready together in my bedroom. My brother was also getting ready in his bedroom. The boy that invited Skye is 17, meaning he's friends with people younger and older, so Cipher was also invited. Isaac Jenka was one of the most popular kids at my school. Every girls either wanted to date him, or Cipher. He had dark skin and curly hair and was really good at sports. His parents were also kind of rich and they were away for the weekend, and were letting him have a couple friends over.

Cipher wasn't too happy to hear that I was going. He tried to tell Dad but Dad told him that he shouldn't be doing anything at that party that he doesn't want me to see, which shut him up pretty quickly.

Skye always got her outfit inspiration from 2000s magazine models. She assigned me an outfit involving a loose black denim skirt, low waisted, and a tight cropped blue t shirt that said 'Playboy' in white writing. It wasn't real Playboy though. She also gave me some boots her Aunty gifted her a few months ago.

Skye wore a black singlet, and short denim shorts and boots. She made sure our hair was straightened to perfection, and that our makeup was glamoured. I felt like a model. For a night, I didn't feel like 14 year old Fiona Glass. I felt like 20 year old Kate Moss.

Cipher basically gagged when he saw what we were wearing. Asked me to remind him how old I was, but I didn't care. I wasn't going to let him bully me out of going to this party.

Skye said she really wanted to talk to Jack Perkins at that party. Jack Perkins was boy that Skye had been talking to for a few weeks. He was 16, but he looked older. He was one of Cipher's best friends. He had a really short mullet, and really nice abs. For some reason, Skye told me he always walks around with a pocket knife. She said it was something to do with dealing, but he wouldn't tell her exactly what the reason was.

Brownie picked us up and drove us to the house. Brownie was a super intimidating person with a really ugly skullet. Brownie and Cipher were always getting into fights together, and from what I've heard, Brownie deals for a super secretive dealer. Cipher said a few things to him in the car about bringing stuff to sell. He made me and Skye swear we wouldn't tell anyone, especially dad, about the drugs. It upset me a little bit that he was dealing drugs to other kids, but I didn't want Cipher or Skye to think I was a snitch. Skye thought it was cool that Cipher and Brownie were dealers. I didn't want to seem like the only one who had a problem with it. I didn't want to ruin everyone's night.

I didn't realise how many people were going to be at that party until I got there. A two story house with a basement and a backyard with a pool that was filled to the brim. Every single person at school, and some Graduates were there. So many private school kids I'd never seen before. Skye couldn't stop talking about how many hot guys there was.

We saw Daine, too. He definitely seemed shocked to see me there, but not so shocked to see Cipher. Daine is the oldest child of Aunt Hannah and Uncle Craig. He's only a year older then me. He goes to private school, and I thought he was a super narrow kid, but apparently not.

The music was loud. Songs ranging from Fred Again, to Tupac, to Lil Wayne, to Chris Brown. So many people were swimming in the pool outside, some were playing beer pong, some were chatting by the fire, some were even cooking sausages on the BBQ by the outdoor entertainment area.

Skye knew so many people. So many boys and girls were greeting her. People I'd never seen before, or recognized from school as bitches that I've always hated.

Brownie and Cipher walked off to their own friends outside. Cipher went straight up to Yana Roche who seemed to be really angry with him. Yana just got prettier with time. I'd always looked up to her, and she was always super sweet to me. Yana used to always ask to braid my hair. Her family moved to a different house right after our Mum left, but Yana, Dare and Mauve used to always come over and ride dirt bikes. Even after they moved. I've always been jealous of Yana. Her hair is so long and has so many different shades of brown in it, it's hard to explain. Her eyes are super green, more then Dare's. And she was Indigenous, so her skin was dark. She's gorgeous, and the nicest girl Cipher has ever spoken to. I wonder what he did this time to piss her off.

Jack Perkins finally found us close to an hour later. He walked us up toward his group of friends who shared their drinks with us. The only time I'd ever drank alcohol was when I was 7 and I accidentally drank one of my dads beers because he had it poured into a plastic cup, I thought it was juice.

The vibe and the music bouncing around the yard hyped me up to do what everyone else was doing, so I didn't hesitate when Jack offered me a can. Jack seemed super nice, but honestly, Skye seemed more interested in his friend, Daniel Evans.

Jack convinced us to play a round of beer pong, and after that, I can't really remember much, to be honest. I remember so many people crowding around to watch the game. I remember it was me and Jack against Skye and Daniel. And I remember winning.

I know Skye spoke to me after and told me she was gonna go somewhere private with Daniel. I remember not wanting her to leave, but she was super eager to talk to him more. So she kissed me on the cheek, and was whisked away into the crowd.

Jack found me standing by myself and offered me a seat beside him. I wasn't expecting him to be so nice. He's one of Cipher's good friends, and most of the time, Cipher's friends are awful humans. But Jack was sort of sweet.

We chatted for hours. It was the longest I'd ever talked to a boy who wasn't related to me or my teacher. I remember he had a really nice husky voice. I'd never noticed it before, because in my mind, he was always Skye's boy or my brothers friend. But he's actually super attractive. He made me laugh so much, and he kept offering me drinks which just got me more and more drunk. I didn't realise how fun it was to be drunk, no wonder people drink so often.

"I swear I never realized you were Cipher's little sister." he told me, rubbing his fingers against his lips.

"Really?" I asked surprised. I thought everyone knew me as Cipher's little sister.

"Yeah. I knew Ciph had a little sister, but I didn't realize it was you until you walked in together tonight." he explains. "Makes sense though, you guys look similar."

I laughed, I don't know why. He just made me feel so giddy and giggly.

"You wanna go talk somewhere more quiet? It's getting crowded out here."

Not a drop of hesitation in my body as I agreed to his request. Even though I wasn't completely sure of what it meant. All I knew is that I was willing to do anything to keep talking to him.

He held my hand as we made our way through the crowd toward the house. We passed Cipher and Yana who were cuddled up on the outdoor couch by the BBQ making out. Yuck.

I still couldn't see Skye or Daniel anywhere. Jack told me he'd been to Isaac's house thousands of times so he knew exactly where we could go for some quiet.

He led me downstairs into the basement, where only a small group of people, including Brownie and Isaac, were seated on couches and beanbags with Lil Peep playing on the TV as they smoked weed and passed around a plate with even piles of white powder. To my surprise, Daine was there too.

Brownie and Jack fist bumped each other as Jack led me to a spare seat on the couch. We stayed there for a while. Jack was snorting coke with the others, and kept offering me some, but I didn't want any. Brownie kept getting pissed off that Jack was offering me some, but Jack played it off well.

I wanted to talk to Daine, I hadn't seen him for a while before this party, but he and his friends didn't stay down there for long. Brownie left at some point too, told me that he'd be back.

I thought Jack and I would stay there for a while, at least until Brownie came back, but I was wrong. Jack stood up, and held his hand out to mine. Before leading me further down a hallway, and into a small room, closing the door behind us. He turned on the light but it was quite weak and super orange.

"It's their spare room. I've stayed in here heaps on weekends." Jack explained, sitting on the end of the bed with a lean.

I looked around the room, it was rather bland and boring. Nothing much on the walls to look at. The smell from outside almost suffocating me. I'd sort of grown used to the smell of weed. My dad used to smoke it all the time, and I knew Cipher smoked it because I could always smell it on him. But I hated the smell, always have.

I sat beside him on the bed. The sound of Lil Peep blasting through the walls.

"So, since when did you grow up?" Jack asked, smirking.

"What do you mean?"

"I just remember you as Cipher's little kid sister- nothin' like you are now."

"I thought you didn't know I was Cipher's little sister." I reminded, smiling as I feel I've caught him in a white lie.

Jack laughs. "Nah, I knew Cipher had a little sister- who I've seen before- but I didn't realize it was you, 'cause you look so different."

"Makes sense." I nod. "Skye dressed me tonight." I admit.

"Yeah, I can tell." he admits, leaning forward and moving my hair behind my ear, sniffling in his nostrils. "You look good."

I could feel the deep pits of my stomach brewing, and my heart beating a million miles an hour. The eye contact alone could've sent me to a hospital, but the fact that his hand was still against my face was enough to bury me 6 feet under.

I'd never been alone with a boy before, let alone kissed a boy. I had no idea what to do in this moment, or if I should do anything at all. I was frozen.

Suddenly, he leaned in. The smell of his deodorant gluing into my system as his lips connected with mine. It was amazing, and terrifying. He was a really good kisser, I think?

I basically let him do everything, because I had no idea what I was doing. He laid me down on the bed, his hand trailing against my body as he kissed me.

"Have you ever done anything before?" he calmly asked.

I didn't say anything. What if he thought I was a prude, or weird for not having done anything before. So many things are running in my mind. Suddenly all the alcohol in my body has evaporated and I'm freaking the fuck out.

I shake my head.

"That's okay." he smiles, before leaning in to continue kissing me.

We did everything that night, I think. He showed me how to do things, things I'd never known to do. He talked me through everything. It was really nice, he made me feel comfortable. Some things hurt, some things felt weird, some things felt good. It was strange, I was feeling everything all at once.

4/June/2019

Cipher and Jack got into a really big fight at school today. I didn't even know until one of Skye's friends told me. Apparently they both got suspended, and everyone knew it was because Cipher found out about Jack and me on the weekend.

WHAT THE FUCK!

The only person I was worried about finding out was Skye, and she didn't even care because she got with Daniel that night. I don't even know why Cipher cared considering he gets with a new girl every weekend.

When I got home he'd already told my dad and my dad was pissed. I don't understand! I'm fourteen now, not twelve. I'm allowed to talk to boys and kiss boys. Everyone else does.

Cipher told me I looked like a slut, and that Skye was making me act like one. He said that Jack was telling everyone at school that he'd gotten with me, and that if it weren't for him, he would've convinced everyone that I was easy.

It can't be true. Jack was so nice. He was so sweet. Cipher is just a dick! They need to understand that I'm not a kid anymore. I'm allowed to do things and explore with other people. I'm growing up! Cipher has gotten teachers fired for sleeping with them in their cars. Cipher has broken so many girls' hearts and he's just allowed to do it, but the second I spend the night with one boy, suddenly I'm a slut! Fuck that!

Cipher is fucking dead to me!

14/June/2019

Cipher cheated on Yana. She slapped him in the face at school. Clearly he has no room to judge me.

I didn't even know they were dating.

15/June/2019

Skye and I went for a drive tonight at like 8pm. We snuck out through my window and got picked up by Curtis Black, 18. And Sammy Oblein, 19. They took us driving super fast down the bush. I tried weed for the first time. It was actually amazing, better then being drunk.

We'd been driving for hours, before Curtis drove us back to their house. Skye went into Sammy's room and I went into Curtis' room. It felt so fun. We barely knew these boys and now we were having sex with them. And they were older!

I felt so grown, I felt like the hottest girl in the city. And Curtis was so so attractive, way hotter then Jack.

23/June/2019

I'm so glad I met Skye. I'm so glad I finally have a best friend. I slept over at Skye's house last night. She finally convinced me to dye her hair. She'd been begging me for weeks but I've never dyed anyone's hair before so I was scared of ruining it. She told me she's only ever put pink streaks in her hair, and that she'd grown bored of her natural colour.

Nancy tried to convince her otherwise. She was happy to help, but she reminded Skye that she might regret it, and that it's not gonna be fun to grow her hair back out. Skye reminded her that it's only hair, and she knows it'll look good. Said the dark hair will compliment her eyes. She also said she's always been obsessed with my dark hair, and that it would be fun to match.

Nancy is super fun. I wish she was my mum or Aunt. I never see my Aunties. I used to see them every Christmas at my Grandma and Grandpas house. Aunt Hannah was always nice. She's a stay at home mum, and her Husband, Uncle Craig, is a University Teacher. They live on the other side of the city, which is why I never see my cousins from them. Daine, who's 15, Tommy who's 13 I think, and Malia who's 9.

Aunt Charlotte was okay. She never went out of her way to talk to any of us. Cipher said it's because she used to date dad, and that Mum stole dad from her. I don't know how Cipher learns all these family secrets. He must have ears in the walls.

Aunt Charlotte always loved drinking wine. She and her Husband, Uncle Waylon, have been on and off for a few years. I remember a few Christmas' ago, he wasn't allowed to drink, Aunt Charlotte forbid it. Probably because every Christmas he'd drink and he'd end up arguing with either my dad, or calling his brothers and arguing with them. Of course, he ended up getting drunk, and he and my dad got into a big fight. I remember, Uncle Waylon had just changed the Christmas songs to Thunderstuck by ACDC when he started arking up to my dad. Every time I hear that song I think of them.

Uncle Waylon has an older daughter from a previous relationship named Tia, 20. But with Aunt Charlotte, they have Easton, who's 10, and River who's 7.

Nancy put on some older songs by Kate Bush, said her mother and older sisters loved Kate Bush growing up. It must be so nice to grow up with sisters. I hate only having my older brother and my dad. I mean, they're not bad. But I wish I had a sister, or I wish my mum would come back.

30/June/2019

Skye finally told me what happened with her parents. We were driving around with Curtis and Sammy again. They picked us up from my house after school on Friday, I've never gotten changed and ready so fast in my life.

We'd parked out by the waterfalls. I finally understand why Cipher loves this place so much. Sitting down on the dark sand, beneath the sun. Sharing a rolly and smelling the air of the lake, it was amazing. Sammy was playing Lil Peep albums from his car speaker. The sound of the waterfalls almost blinding

We started talking about our pasts, our struggles. Curtis told us that his dad had cancer when he was 3, and died when he was 5. He said he cant remember his voice, and has no idea what kind of person he was, besides what everyone tells him. He said he loves his mum more then anyone, and admires her for everything she's done in raising Curtis and his older siblings. Said he also hates his step dad.

Sammy lived with his sister, her partner and their kids until he moved out with Curtis. Said his parents were drug addicts, and he hadn't seen his mum in years. Sometimes he sees his dad walking around the city talking to himself, but he never speaks to him. He doesn't even know if his mum is alive.

Sammy said our dads used to be friends, when they were young. He said his mum was older and got his dad hooked when his dad was 18. Said he has photos of our dads doing drugs together. Sammy said he still talks to his dads parents, that they're really nice people. He said he'd never talk to his mum or their side of the family again.

Skye asked me about my family, and I told them about my dads crash, and my Uncles death. About Nicole, Aunt Charlotte, and about my mum leaving with Blue. I told them about how my dad basically gave up on life after my mum left. How my dad holds a lot of pressure on Cipher to keep the house running, and how I don't even know who my dad is anymore. I miss my brother Blue.

Skye finally revealed her truth. She said her Aunt, as a CPS worker, assisted CPS from her old town in removing Skye from her parents' home. Skye's dad had been sexually abusing her, and Skye had been sending Nancy letters, asking her to help. After her dad was arrested, Skye's mum blamed Skye and happily let her leave.

It makes me so sad to think. So many people have dealt with such shitty lives. If you really think about it, you truly never really know whats going on in someones else's mind, or home.

Curtis also talked about his ex girlfriend, Elia. Said she was a psycho, and that she accused him of a lot of things he didn't do.

Following our conversations, Skye and Sammy ended up making out in the sand, and having sex. Curtis and I giggled our way to Sammy's car, and spent the rest of the night in there.

My dad didn't even notice I was gone. By the time I came back, soaked in lake water from skinny dipping in the waterfalls, and sand in every crevice of my body. My dad was still passed out and snoring in his chair. He must've had one too many beers because as a result of the empty fridge, it appears he has none left. Cipher wasn't home either, probably at some girls house.

I'd never gone skinny dipping before but all day, no matter how exhausted from my lack of sleep, all I could think about was how fun it was. Skinny dipping with a small group of friends beneath a waterfall truly is a feeling to die for.

14/July/2019

I had to block Curtis on everything. He started getting super obsessed. He was acting like we were dating. He was buying me necklaces, perfumes, and randomly sending me money. Then he'd use it against me when I'd tell him I'm too busy to see him. I'd only ever seen him once without Sammy and Skye. I don't know why he was going so crazy. Hopefully he leaves me the fuck alone now.

I think Skye still wants to see Sammy though. She even asked me to go for a drive with Curtis and Sammy again, but I refused. The last time I saw Curtis, he grabbed my arm so hard it bruised. Cipher saw it and he nearly lost his shit. I thought Cipher was still mad at me for what happened with

Jack, but he was practically begging to hurt him back. I refused though. I can deal with my own problems, and I choose to deal with it by avoiding Curtis fucking Black.

28/July/2019

Curtis has a new girlfriend somehow. Good luck to her. He literally still tries calling me on random numbers sometimes. The only way I know it's him is because he's always leaving me fucking voicemails of him screaming at me calling me a liar and a slut one second, and then leaving another one crying and admitting that he's drunk.

Men are fucking crazy. Skye isn't seeing Sammy anymore either, said she got bored of him. Instead she's been talking to a boy named Kash Grogan, who's in the year above us. His older brother, Seth, is friends with Cipher.

2/August/2019

It's Blue's birthday today. I wonder where he is. I hope mum gets him something good. Something he will enjoy.

11/August/2019

Something insane happened. Skye and Kash started officially dating on the 5th. Last night Skye invited me to Kash's house to hangout with Kash and his friends Jonah and Noah. We were drinking for hours, and for the first time I tried cocaine. Kash said he and the other boys do it all the time, and that I had nothing to worry about.

I really didn't want to, but everyone else was, and he said that I can't get addicted after doing it once. But I did it more then once. We did it the entire night. My jaw hurts so much today.

But the coke isn't the only thing I tried. Jonah and Noah ended up going for a drive, they said they'd only be gone an hour, but they didn't end up coming back.

While we waited, Kash, Skye and myself sat in Kash's room on his bed. We started talking about sex, and Kash asked if Skye and I would ever get with a girl. I'd never really thought about it, but Skye said she kissed a girl back in her home town. Kash said he didn't believe her, so she proved it by kissing me. It caught me off guard. I wasn't angry, I just wasn't expecting it.

Kash had a bunch of rap songs playing quietly in the background. He asked Skye if he could snort a line off of her chest, and Skye didn't hesitate. She immediately took off her shirt and laid down so that Kash could form a line of coke between her boobs. I felt so uncomfortable, like I was intruding.

After he snorted the line, he started kissing her body. Skye looked over at me, and asked If I wanted a turn. Both of their eyes on me, but I couldn't quite understand what she meant. Not until she sat up and pulled me closer, convincing me to try. She took off my shirt for me and asked me to lay down. Skye formed a line on my stomach, and Kash formed one between my boobs. It felt so promiscuous. I felt like a sexy magazine model. But at the same time, I felt.. I don't know. Off.

Skye and Kash started kissing, with me still laying in between them. While they were kissing, I felt Kash's hand moving up my thigh, and undoing the button on my shorts. I didn't really know what to do. It was a different feeling to anything I felt with Curtis or Jack. I felt awkward. My heart was beating so fast and my entire body felt hot, like I was lying in a sauna.

Skye took off her bra first, and Kash took off his top. Skye told me to take off my bra too, but I hesitated. I didn't really want to, but they were both staring at me. Kash looked like he wanted to laugh at me, and Skye looked angry. I didn't want to disappoint anyone, and I don't want to look like a prude. I don't know. I should've just left, but I didn't want Skye to be mad at me. So I did it. I took my bra off, and Kash immediately started kissing me, while Skye kissed my body.

We all had sex that night. I didn't really enjoy it, because I was too busy thinking about how weird I felt. I don't know how to explain it. I'm at home now. I just feel so numb.

I also realized just now that I haven't eaten since Thursday, and I'm still not hungry. My stomach feels brewed.

13/August/2019

Kash is acting strange. He's not answering any of Skye's texts, and he ignored her at school all day today.

Skye came over after school and we talked about it. Skye kept rambling and becoming worried that maybe he liked me more. Some of the things she said kind of hurt my feelings. Like saying that she's more his type, and that I didn't do as much stuff with him. I don't know, It just felt like she was trying to make herself feel better by putting me down.

14/August/2019

Kash recorded it. The entire thing was set up by Kash, Jonah and Noah. Kash told all of his friends that he bets he could get a video of him having sex with two girls, and that me and Skye seemed like the easiest targets.

I haven't stopped crying. I left school at lunchtime because Skye came up to me screaming at me and crying telling me it's all my fault. She said if it wasn't for me, Kash would still be talking to her and he would've never gotten the idea in the first place. She accused me of setting her up, and said I probably just want Kash to myself. Yana and Mauve showed me the video that Kash had sent in a group chat with a bunch of boys.

My dad was so shocked to see me home. At first he thought I was Cipher and yelled at me to stop slamming doors. He knew it was me when he heard me go into my room instead of Ciphers.

I can't believe Skye is blaming me. I'm her best friend. And what if everyone starts believing her and thinking it was my idea and that I was trying to steal her boyfriend. I've never cried so much. I feel awful.

Maybe it is my fault. Maybe I should've just left. I'm an idiot. I'm an IDIOT. I hate myself. I hate myself and everything I've done! I'm a terrible person, and I don't deserve to live.

15/August/2019

My dad somehow made it into my room yesterday after I came home. I didn't even know he could still walk on his own. He smelt like he hadn't showered in days. I used to help him to the shower, but I haven't been home in a while so he's probably been stuck in his chair.

When he made it to my room he was whimpering and out of breath. He knew I was crying.

"What's wrong, kid?" he asked as he planted his heavy body onto my bed.

I told him the truth. I didn't want to, but I couldn't think of a good lie in the heat of the moment. My dad made his way back to the lounge room, leaning against the kitchen bench as he slowly called the school. I could hear him screaming from my bedroom, demanding the principle do something. By the sound of how the call ended, I'd assume the principle didn't say something to my dads satisfaction. He hung up and he immediately called Cipher, and with the help of his walking stick, he made his stiff way out to the backyard for the first time in over a year, and sat down at the outdoor table to smoke a cigarette.

I don't know what he and Cipher talked about. All I know is Cipher didn't come home until late at night. By that point, I'd decided to help my dad to the shower, and I cooked us a microwave dinner.

Cipher and Brownie both walked in the front door together. Their fists bruised and their bodies rattled. My dad ordered me to go to my bedroom. Even though I didn't want to, I was trying really hard not to upset my dad more then he already was.

26/August/2019

Today was my first day back at school. Kash had been expelled while I was away. Apparently Skye's Aunt and Uncle complained too, and with their calls and my dads calls, the school had no choice but to do something effective.

I saw Kash with his dad at school collecting his stuff from his locker. His entire face was bruised and welting. My guess; Cipher and Brownie did that. It felt good to see him hurt, humiliated. Maybe now he knows what it feels like to be me and Skye.

I hope she forgives me soon. I miss her.

31August/2019

Skye is dead. She killed herself last night. I woke up to a message from her this morning. After not talking to me at school all week, she sent me a message saying she was sorry and that she forgives me, and that she will miss me. What kind of fucked up goodbye is that. Why the fuck did she kill herself?

I know things were getting rough, since the Kash thing. People were leaving pictures in her locker. People didn't do it with me because they knew Cipher would lose his shit. I tried talking to her. I tried telling her that it would be fine, that everyone will move on eventually but she refused to even look at me.

Why did she do that? Why did she kill herself?

8/September/2019

I haven't stopped crying since that day. Nancy and Ben invited me over for dinner after the funeral. Cipher came with me. Being in that house, I felt sick. I spoke at the funeral, but I can't even remember what I said. I didn't write anything down. All I keep thinking is there had to be more going on for her to do that. Someone doesn't just end their life because of one incident. I know it was bad, and I know her parents fucked her up, but so did mine. I thought she was happy.

What if it was my fault? If I'd just left the room like my gut was telling me to, maybe he would've never shown anyone the recording. Maybe none of this would've ever happened.

Maybe If I forced her to talk to me, to tell me what was wrong. Did I miss something? Was I ignoring the signs? What even are the signs?

I don't know what to do. How am I supposed to move on from this?

Skye's Aunt and Uncle handed me a note that was addressed to me in Skye's handwriting. Nancy admitted that she'd read it, and she debated giving it to me because she was scared it might upset me more. She told me I deserved to know why she did what she did.

But now that I have the answer. Now that I have it written in my hands, I don't know that I could open it.

9/September/2019

I was lonely in my room, sick of crying. I went to see my dad but he was asleep. It was a long shot, but the next door I knocked on was Ciphers. He was listening to sad songs, Lil Peep. Seems like everyone was listening to Lil Peep.

He was sitting on the end of his bed, smoking a cigarette and drinking a beer. He was crying.

"Whats wrong?" I asked, walking further into his smoke filled room.

He hesitated for a moment, silence. Struggling to even speak.

"Yana's pregnant."

2

Chapter Two- Baby

26/April/2020

It's been a while since I've written in this. It's my birthday today, I'm fifteen now. Yana is due to give birth in a month. Cipher is 17 now, and he dropped out of school back in December. The second he left, he started working, apprenticing toward a Diesel Mechanic. He's been saving money, he promised Yana he'd get them their own house. For the moment she's still living with her parents. Luckily they have spare rooms from all her older siblings that have moved away. She's having a girl.

I started working at a diner called Opal Bakers. I don't make any of the food or whatever, I just serve customers and greet people as they come in. It's a family owned bakery, they only gave me the job there because they knew my Uncle that died.

I thought I'd hate it, thought it would be boring. But it's not bad. It's a job. I needed to be making my own money. This way I'd be able to bring good food home like groceries and stuff to clean the house with.

My dad qualified for a home support worker, someone to help him bathe daily, and help him to the toilet and to make him meals. My dad had gotten so skinny. I never even thought about how he was going to the toilet while Cipher and I were at school. I guess he managed. But my dads at the point now that the walking stick wont help.

It took a lot to convince him to accept the offer of the support worker.

He wanted to say no. But I didn't let him.

I still see Nancy and Ben occasionally. Sometimes Nancy invites me over for dinner, or she visits me with the girls at the bakery. I always give the girls free lollipops and stickers. They've always loved putting stickers on their school books.

I wanna move to New York. I'm trying to save as much money as I can to move to America and become a famous Writer.

After Skye died, I went back to having no friends at school, and nothing to do. I started borrowing books from the library again, and taking extra work from Mr Eden. I've started writing down some ideas too, and I'm trying to save for a laptop so I can get to actually writing books with all these ideas. I'm so excited. Finally, I have something to live for.

3/May/2020

I bought myself a glass piggy bank, it's one of those piggy banks that has to be smashed to open. I'm hoping it'll help me save as much as possible without spending it on groceries or other things like makeup.

Ever since I started making my own money, I stopped stealing. I've bought heaps of clothes that I like. I think Skye would like them too. I bought heaps of makeup, skincare, and body washes. I bought stuff for my room too like new bed sheets. The house is actually starting to feel like a home. Nadia Bakshi, dads support worker, said she's proud of me for how mature I am. Said she would've never been so grown up at my age.

19/May/2020

Yana gave birth this morning. Cipher had been staying the night at her house when Dad got the call. We had to wait for Nadia to arrive before we could go to the hospital to see the baby. It was the first time Dad allowed Nadia to take him out in public, and the first time anyone outside our family have seen him in his new wheelchair.

My dad can still move his arms, stiffly, but still able. Yana let him hold the baby first. She was beautiful. He said she looked just like Yana, and I agreed.

Her name is Alina Naomi Glass-Roche. Her middle name being the same as Yana's middle name. She was perfect. I'm happy for Cipher. He's happy too.

5/June/2020

My mum came back. My dad and Nadia were inside. They didn't even know until I came home from work that my mum had been sitting at the front door. She was rocking when I found her. I almost didn't recognize her. Her hair was damp and patchy. Her eyes were red and her skin was thin and all of her bones were sticking out of her dirty clothes. She was nothing like the pretty woman I remember from all her photos.

I thought it was a toddler, sitting behind her. A tall 5 year old, maybe. But it wasn't. It was Blue. Seven years old and he looked like a toddler. He was skinny. His hair was dirty and long and he had big bruises on his knees and holes in his clothes.

I almost cried when I realized who they were. Cried, because of how awful they looked. How awful they smelled.

My mum was making a clicking noise with her tongue before she realized I was there. She stood up so fast it looked like she was almost lightheaded from the action.

Blue didn't look at me. He didn't look at anyone.

My mum hugged me. Expressed how fond she was of me and exclaimed about how much I've grown and how different I look. I didn't know what to say.

I'd always dreamed of this moment, the moment she'd come home. I thought I had every detail and interaction thought out. I thought I knew exactly what I was going to say and do. But I froze.

My dad was worse. He nearly had a heart attack when I walked in with mum and Blue. Nadia had just finished washing him, she was preparing to leave for the night. She was horrified by the sight of the people that had walked in. The sight of the child.

"Mum's back." I said lightly. The first words I'd spoken since I got home.

My mum took it upon herself to shower. While she did I tried talking to

Blue. Asking if he was hungry, or if he wanted some clothes or a bed, or anything. He didn't even look at me. I was a stranger to him.

I called Cipher. Dad was far too in shock to do anything. Cipher didn't believe me when I told him what had happened. I could hear Yana feeding Alina in the background. I heard her ask Cipher what was wrong as he stood silent.

None of us knew what to do. None of us knew what to say. My mum was acting like it was normal. Like she hadn't disappeared for 7 years, but instead took a little walk.

It took an hour for Cipher to get to the house. By that time, Mum had already raided our cupboards and was eating a whole packet of Doritos to herself. Blue hadn't moved from the spot she last placed him in. Hadn't said a thing.

Nadia stuck around until Cipher came home. Filled with people, the house felt empty. Quiet. My mother was laughing hard at the scenes on the TV. My dad could barely drink his beer straight.

Cipher tried asking me what we should do. Do we call the police? Blue looks awful. Abused, starved. He wasn't speaking and he wasn't taking any of the food we were offering.

I think my mother could sense that something was wrong. She finally stood up with her orange fingers and admitted to us all where she'd been.

She said she'd been jumping between towns, staying at shelters and living with friends she made along the way. She told us she left to run away with a man named Chris because she felt it was her destiny. My dad couldn't bare to hear the truth. My mother told the story like it was normal, average. She said Chris ended up stealing all of their money, but not until he'd introduced her to meth. After that, she was addicted.

But it was hard to know which story was the truth, and which were lies. Because some time after she told the tale about Chris, she changed her mind and said it was actually her cousin from another city, named Adam, that got her addicted. Then she said she was trying to find the hospital, and got lost. She never stuck to one story.

She told us that she came back because she wanted to make things right.

She said she wants to be sober, and that she's sick of the life she's paved for herself. She said she wishes to do everything she can to have us forgive her.

She didn't say anything about Blue. About why he wasn't speaking, or why he was bruised and dirty.

My mother was zooming around the house like a child with ADHD. Looking at every picture, wall crack, every mat and item on the shelves. She became so pestered when me and Cipher would try to use our phones. She literally tried to take them from our hands every time. She also ran around the house, unplugging everything and ensuring all the power points were turned off. And she tried to turn the oven off like 10 times because she kept thinking it was left on.

For hours, Blue didn't move. While she looked at all my makeup, I asked her. I asked why Blue wasn't speaking, why he wasn't taking any of my offerings.

She said that he was just shy, that he'd always been that way. She admired my piggy bank, and asked me about work and school. She asked me how old I am and what Grade I'm in. She tried asking Cipher the same, but Cipher was less interested in humouring her behavior. I didn't know how to feel.

11/June/2020

I haven't been to school or work since my mother came home. I've been trying to help her. She's been vomiting on the bathroom floor, shivering uncontrollably. She warned me things would get bad, and I told her I could handle it.

She'd slap me when I'd get too close. She yelled at me. Told me I was worthless. That I was a terrible daughter and that I was torturing her. She told me she never loved me, that I'm not worthy of it. Every time I'd have to slam the door shut and lock her in the bathroom.

I'd cry on the other side as she screamed and hit against the door and continued screaming at me and begging me to let her out. Apologizing to me and telling me that she gives up and wants to leave, and she promises to never bother me again.

I couldn't listen. I wouldn't. Blue still wouldn't let me bathe him. He cried hearing his mother crying. But I told him that it would be okay. That I was fixing her. For the first time he actually looked at me.

Like dad, he stays stuck to the beanbag in the lounge room. The two of them not speaking a word, or mere look. Their eyes glued to the TV.

19/June/2020

My mother is doing better. She's been begging Cipher to meet Alina, and to see Yana again. He still doesn't trust her yet.

I told my mum about Skye and what happened to her. My mum told me she was the exact same when she was my age. Said she used to sneak off to meet boys all the time with her best friends. She said she misses them, her friends.

She told me that my dad was always super handsome. Said she fell in love with him the second she laid eyes on him.

She told me stories about her sisters, and my Grandparents. I asked her if she wanted me to call them, considering she seemed so interested in how they were doing. But she didn't want to talk them, didn't want them to see her like this.

Cipher brought us dinner. Blue finally let me feed him mashed potato. It felt like the greatest accomplishment of my entire life, like I was finally winning. Like everything was finally proving to be worth it.

20/June/2020

Last night, I read Blue a bedtime story to sleep. Goodnight Moon. He laid in my bed, allowing himself to sleep for the first time since they arrived, that I'd seen. He looked so sweet, so innocent, asleep.

I'd left the room to shower. My dad had already gone to sleep and Cipher had left to sleep at Yana's so he could be with Alina in the morning before he had to work.

When I returned to my bedroom, something was different. Blue was still asleep, but there was glass on the floor. My piggy bank.

I ran into my dads bedroom, where my mother had been sleeping, she was gone. She was gone, my money was gone. The front door was wide open. I was the only one that knew. I didn't bother running outside and calling her name, or calling Cipher to look for her. I was out of breath just standing there. Heartbroken. She used me. She stole my money. How am I supposed to tell everyone? To tell Blue?

13/July/2020

I've been going to school and work again. Yana's mother told the police about what happened with Blue and my mother. They came for a welfare check. Nadia vouched for us, said that we were good people with incomes, a home, food, water. I told them that my mother had stolen my money, and I have no idea where she'd gone. I told them I didn't miss her. Not anymore.

The welfare people said they'd try and find my mother. After all, it was obvious Blue had been abused and neglected. Anyone who looked at him could see that. It'd been over a month since he'd been back, and he still hasn't said a word. He still refuses to shower, and he barely eats unless I feed him. The Welfare people told Dad that Blue would have to be enrolled into school, and that they'd organize therapy for him once he started. They said they'd be back soon for another welfare check.

I hope I can help him. I hope he can trust me, one day.

15/July/2020

The welfare people sent someone today to try and help Blue shower. They said he had visible wounds on his body that could possibly get infected if they're not treated, and that they needed to clean him in order to get a doctor to treat him.

The second that lady touched Blue he started screaming. It was the first noise he'd made since he returned. I'd never heard someone scream with more terror, more fear. Her simple comfort was enough to spiral him, and it completely set him back from all the progress we'd made.

It took hours to calm him. The lady stepped away and Blue immediately stood up from the beanbag and accidentally knocked over an empty flower pot sitting on the TV stand. The loud smash of it hitting against the floor boards startled him even more. He looked at my dad and Cipher, the only men in the room, with a different kind of fear. He sprawled into a ball in the corner of the room, hiding his eyes behind his knees and shaking profusely, almost sweating.

It was hot outside today, and our air conditioner wasn't that great. He wouldn't let us change him into shorter clothes, and his hair had gotten even longer since we first saw him. I knew he was overheating, but the welfare lady said his body lacked water and nutrients to be able to sweat, and present with red cheeks like Cipher and I always did when it was hot.

I overheard my dad, Nadia, Cipher and the welfare people on the porch talking. My dad hadn't sat in that rocking chair for years. The front door was open and I heard them discussing different strategies. They were hoping to get him into a psychologist or an OT faster, but my dad could only afford to send him to the schools psychologist. But in order for Blue to be able to see that psychologist, he'd have to go to school.

I knew Blue could hear them, but I wasn't sure if he understood what they were saying. I wasn't sure if he understood anything. He was still hiding in the corner. I wanted to do something to make him see. For him to understand that we weren't going to hurt him.

I wonder If he was scared of me. I wonder if he thought anything at all.

24/July/2020

It's cold outside today. It's the first time we'd seen frost on the grass in years. I had no work after school, and my dad had left with Nadia to go grocery shopping. I was surprised when she told me. I didn't want to make too much of a fuss, because I didn't want to upset my dad. But I was proud of him.

It was just me and Blue. Cipher was working late, and he'd be spending the night at Yana's house.

I decided to try and cook some rice on my own. Nadia had taught me how to cook rice in the microwave a few weeks ago. Next she was going to show me how to cook chicken.

I made extra for Blue and my dad and Nadia when they came back. I wasn't sure if Blue was going to let me feed it to him. He was still laying in the corner. Sleeping on the floor.

I'd noticed his eyes were slightly open, staring into the oblivion as I poured some of the rice into a separate container. I grabbed out two spoons, and grabbed the last two juice boxes from the fridge. Orange juice was my favorite.

I sat in front of him, the juice boxes and the container of rice between us. It was like I wasn't even there. He was looking straight through me.

I ripped off the straws from the juice boxes, and I stuck them in through the circle foil. He still wasn't looking at me but I tried to demonstrate how to use the straws. I wasn't sure if he'd ever used a spoon on his own, or if he'd ever eaten rice. I was hoping he'd like the smell of it enough to eat it.

"My-" I hesitated. "Our dad- he used to cook Cipher and I rice all the time for dinner. It was the easiest thing to make, for someone who couldn't stand without a walking stick."

I ate a spoon full of the rice.

"I prefer mac and cheese though. I told Nadia to buy some at the shops, so hopefully you can try some of that too- If you want."

I waited. I waited for what felt like hours for him to say something. Do something. Until finally, his eyes shifted from staring into the abyss, to looking at me. I smiled, a genuine smile.

"Do you want to try?" I asked. But nothing.

I sat there for a while, eating small spoonfuls, hoping he'd eventually sit up and ask for some. I was thinking to myself about what I'd want if I was in his situation. What I'd want someone to say.

Suddenly I came to a realization. He'd probably never eaten rice, or drank from a juice box. He's probably never used a straw or eaten with a spoon.

I stood up, and I walked into the kitchen to grab a plastic cup. A yellow one, my favorite plastic cup when I was little. I took it back to where I was sitting with Blue, and I poured the juice from the juice boxes into the cup. Then I showed him how to drink out of it.

He still didn't move, but I didn't give up on my plan yet. His eyes synced on my fingers as I grabbed a small hand full of the rice and fed it into my mouth. The shape of his big blue eyes changed as he watched. Something different, something familiar to him.

He looked weak as he slowly sat up. His small and pointy bones grinding against his thin skin as he mimicked the way I sat.

I gently push the container of rice closer to Blue. I could hear his stomach growling. His frail hand moving with precaution, his eyes glued to my face as if testing my reaction. Fearful I'd suddenly change my mind. I could see it behind his eyes. He was scared of me. I've never experienced that feeling before. Knowing that someone, especially someone smaller and weaker then me, was afraid of me. Afraid of what I'd do, what I'd say. Afraid I'd suddenly change my mind, and I'd take the offer of food away from him. Or worse.

I didn't like that feeling. It felt like the opposite of power.

But he did it. I was so proud of him for doing it. He grabbed a singular piece of rice with his fingers, and he fed it to himself. His stomach immediately growled harder, and he slowly began to pick up bigger hand fulls. I knew he was starving. I knew he wanted to eat more then he was grabbing. I stopped eating the rice because I wanted him to eat as much of it as possible. I was hungry, but I wasn't starving. He needed it. I didn't.

While he was eating, he kept looking at the straws with the corner of his eyes. But it didn't look like intrigue. I can't describe the look in words. It's more something you have to see with your own eyes, to feel it yourself. It was like a spider was inching closer toward him. He was too afraid to move, but not afraid enough to kill it. I don't know. I can't explain it.

Something inside me told me he didn't want the straws there, to be near him. I grabbed them, and he flinched as I moved. But I assured him it was okay. I stood up. He stopped eating as I did, and he watched as I placed the straws in the bin. His eyes wide and glued as I walked back over to him, and sat in front of him.

His eyes softened. "Do you want to try the juice?" I asked, pointing to the plastic cup. I think he understood me. His eyes moved to the space of the cup.

I think I was proving to him that I'm not someone to be afraid of. That

I'm someone who means it when I say it's okay. My heart was beating fast in my chest. Anticipation, I think. Hopeful he'd finally understand me, so that maybe I could understand him.

He struggled holding the cup, as if it were heavy. I supported the bottom of it with my hand, while both of his gripped around the cup. His body almost feining for the drink inside. I could hear the gulps as it made its way down his small throat. His eyes were squinting and it was like he struggled to stop himself from consuming the juice. But I didn't want him to stop. I'd never felt so rewarded by something that wasn't benefiting me. I loved that feeling.

He was startled as Nadia pushed my dad on his wheelchair through the front door. Bags of groceries in his lap. They both halted their conversations and looked to Blue with shock to see juice dripping from his mouth, and rice stuck to his hands.

Blue's jaw was shaking. That fear had overcome him again. Nadia cleared her throat as she continued her conversation with my dad. They walked into the kitchen like everything was normal, giving Blue the impression that it *was* normal, that it *was* okay. They knew exactly how to react to Blue finally eating, to not react at all.

He watched them packing away more food into the cupboards and fridge. He saw that they weren't upset, that they weren't angry. They weren't even looking at him. They weren't phased by his actions. They weren't disappointed. They weren't hurt by his choice to eat that day. So he did. He ate. He ate the entire container of rice. He drank the entire cup of juice. His stomach looked bloated from the small amount of food he'd consumed.

"Do you want more?" I asked, on a whim. Unsure if he knew what I was asking. But he did, he shook his head. He didn't want any more. Was that a good sign? Was it bad?

"Okay." I responded gently, stacking the cup inside the container, preparing to take it to the sink.

I wasn't sure what to say or do next. I wasn't sure if I should say or do anything else. I didn't want to overwhelm him. But I also didn't just want to give up.

"Do you want to see something cool?" I finally asked.

He looked over at my dad and Nadia. Still, he saw that they were busy. They weren't looking for his response, they weren't watching his reaction. I think he liked that. I think it made him feel safe, the lack of attention.

He nodded his head. "Okay." I said. I reached out my hand. A gesture of kindness, I hoped. Surprisingly, he took it. His hand was so small. Sticky from the rice, and rough to the touch.

It took him a while to stand up. It seemed like he needed help, but I was scared If I ran to his rescue he'd abort away. So I waited. I was patient.

I guided him outside. The sun was hidden behind clouds, and he immediately got goosebumps. But he didn't act cold.

I showed him the frost on the grass. I told him that I loved winter more then summer. And that I'd always dreamed of visiting America during Christmas and to see the snow. I dreamed of snow.

I sat on the grass, and he followed. I told him that It was cold to touch, but it was interesting to me to feel all the small shards of frost.

He touched it too. He was sort of washing his hands in the frost. A strange thing to see, really. I've never seen someone wash their hands in grass before.

2/August/2020

It's Blue's birthday. I took the day off of work to spend it with him. Whenever I wasn't home, my dad would refuse to leave the house because he didn't want to leave Blue alone with the welfare people. My dad knew Blue didn't trust the welfare people, no matter who they brought. Cipher said that maybe it was their uniforms. Maybe he didn't trust people who wore certain clothes.

They visited yesterday while I was at school. They never see any progress when they try to approach him, but they're glad that Nadia is an out of family witness to see how Blue responds to me and my dad. Cipher never makes much of an effort. I think he wants to, but I think he's afraid.

Cipher has never been great with comfort. He's never known how to talk about emotions, or how to be patient with people. He means well, he's just afraid of doing something to set Blue back. And he doesn't want to be labeled as someone that blue is afraid of.

Cipher and Yana brought Alina over to meet Blue for the first time. They brought him presents wrapped in blue birthday paper. I don't think Blue has ever seen wrapping paper. He turned 8 today, and he'd never received a gift wrapped in birthday paper.

He still hadn't let us clean him, so his odor was undeniable. He couldn't peal his eyes off of Alina. It's like he'd never seen a baby before.

I had to show him how to rip off the presents. It was awkward. Silence ripped through the room as everyone watched him watch me rip open Cipher's gift for him. It was a soccer ball. Yana's parents also gave him new clothes, clothes just for him. I don't think he understood that though, that the gifts were for him.

"Do you want to try it on?" I asked. The welfare people watching for his reaction. Waiting to see if he'd except my offer of trying on a new Rolling stones T-shirt.

I hated that they were there. His birthday was supposed to be for him, and it felt like they were making it about them, in a way.

He didn't respond to my offer. I wonder what he was thinking. Whether he was thinking anything at all.

I'd brought a cake home from my work. We debated singing him happy birthday or not, or using candles. But we decided we should, just to see.

Cipher lit the candles with fire. Blue's eyes rushing with the click of the lighter. I could see he was getting scared. I approached him. Sat by him beside the beanbag. He flinched as I held his hand, but it got him to look at me. And he knew he shouldn't be afraid of me.

"It's okay." I reminded him. "Cakes mean good." I told him. "Cakes make people happy." I nodded.

I think he understood me, because he let Cipher bring the cake over toward him. Everyone singing happy birthday, but quietly. Because the welfare people said that loud sounds could disturb him.

He didn't know what to do when that yellow and blue cake was in front of him. But he wasn't looking at the cake itself, rather the burning candles.

He knew everyone was smiling, he understood that I said it was okay. But the fire, the fire was all he could focus on.

At the end of the song we waited for him, but he didn't do anything. Instead, Cipher blew the candles out. It took everyone by surprise, and we waited for Blue to react negatively to Cipher's abrupt action. But he didn't. He didn't do anything.

He let me feed him his chocolate cake, I'm glad the welfare people got to see that. I saw Blue looking around, watching everyone eating that same cake. He saw everyone's smiles, heard everyone's chatter.

Later that night, Nadia, Cipher, Yana and Alina had already left. My dad was sitting in his chair and Blue was sitting on the couch. He'd moved there to sit beside me. Perfectly within arms reach of my dad.

It was the perfect time for my dad to finally give Blue his gift. Blue watched intently as my dad struggled to rip the wrapping paper off on his own. I could see my dad felt embarrassed. Embarrassed he couldn't do something so simple himself. But nobody could understand him, more then Blue.

Just like I'd done with him earlier, he helped my dad. My dad froze, trying not to startle Blue as he gently helped my dad rip off the wrapping paper from the square gift. My dads hand shaking as his hands weakly grabbed a hold of corners, while Blue took most of the work in helping unwrap the gift. I felt my throat churning as I watched. My eye's beginning to water. He was so kind in that moment. He was doing something, not because he was eager to see what was in the gift, but because he could see that my dad could not do it on his own.

I saw tears roll down my dads old cheeks. Unable to wipe them away. Finally we could see what my dad had gotten him. A photo album. A yellow and white striped album, with a teddy bear on the front.

My dad moved his hand to try and lift the cover open, with Blue's support, they got it done. The first page had Blue's name, his weight and height as a baby. It had his birthday, his mum and dads names, and the names of his siblings.

My dad opened the next page, which contained a small lock of Blue's infant hair. Blue's umbilical cord. Some things my dad had kept from the hospital when Blue was born. The page on the right had a handwritten family tree, with Blue's name in the middle.

My dad started pointing at the different names, explaining who they were. Talking about his parents, his voice shaking as he talked about their deaths. Shaking as he talked about his twin brother. Shaking as he talked about our mum.

My dad moved onto the next page, which was full of baby pictures. Photos of Blue when he was just born. My dad explained each and every picture. Telling Blue the story behind every one. He showed photos of Cipher and I holding Blue hours after he'd been born. Photos of Uncle Ronny, Grandma and Grandpa. Our Aunties. Our cousins. He pointed out every single person on every single page. Showing Blue some of dads old friends who'd held Blue before he disappeared.

I couldn't stop the tears from falling from my own eyes. Wiping them away the second they broke free. Trying to remain silent as my dad retold some of the brightest stories, during the darkest time in his life. Showing Blue that he is loved. That we have loved him for 8 years, even if he didn't know it.

Blue cried too. A different kind of cry. It wasn't a cry of fear, or hungry. I don't know what it was. I guess only Blue could really know how he was feeling in that moment. I could only imagine.

Blue slept on the couch beside our dad that night. They both snored as they dreamed of tomorrow.

4/August/2020

Blue is expected at school orientation tomorrow. Myself and Cipher had to take time off of work and school to take Blue to the Primary school for a walk through with the principle. One of the welfare ladies would be joining us too. But Blue couldn't go to school without cleaning himself.

My dad had been showing Blue a bunch of different movies that my dad and his brother loved to watch as kids. It was rewarding to see my dad hand Blue a VHS tape from the pile he asked Nadia to collect from the TV cabinet. We were pretty sure Blue couldn't read, so my dad had to point out which VHS tape for Blue to grab, and he taught him how to play VHS tapes on the TV.

They watched The Goonies, The Land Before Time movies, Labyrinth, Back to the Future, The Never Ending Story, The Secret of Nymph, E.T, and had so many more movies on the list left to watch. My dad seemed super happy to have someone to talk to these movies about. Even if Blue never said anything back, think my dad and Blue turned out to be quite similar. The same facial reactions to certain scenes, even laughing the same. Blue's laugh was something to cherish, something magic, even.

Nadia had cooked us butter chicken and rice for dinner. Blue loved it, it was his first time eating chicken with us. He also loved orange juice, almost as much as me.

After dinner, Nadia helped my dad to his en suit shower, while I held Blue's hand and took him toward the shared bathroom. I wondered if Blue had ever seen a bathroom before. If he'd ever taken a bath or showered.

He was startled as I turned the bath on. I was asking him questions, seeing if he wanted to touch the water first in case it was too hot or too cold, but he didn't respond. I could tell he didn't want to do it, take a bath. I didn't want to force him, but I knew if he didn't do it with me, the welfare people would start to get worried. I didn't want to traumatize him more then he already was, but I did want to try and help encourage him. Support him.

I told him that I loved taking baths as a kid. I reminded him of the photo of him as a baby in the bath with Cipher and I. I told him to watch as the soap I poured into the water turned into bubbles. The smell was amazing.

After I finished filling the bath, I ran my hand through the water, and grabbed a handful of bubbles and blew them at Blue. I laughed, and he smiled.

"Do you want to try?" I asked, and his smile disappeared. He was scared.

Suddenly I got an idea, it was a long shot, but it was all I could think to help him in that moment. I stood up, and I stepped into the bath, fully clothed. I sat down, and felt the uncomfortable texture of my wet clothes sticking to my body. The water temp was perfect.

Seeing me get in, Blue started to inch closer. He gently touched the water with the tips of his fingers, perfect temperature.

He lifted his foot, I could see old scars and dirty cuts on the bottoms of his feet as he stepped in. He stood there in the bath for a bit, looking like he was debating whether to go further or not. I was shocked to see him slowly take off his ripped long sleeve top. I think it used to be a white top. I could tell he felt uncomfortable by the bottom of his heavy pants getting wet, so he stepped back out, gently placing his dirty t shirt on the sink, and slowly taking off his pants.

He looked awkward, uncomfortable. I looked down at the bubbles, popping them and giving him the privacy of stepping into the bath without me looking. He sat down and the water level rose.

I showed him again how you can pick up the bubbles and blow them. He smiled and gently tried it himself. Everything he did was always so gentle, so careful. He smiled more seeing he could do it too. Like magic.

His teeth were so yellow, and they seemed so small too.

I adjusted myself to sit on my knees, my clothes still sticking to me. I asked him if it was okay if I washed him with a sponge. I showed him the sponge and let him feel it. I showed him how bubbles and soap drip out of the wet sponge when you squeeze it. He nodded his head, and without me telling him to, he turned around and wrapped his arms around his knees as I started scrubbing his back. His back, filled with cuts and infected wounds. The welfare people were right.

I could see so much trauma written on his back. I nearly choked on my own source of oxygen, seeing it. Suddenly all my biggest traumas were miniature to his. Cigarette burns, thin and long scars. Bruises that look like the buckle of a belt. Puss was oozing from some of the burns. His spine staring at me as I ever so slightly washed the dirt from Blue's skin. His shoulder blades on his back pointing as a slope for the water to drip from. Only as I washed his hair did I realize there were many bugs living inside. A welt rising around the back of his neck, like something was wrapped around it.

I helped Blue put on the clothes Yana's parents bought him for his birthday.

A rolling stones T shirt and black track pants that fit his waist perfectly. He looked at himself in the mirror as we heard Cipher enter through the front door. He was dropping off oranges from Yana's parents orange tree. I told him that it would be fun to make real orange juice with Blue, considering he loved it so much.

As he walked through the front door, Blue and I both looked at Cipher as he stopped at the open bathroom door. Me, soaked and dripping water from my heavy clothes. And Blue, clean and wearing his birthday outfit. A smirk rose from the corner of Cipher's mouth.

"He has head lice." I told Cipher. His smirk faded away.

Cipher took the bag of oranges into the kitchen, and then found his old electric razor in the bathroom cabinet. Blue watched as he plugged it in, and was frightened by the sound of it turned on. Cipher was quick to turn it back off and we comforted him promptly. Cipher explained to him that we had to shave his hair, so that it could grow back clean. But Blue didn't want to. He was afraid.

Cipher caught an idea in his mind, a split second decision. And suddenly, Cipher was looking at himself in the mirror and shaving his own hair off. I gasped at his decision. Cipher had always taken care of his appearance. Always made sure his curly mullet was perfect since the day he turned 13. He'd never shaved his hair, and never even considered doing it until today.

Blue watched and slowly calmed as Cipher continued shaving his hair until it was all gone. His lost hair coating the floor and sticking to the dripping water. Jo March. Cipher reminded me of Jo March in that moment. Cutting his hair solely for the intent of supporting someone else. I'd never seen Cipher so selfless.

After that, Blue let Cipher shave his hair off too. After a short amount of time, I soon saw two new brothers, with two new matching hair cuts. I realized how similar their faces were. I could finally see what Blue truly looked like under all that dirt and hair. Identical to Cipher, and Identical to our dad.

Nadia helped our dad to the couch, wrapping a blanket over his legs. Both of their eyes lifting as myself, Cipher and Blue walked into the lounge room.

Their eyes staring at the new hair cuts, and Blue's new clean appearance. My dad nearly teared up again. And me, no longer aware of the damp and uncomfortable feeling of my soaked clothes.

5/August/2020

Cipher picked Blue and I up from dads house this morning. The social worker, Emma Zane, was going to meet us at the school. Cipher was wearing his work uniform. Dad and Nadia waited outside as we approached Cipher's car. I know my dad wished he could go too, but it's just easier if Cipher and I do. Once Cipher is of age, he will be considered one of Blue's new guardians, alongside my dad.

Blue looked at the logo on Cipher's shirt, and the same logo on his hat. I asked him what Yana thought of his new haircut. "Handsome." he laughed.

Cipher saw Blue's eyes glued to the logo on his hat.

"It's where I work." Cipher explained. "Do you want one?" he then asked, not bothering to wait for a response as he reached into the back of his white ute and pulled out an identical hat.

Blue took the hat from Cipher's hands. He inspected it, then looked up at the one on Cipher's head, before placing his own on his head in the exact same position. My dad forced them to get a photo together, Blue copying the exact way Cipher crossed his arms and looked with a stern face instead of a smile.

Emma and the Principle of the Primary School, Mr Nyick, met us at the front of the office. Mr Nyick, who was once Cipher and I's Principle, met Blue with a big smile and tried to shake Blue's hand. Emma reminded him that Blue might not be susceptible to new people, and was unlikely to accept gestures, physical touch, and communication.

Blue held my hand tightly as Mr Nyick took us for a tour around the school. He showed us the classrooms of the Grade Blue would be in. Every child staring through the windows and the open doors as we passed. Blue barely looking up from the sight of our hands gripped together. He showed us where the two different boys bathrooms are, where the canteen was, where children liked to sit and play during breaks. He showed us where the music room was, the Drama rooms, the art room, the playground. Never once did Blue seem interested. I think Mr Nyick and Emma discussed making sure the school wouldn't be too disruptive during the tour, ensuring no music classes were in play at that time of the day, and simply pointing out the Gym and basketball court, rather then actually approaching them.

The final place he took us was the well being building. In there was the first aid rooms, and two different rooms with two different counselors. Mr Nyick introduced us to both, but explained that Mrs Keen, a short indigenous lady with a kind smile, was the only counselor with an advanced psychological training background, and that she'd be Blue's assigned counselor at the school.

"Hello, Blue. It is so wonderful to finally meet you." she greeted. "My name is Mrs Keen, and I want you to know that when you officially start school, If you ever need anything- a time out from class, someone to talk to- I'll be here. My door will always be open."

She seemed gentle, sweet. Blue looked at her as she spoke. I was proud of him for acknowledging her.

After the tour, Emma informed us that the school would fund his books and a pencil case with all the things he needs. She said that all we'd need to ensure is that he had a backpack, a lunchbox, his uniform, and food to eat during breaks. She also explained to us that Blue's classes will be different sometimes, that he'd be able to attend music and art classes like normal. But depending on how he responds to English, math and science classes, he might have to receive additional care.

At that point in time we had no impression on whether Blue could read or count, or if he knew colours, or sound. We knew he wasn't deaf, but we had no idea if the reason Blue didn't speak is because he chooses not to, or if he just doesn't know how. Emma told us it would be Mrs Keen's job to help us determine that. She said that Mrs Keen was also licensed to diagnose and medicate children, and that Blue's life would become a lot easier once he starts seeing Mrs Keen.

Emma also told us that she would be Blue's assigned social worker from then on. She said she'd already had this discussion with our dad, but thought it would be best to inform us as well. She said she would be visiting Blue at school once a week from the moment he starts. She told us that if we ever had any questions to speak to her or Mrs Keen.

Emma finished the conversation by telling us that starting tomorrow, Cipher or another adult in his family would be required to take Blue to Mrs Keen's office on Tuesdays and Thursdays, up until September 2nd, when Blue would officially start school. She said she discussed with our dad getting Blue an in-class support worker, and that she would try her hardest to get someone as soon as possible. But even then, no one knows if Blue would even take to another support worker.

Emma knows Blue, and she knows to wear certain clothing when around him. For some reason, he doesn't like the purple uniform the people from her company wear.

Cipher drove Blue home after that, while I walked a few minutes back to my school.

13/August/2020

I've almost saved up enough money to buy a laptop. Cipher has been taking Blue to Mrs Keens office on Tuesdays and Thursdays. His boss understands. Cipher isn't particularly happy about the 2 hours of lost money hes facing doing it, but he knows it's important. He sits out in the hallway for 80 minutes while Blue talks to Mrs Keen. No idea if he's actually talking, or if it's just Mrs Keen doing the talking.

Blue and I have started a routine. Nadia always makes him and my dad breakfast, and she helps feed him lunch during the day. I often work straight after school, but when I get home, Blue and I start his bath time. I think he's starting to enjoy the bath.

17/August/2020

Our Grandma and Grandpa visited Blue today while Emma was over. None of them have seen Blue since he came back. I think maybe it was too hard for them, or something.

My Grandma was excited to see him, she talked about a bunch of different stories about our mum and our aunties from when they were kids. Showing Blue photos from her own albums.

My Grandpa didn't say much to him. I don't think he understands why Blue doesn't speak. My mum and my Aunties have always been chatterboxes. They'd never stop talking if they could. Blue was different, and my Grandpa didn't know how to handle that.

"Maybe you should ask Merry." My dad said with a snarl, sipping from his coffee.

My dad hadn't drank a beer since Blue returned, to my knowledge.

28/August/2020

Cipher told my dad that Mrs Keen has diagnosed Blue with PTSD and Selective Mutism. My dad hates that he couldn't be there to hear it from her himself. She said he has a clear anxiety disorder that restricts him from speaking. She's certain that it is anxiety, he chooses not to speak. She said it would take a lot to get him to speak. And even then, he may not.

My dad broke down. Knowing that Blue was born perfectly normal, that something traumatic enough to cause Mutism happened to him was something completely unbearable. The thought of knowing he may never speak, was almost deafening.

Blue's wounds have been treated. They're starting to heal from the ointments, and the bruises were starting to fade. Emma had photos taken of his wounds, and was working with Mrs Keen and my dad to write up a report against our mum, if we can ever find her.

Nadia and I made sure to collect Blue's uniform today after I finished bathing Blue. We bought him a pair of sneakers with laces, but Blue freaked out when he saw them. I asked him to show me what it was. I told him that he was safe and that I just wanted to see what was scaring him. He pointed at the shoe, I thought. I thought maybe he didn't like it, or something. Until I looked again, and it was the shoe laces. I plan to return his shoes tomorrow, and buy some shoes with Velcro straps instead. Hopefully he likes that better.

29/August/2020

Cipher let Blue have his old backpack and lunchbox as his own for school. He said Blue is also welcome to sleep in his old bedroom, considering Cipher is never home. He showed Blue around, he's gotten more comfortable walking freely in our home.

Cipher let him look at all of his belongings. All of the things he loved when he was Blue's age. Blue fixated on the stereo. Cipher asked him if he'd ever heard music before. Of course, he didn't answer. But Cipher took the opportunity to show him some of his favourite music.

He explained that the stereo used to be our dads, and that he'd been buying CDs for it for years.

He showed Blue how to use it. He put on a CD with November Rain by Guns n Roses. The sound was high and at first frightened him. But Cipher was quick to turn it down. Only then could he actually allow himself to listen to the song that was playing. Cipher waited with anticipation, hoping he was doing the right thing in that moment. Praying he wasn't pressuring Blue. Praying he wasn't scaring him.

It was a sweet moment, one I'm sure the two of them will remember forever as the day Blue discovered music.

7/September/2020

Its been a week since Blue started school. Monday was hard. Our dad and Nadia took her car so that dad could bring his wheelchair. Myself and Emma walked in with him, taking him first to Mrs Keen's office. The only problem is, he'd only ever stayed with Mrs Keen because he knew Cipher was right outside the door. My dad had to ask Nadia to take him outside, because he couldn't handle Blue's screaming. He wanted to take Blue home but Emma wouldn't let him. She warned him it would be hard.

Blue held onto my arm so hard it hurt. Emma and Mrs Keen kept trying to talk to him, but it was only making things worse. I lost my temper. I shouted at everyone, I told them all to stop talking because I could see they were overwhelming him.

I knelt down and I held Blue's shaky hands as I looked into his eyes.

"I know you're scared. I know you don't want to-" His tears dripping down to my hands. "-I hated school too, you know- when I was your age. I hated going, but I knew I had to. But you know you're not alone. I'll be at school too- just up the road. Emma is going to be with you all day, and Mrs Keen is here to help as well. You wont ever be alone."

I could see my words were helping, slightly. Suddenly my eyes caught a glimpse of the bracelet on my wrist, the same one Skye gave me a long time ago. The handmade one on a brown string with yellow and green beads. I know I made a promise to Skye, I said I'd never take it off. But this is a promise I'm willing to break, for Blue.

"Here." I said, taking the bracelet off of my wrist and showing it to Blue. "I made a promise a long time ago to never take this bracelet off. It's from someone very special to me, that no longer gets to see it. Will you promise to keep it safe- and in return, it'll keep you safe too."

Blue looked at the bracelet convincingly. He truly believed me when I said it. He let me put it on his wrist, and he immediately began fiddling with the beads.

"You've gotta be brave, okay? And I'll be here at 3:15 to pick you up. Then we can walk home together. Okay?"

He didn't say anything, he didn't even nod. But I could read his face, and I knew he was going to try.

Emma took out her hand for Blue. He hesitated, but the bracelet gave him the confidence to go. I waved him goodbye, and I spent the entire day at school barely able to focus. Fearful he wasn't okay.

He did better then anyone expected. He was quiet, didn't participate in class and of course, didn't speak to any of his peers or teachers. Emma observed him all day, and took him to eat with Mrs Keen during breaks while Emma left the school. He was never left alone, just like I said.

He went to school everyday this week. I rewarded him on Friday afternoon, bringing him home a chocolate cake slice from my work. Chocolate cake was his favorite.

11/October/2020

It's been a while since I've written in this, I've been so busy with school, work, and Blue. I'm so close to buying a laptop. I've been writing down and discussing so many book ideas with Mr Eden.

Cipher and Blue's hair have been growing at the same rate. It's sort of a mess at the moment, but Blue loves wearing Cipher's old hats he finds in Cipher's bedroom.

Blue's been doing well at school. Emma doesn't have to shadow him anymore, but she's still trying to get him an in-school support worker to help him engage in class work. Mrs Keen is still working with him too.

Sometimes Blue wakes up in the night screaming. He has nightmares a lot when he sleeps alone. Sometimes he doesn't even try to sleep in Cipher's room. But I don't mind when he wants to sleep with me. I don't like sleeping alone either. I hate seeing Skye in my dreams. Blue makes me feel okay when I wake up and see him sleeping too.

I had to work unexpectedly today. Blue had to come with me because my dad and Nadia had to go to see a doctor about my dads paralysis. Yana, Cipher and Alina visited me in the shop today.

I gave Blue so many free lollipops. My boss also cooked him ham and cheese toasties for lunch. While he sat there, he drank hot chocolates and worked on the learning book Mrs Keen gave him. The first few pages of the book are about identifying colours. There's some pages about identifying numbers and words as well. Mrs Keen made sure to block out the colour purple with a black marker before giving it to him. We still don't know why that colour frightens him. She also blocked out word sections in the book that discuss mum's and mothers. We're not sure if he can read that word, but if he can, we just want to do everything we can to avoid upsetting him.

I think he liked the peacefulness of the bakery. My boss is a super nice old man as well, and he always talks about his Grandkids. He told me at the end of my shifts that Blue is always welcome to come to work with me. He said Blue was incredibly kind and soft hearted.

23/October/2020

It's Cipher's birthday today. My dad, Nadia, Blue and I visited his house with Yana and her family after school. I brought a rainbow cake from my work. Blue also handed Cipher his birthday present. We were scared Blue would be afraid in an unfamiliar place, but I think school has helped him get used to that.

9/November/2020

The end of the year is approaching. I cut Cipher and Blue's hair today. They'd both grown out enough for me to give Cipher his mullet back. Blue wanted the same haircut.

Blue is doing really well with the books Mrs Keen has been giving him. He does really well at identifying colours. He's working on his writing and spelling now too.

I also bought myself a laptop today. A cheap one, but it'll work. Something is better then nothing. And now I can finally start writing my books, meaning I'm one step closer to being a famous author.

25/December/2020

My dad and Nadia bought Blue a chalkboard and chalk a while ago, so that he could continue working on his spelling and writing. He started covering the pavements in front of our house in drawings and words. He loves drawing his family, especially Alina. He loves Alina. He gets excited when we get to see her. Blue still doesn't talk, but we're starting to understand him based on his expressions.

His love for the chalkboard gave me an idea for Blue's Christmas present. I knew Blue wouldn't like something unless its familiar to him, and the only thing I could think of, the thing I know he's seen me use and carry around with me. Something of mine. Something I know he will love, and I know he will use. Something that will benefit him in so many ways. My journal. The same one Cipher gave to me once upon a time.

So this is my formal goodbye. Thank you, my beautiful journal for everything you have done. I hope you help Blue express himself, and regulate as much as you helped me.

Goodbye.

3

Chapter Three- Cornflower

Cipher Glass

The Monologue

My mum left when I was 9. I do believe I got to spend the better half of life with her. Fiona wouldn't remember her much from before, and Blue only got to see her after she fucked her life up. I don't really know what Blue saw, but I know what I saw.

My first few memories of her, I remember she used to love wearing long floral dresses and big sun hats. She used to like wearing lip gloss too, and sometimes would have me put it on when my lips were dry.

My mum and dad bought me my first bike when I was 5. I started becoming good friends with the family from across the street when I was 6.

Melody Roche and my mother both liked gardening. They bonded over it. They used to give each other tips and help each other out with their gardens. Back then the houses looked bright. I remember once, when I was about 7 years old, my mother invited all the Roche family over to listen to music and help her paint the outside of our house. My dad hated it, but he never told her no. He knew she enjoyed it. Even if she picked ugly colours like yellow for the panels, and blue for the door. Nobody would ever look at our house and think it was boring. Even years later, after some of the paint had chipped off or warn out.

Jerome, Zain, Cruz, Dare and I used to ride around the neighborhood a lot. School holidays and weekends we spent all day on our bikes. We started building dirt tracks behind my house, past the creek. Used to spend all our time learning tricks.

Fiona was always the youngest of all the kids- Yana's sisters used to love doing her makeup and hair. They always laid on their stomachs in circles, drawing chalk all over the pavements and roads between our houses. Always having to move when a car came through. Sometimes we all played football too. I remember Mauve used to always get super sooky when she didn't understand the game. Dare used to pick on her all the time. She and Fiona usually sat on the sides and watched, making sure no one was cheating.

I remember the first time Yana's oldest brother, Jerome, told me that Melody wasn't his mum. He said that Justin, their dad, had Jerome before he met Melody. It was around that time that I met Daniella and Sophia too. They were kids Jerome's mum had to another bloke. They came around to stay with Jerome once a month. That's when our football games were the best, because we had more people. My dad and Justin used to play goal keepers. My dad loved football when he was in school, and he was always tackling us down. It was almost impossible to win if you were going against my dad.

I'd been friends with Brownie since we were babies. Our dads were childhood friends, and Eyeball was at our house more often then his own. When Brownie and I were 8, his mother, Veda, died from breast cancer. I remember me, Brownie and Dare sitting at the creek behind my house right after the funeral. Dare throwing stones into the water while Brownie and I hung our shoe less feet in. That was the first time I'd ever experienced death. I'd never thought about it until that day. I'd never grasped the concept of it. Still don't.

My first kiss was down by that creek too. Yana and I always had a crush on each other. She used to come and watch us boys on the dirt tracks. I used to always catch her down by the creek, looking for ladybugs too. I never understood why she collected them. She always used to get so fucking mad when one of us would accidentally step on an ant. Dare was a cruel motherfucker and would start doing that shit on purpose to piss her off.

The day we kissed, Dare had gotten into Yana's collection of ladybugs, and killed them. She was back down there, sniffling in her own thoughts, burying all those dead ladybugs like they was people.

I sat down by her, watching her bury small holes in the wet dirt with the tip of her finger, as she listed off their names as each body was buried.

The pure red ones were named Buggy, Buck, and Rudolph. The orange ones were called Orange and Juice. Fiona named them. And the yellow ones were called Socks and Sunny. I thought the names were ridiculous, and she just about lost it at me when I laughed.

But I wasn't laughing because I thought it was stupid, I was laughing because I thought it was cute. Even at 9 years old, I knew what I was looking at.

I used to love that she never had her hair up like the rest of her sisters. Always keeping it down, simple. And I liked like she had green eyes instead of brown like the rest of her sisters. It made her seem different. Unique. Never had as much game as I did when I was a kid, I tell ya that.

First time I smoked a cigarette was when I was 12, Yana thinks it was when I was 13. I did smoke when I was 13, with Eyeball and Brownie. But the first time was when I was 12. I'd stolen 3 of them from my dads pack, and took them down to the creek where Brownie and Dare met me after school. Coughed our cunts up. We still laugh thinking back to that day.

Yana's never understood why I tried all that shit, smoking and drugs. But she doesn't get it. Hate to say it but her life has been pretty close to perfect. I remember the day my mum left. Dad was in hospital. Fiona and I had been dropped back at the house by Grandma Uma. It was late. Fiona was calling mum's name, probably wanting to sleep in the bed with her. I remember at the hospital listening to Eyeball asking Grandma and Grandpa why my mum wasn't there, why she wasn't answering her calls or texts. I remember being scared that maybe she was hurt too. Worried something bad happened to her and Blue.

When we got back to the house, Grandma Uma searched the house with Fiona. Little Fiona, crying for the comfort of her mother. I had to hug her while Grandma called the police, when she realized that my mum and Blue weren't home. Everyone really thought something bad had happened. No one could believe that she might've left willingly. Not while her partner was in the hospital. Not without her other two children. Right?

I remember having to stay at Aunt Hannah's house for two weeks. Her house was nicer then ours, but less colourful. Aunt Hannah and Uncle Craig were engaged at the time, and had only one son, who was about a year older then Fiona. His name's Daine, and he went to private school, while Fiona and I went to public school.

I hated staying at that house. I hated hearing Fiona crying every night because she missed our parents. Every morning she would ask Aunt Hannah if Grandma found mum, and Aunt Hannah would always say no.

I remember teachers constantly pulling me to the side after classes to ask me how I was doing. I fucking hated those question. Like seriously, how do you think I'm fucking doing? My baby brother and mother was missing, and my dad was in the hospital. Oh, and my Uncle was dead.

Uncle Ronny's funeral was the first time I'd seen dad since the accident. He looked awful- different. He was in a wheelchair, and he refused to talk to anyone. After that we stayed with Grandma Uma and Grandpa Rupert for a few more weeks before moving back in with our dad. At that time, dad was still walking, and he was supposed to be attending physical therapy. Which he was, for a little while. I guess after some time the beer became more important.

I have a faint memory of the few times he'd leave for a couple hours, and then he'd come back like nothing ever happened. I always suspected he was looking for mum. I just wish he'd let me know before he left.

I always wondered if dads paralysis was more of a mental thing, rather then a real physical issue. I don't know, I've just never believed that one day his body just decided to stop working. I know the doctors said that his spine was a little fucked after the crash, and that he'd need physical therapy and treatments to fix it. But for a while there, he was walking around and moving like nothing had happened. He was a little wobbly, and maybe drowned his pain in alcohol, but he was fine. Then suddenly he just started to get really bad out of no where. I don't know, maybe I'm an unreliable source. I'm just explaining what I saw. Maybe he became so filled with self hatred that he let himself waste away until he was close to nothing. Maybe it was easier to slowly die, then to try and fix his life.

After I turned 12, I started looking at life a little differently. I started questioning why anything was important anymore, if it meant that one day It could all be for nothing. Uncle Ronny was doing great in life. He had a business, a wife, friends, family. He had money, a home, a future, and one day he just fucking died. What a waste of a life. All because his wife decided to cheat on him.

I hated her for a long time for that. Sometimes I fantasized about what I'd do If I ever saw her again. The hatred I had for her only grew, and grew until it reached my mum and every other woman in the world. Maybe that's why I'm terrible in relationships. Maybe I'm just filled with so much hatred I could never truly love someone. Not even myself.

I lost my virginity when I was 14. It was around that time that Brownie had introduced Dare and I to Beau Jones. I used to admire the shit out of him. He was like 3 years older, and his Aunt sold the best drugs in the city. His brother, Link, was a year older then me. Us boys used to go to Beau's house after school almost everyday. Fiona always used to ask to come, but I knew she'd snitch on me if she saw what we were doing there.

Jasper Krike was a mutual friend of myself and Link, and he used to bring his little brother Jordan around too. It was the designated hang out spot. And it was perfect, because Beau and his Aunt would throw the best parties there that would last from Friday to Monday morning. At the ripe age of 14, we were sneaking back into our houses still drunk and walking to school. It was a time to be alive.

I met Virginia Joste at one of those parties. She was like 18 and at the time I looked a lot older then 14, so I lied to her and said I was 16 and she believed it. She was literally one of the hottest girls I'd ever seen at the time. Older, long black hair and bright blue eyes, naturally thick lips and an insane body. Best believe I was seen as a fucking king when I finally bagged her. Never lived it down.

She and her friends came around for those parties like every weekend. While I was hooking up with Virginia, Beau was hooking up with her cousin Lacie. It wouldn't take long for Dare and Brownie to rush the opportunity too. Brownie took the longest- I reckon he was nervous about it, scared the girls wouldn't like him or something. But he always said he just hadn't met the right girl yet.

First time I tried weed was at that house, same with cocaine, and pingers. It didn't take long before that shit was on the regular. I enjoyed the company of being surrounded by people who were just as fucked up as me. The older we got the more shit we got to experience. Sneaking out to drive up to the water fountains with pretty girls. Skipping class to smoke weed. Sleeping with girls who had boyfriends and getting into fights. It was all for our own enjoyment. Nothing meant anything. Nothing but good times.

Even when I'd lie on the floor in Beau's house, looking up while my eyes are spinning out of my head. I'd sometimes be reminded that this is it. This is my life, and If I died tomorrow I'd have nothing to regret, because I never did anything without making sure it benefited me. What's the point in pleasing other people if it meant I wasn't happy? What's the point in wasting my life on school and money and work if it meant it might all be for nothing tomorrow? I didn't want to live like that, I wanted to live freely.

I remember when Fiona started hanging out with Skye Sallow. She was pretty, but too young. She used to always try and talk to me on social media, it got a little weird. If she'd been around long enough to turn 16, who knows.

But I hated the way she was changing Fiona. Fiona used to love wearing my clothes. I fucking hated it at the time, but once she started dressing and acting like Skye, I missed it. She was too young to be dressing like a prostitute. Not that I could do anything about it. Just didn't want to think about her entering her a life where she starts thinkin' about boys. And best believe if any of my friends ever tried to go there I'd kill em.

I remember finding out about Jack Perkins. I met him for the first time in High school, he was year 7 and I was year 8. Funniest cunt you'd meet. One of those kids that sat at the back of the class with all the boys. Usually favored by the female teachers.

I'd been friends with him for 2 years before I found out he'd hooked up with Fiona, who was only 14 at the time. Sick fuck. He was lucky I ever started inviting him to any of those parties. If it weren't for me he wouldn't be known by half the people he is now. And you know what, after I kicked his ass for getting with my sister, don't nobody give a fuck about Jack Perkins. Fucking pedophile.

I was pissed at Fiona too. Doing that shit at 14. I knew it was because of Skye Sallow. Fiona never cared about any of that grown up shit until she became friends with Skye. Around that time I found out she'd been sneaking out too, getting picked up by boys and driving to the waterfalls. I didn't want her to fucking hate me, but I also didn't want her gaining that kind of reputation, you know?

I knew I didn't have the greatest reputation either, but it was different for me. I could handle my shit. If someone had something to say, they'd either say it or they'd fuck off. Girls were different. When girls do shit, people hold onto it for years. I mean, Yana and I had been on and off for years. Then she finds out I hooked up with Stella Heistery at that Isaac Jenka party, and she fucking slaps me at school for it. She just walked up to me crying, surrounded by her friends, and slapped me right in the face without a single word. I wouldn't say that Yana and I were actually together at that point, but I get why she did it. It would piss me off too to hear she'd gotten with someone else. But I never had to worry about that, because Yana wasn't like that.

Anyway, after that, the only thing anyone could talk about was her slapping me. I'll admit, I fucked up that weekend with Stella. And I honestly thought I'd never hear the end of it either. Stella Heistery was the kind of girl to dangle a carrot. She knew how to push the right buttons. But all anyone focused on was what Yana did. That's how I knew I couldn't let Fiona make the same mistakes I was making. Of course, I didn't fucking know Kash Grogan would film her and Skye naked and send it to everyone in the entire city.

Honestly, I don't think I was home enough those years to tell her otherwise.

My dad and I fought nearly every day and sometimes I just couldn't fucking deal with it. Fiona never got to see the sides of dad that I did. She never had to deal with his backhands and the sound of him beating down her bedroom door because I forgot to buy him a 6 pack after school from the fucking petrol station. She had it pretty fucking easy if you ask me. Daddy's little girl, and I was just a son. The wrong son. The one mum should've taken with her instead of Blue. Then at least my dad mightn't have turned into the thing he is today.

That's why I loved the escape. Focusing on something bizarre and fucked up. Like not giving a fuck about the repercussions of sleeping with every pretty girl I see- even if she's married, even if she was a teacher. Or getting rides from Beau and drinking the night away at the waterfalls. Listening to blasting music and forgetting about every fucked up thing life has to offer. That's why I fucking loved that cornflower shit. Cocaine crumbs and the taste of marijuana. Because who gives a fuck?

I don't know that I necessarily wanted to die, but I didn't care to live either. That night at Beau's house, when his brother climbed up on the roof. Everyone else was chanting for him to jump, thinking maybe he was just fucked up too, and wanted to see if he could hit the trampoline. But I knew. I was fucked up and I knew from the look on Beau's face that it wasn't a dumb joke. Linkoln made that choice. He chose that he didn't want to live anymore. I've never made that decision, but I'd be lying if I said I never thought about it. I'd be lying if I said it wasn't constantly on my mind.

Every time I'd fuck up, like the day Yana slapped me. I could've cared. I could've changed and tried to be a better person, but I didn't want to. I didn't want to because I didn't give a fuck about my life. I didn't care because I don't care if I die tomorrow. And if I do, then it's not my problem anymore. Nothing is.

I felt that way for so long, and I truly thought it was normal. I thought everyone felt that way. I thought it's just something you've gotta learn to live with. Maybe it is, but if that's true, then maybe this life isn't worth living. Or it truly isn't worth caring about.

Eventually I just became numb to it all. There's so many chunks of time I just can't remember, because my brain stopped creating memories because I truly didn't think I'd ever want to look back on life. Until the day I found out Yana was pregnant.

Everything changed for me that day. Of course I was scared, I was scared shitless. But nothing else had ever given me purpose in life, not until that day. Suddenly life wasn't only about me. Suddenly it was about someone else. Suddenly, every mistake, every decision I made contradicted someone else entirely. Suddenly I was biologically responsible for another person. And that thought fucking freaked me out, but it also gave me something to live for. Something to care about.

I thought, maybe this is it. Maybe this is what I need to get me the fuck out of this deep and dark hole. Maybe this is my purpose. Maybe this is why I'm still here.

I thought, finally. Finally I might feel something again. Finally I might *want* to feel again. And I did. I felt so fucking much, until it was too much. Overbearingly too much. Because what do you mean I have a beautiful fucking girlfriend, and the most beautiful daughter and I still think about death?

What do you mean my little brother finally came back from the abyss, and I still think about death?

What do you mean I'm sober, living in a fucking great house, and working for good money, and I still think about death?

I thought, Is this it? Is this all I'm meant to live for? Every day passing and wishing that maybe one day I'll feel differently? Wishing that one day this overwhelming thought of impending doom might subside?

What do you mean life doesn't get better? What do you mean I was wrong? What do you mean It was all for nothing?

It was an endless cycle, and no matter how hard I tried, I couldn't control it. And I just thought, well, If I'm gonna be depressed either way- I might as well be depressed, and doing things that make me feel happy. Even only for a moment, or a second.

I wondered, why did I ever start caring? Why did I ever try and change myself, because clearly I'm biologically meant to be this way?

And then I wondered, does that mean I fucked her up too? My daughter, the one I fought so hard to convince Yana to have. The one I decided to dedicate my life into getting better for. Did I sentence her to a lifetime of whatever the fuck it is I've been living with from the second she entered this world? Is my DNA poison?

Reliability. Responsibility. Accountability. Ownership. It is all me. It is all my fault. And that.. that is a burden I could not put into words. That is a burden I simply cannot explain.

It is deafening. It is controlling. And it might just kill me.

4

Chapter Four- Beau

Fiona Glass

I turned 17 a month ago. Alina turned 2 three days ago. Cipher, Yana and Yana's family came over to the house to celebrate. I brought a cake home from work- a pink princess one. Cipher brought his stereo outside and played loud music while cooking a BBQ. My dad smoked a cigarette at the outdoor table with Yana's father. Blue was playing soccer with the goal my dad bought him last Christmas.

Brownie came over too. He was smoking and laughing loudly with my dad and Yana's. Even my Aunt Hannah and her family, and our Grandparents came for Alina's birthday. Aunt Charlotte said they couldn't make it.

Alina looks so much like Yana. Today she was wearing her new Princess Rapunzel dress and sparkly dancing shoes. Yana let me brush Alina's hair into two pigtails with plaits and bows. My dad can't help but take a million photos.

Alina is obsessed with Blue. Everything he does she likes to do too. My family has been super happy the past two years. I would've dreamed of days like today when I was 13.

I had to work after school the following Monday. School has been okay. I don't really talk to anyone. Even at Senior School, everyone still knows me as Skye's best friend. Skye, the girl that killed herself. I'm the girl that made a sex tape with Kash Grogan and Skye Sallow- the girl that killed herself.

Nadia is a half Indigenous, half Indian woman with short curly brown hair and a septum piercing, has been my dads disability support worker for a few years now. Blue never got approved for his in-school support worker. I think he'd rather without it now anyway. He's doing really well at school. He's smarter then anyone else was expecting him to be. Especially as someone who only learned how to learn two years ago. He loves drawing, and he loves coming to work with me.

On that Monday I sat with Blue during my break. He was writing in his journal, and beneath was an open homework book from Mrs Keen. I brought him over a hot chocolate, and myself an iced coffee. He's very secretive about the things he writes in the journal, but I'd never attempt to read through it. When I was still writing in that journal, I would've killed anyone who tried to spy on me.

Sometimes I wonder If Blue has read through the pages that I'd written in- by now he'd understand most of the common written words, and surely the curiosity would intrigue him.

"How's school been?" I ask.

Blue closes the journal, and starts flipping through his home work pages. He prefers art- he always finishes the art homework before any of his other classes.

"I'm glad you're liking school, Blue. You're way smarter then I was at your age." He smiled in response. "Speaking of, I have a gift for you."

I reached into my bag I had placed beside me. Blue watched intently as I searched through. He looked with interest as I pulled out two books.

Holding up the first book, I explained "This was my favorite book when I was like.. 13." I showed him the front cover; Little Women. "I borrowed it from the library, so let me know when you're finished, okay?"

Blue nodded. He reached out and took the book from me, inspecting it. "There might be a few big words in there that are a little hard to read, but someone is always around to help if you need it."

He seemed happy with my first gift, so I was eager to show him the second book. I placed it down on the table between us, and I flipped through a few of the pages.

"It's a book of stickers. You can put them on the covers of your school books, or even the cover of the journal- if you want." he inspected that book too, flipping through the pages and looking at all the different stickers.

He looked up at me with a smile- Blue's way of saying thank you.

Every day sort of looks the same in my life these days. Nothing truly exciting. The police have been looking for my mum for the past two years, trying to get some kind of explanation or justice for whatever the hell happened to Blue while they were away. They've had a few sightings, but somehow she always seems to slip away. She probably knows its best for her to not be found. Assuming she has some sort of brain function left.

My dad was given full custody of Blue, but Cipher is always listed as Blue's top emergency contact- due to my dads disability. My dad is second, and I'm third. When I turn 18, we plan to change it so that I'm at the top. Cipher has his own daughter to worry about.

My dad can only move his forearms, fingers, mouth and eyes. He can barely move his neck. Doctors say his life expectancy is shrinking more and more each year. I know it's only a matter of time before my dad dies. Then it'll only be up to me to take care of Blue, and I'm scared of that thought.

Blue's a good boy. He's easy, now that he trusts me. I look forward to spending time with him, and I think he feels the same way.

Blue sat beside dad tonight, colouring in his home work book and using the new stickers I got him while I cooked dinner. I picked up some cold meat pies from my work, all I had to do was heat them up, and cook some veggies on the stove. An easy dinner, one of the best things about working at a bakery.

My dad and Blue are so similar in manner. They eat the same, laugh the same, smile the same. Blue, my dad and Cipher are like triplets.

Blue still sleeps with me at night most nights. Even then, sometimes I wake up to him sweating and making noises in the back of his throat. He's easy to soothe back to sleep, but it breaks my heart to know that something still eats at him, even after all this time.

Cipher finished work early on Thursday, so he offered to pick up Blue with Alina while I went to work. Thursdays always seem so boring. It's the least busy day of the entire week. I'm happy Blue gets to spend some time with Cipher and Alina, but it would've been nice to have someone to talk to during the quiet hours.

Although, my afternoon started to seem a little more exciting as a particular boy walked through the doors. The ring of the bell echoing in the tiny bakery.

There was two of them. His friend had darker skin, light eyes and earrings. He was tall and skinny and had tattoos all over his body. But the boy who caught my eye had fair skin, blue eyes and a dark blonde overgrown mullet. I didn't notice until he turned back to talk to his friend, but he had random braids in the back of his mullet as well. He had tattoos too. A really large one on the front of his neck and hands. He seemed shaggy- kind of feral, but in a cute way. He was also missing part of his left ear, which I wont lie- was kinda hot.

"Hello, gorgeous." he spoke confidentially, chewing on gum and leaning against the serving register.

"Hello. What can I do for you?" I responded with a service worthy smile.

"Well, there's a lot of things you could do for me, really." his friend chuckled. "But what I really want, is to organize a cake. Can you do that for me, gorgeous?"

He was starting to seem a little bit over-confident. His face was cute though. I grabbed out the cake requests book, and we discussed a date for collection. I then asked him what flavour he wanted the cake to be, and specific decorations- if any.

"Chocolate. He likes chocolate." his friend answered with a childlike smile. Their deodorant infiltrating my nose.

"And if we're being totally honest- I don't care what's on it. I just want it to be some kind of 'Welcome Home' cake." he explained with expression in his hands.

"No worries, we'll have it ready by then." I confirmed, writing the details down in the book.

"And can you make me one promise?" he asks with a smooth eyebrow raise.

"Depends what It is." I responded quickly.

"Can you make sure it's done by you. I'm sure he'd like it better if it was made by someone as pretty as you."

I honestly couldn't tell if he was joking, or if he's just naturally this bad at flirting.

"I can do that." I smile. "What name would you like me to put that under?"

"You can put it under Beau Jones, kindly." he answers, rising from his lean. "Do you mind me asking, whats ya' name- other then gorgeous, of course?"

"Fiona."

"Right." he responds with a smirk. "Do you have a piece of paper and a pen I can borrow?"

I was sure he was going to write his number down, but I gave him the pen and paper anyway. To be honest, I sort of enjoyed the attention. Especially coming from someone who was actually attractive.

The two of them sort of reminded me of the boys Skye and I would run away to see. Skye would've loved the friend, that is something I'm certain of.

I leaned forward slightly to read the note in front of him as he scribbled, and to my surprise, it wasn't his number. It was an address.

"Saturday night, come whenever- we don't care."

"Whats on Saturday night?" I ask, taking the note.

"Last party before my brother comes home. Should be a good one." he responds with a menacing smirk.

"See you there!" his friend adds, before the two of them depart out the bell door.

I wasn't gonna go. I was gonna stay home and spend some time with Blue and my dad- considering I wasn't working. But on Saturday night, I walked out to find Blue and my dad watching movies together and eating popcorn. They looked like they were in their own little world. And to be honest, I didn't feel comfortable interrupting.

Maybe it was just an excuse. Maybe I was looking for a reason to go, upon my prior judgment. I can't change what the heart wants.

I started doing my makeup at my desk- doing it brought me back to when Skye always used to do my makeup. I wish she was still here, then maybe she'd be able to go to this party with me. I'd never just gone somewhere unfamiliar by myself. The anxiety I felt was undeniable. Insane.

I was basically shaking as I straightened my hair. I nearly convinced myself not to go a few times, but I kept reminding myself that maybe this party could change my life. Maybe I might meet people, good people. Fun people. Maybe my life might change for the better. I already know school wasn't going to do that, maybe this party would. Maybe stepping out of my comfort zone would be beneficial, like it had in the past.

It was cold outside, so I put on my favourite baggy low rise jeans, and a light brown licensed tank top. I told myself that if I looked good, I'd feel good. So I made sure I was absolutely certain before stepping out of my house.

I didn't say goodbye before I left. I couldn't think of a good excuse for where I was going. My dad probably wouldn't let me go If I told him I was going to a party, considering what happened last time I went to a party. Even though it was years ago, my dad knows how to hold grudges.

Luckily the house wasn't too far from mine. A fifteen minute walk, if that. I could hear the music from up the road. It was loud. Rap music, specifically artists like Tupac, 112, Biggie, 50 Cent. It was so loud, like a club.

I was freezing on the walk, eager to get by a fire. I passed an old house that burned down many years ago. Only a few plots up the road from Beau's house. The same house my dads friend died in all those years ago. Left to rot with burnt char and forgotten wood.

People were outside, drinking, dancing. It felt so strange just walking into a random persons house. I recognized a few people from school. Some of them were people that Cipher used to be friends with. I saw that Victoria girl Cipher dated making out with someone on the hammock by the door.

The front door was wide open. The lounge room was to my left. A lot of people were in there, smoking. I could smell the weed from outside. A small hallway led toward the kitchen, which is where the friend from the shop saw me.

"You actually came?" he said, his breath wafting of beer.

"Well, I had nothing else to do." I admit awkwardly.

"Go sit down on the couch- I'll go get Beau." he requests eagerly. "I'm Jasper, by the way." adding with a smile.

Walking away to go find Beau- like he said. And I did as he told me, I sat down in the crowded lounge room. A rectangle room with a mounted TV facing a brown stained L couch, opposite a velvet two seater.

As I sat down on the two seater, I looked around the room admiring the walls. A few fist holes, some old black spots like the tip of a cigarette. Tobacco stains and some random stolen street signs. Scratchy blankets roughly folded on the arms of the couches, and pillows that look to be close to 30 years old with teared lint. A black coffee table in the center of the room with a bong, a couple lighters, and filled with half empty cups.

To my left sat a girl. At first I thought she was asleep, but she was just sitting with her eyes closed and her head leaned back. She was pretty- skinny with long blonde hair, wearing a white laced top and jeans. I remember admiring her button nose. Her side profile was beautiful- just like the magazine models.

She must've felt me staring at her, because her eyes suddenly opened and looked at me. Her jaw was rocking, and her eyes were red.

"Hey." she greeted, smiling.

"Hey." I responded.

"Whats your name? I've never seen you around here before." she asks, with a subtle croak in her throat.

"Fiona, and yeah, It's my first time here."

She chortles, laying her head back against the couch. "So which one invited you?"

"What?" I ask.

"Thing one or thing two?" her smile widens.

"Oh, Beau." I admit. "He came into my work, ordering a cake."

"Mm, Beau is such a flirt." she huffs, sitting up to grab a cup of water from the coffee table, sipping it. "That cake was probably for his brother.

He's getting out of prison next week."

Lovely.

Suddenly, Beau and Jasper rip from around the corner. Beau barely standing up as he approaches me.

"Hello, gorgeous! You look even better out of your uniform." he greets, as he plants himself between myself and the other girl, kissing my cheek and laying his arms behind our heads. At least he smells good. "I'm so glad you came." he exclaims, while Jasper sits on the L couch and lights another joint.

"Do you smoke?" he asks me politely from across the room.

"Not actively." I respond.

"Do you *want* to smoke?" he clarifies.

I debated it for a moment. It'd been a while since I smoked marijuana, and sometimes, I really did miss it. "Sure."

He took a puff himself, before handing it over to me. I was so scared of coughing in front of all of these people, but luckily enough I think my lungs preserved me. Beau and the girl took a puff too, before handing it back to Jasper.

"Jasper-" the girl gargled beneath her dry throat.

"Yes?" he responds politely.

"-Can you be a gentleman and get us ladies a cold drink?" she requests, opening her eyes for a moment to address him.

"At your service." Jasper responds, handing the joint to Beau, and standing up to grab us drinks from the kitchen.

The girl sat up, squirming in her seat and smiling at me. "I love Jasper."

"Are you guys dating?" I ask.

"No." she and Beau giggle. "We're not dating. We used to be in laws, so that would be a little weird." she jokes mockingly.

"It would be hot though." Beau injects, handing the girl the joint.

She shakes her head, still smiling. "I used to date his little brother, Jordan."

"Used to?" I ask curiously.

"Yeah- nice guy, but, waaay too plain for me."

I chuckle- she seems nice. Funny.

"What was your name, by the way? I forgot to ask." I questioned gently.

She takes a long puff of the joint, and then finally responds- her eyes closed again. "Maddison Sterling, but everyone just calls me Maddy."

At that point Jasper returns, handing us both a drink, before sitting himself back down and taking the joint.

"Hey, Fiona- What was your last name again? I feel like I recognize you from somewhere." Jasper queries randomly, as I crack open my can.

"Glass." I say, igniting a reaction as both Beau and Jasper and a few of the other people in the room turn to look at me.

"Denny or Ronny?" Beau asks, shocked.

"Denny." I say, also stunned.

"So your Cipher's sister?" He asks.

I nod.

"So how old are you?" Jasper urges.

"18." I lie. Fearful they might kick me out if I tell them I'm underage.

"Only a year younger then me." Maddy injects.

"But you wouldn't know her- Maddy went to private school." Jasper adds.

"Yes, Jasper. I went to private school. I am sorry." Maddy responds with sarcasm. The boys chuckling. "You know what, I've accepted my fate. Being a privy is embarrassing, but I am who I am." she taunts jokingly.

"How old are you guys?" I ask, attempting to further the conversation.

"I'm 20- Beau's an old fuck." Jasper jokes.

"Fuck you, I'm 23!"

"How do you know Cipher then?" I ask. Beau's eye contact, by the way, is insanely intimidating.

"Cipher was a reg, before he had his kid- ya know? I get it though. Miss havin' him and Brownie around."

Our conversation was quickly interrupted by the entrance of someone who caught Beau's eye. A woman at the door. She was older- my dads age. Tall with dark hair tied back. Accompanied by a man so tall he had to duck down at the front door with dark skin and no hair. The other man incredibly muscly with islander features. The three of them entering with a very intimidating manner.

Beau immediately stood up and approached them. Jasper and Maddy kept talking, but I couldn't help but find myself more interested by the woman Beau was talking to- whispering, more like.

"Hey, Jasper- Who's that?- The woman Beau's talking to." I probe.

Jasper turns around to have a look, and turns back quickly to answer me.

"Tarn Lavery, Beau's Aunt." he responds, reaching into his pockets, searching for something.

"Who are the guys?" I ask further.

"I think the tall ones name is Carter, but everyone just calls him Cart. The other one is Silas." he explains, finally finding what he's looking for. His wallet.

He opens it, and pulls out a small bag with two clear pills.

"You ever had MD before?" he asks.

"No." I respond honestly.

"Oh my god, it's the best." Maddy exclaims.

"Says the nurse." Jasper chuckles, opening the pack and cracking open the pills, pouring the brown substance on a plate that's on the coffee table.

"Training, nurse." Maddy defends subtly.

"What is it?" I ask, as I watch him crush the brown rocks until it looks like dirt with his ID card.

"Caps- technically. But it's MDMA rocks. You can swallow the pill without cracking it, but I prefer to crush it- works faster." Jasper explains.

"Where did you get them from?" I ask curiously.

"Beau's Aunt." Jasper explains, gesturing over to the woman talking to Beau with the flick of his head. "Beau and I sell for her- Beau more then me- but she gives us bonus' all the time. Free drugs, free beer. Money. It's a pretty great trade."

I guess now I know who Cipher and Brownie used to sell and get their drugs from.

Intrigued, my eyes look up as Beau and Tarn both look over at me. She smiles, and together they walk over.

Beau sits back down in between Maddy and I, lighting a cigarette, and throwing a small bag of white power- which I immediately recognized as the same powder I had at Kash Grogans house- on the plate Jasper was working on.

"Hello, how are you?" Tarn greets, sitting on the unstable wooden chair beside me, lighting her own cigarette.

"Good, thank you." I respond, curious as to why she's talking to me.

"Beau told me he met you at Opals. You'll be making my nephew's 'Welcome Home' cake?" she smiles. She seems sweet.

"Oh- yeah!" I respond, as Jasper mixes some of the white powder with the crushed MDMA.

"You know," Tarn begins. "You are quite beautiful- gorgeous."

"That's my nickname for her." Beau interrupts.

I chuckle. "Thank you, you're very kind."

"You look just like your mother, you know."

"You knew my mum?" I ask, surprised.

"Everyone knew your mother, because everyone knew your father- and his brother." she explains. "Sorry, for your loss by the way." She adds, leaning forward and placing her hand on mine. "He was a pleasant man, from what I've heard."

"Thank you. From what I remember, he was." I respond.

But while having this discussion with Beau's Aunt, I can't help myself from looking at what Jasper is doing through the corner of my eye. Something about it- almost, magnetizing.

"I meant what I said. You are absolutely stunning."

I couldn't say thank you- it felt sort of.. repetitive. Instead I smiled, and caught a glimpse of one of the men, Silas, as he handed more of those small bags to two other boys, and they handed him cash back. It was then that I sort of realized why they were there. I mean, it's not often you see someone over 30 at a party with a bunch of early 20s. It's not often someone invites their Aunt over to a party they know people will be doing drugs at. I know my dad would kill me if he knew.

Suddenly, Tarn grabs out a small white rectangle card from her own purse. I watch as she writes something on the card, with a pen from her bag. Before handing it to me. I read it straight away, to find her phone number and her name.

"Call me, if you ever want to use that beauty of yours for something worth your while. You know, something greater then my nephew."

Jasper snickers at Tarn's insult, and Beau flips him off as Tarn walks away. I watch as she spoke to both of the men, and they followed as she walked into a different area of the house.

The distracting sound of Jasper snorting a line of the mixed substance through a 5 dollar note became irresistible. He scrunched his face and hugged his nose with his hands before he pushed the plate toward Maddy. She did the same, making the same face as she handed it to Beau. He snorted a line too, but he didn't have as much of a reaction as the other two.

But there was one more line that Jasper had carved.

"Ya' want some?" Beau asks, looking at me while wiping his nose.

"You can have some, I'm always willing to share." Jasper offers, leaning back in his seat.

I think they could see I wasn't sure. Maddy encouraged me to do it too. Said she was nervous the first time, but it's worth it. Beau asked if I'd ever done any drugs before, and I told him truthfully that I'd only ever done cocaine and marijuana.

"Well, you're already halfway there then. It's coke, with a little extra spice." he explained.

Half of me wanted to say no, but half of me wanted to say yes. The half of me saying no was thinking of my mother, and the damage drugs did to her. But the half saying yes was reminding me that Cocaine and MDMA aren't as bad as something like meth, right? And I'd never ever say yes to meth. But cocaine and MDMA aren't as bad. Lots of people do it?

Everyone at this party was doing it and they all seemed normal. Cipher's probably done it before too, considering Beau and Jasper said Cipher and Brownie used to come over all the time. What harm could it really do?

"Okay." I finally say.

I take the rolled up note from Beau, and I place it slightly inside my right nostril. Leaning forward, I snorted up the line from bottom to top. Immediately it burned- burned way more then I remember it when I did only coke. It burned for a while, all the way up my sinuses. Almost forming a sharp headache behind my eyes.

But the more lines I did, the less it hurt. Like my face was slowly becoming numb to the pain. I also noticed the more I did, the more I wouldn't shut up. The more no one would shut up. Suddenly, I was talking to every person in that house, and they were talking to me. I kept telling myself in my head to stop talking so much, but I couldn't stop. My mouth wouldn't stop running.

8 hours felt like 2, and suddenly it was 6am. The skies were ready for the sun to rise. No one had slept. I feel like I learned more about Beau, Jasper and Maddy then I learned about anyone in 8 hours ever. Truly an in-explainable experience.

By the time I checked my phone, it was 6:30am. I knew I had to get home before Nadia got to my house to help my dad, or before Blue wakes up. I hope he slept okay, without me. I wasn't supposed to be out all night. I don't know where the time went.

Beau noticed me putting my shoes on, and looking for my bag and phone.

"Ya' leaving?" he asked.

"Yeah, I've got to get home before my brother wakes up." I explained. I felt like I was still talking super fast. My body also felt super warm and fragile.

My tongue felt tingly and dry, and I could already feel bumps forming on the inside of my mouth. I could also firmly feel the makeup on my face- as if I'd caked more on without realizing.

"Cipher?" he questions curiously.

"No, my little brother. Blue."

"I didn't know you had a little brother." he admitted.

"Is his real name actually Blue?" Maddy asked.

"Yes, that's his real name." I laughed.

Beau stands. "Surely you'll let me get your number?"

I smile at him- he's taller then me. "Fine. Give me your phone."

He hands me his phone, and I type my number in- creating myself a new contact. "There." I say with a smirk.

"I'll message you." he promises.

"I'm sure you will." I say, before waving everyone goodbye and walking toward the front door- Beau following me.

"And you know I'd drive you home If I could-"

"It's okay, I need the fresh air." I assure, smiling up at him. "I'll see you when I see you."

"Yeah, see-you." he waves, watching as I walk away.

"And good luck with your brother!" I wish, turning back to shout with a smile, before disappearing into the distance.

Luckily I made it home before anyone was awake. Even then, I moved quickly to get into bed before giving them the chance. I rushed to wipe off my makeup, and get into comfortable clothes. Trying so hard to remain silent, as Blue had fallen asleep in my bed.

I felt so bad, looking at him fast asleep- alone. I wonder if he waited up for me. I wonder if he was worried about where I went. I hope he wont be mad at me.

Getting into bed felt amazing, it was the perfect temperature. Blue moved as I laid down. I was so scared of waking him up, but he didn't. I'd never fallen asleep so fast in my life, even though it felt like I could stay awake for another 8 hours. My body internally must've been exhausted.

I didn't wake up until after lunch. Blue laid at the end of my bed, writing in his journal silently. I could hear my dad and Nadia talking in the lounge room- she was probably feeding him his lunch- I could smell food.

I turned over to check the time on my phone, then sat up to greet Blue.

"Afternoon." I said, with no response. "Did you sleep okay?" I ask, hopeful for a smile.

But I didn't get a smile, instead Blue turns over from laying on his stomach to look at me with a frown.

"Whats wrong?" I question, praying he's not upset with me for disappearing. Praying he'll forgive me if he is.

Slowly, Blue sits up in front of me, holding the journal and a pencil in his hand. He switches from looking at me and looking at the journal, before finally deciding to show me what is wrong. He opens the journal to one of the earlier pages, a page with my hand writing. Pointing to a singular word.

'Skye'.

"Skye?" I say, confused about what he could be asking. "Did you read the pages about Skye?" he nods.

No idea what to do in this situation. I considered him reading those pages, but I never considered the after. And what I *would* say if he ever did ask.

"So you know.. what happens?" I ask, trying to further understand Blue's point of view. He nods again.

"Are you okay?" I ask, having no clue of what else I should say. I should've ripped those pages out before I gave him the journal.

Blue doesn't nod this time, instead, he pointed to the bracelet I gave him, still sitting on his wrist. The same bracelet Skye gave me, once upon a time.

"Skye gave me that." I admit. "It's a friendship bracelet. But I am proud of my choice of giving it to you." I continue.

Blue looks up at me. I can't describe the look.

To be honest, I wasn't really sure of what he wanted to hear or know. He bowed his head, and I placed my hand in his as he fiddled with the beads- causing him to look up to me once more.

"I'm okay, you know." I assure. "I miss Skye- I miss her everyday. And to be honest, I don't know where I'd be in right now… If I didn't have you in it. I guess you kind of saved me- in a way."

His eyes started to welt, but before a tear could drop, he rushed in to give me a hug- the tightest hug I'd ever received. The only hug by that point I'd ever felt by the hands of my baby brother Blue. The best hug I will ever receive in my entire life. A hug to never forget.

Cipher Glass

It feels like time has flown since my little girl was born. I never thought I could love someone as much as I love Alina. I see pieces of myself in her, but I do admit, she looks the most like her mum. And I love her mum.

I want to get us our own house. I saved to get a car, a white ute. I'm trying to save to put a deposit on a house. My dream is to renovate the entire thing, and make it our own. Yana shares the dream too. Says she wishes to be an interior designer, and to decorate our house with gold accents and floral wallpaper.

It's been hard since Blue came back. I never really know what to say to him. My hair has finally grown back- but I don't regret shaving it. I think I did what I needed to in that moment to get it done.

Whenever I'm on the other side of the city collecting parts for work, I always make time to visit the CD store so that I can buy him a new CD album to listen to. He's started going through all of my old CDs I used to blast when I worked out as a kid. I still workout, just not in my dads house. I go to the gym.

Yana's parents- Melody and Justin Roche- have a pretty big garden outside the house, in the backyard. The older Alina gets, the more Melody involves her in tending the garden. She's trying to create a sort of magical walk through garden. She's been working on it for years and at night the fairy lights, flowers and green bushes really do make it feel that way. Alina loves it- so I love it.

My little sister and brother love orange juice, and Fi likes making fresh orange juice with my brother. So every time the orange tree grows out I take a plastic shopping bag of them and bring them to my dads. I usually do it on weekends but sometimes If I finish work early It gives me extra time to get it done. Yana hates that I'm gone so often- gym, work, double shift, my dads house. But I'm always there to read my little girl a bedtime story. I'll never miss out on that.

She's been begging me to have another kid a lot recently. I loved growing up with a little sister- as much as she pissed me off. And Brownie and Dare were like brothers to me, and I don't want Alina to grow up missing out. But every time I think about havin another kid, I think about the little girl I've already got. And that thought in the back of my head- the wonder, if I fucked her up enough internally with my DNA. Debating whether I have the heart to take that risk with another kid.

Luckily enough for Alina, I think she resembles her mother a lot more then she resembles me. I just hope that's enough to keep her safe from the curse that is me.

I'd have a whole football team if I could- like Yana's family. Yana's the youngest. Zain been in jail for three years now- we took Alina to visit him twice, on boxing days. Cruz is around, he comes over every time his woman kicks him out. He's got two little boys- Jag and Jothry. Dominica lives a few hours from here with her Husband she been dating since she was 15, they got a newborn named Isla. Dare tryna be a rapper, and Mauve lives with her boyfriend, they tryna have a baby.

Dare's my favorite, even though he never stops talking. He's fun to smoke and drink with. Usually, on Saturdays he invites me to the pub with the boys.

Brownie's always around. Yana's dad always uses Brownie's job as a plumber when It comes in handy around the house. I could do the same shit, but Yana's dad rather have me help him fix his cars.

Justin own his own car garage- Roche Cars- where he fixes cars, especially old ones. He taught me everything I know about fixing cars of any engine, shape, and age. He gets me in there most Saturdays and Sundays. Bein' there after drinking all night with the boys isn't fun, but Justin would kill me if I didn't do it.

Sometimes Alina comes with me too. I've brought Blue a few times, taught him a few things about cars. But a lot of the boys that work there are old, they don't understand why Blue don't speak, or barely laughs at they're jokes. I mean, I wouldn't laugh either, but If I don't I look bad.

I think Blue would rather spend the time with Alina in the garden, but it's good for me to pass down the stuff I know to a boy- ain't it?

Yana's been on my ass recently about drinking too much, says I'm not home enough and Alina misses me. Yana works too, at a restaurant as a waitress. But she can only work when Melody's home. Justin's always at work, and she's not gonna trust Dare to take care of our kid. Melody is the only one around that could watch her while the rest of us make money. I could ask Fi, but she got school and work too. And a lot of the time she's watching Blue.

Sometimes I feel bad for Fi. I had a kid young, but Fi been looking after Blue since she was 15. When I was 15 I was sneaking off to the lake with the boys to meet with older girls. I did so many crazy things before I got Yana pregnant. Brownie and I used to sneak our dads beers and drink before school started. We thought we were so fucking cool for that shit too.

Brownie's dad- Eyeball- they got the same name, which is why Brownie goes by Brownie instead of Cooper. Which I guess, doesn't really make sense, considering his dad goes by Eyeball instead of Cooper anyway. He got the name Eyeball when he was a kid, cause he's blind in his left eye. It's fucking sick if you look at it. Missing most of its colour. Like a comic bad guy or some shit.

My dad was way more strict on Fi then me, but I think he regretted that once I got older. He started hitting me a lot, used to throw me into walls and shit and threaten to break my stuff. He was an angry mother fucker growing up. Used to piss me off. He was stricter on Fi, but he would've never yelled at her like he yelled at me. He woulda never hit her.

My dad just didn't want me in jail or getting any girls pregnant. I knew I woulda never gone to jail. And I thought I wouldn't get a girl pregnant either *but*, here we are.

We've been going strong for a few years. We fight sometimes, but Melody hate to hear it and I don't like to fight in front of our kid. Sometimes when I need space I just go to Brownie's or my dads.

I came back from the garage today. Justin headed straight for the shower. Yana was sitting at the kitchen bench, reading a magazine. Alina was outside helping Melody.

I always give Yana a kiss when I see her.

"You have a good day?" I asked, kissing her forehead more. Smelling her hair- lavender.

"Yeah-" she begins, but she's cut off by my phone ringing.

I answer it, it's Dare. He's asking me to come to a club with him tonight, said he already called Brownie and he's got a few other friends for the ride too. I said I could come after I put my kid to bed- like always.

"Who was that?" Yana asks as I hang up. I can tell she's mad.

"Your brother."

"Of course." She snarls, turning back to her magazine. "Where you going tonight?"

"Some club he said."

"Better not be some slutty-ass strip club."

"Why would I go to a strip club?" I ask, leaning over her.

"Because, I know my brother. Dare's a whore for a slut."

"Well, I ain't Dare."

"Right, but you're friends with those Jonesy boys too- and best believe I know the trenches they came from." She responds, looking up at me with her beautiful green eyes. I love those damn eyes. "You be drinking too much, Ciph." she tells me. Same thing she says every time Dare calls me.

"Saturdays." I respond, as she stands and distracts herself with cleaning.

"And every time you go to your Dads." She adds.

She got me there. My dad always got beers, and it's the only way I can deal with bein' in that house.

Don't get me wrong, I like goin' there and seein' everyone. But fuck, sometimes It's hard to be back there. Mentally. So much shit is written on those walls. So many bad memories.

It's like a ghost house. My brother and my dad are there- physically. But they ain't really there. They haven't been there for years. I don't know how Fi does it.

"Speaking of, I've gotta go drop some stuff at my dads. But I'll be back in time to read Lina a bedtime story."

Yana rolled her eyes, pushing through with her cleaning to load the half full dishwasher.

"Are you mad?" I ask, kissing her head.

"Not mad. Just annoyed."

"I can make it up to you."

"How?" she asks, looking back up at me.

I didn't really know how to answer her. Yana ain't a materialistic girl. She's more about gestures- and I'm shit with gestures. Yana is sort of like the opposite of Blue. In a way. Everybody is so fucking different it's hard to please everyone. Except Alina- my little girl will be happy with anything simple.

I had to leave quick in order to make it back it time for dinner and bedtime.

The drive to my dads house isn't far- like 20 minutes with good traffic.

Fiona was in her bedroom, typing on that laptop she bought herself. My dad was working on squeezing that ball the doctors gave him to work on his grip.

Blue was in my old room. He's always sitting on the floor in front of the bed, hitting my old down ball against the wall, listening to some of the CD's. Today he had on the Appetite for Destruction album by Guns n Roses. He loves their shit.

"Hey." I greet, knocking on the door.

His face lights up so quickly by the sight of me. He stands up immediately, probably eager to see what I brought him.

I grab out a CD package from my back pocket. No Need To Argue, by The Cranberries.

"I got you a new album to listen to." I say, taking out the CD he's got in, and putting in the new one.

It went in order. First came Ode To My Family, then I can't Be With You, Twenty One. Everything was going so well with the album- I think he likes the first one the most. He appreciated the CD, until the fourth song came on- Zombie.

It was sort of like a movie. It started and Blue's smile immediately disappeared. I could see him freeze and eventually goosebumps started rising all over his body. Without a single sound exiting his mouth, he started to cry. His eyes were open, but it was like he was asleep. Caught in a nightmare. A trigger.

The second I realized I quickly stopped the song.

"Hey. Hey!" I say, grabbing his shoulders and trying to get his attention. "It's okay, It's off." I assure, guiding him to sit down on the bed with me.

It's always hard to know what to say in these moments. I'm not good with feelings. Fiona's usually there to help when we discover a trigger- but I don't wanna seem like I can't handle this shit.

Purple uniforms, yelling, fire, belts, shoe laces, straws, spoons, and now Zombie by The Cranberries.

"You don't like that song?" I ask gently.

He looks at me with his watery eyes. A fearful expression.

"Does it..- does it take you back there?"

He nods ever so slightly, wiping his tears with a fist.

"Okay. How about this, I'll take it back to the shop, and see if they can remove that song from the CD? Will that make you feel better?"

He nods. Thank fuck.

"How about, we listen to the rest of the songs on the album, so that you can let me know if I need to remove anymore songs. Is that a'ight?"

He nods. Okay. I skip that song, and we move onto the next. Empty, Everything I said, The Icicle Melts, Disappointment, Ridiculous Thoughts, Dreaming My Dreams, Yeats Grave, Daffodil Lament, and finally, No Need To Argue. All of the tracks were perfect, except for that one song.

I told him I'd get it removed, then I'd bring the CD back. He liked the rest of the songs, and listening to the others helped him calm down. I stayed with him for a little extra time after that. We listened to some of the old CD's I used to love as a kid. I talked to him about how I used to blast music in here, and lift the weights still sitting on the floor- collecting dust. I told Blue that sometimes, working out helped me to feel less stressed. I told him that lifting weights helped me not only become more confident, but it helped let off some steam whenever things made me mad.

"Does anything ever make you mad?" I ask.

He hesitated, but he nodded. I showed him a few different ways to lift the weights, and how to make them heavier once he gets stronger. Bicep curls, tricep dips, chest press on the bench, lateral raises. All of that simple stuff.

I think he was actually interested in learning. I think Blue is very impressionable. Sometimes I think what I'd be like If I'd spent years of my life not learning nothing. Wonder If I'd take the opportunity to learn new shit or if I'd just- I don't know.

I put my little girl to bed when I got home. To be honest it was kind of hard to leave Yana that night. She always dresses in something nice to bed when she knows I'm going out with Dare and Brownie. But I knew they'd give me shit if I chose to stay home with my woman after already saying I could go.

I met with the boys at the same pub we always meet at. Brownie's dad came with him too, but he was sitting with his own friends smoking cigars and playin' poker. As kids us boys used to pick on Brownie a lot because his dad is this big ass muscly man with a thousand tattoos and a wicked eyeball. And Brownie is this stubby dude with a skullet and freckles. He used to play rugby back in the day, so he's a pretty sturdy guy. But they're such opposites.

Dare is exactly what you'd expect him to look like. Shorter then all his sisters, dark skin, certain parts of his hair on his head grows faster then the rest. Always got beanies or backward caps on, sagging pants and tight tops. Loves his jewelry as well. He looks a lot like Yana though, same eye colour. But Yana's a lot quieter then Dare. Dare's a performer. He makes his presence known.

We drank there for a while. Dare had been ranting and ravin' about this club he visited the other night with some other guys, saying it had the hottest ladies working there. Even Eyeball said he and his boys went there and their drinks are better then any other club around the city.

"Ay, you remember Beau and Link Jones?" Dare asks, using his expressive hands to talk.

"Course I remember them." I respond, sipping my beer.

"They Aunty run it."

"Big Tarn Lavery run a new club?" Brownie asks, chuckling at the conversation.

"Yea. Beau and Link waitin' to meet us there."

"Isn't LJ in jail?" Brownie asks.

"Nah, man. He got out Tuesday. Hit the clubs on Thursday."

"Well, shit." I say, surprised. I hadn't seen Link since before last Christmas. They must've let him out early for good behaviour.

"Lowkey wouldn't mind goin' to see old Link." Brownie speculates.

"Trust me, you wont regret it. Queen got the baddest bitches in town workin'."

To be honest, it didn't take much convincing to get us to go once we heard Link was back from prison. Brownie and I used to chill with Beau Jones and Jasper Krike all the time on weekends and after school. Their Aunt Tarn and her boys sold the best fucking coke I've ever tasted, straight from the brick. Expensive shit but worth it. I stopped going there when I found out Yana was pregnant. Needed the money for my kid.

The other boys hadn't seen Link since the night he got arrested four years ago. Can't imagine being freshly 18 and going to jail for 4 years. Wasting your golden years on prison life.

Beau had gotten Brownie and I fake ID's when we was 16. We were there in the pub when Link got arrested, and we had to run the second we heard someone calling the police. Once I turned 18 I visited Link a few times. He was at the same prison Zain's at, so I'd see them around the same time. I was so scared after that Link would be pissed at us for running, but he told me he understood and he woulda done the same.

I didn't know until we got to the club- Queen, Girls Girls Girls- that it was a strip club. There was already two lines out the front of the building. Took 40 minutes before we were even able to get in. Dare said all the security guards are hired by Cart and Silas. Most of them are related to those big boys, and they definitely look the part. Junkies in the city still try and arck up though. Ain't nothing stopping them.

The second we got in it took a minute for me to take everything in. That place was massive- two stories high, visible second floor. Two stair cases- one spiral and one grand. Aerial Spheres with poles and dancing girls, and a center square bar with four poles on each corner.

There was another bar right at the entrance where Beau, Link and Jasper were waiting. I could see another bar upstairs and toward the back of the building with more poles too. The whole club was bright with pink and blue LED lights. The place reeked of perfume and vodka and the music was so loud you could hear it vibrating against the city, like an underground rave.

"Shit- Little Link is back!" Brownie greets, rushing to bring Link in for a hug.

"Hey Browns, long time no see."

"How was prison life?" Brownie asks, as Beau orders us a round of drinks at the bar. Dare admiring the dancing girls in the distance.

"Different to what I was expecting." Link responds, turning to Dare. "Ya brother said he misses you. Said you should visit him more often."

"That mother fucker is full of shit! Used to steal my scooters and shit- he a dick." Dare responds boisterously. "But I'll try and make some time."

"Anyone want a private dance?" Beau asks, handing out drinks.

"We ain't cool like that, B." Dare responds jokingly. We all laugh.

"Real funny. Hey, you know me and Jasper was hanging out with your sister last weekend." Beau adds, looking to me.

"What?" I say, shocked. Nearly choking on my drink.

"Yeah. Met her at Opals. She ended up coming back to ours Saturday night. She cool, you know. Reminds me a lot'a you. Except, she's hotter."

I punched him in the arm, jokingly. But I was lowkey pissed that Fiona went there. I know what they get up to there, and that ain't Fiona. That's the kinda shit Skye Sallow would've convinced her to do.

"There's private dancing rooms in the basement. I rented one out for a few hours, unlimited drinks- welcome." Beau tells the group, before leading us toward the downstairs access area.

The security guards by the downstairs entrance didn't even flinch as Beau approached with us. Of course, everyone would know Beau and Link Jones are Tarn's nephews. I wonder if their mums back in town.

There was three girls in the room, serving us drinks in lingerie with high heels and dramatic makeup. One of those girls I recognized. I used to think she was so hot when I was 15. I nearly had her once but then she realized I was a kid and she turned me down. Her real names Grace, but the name she was using was Frosty. I think she recognized me too.

Eyeball was right. Their drinks are insane. Felt like I barely drank and I was already fucked up. Beau had like 8 bags of coke too- I think some of them was mixed with Ket as well. Felt like I was robbin' him, but he said it was fine. Can't pass up an opportunity like that.

I don't remember how I got home. I don't really remember much past getting into the private room. I don't remember if I even did anything- hope not.

I slept in that morning. When I woke up and realized Yana wasn't there, I knew she'd be pissed. My jaw was fucking aching. Had so many sores inside my lips. Reached to my bedside table for some water that wasn't even there. Definitely got fucked up.

Was kind of embarrassing to walk into the backyard where Yana was sat watching Alina play with Melody in the garden. Justin must be at the garage. Yana didn't even look at me when I sat down. I lit a cigarette, gave it to her, then lit another one for myself. She still didn't acknowledge me.

"You mad?" I ask, barely able to open my mouth to speak. Haven't felt this stiff in years.

"Where'd you go?" she interrogates. Speaking quietly so Melody wouldn't hear our conversation.

"The pub." I lie.

"All night?" she asks, finally looking at me. I felt caught.

"You remember Linkoln Jones?"

"What about him?"

"He was released on Tuesday. Dare surprised me and Brownie at the pub. When we realized he and Beau were comin' for a drink, we didn't want the night to end." I say, trying to convince her of my truth. "We took the party back to Beau and Jasper's- nothin' crazy, you know?"

The way she's looking at me- like nothing I'm saying is a surprise. Maybe she already knew Link was released.

"You didn't even send me a text, Cipher. I woke up at 3am and you still weren't home. You're a dad now, you can't be playin' around all night with ya boyfriends." Fuck.

"I don't know where the time went. I haven't had a night like that in ages, Yana. You can't be that pissed at me for it."

"You go to the pub every weekend, Ciph. I ain't never been to a nightclub with my friends."

I knew It would be better for me to just stay quiet in that moment. Yana was always really good at hiding her anger on the outside, but you can always tell when she's about to kill you- based on her tone. She can be smiling and waving while threatening to make you disappear. It's kind of sexy.

Denny Glass

Doctor gave me a ball to start squeezing. Said it might help get my grip back.

The truth is: During the car crash, I suffered a spinal injury. Don't ask me to explain the exact spikes of my fucking spine I battered- cause all I know is my spine got fucked up.

I had to get surgery after that to try and fix it. Doctors don't know if the condition came from the injury itself, or the surgery, but I ended up getting diagnosed with Guillian-Barre Syndrome. Some disorder where my immune system attacks my nerves.

When I left the hospital- after I found out Merry had taken off with my little boy Blue- I left with tingling in my feet and some of my joints. Thought it was cause I'd been bed ridden since the accident.

Doctors wanted me to do physiotherapy, and start a treatment that had a good chance of fixing me. But I left.

I remember them telling me my twin brother was dead. Ronny was my best friend- no matter what anyone tells you. I loved Ronny more then I ever loved anyone. Ronny got me sober. Ronny was the reason I dated Lottie, which was how I met Merry, who gave me my children.

After I found out Ronny died, I blamed Nicole. Ronny and Nicole had just gotten into a fight over her cheating on my brother. Ronny struggled tryin' to have kids, so she cheated on him and tried to say it was his. Ronny was smart, he knew he wasn't even in town around the time she got pregnant. She married that man he cheated with, and she had that kid.

Merry leaving with Blue was my last straw. No one understands what that does to you- not knowing where ya kid is. My twin brother was dead, and now my woman was gone with my baby.

I used to drive around the city at all hours of the night trying to find Blue. I didn't care about the numbness I'd feel in my body. Honestly, my condition wasn't really my biggest concern.

I wanted my brother back. I wanted my baby back. I think I was a little hard on my other two kids after that. I always felt bad every time I'd yell at them, but I couldn't help it. Feeling my body slowly giving up, and knowing I could've done something about it sickens me.

I'll forever blame Merry for that. She took my child, and she took my life with her.

For a while I had to get around with a walking stick, before Nadia was around. Everything used to make me angry back then. I had to drink to keep the nightmares away. Some people say they see they dead relatives in dreams, I see them in my nightmares. I don't dream. While Blue was gone I either saw Ronny dying, or all the shit that could've been happening to my baby while I sat in my house slowly fucking dying. Couldn't even drive after a few months.

I started losing weight, which was making my muscles shrink- so I started getting weaker.

My feet went first. Then it was my legs, my shoulders, my back, my neck. My hands and arms are almost gone now too.

Nadia and the doctors keep telling me to squeeze the ball in hopes I wont lose my grip. They're starting to get concerned my face is gonna go- then my lungs. And I know that they will, one day. I know that's how I'll die.

I'll be sitting in my chair, eyes open, mouth open. No one will even realize I'm dead until they see my lungs ain't moving. I think about who that'll be all the time- Blue, Fiona, Nadia. At least I know it wont be Cipher. Wish it was none of them. I hope it happens after they've all left.

I think my condition is irreversible now. I'd given up on it a long time ago. Only reason I agreed to start trying again is because of Blue. Blue came back and suddenly I allowed disability support into my life, and started going back to doctors appointments.

But I can't go to hospitals. I don't want surgeries. That shit just brings me back to the day my life ended. If that crash never happened, Merry might have never left. Or if she did, I would've been there to save Blue.

After I stopped blaming Nicole, I started blaming myself. I know It wasn't my fault the truck crashed, but I should've seen it earlier. The headlights were bright- it was night. I should've seen that they were getting a little too close. I don't why I didn't. I think about that all the time, and I have no idea why I didn't see those headlights before it was too late.

I hate myself. I hate myself for destroying this family. I could've saved Ronny. I could've saved Blue. I could've saved myself.

People always say to not live with regrets- but those people can suck my fucking dick.

Every time I look at Blue I have regret. Every time I look at him, he looks the same he did the day he came back. Broken, beat, dirty. So skinny even police thought he was a toddler. When I first saw him I thought Blue was dead, and that he was some other little boy Merry had with some other junkie.

When I die, I hope Blue, Fiona and Cipher forgive me for the father I've given them. I wish I could've done better for them.

Fiona Glass

I had work again today after school. Cipher texted me Sunday morning losing his shit at me for going to Beau Jones' house. Honestly, I didn't text him back. Cipher does this. When he gets angry at me he will go on and on screaming at me and calling me the meanest names he can think of and then suddenly the fuse will blow over and he'll act like nothing happened. It's easier to just ignore him until he takes a fucking nap.

Blue came to work with me again. He's sat in the same spot he always sits in. Writing in his journal. He's getting better with his handwriting. It's getting a little easier to understand.

Maddy came in this afternoon as well. The shock on my face would've been extremely visible by the sound of her voice. She looked so different. The average University school student with her hair tied neatly back, wearing a button up white top and black pants. A book bag hanging over her shoulder and blushy makeup making her appear so incredibly innocent.

"Hey Fi. You don't mind If I call you Fi, right?" she greets as she walked through the bell door.

"No." I said with shock, seeing her so abruptly. "Most people just call me Fi."

"Cool. By the way, I'm not a stalker- Beau told me you worked here."

"It's okay." I assure. "How've you been?"

"Ugh, bored! University is definitely not all its hyped up to be." she exaggerates, leaning against the register.

"How long until you're finished?" I ask curiously.

"A while, and I'm already over it. I wanted to be a midwife, but my mum would only pay for the nursing course- so, here we are."

"I wish I was smart enough to do something like that."

"Why, what do you wanna be?"

I hesitated telling the truth- It's not often someone gets to actually be a famous author, no matter how bad they want it.

"An author."

"Really? I thought you were gonna say a model."

"Really?"

"Yeah, are you kidding? You're so hot. I'd actually read Playboy if you were in it."

Her compliment made me laugh- maybe blush?

"Anyways, I have to get back home before my mother sends a rescue team to come a find me. Beau was gate keeping your phone number so I was just wondering If I could have it? I could use a new friend."

I was flattered by her question. She was so confident and witty, and it was flattering she went out of her way to try and be my friend. I gave her my number without hesitation. She told me she'd text me soon about seeing each other. As she went to leave she stopped as she sighted Blue.

"Is this your little brother?" She asked.

"Yeah, how'd you know?"

"You look alike." she said, smiling, before exiting the store.

I closed the bakery at 7pm. I don't usually get many customers that late anyway so I'd been packing up and cleaning the store for over an hour. I wanted to get out as soon as possible so Blue and I could get home.

I usually lock the door when It's closed, but I forgot to today. All the lights were off- food was packed away- and I was wiping down the tables when I heard the bell ring of someone entering. It made my skin crawl. It's scary being in the store that late- the city was kind of intimidating at night.

"Hello, Fiona." Tarn greeted eerily. "You aren't closed, are you?"

"Sorry, we closed at 7." I smiled.

"Ah, that's too bad. Thought It would be nice to bring my girls some cake."

"You have daughters?" I ask kindly. I felt an urge as soon as she walked in to stop cleaning, and instead bring my full attention to her. A strange urge.

She chuckles. "Think of me as sort an.. agent."

"An agent?"

"Right. Sort of like an acting agent, or a modeling agent."

"Really? That's so cool."

"It is. It's an honorable career, truly." something about her smile in the dark sent shivers up my spine.

The way she described herself made me remember how interested she was in the way I looked. Maybe she meant it when she said I could use my beauty for good.

"I'll be honest, Fiona. I came here hoping you were working."

"Really?"

"Yes, because I've been waiting for your call."

"I know, I'm sorry. Life has been super busy-"

"I'm sure it has." Tarn agrees, peering over at Blue, who's stuck in his work. "As it turns out, there happens to be an opening in my agency, and I am convinced you would be perfect for the job. Now before you say anything, may I ask, how much do you make here an hour?"

"$11." I answered honestly.

Tarn smiled ludicrously. "Well, if you worked for me, you'd be making up to $25 an hour- certainly- plus tips. And there are many other ways to make up to hundreds of dollars extra a night- and based on your beauty, I'm sure you would thrive."

Tarn talked with such convincing nature. Honestly, she could convince me to sell my dads house if she talked for long enough. She seemed like the kind of person that didn't take no for an answer, and that pay sounded incredibly tempting. After all, life is all about money.

"What would I be doing?" I ask curiously.

"Well, that's for us to discuss at a later date. But I will give you the time to think on it. Remember, you have my number- call me when you have an answer." she said finally.

She placed her cardigan hood over her head, preparing to walk into the cold night. She turned back at the last second to say one final thing.

"Have a splendid night Fiona, I really hope to be hearing from you soon." she smiles, before walking out of the store.

I looked through the windows as Silas opened the black tinted car door for Tarn to step inside. So mysterious.

The entire way back home, Blue and I walked silently. All I could think about was Tarn's offer. That money could get me so much closer to moving to New York- and maybe, if she's right about my looks, maybe I could model too. Maybe one day I will be on the cover of Playboy, or even Vogue!

5

Chapter Five- Queen

Fiona Glass

Times have changed a lot. After Tarn visited me at Opals, I took her offer- calling her the following day. I'd be a fool to pass up that kind of money.

I'm 18 now, Blue just turned 12, and Cipher will be 21 in October. I've been working as a bartender in Queen Night Club, under Tarn's management. I didn't know it was a strip club until after I called Tarn that following day. She had me meet her at the club before it opened for the night, and asked me to start training behind the bar an hour later.

I didn't stay in school for long after that. It became too difficult to work until 3 or 4 AM and then walk to school at 8:30. My English teachers were sad I was dropping out, but there's nothing more that school could teach me that I don't already know.

Tarn told me that every girls who worked there were hand selected specifically, that she didn't just let anyone work there. The bartenders and dancers are only female, and the security guards are only male. I've primarily been working at the front bar, and occasionally worked in the center square bar- also known as the main bar. I've never worked the back bar or the upstairs bar. I've never been in the VIP upstairs area or downstairs in the private rooms. I told Tarn I didn't want to be a dancer. I told her I wasn't confident enough for that. She told me that all girls start out as bartenders, that they have to earn a promotion to be a dancer.

For a long time, I didn't want that promotion. Bartending was fun, and I was making way more money then I was at Opals. I was gonna keep it a secret from my family- except Blue- that I'd changed jobs.

It went well for a while, of course, until Beau told Cipher. I've learned pretty quickly that Beau doesn't know how to keep his mouth shut about anything. Worst secret keeper in the entire world.

Cipher nearly killed me, dobbed me out to our dad. At the time, I was still 17, so my dad was angry. But my dad doesn't have the energy to yell anymore. My dad doesn't have the energy to do anything anymore.

I think he was more disappointed, if anything. If I'm being honest, that didn't feel great. I think Nadia was starting to notice the difference with my dad. He was more depressed then ever. I think he misses the freedom.

I started feeding my dad beers through straws whenever Nadia wasn't there. I knew she'd be disappointed if she knew. My dad hadn't looked so happy in years, but I couldn't stop after doing it the first time. It sort of felt like we were bonding over a secret no one would ever know- except Blue, of course. Blue was always around, it was impossible to hide anything from him. But he didn't seem to care though, really.

Tarn told me a few months ago I was one of their best bartenders, that I was making them more money then the others. She gave me an ultimatum- either I start my training to be promoted as a dancer, or I be sent to the back bar. The back bar is known in the club to us girls as the 'dog house' of the club. You make the least amount of money back there, and its right by the entrance to the private rooms, so most of the fights from men trying to sneak into the private rooms happens.

A lot of the time the girls back there get roughed up by customers. Of course, not enough to cause any damage, because the security here are the best security I've ever seen. I, for sure, wouldn't mess with them.

Cipher hated that I was working there at first, but he got used to it eventually. He started liking the free shots I was giving him.

Yana and Ciph have been arguing a lot recently. She's been threatening to kick him out for months. Ever since he reconnected with Beau and I started working at Queen, Cipher's been spending more of his off time out on the streets, rather then at home.

I don't know what's going on with him. He tells me only light details, rather then the specifics. I hope they don't break up though, I like Yana, and I wouldn't want to lose the option of being able to see Alina.

In the end, I took Tarn's offer. I was loving the money, and the option of making less didn't look as appetizing. She told me that I'd be trained, that she wouldn't let me up on the stages until she felt I was ready. That sort of made me feel a little better, I guess.

I've been training for a while now, and I know a few tricks and routines. I've even been meeting with some of the girls outside of work hours so that they can train me to perfection. I started looking up to some of these girls, manifesting that one day I'd be as great as them.

I mean, there is a bigger picture here. It was all for money. One day I'd get to leave and pursue my dreams in New York. It's so close, I can feel it.

All of the girls have their own names they give themselves once they start working as dancers. The bartenders use their real names, but it's not often customers are asking the bartenders their names. I don't know why the dancers do it, but all of them have one.

Star has been my top inspiration for dance. Her real name is Yusra Fadipe. Her parents were from Nigeria- she still has the accent. One of the prettiest girls at the Club in my opinion. Yusra has 4 kids to her baby daddy. They ain't together no more but they co-parent so that both of them can work. They even live together. They live together and they have their own rooms on opposite sides of the house. Yusra also has a dancing room at her house, which is why she invites me over a lot during the day to continue practicing. Her kids are also close in age to Blue, so he always enjoys coming with me so that he can play with them.

Roxy is another good friend from the club. She's only been a dancer for a year, which is helpful coming from someone who is only just starting. Her real name is Letty White- she's the same age as Beau, and Beau's favorite dancer. She dyes her blonde hair red and keeps her brows blonde. She also has really big fake lips and boobs. She always has long nails on too, and she's the best at rolling in the entire city.

Maxine Saigar is who trained me in bartending. She's one of the few bartenders Tarn wants to keep as a bartender. She primarily works in the front bar.

The girls have been giving me some ideas for names, but I have nearly an entire year to decide before Tarn will actually promote me to a dancer.

The club is open Wednesday - Sundays from 4pm to 7am. It's still kind of new so its a pretty big hot spot in the city these days. Shit gets pretty busy at certain times of the nights. Sometimes it reminds me of 90s club movies.

Music blasting, girls dancing, guys smoking, rapping. It's pretty much everything you'd expect a massive and expensive strip club to be.

The VIP area is for celebrities and high paying clients. A lot of the time they rent out the entire private floor for themselves and their friends for secret services. Everyone does drugs too. Tarn doesn't care if people are doing drugs, unless there's undercover cops. We all wear earpieces so that Tarn can communicate with us from her office where all the security cameras are.

Police have been trying to bust Tarn for years. The girls talk about it all the time when she's not around. Police think she's laundering money somehow, dealing drugs within her business too. Tarn also owns a few hotels and restaurants around town. All of these places under her name are always being watched. But it's always pretty obvious when undercover cops are in the building. It is only when there's undercover cops that we're not allowed to let customers openly do drugs, or buy drugs from the security guards.

I couldn't imagine how much money Tarn would be making. The adrenaline of knowing that she's doing something that could get her in massive trouble. She's smart, though. She knows how to get away with everything. She knows exactly what to do, how to act, and how to control us like puppets to deter the police when it's needed.

The girls aren't supposed to talk about the private rooms, but Star told me that Tarn makes all the customers renting rooms sign 100 page disclosure agreements that no one reads. Some people rumour that there's consent forms for things that people wouldn't usually consent to when they're sober.

Another rumour- one that also interests the undercover cops- is one that claims there's roofies in our drinks. Just enough to make people keep spending their money, but not too much to take anyone out. But it's just a rumour of course. I've drank our drinks before- and I'll admit, I get drunk quickly. But I think that's just because we make them strong.

It's Saturday night, our busiest night of the week. I've been working since open, primarily on the front bar. I had to help out in the center bar for about an hour because customers were getting rowdy. Cart had to kick a few people out earlier for making too much noise.

Blue still comes to work with me. He stays in the girls pamper rooms which is behind the front bar. A hallway that leads to Tarn's office as well.

The girls love Blue. A lot of them have kids so they're always offering to help him with his homework while they get ready and during their breaks.

Blue loves coming too. I'd never force him to go if he didn't want to, but on Friday's and Saturdays he usually gets himself ready in time to come with me. I don't let him go during the week though, otherwise he'll be up too late and wont go to school. I think Blue loves seeing the girls because they help him feel more normal. He still doesn't speak- but the girls don't care. Everyone is different, and most people wouldn't expect it- but club girls are some of the nicest girls you'll ever meet. They accept everyone for their differences- at least, these girls do. I don't have a problem with any of them.

"Hey, Fi." Eyeball greets, accompanied by his friends. Awaiting me at the front bar.

"Hey Eyeball, what can I get you guys?"

"Two whiskey cokes, and two gin an' tonics please, sweet'eart?" he asks, already getting his card out while I start making the drinks.

Pet names. Men love them. Sweetheart, gorgeous, baby, baby doll, pretty eyes, you name it. I hear it all. After a while it starts to get a little repetitive. I wish they'd come up with something more creative.

Even as bartenders, us girls have to wear super revealing clothes. Heels or boots are a must. Makeup is a must, and our hair always has to look neat too. Tarn would also fire us if she ever got a waft of us smelling bad. Us bar girls keep perfume and deodorant behind the bars and use them constantly.

Dancers are more nude then us- sometimes, literally nude. The most being stickers. Compared to the dancers, us bartenders dress extremely conservative.

"There you go." I say as I hand them their drinks. Eyeball scans his card on the eftpos machine, then hands me a $10 bill as a tip.

Eyeball and his friends usually spend their time at the poker tables, betting all their money away and smoking cigars.

It was after they walked away that I saw Cipher enter with his usual group- Dare, Brownie, Jasper, Beau and Link. Today they brought Archie Hatt with them too.

Archie is like the odd one out of the group- seems like the best way to describe him. He'd get sunburned from snow, has orange hair and massive freckles all over his face. He dresses like Dare, though. Talks like Beau. It's a strange combo.

They always shout out to me the second they see me, always seeming so excited by my presence.

"Hey guys. Do any of you want a drink?" I ask with a grin, knowing they'd never pass up the offer.

"Just some Great Northern's, please Fi." Beau requests, handing me too much cash like he always does.

When I first met Beau I thought that I'd probably end up liking him. I mean, he was cute, confident, and not hard to talk to. He was okay. But that was until I met Link. Link and Beau look so similar, yet so different.

Link's blue eyes are something you could see from across the club. Of course, he has a mullet too- don't they all? Link's got a few tattoos from prison- nothing as big as Beau's but, visible. Link was also way quieter, and way more shy then Beau.

Every time I talk to Link he blushes. I know he likes me, but I don't know if that's just because I'm a half naked girl giving him alcohol or not.

He's cute, but he's Cipher's friend. It might be kind of weird.

He's also Tarn's nephew, and I feel like it would look off If Tarn met me because of Beau, and then I started seeing Beau's brother. I don't know. I don't want that kind of reputation, you know? And like I said, Link's hot. I'm sure he gets plenty of attention from way prettier girls then me.

"Are you alright?" I asked Cipher as he sat down at the bar. Some of the other boys turned to admire the dancers, other's chatted with one another.

"Yeah." he responded with shortness.

"Where's Yana?"

"Same place she always is." he responds, bags beneath his eyes.

"You look like you haven't slept." I respond, as he lights himself a cigarette.

"Yeah, well-" he begins, cutting himself off.

"Are you guys fighting again?" I dig. But every time I ask these kinds of questions, I feel like I'm walking on eggshells- but I kind of like to hear what's going on.

"Where's Blue?" He finally asks, avoiding my question.

"Out the back. Do you want to see him?"

"Nah." He groans, clearing his throat. "Is he reading?"

"Homework."

"Good." he nods shortly.

Suddenly Link turns from talking to Archie to lean over the bar, looking straight at me.

"So, Aunty Tarn told us you been practicing. When're you getting that promotion?"

"Well, technically I've already got it. She just wants to see that I can actually dance before she lets me on the stage."

"Can you please warn me over text before you go on stage- and where- so I know when to leave." Cipher requested grumpily.

"I wont be dancing every night, you know. Just depends on when Tarn needs me."

"Exactly." Cipher responds.

"Hey, boys!" Beau shouts, capturing everyone's attention. "Come for the show." he invites, seeing Roxy is about to go on stage.

"You guys go ahead, I'm gonna get another drink." Link responds hastily.

The other boys stare at him with wonder. Beau looks at him, then looks at me, and leaves with a smirk.

Cipher stood from his seat, sluggishly, following the other boys toward one of the stages where Roxy was dancing. Link sat where Cipher was sitting- drinking his beer quietly.

"Not in the mood for dances tonight?" I joke.

He giggles- he has a really awkward giggle. Always covers his mouth when he smiles- I've noticed.

"Nah- Nah I usually don't come here for the dances." he responds. God he's hot.

People that hot usually don't act so awkward. But the presence of awkwardness is not to be confused with a lack of confidence. Every girl that walks past him looks his way- someone who receives so much attention would usually be a cock head. I know he sees it, but maybe he's just really good at pretending he doesn't care.

"What do you come here for then?" I ask.

I could see him deciphering in his brain trying to think of a response, but Jasper interrupts him. Walking back over to buy another beer.

"Thanks, Fi Fi." he obliged, before joining the boys back in a hurry.

Link still sat there while I served other customers. He ordered another beer and that's sort of the only conversation we really had for that time being.

We looked over a few times, laughing as Beau cheered and threw money at Roxy. $50 bills.

"He's such a flirt." I joke.

"Yeah. Yeah, he's always known how to put on a show- It worked on you, didn't it?" he tantilizes, turning back to look at me with a suppressed smirk.

"Wow." I laugh. "You almost sound jealous."

"A'right, gorgeous." he jokes, picking fun at his brother and laughing into his beer.

It was at that point that Maxine started her shift- around 10pm. Peak hour.

"Hey Fi- hey Link." she greets, approaching us from the glamour room.

"Hey Max." we both respond.

"I didn't realize how great Blue was at drawing." Maxine expresses, as she serves another needy customer.

"Oh, yeah. Blue has always loved drawing- pencils, chalk. All that." I explain, serving a different customer.

You sort of learn on the job how to tune out the obnoxious compliments, demands and stares from old men.

"Hey, how's Damon, Max? He's been okay?" Link asks- Damon is Max's son.

"Yeah- he's loving kindergarten. He's so good at making friends."

'That's great." Link agrees. "What about- what about Will? He's been leavin' you alone?"

Max hesitates for a moment, distracting herself with wiping down the bar.

"Yeah. Thanks Link." she finally responds.

Will is Damon's dad. Max used to come into work with bruises all over her, especially her neck. She used to get me to cover her with makeup and wore scarves in summer. Of course, until the boys found out.

I was the one that told them. She was pissed at me for weeks but after Beau, Link, Jasper and Cipher.. dealt with it- she realized it was the right thing. Tarn told her to let them know if he ever shows up again.

After she forgave me she cried in my arms in the glamour room and thanked me. She said he used to hit the kid- but she'd beg him to hurt her instead, whenever Damon did something to upset him.

"What about you, you been staying out of trouble?" I hear Max ask, as I serve a big group.

I've never asked anyone about why Link was in prison for four years. I never really felt like it was something I needed to know. He didn't seem like a bad person, you know?

"Yeah- nah, I'll never go back." Link responds, lighting a cigarette. "I'd never go back."

"Well, good. I'm proud of you." Max responds, nodding with approval and grabbing him a new beer.

I was working until 4am. Cipher was supposed to take Blue home at 12, but he was clearly, very intoxicated.

"Cipher! Cipher!" I shouted, calling Cipher over as I approached him by the center bar.

"What?" he responds, turning around with a pink mixed drink dripping down his chin.

"What the hell are you doing? You were supposed to take Blue home!" a sudden gasp washed over his face as he remembers

"Shit! I forgot, Fi."

The club is packed. People bump around us. Spilling cups and admiring lights.

"You forgot? Are you fucking serious?"

"Why do you even bring him here, Fi?"

"No, don't turn this on me! You said you would, that was the only reason I let him come." I shout, but in a hush so other customers don't intervene.

"Well.." Cipher responds, unable to come up with a reasonable explanation.

"I can take him home." Link offers, overhearing us from the poker tables.

I looked at him, trying to remember how many drinks he'd had. He hadn't done any drugs- I think. He wasn't slurring, he could stand straight. He seemed sober.

"Are you sure?" I ask, just in case he wanted to change his mind.

"Yeah, If Cipher's okay with it."

"You gonna come back?" Cipher asked.

"Someone has to take you losers home." Link jokes.

"Are you sure? You don't have to." I assure, giving him another chance to back out.

"Just- take the offer." He smirks.

Okay. Someone has to, and it can't be me. I walked into the glamour room. One of the other girls was on break- fixing her hair- and helping Blue answer some of his math questions. He always hated math.

"Hey, Blue. Time to go." Blue waved goodbye to the girl, and she wished him luck with his homework.

Blue was quick to pack up. He followed me out to where Link was waiting by the front bar, holding a jacket.

"Link is gonna take you home, okay?" I told him. I could tell he was confused, I sort of expected that, though. "Cipher can't drive at the moment, but Link can."

"Here." Link says, as he wraps his jacket around Blue. "It'll be freezing outside, you'll need it."

Blue smiled awkwardly.

"I'll see you in the morning, okay?" I told Blue, before he and Link walked out together.

I sort of wanted to rush them out the door before Blue had the chance to refuse.

The remainder of the night only worsened. Thank fuck Blue went home when he did. I don't even remember everything that happened- or how we got to such a point.

I remember some time had passed since I'd seen the boys, and when I did their heads were in the clouds. I could tell the second they walked by.

Tarn must've given them something new. They were staring at the lights. Pupils massive. It was way too busy for me to even take care of that. A bucks party was attending- plus free pupils. It was busier then any Saturday night I'd ever worked.

Security had already kicked out two separate groups during the night for fighting. Tarn was yelling at the girls in the glamour room because of their outfits, telling them to change- fix their lip colours. Pick a different hair style. It all felt so stressful- It not often it's like this.

Bucks parties are always hard- the guests are always so fucking greedy. Always expecting everything handed to them on a golden platter. Expecting drinks within seconds, and for dancers to take them to the private rooms free of charge. Always trying to get in our space, some of them even trying to get behind the bars to make their own cocktails. The security were starting to get fucking pissed.

Cipher, of course, only made it worse. Every time one of those drunk fucks came near me he lost his shit. He was only doing it because he was pissed at Yana and he needed someone to yell at. It was fucking embarrassing. And all the other boys kept feeding him drinks and by 2am he was barely fucking standing.

He came to me begging for more and I told him no, said I was cutting him off. By then, Link had come back and was just waiting around for the boys to ask to leave.

"Fine. I'll just go to the other bars." he threatened with a stumble.

"They wont serve you, I told them you're cut off." I lied, but I knew he'd believe me.

"Why do you always have to be such a bitch, Fi?"

Link and Jasper walked over, they saw how fucked up he was and knew the angry part of Cipher was about to come out- the messy one.

"Hey, Ciph, how about we take this back to my place-" Jasper offers, trying to take Cipher away but Cipher shoved him. Everyone who knows Cipher knows not to take that shit to heart when he's like this. Other's don't.

One of the bucks boys started cat calling me, whistling at me and laughing in an attempt of getting my attention. I usually ignore guys like that- let the security deal with it. But of course, Cipher had to get involved.

"Hey!" he shouted, approaching them with his shoulders broad and his fists tensed. "Watch who you fuckin' whistle at!"

"What you gonna do, dick? You in love with this slut or somethin'?" the man responded with a pestering tone.

Cart and two other security guards were on their way over, but they just didn't make it in time before Cipher punched him in his fucking face. A brawl started. The boys were trying to help the security guards get Cipher off of him. The guy from the bucks party- a bleeding nose and lip- got kicked out. All of his friends testifying but Cart told them that if they wanna argue, they can go too. They went real quiet after that. Then Cart turned to Cipher- who now had a bruising eye- and told him that he knew the other guy started it, but if he did it again he'd be kicked out too.

Link pulled Cipher to sit down at the bar, asked me to get him a glass of water.

"I'on't want a glass of fuckin' water." Cipher snarled.

"I finish in one hour, can you not be a dickhead until then, please?" I beg, hoping something will go through to his thick fucking skull.

In case you were wondering, he didn't stop. Link and Jasper basically had to hold him down to keep him from leaving his seat. He kept trying to get up- wanted to *talk* to those guys outside. Beau came over after narrowly missing all of Cipher's fucking rants.

"Yo, what the hell is goin' on with ya' brother?" he whispered with a smirk. I think Beau deep down loved the drama- loved that his friends are the type of fuckwits to fight other fuckwits.

"You know as much as me, Beau." I huff, wiping down the bar while Max rushes around unpacking boxes of low stock. Her long orange braid getting in the way.

All I wanted was to get the hell out of there. But I basically had to drag Cipher out of the club. All of the boys came with, at least. Silas warned me and Link at the door that the bucks guys were still outside.

"Well-" I sighed. "Let's just get it over with."

I knew what was going to happen- and to be honest, I couldn't be fucked dealing with it, almost as much as I couldn't be fucked trying to avoid it.

The second we walked out, Cipher and the guy from before immediately started screaming at each other. They were on the road so it was out of the security guards' responsibility. So you know what, I decided too that I was just gonna stand there and watch. Let Beau fix whatever the fuck is wrong with Cipher- lighting a cigarette for myself, like popcorn.

Eventually the boys got Cipher away and brought him to our cars.

"I can't take him to Yana's like this, and I can't take him home either." I told Jasper, after he finally got Cipher inside my car.

"You can bring him back to mine." Link offered. "It'll be more quiet there then at Jasper and Beau's place."

"That's true." Jasper agreed.

"Okay, might as well." I huffed, getting into the car. I was prepared to agree to anything that would solve this hopeless night.

Link drove with me and Cipher. The other boys said goodbye and all headed back to Jasper and Beau's in Cipher's car. Beau promised to come by in the morning to check on Cipher, and to drop his car off. Honestly, I just wanted to get the fuck out of there.

I saved enough money pretty quickly to get a car- a cheap black ford, but a car. Cipher took me on a few driving lessons and helped me fake my hours under my dads name, and then I just winged the test and somehow I passed.

Cipher was laying down in the back seat the entire time just ranting about life. Link and I honestly thought it was pretty funny.

I never knew Link had his own place- to be honest, I never really thought of where he lived. He told me in the car that Tarn rented him the place once he got released. Said he's been trying to find a job but it's hard for someone who hasn't got any work experience, and with a criminal record.

Link's place was in an apartment building. The walk up the stairs and the outside was kind of sketchy. It wasn't a tall building, but his room was on the top floor- which was so fun to walk up with Ciph..!

The front reception was merely a small box by the revolving front door, filled with cigarette butts falling from an overflowing empty can of baby formula. We led Cipher toward the back of the small entrance and up the wooden stairs. The inside of this building reflected the outs, and was freezing cold.

Two little girls sprinted past us down the stairs. It seems they were playing a game of tag with a third party we couldn't see. They almost bulldozed us over as they barreled down.

The smell of cigarette smoke and loud TVs from the inside of rooms echoing up the stairs made it all the more overwhelming to carry my brother to the very top of the building.

The inside of his apartment was massive. The kitchen was bigger then my dads entire house- so was the lounge room. As you walk in, the kitchen is to your left. The lounge room is directly open and ahead of you, big windows looking out to the city below.

"Wow." was first thing I said when I walked in. Definitely not the kind of room you'd expect to be at the top of this building.

We laid Cipher down on the couch, he was mumbling something about Yana. There was a hallway to the right of the lounge room- assuming it led to a bedroom and a bathroom-laundry area.

Link went to grab a wet cloth and a bottle of water from his fridge. I looked around- inspecting the room. A photo frame with a picture of two little blonde boys, and a mother sat on the coffee table beneath the wall TV. I guess they grew into their dark hair the older they got. Another photo frame hung on the wall of the same two little boys- but even younger- accompanied by the same mother, and this time, a Grandmother, and another woman resembling a younger Tarn. All smiling.

"Here." Link said, handing me the wet cloth to place over Cipher's welting eye while he placed down the water bottle on a wooden side table.

The second I tried to put the cloth on Cipher's eye, he pushed me away gently, and started crying into his palm. The last time I seen Cipher cry was when he found out Yana was pregnant. A cry of fear- like any young expecting parent might do. But this cry- it was a whimper, a cry for help.

"Cipher- what's wrong?" I ask, a wave of empathy washing over me. What could possibly be making him act this way?

Cipher Glass

Yana and I have been fighting a lot recently. She's been getting fed up with me going out with the boys every weekend.

It started after that first night I'd gone to Queen with Dare. Some of Yana's girlfriends must've been out that night, said they saw me go in.

Yana lost her shit at me. Her parents were out of town- visiting her older sister- the only reason she really let herself scream.

"What the fuck, Cipher!"

"You're gonna wake Alina." I warned with a hush.

"Good, then maybe she can learn from a young age what kind of father you really are!"

"Don't fuckin' bring Alina into this!"

"You're the one that said her name! And don't try and change the subject! Tell me, what the hell were you doing inside a strip club!?"

"I told you, I was seein' Beau and Link!"

"In a strip club, really?" she taunted.

"A *club*, owned by their fuckin' Aunt!"

"You really think that excuse is gonna work, Ciph? Are you fucking kidding me?"

"I went there to drink, Yana!"

"So you do it at a fucking pub, not a place that promotes naked fucking women, Ciph!"

"I don't know what you want me to fuckin' say!?"

She groaned, tensing her hands by the sides of her face. She looked like she wanted to claw my eyes out.

"Do you understand how disrespectful that is? My father would've never done that to my mother."

"Yeah, well I ain't ya' father."

"And you'd do that to our kid? Cheat on her mother?"

"I didn't fuckin' cheat on you! I went there to drink and then we left and took it back to Jasper and Beau's-"

"How am I supposed to believe that?"

"You should trust my word."

"Really? Because I asked you Cipher. I asked you where you went and you conveniently left out the part where you went to a fucking strip club-"

She was so fucking frustrating- felt like I couldn't breathe.

"-Think of it from my shoes, for once in your life just think about someone else!"

"I am thinkin' about you!" I shout, slamming my hand against the bedside table. "I am always thinkin' about you, Yana! I *fucking* love you! I fuckin' *love* you!" shes silent. "I would never do that, you should know that Yana." I assure again, placing my hands gently on her cheeks. Desperately trying to convince her. "I love you and Alina more then anything in the entire fuckin' world. I need you to know that."

She forgave me, over time. I didn't go out for a while after that. Until my birthday weekend. Beau and Link called me and told me that Tarn had sold them pingers- I hadn't done pingers since school.

I dreaded having to ask Yana for permission to see the boys that weekend.

But surprisingly she was okay with it. I told the boys I didn't want to go anywhere but Beau and Jasper's house, that Yana would kill me if she knew I left. They kept trying to convince me- Beau even offered to sneak me in through a hidden door, but I declined.

I was sticking to my word, until the pingers kicked in. Orange pingers. We were fucking sweating at Jasper and Beau's house, so we decided to go for a walk. Fresh air.

Anyone who has done pingers knows that you truly do lose track of time and place- you don't even realize where you are until you're there. And suddenly, I was in Queen again.

The other boys sat by the stages to watch the girls. I stayed with Eyeball playing poker all night. No girls in my sight- I fucking swear it. Fiona was there that night too, she had already started working there by then and even she could promise that all I did was drink and play poker.

The next day I knew Yana knew, but she didn't say anything. She never said anything. She only spoke to me when she needed to. Only touched me when she wanted sex. We were like friends with benefits living in the same house- and also raising a child together.

Life was like that for months, until the night I got into that fight with that dickhead at the bucks party.

I wasn't supposed to go out that Saturday. I was cleaning up after dinner, everyone had gone to bed already for an early night. Beau was spamming my phone, begging me to go out with them.

Yana walked out from putting Alina to bed and sat down at the kitchen bench. She looked beautiful in blue. I could tell there was something wrong. I thought It was about the previous boys night still- but it'd been months since she said anything.

I put down the sponge and dried my hands, leaning against the bench.

"What's wrong, Yans?" I asked.

She didn't say anything at first, just clearing her throat and nervously playing with her hair like she'd always does- the same thing Alina does when she's nervous.

"Please, just talk to me. We used to be so good at talkin', bub." I pleaded, and finally she took my offer and told me what was wrong.

Her throat sounded dry as she spoke. "I spoke to Dominica a few weeks ago. She told me that they were opening up an Interior Design class at the university she works for."

"Okay.." I say, waiting for the rest.

"I applied."

I felt my own throat dry instantly. Dominica? She lives hours away. How is Yana supposed to tend classes there and live here?

"What, do they- do they have online courses or somethin'?" I ask curiously.

She shakes her head.

"Then- what?" I'm confused.

She stands up slowly from her seat. "Dominica has spare rooms in her house. She's kinda rich, remember." she smiles awkwardly.

"What are you saying?"

"Well, If I get in, we'd have to move there."

What the hell is she talking about?

"My- my family lives here-"

A stern frown pierces her eyebrows as she storms around to my side of the kitchen counter.

"No, Ciph. Your family is here!" she objects, pointing at herself. "Your family is where your daughter is!"

"My daughter is here, Yana! You are here!"

"But we won't be if they accept me!" she announces sternly. "I am not asking for your permission, Cipher."

"You can't just make this decision without consulting me. We have a child together!"

"This *is* me consulting you! This *is* me talking to you about it. I am giving you a choice, Cipher."

"I can't-" I say, ripping my hands away from hers and walking toward the front door.

She followed close behind, shouting things in my ear, trying so hard to convince me while I put my shoes and jacket on.

"Where are you going!?" she questions, as I rip open the front door.

"To think!" I shout, before making my dramatic exit and closing the door behind me.

I met the boys at Jasper and Beau's. First thing I did was light a cigarette and ask Beau what drugs he had. Everyone had put in money to buy acid off of him- and there was not a single ounce of hesitation as I gave him cash.

We snorted a lot of coke and drank a lot of beer before we headed out. By the time we got to Queen I'd drank an entire bottle of vodka to myself. Beau kept making jokes about it- but all I cared about was buying more acid.

The lights inside Queen made me forget about everything. There was not a sound in my ears beside the sound of the lights. I don't remember much besides the drinks and shots- and maybe the fights.

Next thing I knew I was lying on a couch in Link's apartment with Link and Fi huddled around me. Something about the way Fi looked at me just made me burst out crying. A moment of weakness I'd hate myself for- once I sobered up.

"I think she fuckin' hates me Fi." I whimpered.

"She doesn't hate you, Ciph. If Yana didn't love you she would've gotten rid of you a long time ago." she jokes.

As much as Fi probably fucking hates me too- she's always been one of my favourite people. She's always had some kinda nature about her that just makes anyone feel comfortable. I fucking hate crying- only reason it probably happened was because of the drugs. I'd never do that in front of anyone else.

Link Jones

First time I saw Fiona Glass was her first night working at Queen. It was a Friday. I remember Aunt Tarn telling me she was still 17. Beau told me that the first night Fiona went to their house for a party, she lied and said she was 18. Beau always liked girls that told white lies. A weird kink he always favoured.

I knew she was Cipher's sister, but I'd never met her before. Cipher used to chill with us a lot. He used to talk about Fiona lightly in conversation, but never anything crazy.

Cipher used to visit me when I was serving time. I've always appreciated that because among all the boys- including my brother- Cipher visited me the most.

First time I saw Fiona, she was training behind the bar with Maxine. That night I was only with Beau, Jasper, Dare and Archie- after Cipher had gotten into trouble with Yana. I thought it was probably a good thing at the time- couldn't imagine how Cipher would react to hearing Fiona was working at Queen.

God she was beautiful- she still is. I'd never ever felt shy around a girl before- until I saw her. Beau picks on me all the time about it. But I don't know what it is, something about her just ruins any kind of game I could possibly possess.

It took me forever to gain the confidence to introduce myself to her. Beau and I usually go to Queen every weekend to support the business. It was around August that I finally went up to her by myself to order a beer.

Her smile nearly made me abort and hide behind my knees.

"Hey." I smiled.

"Hey." She smiled back. Her dimples were so perfect- everything about her was perfect. "You want a beer?"

Same thing I always order.

"I'm Link, by the way." I finally said as she handed me my drink.

"I know." she smiled again as she wiped down the bar.

I felt like she knew she made me nervous. Fuck I don't know what's wrong with me. It was so strange for me to feel that way. Maybe I forgot how to talk to women while I was away.

I've dated girls before. First girl I ever slept with was one of my mum's friends. My mum was young when she had me and Beau, and she used to have parties at the house all the time- the same house Beau and Jasper live in now. My mum lives there too- sometimes. She's always with a man-it's always been about a man. My mum dated so many men I can't even remember all their names. The older I got the more I realized her problem- she moved way too quickly. She fell in love way too quickly. She always gave these men a home in our house- alcoholics, drug addicts, men with anger problems.

Eventually, they'd always end the same. Honey moon phase, the parties, Tarn's drugs, then the fights, and then they break up.

About a year after my dad was arrested- when I was 7 and Beau was 9- my mum was dating a man named Davis. Davis was cool at first. Used to buy us toy cars and bring home race tracks from work. But of course, just like every other man my mum loved, he left. But before he left, he tried to take me with him. I don't know what they were fighting about that day- could've been anything. But while my mum went out the back for a smoke, Davis found me in my bedroom and took me in his car with him. I can't remember where Beau was, but if it wasn't for him, my mum would've never realized I was gone.

Aunt Tarn was the one that found me. I remember watching Cart beat the living shit out of Davis.

I used to think Aunt Tarn and Cart were dating, but later in life I just came to the conclusion that some questions are better unanswered. She met Silas around the time she started dealing. I don't know the full story about that- all I know is Silas has like 13 siblings, and a daughter.

When his daughter was born he was in jail, so the mother didn't put his name on her birth certificate.

When he got out, he came home to an empty house from an impatient partner. She knew Silas would never leave the life of drugs. I think maybe that's why he never tried to get his daughter back. He always talks about her, Summer, and shows me photos of her from before they left. Maybe he's given up on seeing his life any differently.

I know that most of the time when my mum is gone- if it's not for a random boyfriend- it's for Blade. Older brother of Jaxton Ritcher- who was Tarns childhood lover. He's the master of Tarn's enterprise. I guess they're sole partners of all their earnings, but if it weren't for Blade, there wouldn't be drugs. My mum was hired by Tarn years ago to be the direct transport from Blade to Tarn when stock is low. It used to be Cart, but once the Club was opening, Tarn felt Cart was best kept close by.

I don't know where Blade lives- I've never met him before. But I know my mum was his favourite prostitute- back when Tarn's main source of income came from the inside of our childhood home. And I know my mum probably loves him- more then she ever loved us.

Like I said, I've dated girls before. But I've never been very good at staying interested. They always look pretty, until it's been a few weeks and then suddenly an overwhelming fear of boredom hits me, and I leave. I haven't dated anyone since I was arrested. So I guess, maybe I've changed. It's been a long time since I first saw Fiona, and everyday I just become more and more intrigued.

I've noticed she always puts her lip gloss behind the strap of her bra when she works. I've also noticed that she always wears a jumper when walking into work, and when walking out. I've noticed that she talks a lot more about Blue then Cipher ever does. Even when Blue was still missing, Cipher never really spoke about him- not with us, anyway.

I've noticed that when no one is looking, she bites the insides of her cheeks. I've also noticed that she always smiles when she speaks- not just with her mouth but with her eyes too. Most people fake their smiles, and you can always tell by the shape of someones eyes. But not Fiona. I'd never know if her smile was genuine or not, because she's so convincingly good at being happy.

I don't really know how to go about my attraction toward Fiona. I wonder if Cipher would be pissed if he knew. I wonder if she thinks the same about me.

I knew Cipher was pissed that day. I knew he'd get into a fight with someone, and to be honest, I wasn't gonna stop it. No one stops Cipher when he's pissed. Cipher always has to have the last word, and he always has to prove himself- usually with his fists.

It was sort of like the perfect opportunity to be alone with Fiona. To have her finally see that I'm more then just Beau's little brother.

I knew my apartment would surprise her- it surprised me. Aunt Tarn pays for it, on the promise that I'd pay her back one day.

I made a promise to myself that I'd stay clean once I got out. I used to be super dependent on cocaine and alcohol to get through the day. I started smoking cigarettes when I was 12, and started drinking daily when I was 14. My mum gave me marijuana for the first time when I was 11, but I didn't start smoking it regularly until I was 15. Beau and I used to steal chocolate and snacks from small stores, because our mum never gave us money for food. I've never had a real home cooked dinner- only reason I know what that looks like is because of movies. Though, they never actually eat the food in movies. That shit pisses me off. I'd give anything to eat all that food.

CPS used to get called on my mum a lot, but they only ever came for us whenever Aunt Tarn was around- it's like she knew they were coming. House would suddenly be spotless, pantries were stocked, and we were only ever given new clothes during visits. I wore the same pair of sneakers from when I was 10 until I was 16. But I guess It's not my mum's fault.

My apartment was peaceful once Cipher fell asleep. Fiona wrapped him in a fuzzy yellow blanket I'd stolen when I was 15 from a baby pram at a supermarket. I made us both a drink with vodka and orange juice. I've never seen someones face light up brighter by the sight of juice.

"Is that orange juice?" she asked, her cheeks red with a smirk.

"It is." I responded carefully as she approached me in the kitchen. She stood closer then I was expecting- I never usually take much note of that, but It was all I could think about in that moment.

"I love orange juice." she says, taking a sip of the drink.

Taking a quick note of the subtle freckles all over her cheeks.

"You can stay here.. if you want." I told her with as much confidence I could.

The room fell silent.

"I can take the other couch, If you wanna sleep in the bed." I offer.

"Are you sure?"

I chuckle. "You're always asking me that question."

"Well, maybe I'm just trying to be polite." she jokes.

"Nah- not trying." I say, and suddenly our eyes are glued to each other. I can't pull away. I can feel my waist nearly touching hers.

I can smell her hair- some kind of fruit or flower. Her eyes look more green instead of brown in this light. The perfect shade of hazel.

"Okay." She finally whispers. "If you say so."

The clothes she was wearing didn't exactly look comfortable- she must've forgotten her jumper in the pamper room- so I showed her to my bedroom closet, and I gave her a top. I offered her shorts too, but she put them on over the skirt she already had on and we both laughed as they fell right down to her ankles.

"It's okay. The top will do. Thank you."

It was hard for me to leave the room alone and find my way to the couch with Cipher's snoring. Every part of me felt magnetized to her. I knew I'd have to play the waiting game to be successful- but honestly it just felt like I was fighting against this incredible force, and I ain't ever been that strong.

Fiona Glass

A window is placed directly opposite Link's bed. The bright sun woke me up in the morning- even with the blinds down. I could hear the busy city outside. Others in the area were arguing, or yelling at passing cars for a lift.

It was only then that I noticed another picture frame on the bedside table to my left. Holding it in my hands, I inspected it. Two little boys, and two women. One with brown hair- Tarn- and the other with curly blonde- possibly their mother.

Someone else had taken the photo- a picture of the four of them sitting on a rocking bench outside a wooden paneled house- resembling Beau's current house entirely. A bright sun and a lit cigarette in the hands of both the women.

They look a lot like her- the blonde. The same noses, same blue eyes. I wonder who put all these pictures up- whether it was Link, or someone else.

Cipher was still asleep when I walked out, Link was too. I felt kind of rude making myself at home, after stealing his bed for the night, but I was so fucking thirsty.

I tried to remember from last night where his cups were, but I ended up looking in every cupboard ever so quietly before I actually found them. All he had were rum glasses.

I used the water from his sink tap to fill the cup. I think the sound of it turned on woke Link up. He had no shirt on- I'd never seen him with no shirt on. Boys are always blessed with abs without even trying. Before Cipher even started working out, he always had abs. I've been doing crunches on my bedroom floor for years and I only ever see abs when I haven't eaten for days.

"Mornin'." he grunts in a deep voice.

"Morning." I smile.

I watch as he sits up on the couch, and brushes his hand through his hair. His hair is so thick and shiny for a boy. The sun from the big open windows was beaming into his eyes- they looked so blue it was insane.

I could smell his deodorant the closer he got to me- must be pretty strong to last the entire night.

"You want some water?" I ask, as he sits down at the kitchen counter.

"A beer, please. From the fridge."

A beer? At this time of the morning.

"Did you sleep well?" he asks, his voice still deep and croaky.

"Yeah, I did actually. The bed is definitely way better then the couch." I laugh, he laughs too.

I hand him his beer.

"Don't hate on my couch. My couch is comfier then most couches."

"I'm sure my dad would disagree." I respond.

"Whys that?" he asks curiously.

I chuckle at my own unfunny joke. "My dad is sort of a.. couch expert. Spends a lot of his time sitting on one couch in particular."

"Well, If he ever finds his way here, he'll probably never wanna leave my couch. I promise you that."

"I can see why you live alone." I giggle.

"What's that supposed to mean?" he asks, nearly choking on his beer.

"Clearly you're married to your couch."

Fuck. I actually love his laugh. I never took notice of it until right now. It sounds so innocent, so similar to a nostalgic childhood giggle.

I found myself staring into his eyes. They were so blue it was indescribable. I probably look like a freak- refusing to blink- because I'm so intensely studying his eyes.

It was then that Cipher woke up. His phone was buzzing in his pocket, and he was quick to answer. It was Justin- asking where he was.

When he got off the phone he looked over and seemed shocked to see Link and I together in the same private vicinity. He stood up, and slowly walked over assessing the scene in front of him. He saw me- dressed in Link's T shirt. And Link, missing a T shirt, and drinking a beer in his kitchen.

"What the hell happened last night?" he asks, caressing the bruise surrounding his eye.

"You don't remember anything- at all?" I ask suspiciously.

Of all the times I've been drunk or shit-faced, I always at least remember some things- the general nature of the shit I did.

"I remember walking to Queen, and that's it." he explains, starting to get worried. "Did I do anything.. stupid- Did Yana give me this black eye?" he questions, genuinely being serious.

Link and I couldn't help but laugh. While confusing to him, I also think our chuckles made Cipher feel a little bit better about not remembering. He probably also realized that if he and Yana had gotten into a serious fight, I wouldn't be laughing at him right now.

I put down my cup in the sink, and I approached my older brother, placing my hand on his shoulder.

"First, you need to get your ass in the shower. Second, you need to go to Yana's house and convince the fuck out of her mind that you are worth staying." I demand, looking at his face to see If I'm convincing him. "You have to believe it yourself, If you have any chance of convincing her, Ciph."

Clearly my motivation speech was enough, because not long after that Cipher leaped into Link's warm shower without another moment of hesitation.

I told Link I had to get home and get ready for brunch with Maddy. I offered him to come too, but he told me he had job interviews to tend to. I could tell he was nervous- about the interviews.

"Same thing I said to Cipher, Link."

"What?"

"You're never going to convince anyone that you're worthy of something, unless you believe it too."

He smiled. That damn smile.

"I believe it- If it makes you feel any better." I add assuredly.

"Thanks, Fi." He says, putting his hand on top of mine.

A boy has never given me butterflies before. I've felt nervous, but I've never felt real butterflies.

Maddy has only ever visited me at work twice. Mostly because she's exhausted from her study and placement for Nursing, that she'd rather spend her spare nights sleeping- over going to a Strip Club- which I get one hundred percent.

Sometimes I wish I'd done something like Maddison- studied toward something. But then I remember that writing is my life. I remember that the club is only a miniature hurdle, before my big move to New York. Everything will be worth it eventually.

Following my day with Maddy, enjoying Cafe croissants and lattes on the beach. I spent some time jotting down some Ideas on my laptop while Blue scribbled in his journal on my floor.

I've been trying to write a novel about love for a while. I have so many ideas but no clue on how to execute it. Honestly, all I could think about was that night I spent at Link's.

I'd never really thought too hard into his life- into him. But last night inspired so many questions in my head. Suddenly I wanted to know everything about him. Suddenly everything about him was incredibly interesting to me. Suddenly I craved being with him again, and suddenly I was coming up with all these different things I was gonna ask him about.

It was strange, that urge.

6

Chapter Six- Blueberry

Denny Glass

The day Blue came back was the first day I felt alive. The thing that hurt me the most was knowing that I could never be the father he deserved. I could never be there for him, physically or emotionally.

I know I fucked up with Cipher and Fi- I always knew I would. The years I spent wishing for Blue to come back I always told myself that I'd do better this time, that I'd be the father I wasn't for my older kids. But then my body got worse and the universe reminded me that karma is a fucking cunt.

Now I just live in hate. Every time Nadia isn't here I feel all the wrong cravings and suddenly my reasons for quitting drinking don't seem that important anymore. Cipher doesn't live here anymore- I used to hate the pound of his music and weights beating against the floorboards, but now the silence just reminds me that he's gone. Fiona is always working, and when she's not she's hiding in her room or taking Blue shopping.

Blue begs Fiona to let him go to work with her every night. At first I wasn't too sure about it- a kid hangin' around in a strip club. Who knows the shit Blue's already seen- too much for his age. But he likes going, and I don't want to do anything to stop him from feeling comfortable with us. The early years of his return were fucking difficult. Knowing my own kid didn't recognize me, and that I barely recognized him fucked with my head.

These days, every time I try and sleep, my mind makes me think of that look in Blue's eye- the one he gave when he realized Merry wasn't coming back. Must've been something she did often- leaving him alone with people he didn't know. He knew what to do- hide in a corner and seal his eyes shut. Flinching at every stroke of wind. The guesses and assumptions I have of everything that happened to him to make him the way he is, is what kills me at night. When thc house is still, and quiet. When I'm reminded through the echo of emptiness that It is my fault my son is so traumatized, that he can't even tell me what's wrong. I may not have directly done it, but he's my kid- and anything bad that happens to my kids is my fault. Because I should've been there to protect them. I should've shown up. I should've killed every motherfucker that looked at any of my kids the wrong way- but my fucking body wont let me. I'm cursed with stillness, keeping me cemented in one spot. Cemented in memory of everything I should've done.

Knowing I can't even throw one of those glass bottles at the fucking TV kills me. Can't even cut my own wrists- even if I tried. Suicide should've been my first option the second I felt myself starting to numb. Instead I chose to ignore it- pretend it wasn't happening. I got angry, drank, smoked, and suddenly the days turned to years and now I'm stuck in an endless loop of regret. Nostalgia suffocating me every time I remember the evenings my brother and I would spend runnin' around the neighborhood. Ding dong ditching old Maisie Calloway's house and listening to her swearing like a pelican as we sprinted back down the road. The fences I'd jump with my mates while running away from the principle to go smoke. How much I hated having to work- especially for my brother. Fuck, I'd give anything to work now. I'd give anything to do fucking anything. Relying on someone else for fucking everything is almost the worst part. Couldn't even stick a gun in my mouth without asking for help.

I used to wonder why I was chosen to live after that crash. But I've since realized that I wasn't chosen to live at all. I was chosen to suffer. My brother received mercy, he was the good one. No karma, no debts.

But me? I've been arrested. I've jumped cunts in the street for petty cash, or a cigarette. I've stolen from old people and I've cheated and forced children into a world with two kids who were never supposed to be parents. One became a lump of disappointment, and the other became a memory of blurred recollection. Three children destined for nothing because their parents couldn't give them anything. Couldn't even give them the love that they deserved.

My family has never been big on affection. I always thought that shit was gross, even with relationships. I always thought tough love made boys into men. I always thought that If I treated Cipher the way my dad treated me and my brother, he might have a chance of ending up like Ronny. I hit him, and punished him for stepping out of line. I reminded him of his expectations. I told him over and over again to man the fuck up, because I thought it would make him strong. Now I know that Cipher isn't like Ronny, but instead he's like me. He's so much like me that it scares me.

Fiona was always my favourite, my little girl. I never thought I'd want a daughter. Never even thought about how I'd raise one. Never considered what it would feel like to have one, until I did.

No matter how old she gets, she will always be my baby girl. Two wavy pigtails and a smile as beautiful as her mother's youth.

Blue- I don't know what Blue is. I don't know how to describe him. I don't know how to connect with him. He's older now, but I still see him as the baby he was before. It's like two different kids in my memory. The kid I was expected to raise, and the kid Merry created. A kid who refuses to speak- or can't. The kid who has triggers, and who can't make friends, and who can probably never live on his own. All because I couldn't be there for him. All because I couldn't make him a man.

Cipher and Fiona may hate me, but they can never deny that they were a lot better off then Blue was. I know I'm not perfect, and I never will be. But knowing I could never fix whatever is broken inside of Blue is what will eventually end me.

Fiona Glass

It's been a week since Cipher's whole mishap at Queen, which resulted in

Link and I taking him back to Link's apartment. He went home to Yana a few days later, and I haven't heard from him since- I assume she's probably killed him by now.

Blue's in the back working on his science homework with Honey, she's always said how much she loved science as a kid.

I haven't spoken to Link since that night either- he hasn't been to the club and there's never any other chances for me to see him so.. eager, is an understatement.

Maddy came in about an hour ago, said she was bored of studying and needed a long glass of vanilla vodka to calm her nerves.

Maddy has never been so interested in my love life, until tonight.

"Okay, but, boys don't just offer their bed away to any girl, Fi." she urges to convince. Maxine nodding toward her conviction as she serves another customer.

"Some boys can be nice, you know." I respond hastily.

"Have you ever met a Jonesy boy? They don't put them in jail for the fun of it." Maddison jokes, sipping on her vodka and wincing as she evens it out with a cup of juice.

"Why did he spend time in jail anyway, Cipher never told me?" I ask curiously. Seizing the opportunity as it passes.

I'd always wondered what he spent time in jail for- but I've never been ballsy enough to just ask, so I sort of just accepted it might forever remain a mystery to me.

"Who, Beau or Link?" Maddison slurs.

"Who do you think?" I respond with a smile.

"Well, I only know about Beau's holidays- not Link's."

"Why?" I laugh.

"Because I barely talk to Link- that is supposed to be your job."

Maddy has always had a way with words. Something about her cues and the way she delivers herself makes her feel a lot more approachable, and often times, a lot funnier then the average person. Maybe it's her dry sense of humour or bluntness that does it for me.

"Speak of the devil." Maddy stews, as she turns her head toward the entrance to watch Link, Beau and Jasper walk in.

I love it when men wear baggy clothes.

"Maddison Sterling!" Beau gags with excitement. "Never would I think I'd see you here." he exclaims as he approaches her for a one-armed hug.

"Well, a club ain't a club without Maddy Sterling." She responds jokingly.

"So they say." Beau agrees, as Jasper orders the three of them drinks from Maxine.

I can feel Link's blue eyes peering against my left cheek. It feels like my body is literally rejecting me from politely looking in his direction. I probably look like a dickhead- twitching my eye or something stupid.

"How's Ciph?" He finally asks- fuck, now I have to talk to him.

"I wouldn't know- he's been silenced." I respond, taking another customers order.

"Fuck, Yana probably has him locked in their fuckin' attic." Beau and Jasper giggle.

Beau has always been the best at making jokes at someones expense.

"What about you?" Link asks, clearing his throat and leaning over the bar. "Did you sleep well?"

He smells so fucking good, and can anyone else see the way he's looking at me right now? Or am I just imagining that shit?

The others all chuckle, like twelve year old's watching their friends about to kiss for the first time- completely and unimaginably immature, might I add.

"Yes." I smile. "Thanks for asking."

With Beau's peering giggle, interrupted as one of the security guards whispers something in his ear.

"Room 2, if anyone's interested. Link?" Beau asks, referring to the private rooms- he must've rented one out for the night. Not that 'rent' is necessarily the right word. The Jonesy boys never pay for anything at Queen.

Link looks to Beau as he offers, then I swear on my mothers life he looks at me before deciding to deny the offer. Like he's deciding which is more important.

"Nah, that's alright."

"You sure?" Beau smirks.

"Yes, Beau, I'm sure." he responds quickly, as he seats himself at the bar.

"Okay." Beau taunts. "Maddison?- What do ya' say?"

Maddison huffs. "Alright, but don't expect me to dance for you." she agrees, standing to follow Beau and Jasper. "And I sure as hell wont be paying for shit." I hear her mumble as the three of them walk away with the security guard.

"Do you want another drink?" I ask politely.

"Please." he responds- and why the fuck is he so good at eye contact?

For a Saturday night, it wasn't too busy. Most people were using the center bar for orders, but a few people who were only just entering came to Maxine and I at the front bar.

Link kept talking to me- asking about my dad, Blue. Laughing to me about random guests and making fun of how different men acted throughout the night. He was actually quite funny- maybe it was just the charm. And I don't know why, but this night felt so different to every other night we'd spend chatting. It felt so.. jittery. Or maybe that was just me.

Eyeball came in at some point too. It's always nice seeing him. He and his group all sat at the same table they usually sit at for poker and views.

Cart and Tarn pushed through, and Eyeball greeted Cart with a dap up before they parted ways. Tarn looked like she was on a mission, barely acknowledging Link as she stormed into the security room.

"Were you ever close with Brownie, or was that just Cipher?" Link asks curiously, sipping on his beer and smoking a cigarette.

"Just Cipher- but my dad used to be friends with Eyeball when they were in school, so Eyeball and Brownie have sort of always been around."

"What about now?"

"Well, Brownie only really comes around if he's with Cipher, and Eyeball hasn't been to the house in years."

"Why? He and your dad aren't close anymore?"

"It's more like my dad just isn't close with anyone anymore. Once his paralysis started getting bad, he started pushing everyone away. Eyeball helped my dad for those few years that they searched for Blue- Eyeball and the other boys would probably still be hangin' around everyday If my dad could stand it."

And that was the honest truth. I remember constantly seeing my dads phone ring and texts go unanswered while he drowned his thoughts in alcohol and weed. I think my dad was just to embarrassed to let anyone see him get as bad as he's gotten- I honestly think he probably would've evaporated into that couch by now if it weren't for Blue coming back. My dad would've never cut his drinking, and allow for someone like Nadia into the house if Blue had stayed away.

"What about you?" Link asks subtly.

"What about me?"

"Does your dad ever talk to you?"

I chuckle at the thought. I wish my dad would talk to me.

As a kid, I probably wouldn't have been able to handle the conversation. But now, I'd give anything to hear how he truly feels. Even though I know the truth- I know how he feels just by looking at him. I know he kills himself mentally everyday knowing he could've done something to change the outcome. I know he blames himself for what happened to Blue- whatever that was. I know he hates himself for everything bad that has ever happened since that crash. I know the truth, but I'd beg on my death bed just to hear him say it. Just to know that he trusted me enough to tell me what he's thinking, out loud.

"No." I say simply.

Link looks at me with such empathy drowned eyes. So much so, it makes my stomach drop. I want to change the conversation. I don't want pity, and I know my dad wouldn't want it either.

"My dad was like that too- before he left." Link reveals. "I mean, he was an asshole, like, all the time." he titters. "But he was still my dad."

I can tell Link is trying to relate, and honestly, I really am interested in knowing more about him.

"When did he leave?" I ask curiously.

"He went to jail for a few years when I was 6. I know he's out now, but I haven't heard from him since." Link explains solemnly.

"Do you ever wish he'd come back?"

"Fuck no." Link responds without hesitation, suddenly disposing every bit of sadness from his expression- excluding his wilting eyes. "I mean, he *was* still my dad- *is* still my dad- but after a while, there's only so much fucked up shit a person can do before there's no forgiving to forget- ya know?"

I agree. Link's short sniffles ignite some kind of maternal warmth beneath my heart. He stands up abruptly from his chair, almost stumbling.

"I'll be back." he claims quickly, before heading directly for the men's toilets.

I've never felt so fascinated by another persons brokenness. The way he spoke about his dad, and the response he gave me when I asked him about his dad coming back. The abrupt and almost sarcastic reply to deter from what his eyes were feeling. You can always see how a person is truly feeling, based on their eyes.

It was a while before Link finally came back. And when he did, he was almost like a whole new person. Smiling and charming again. No sniffles, or darkened tones- but still, those same drooping eyes he fails to disguise.

"What are you doing when you finish?" he asks curiously, sitting back in his seat.

"Probably taking Blue home to bed." I chuckle.

"You want to do something?" He asks eagerly.

"Like what?"

"I don't care, anything. I can drive." he offers. Truly, something I couldn't fathom passing up.

I finished work at 3am that night. Blue had already passed out on the couch in the back. The girls had tucked him under a green blanket and had dimmed the lights for him. It didn't take much to wake him up though, I think he was eager to get home.

Beau and Jasper took Maddy home, and Link followed close behind as I drove Blue home.

Link came inside with us as I guided Blue to bed.

Link Jones

I've never been in their house before- I was sort of curious to see what it looked like.

To be honest, I was expecting more of a mess- something similar to Beau and Jasper's house. Beer cans on the floor, old food rotting in the sink. There were a few holes in the walls, and the doors were rusting- but it was nothing compared to what I was expecting.

The outside colours of the house were interesting though, to say the least. Even in the darkness of night, I could still see the yellow chipped wood panels that frame their small home. As well as their blueberry shaded door- I've never seen a blue door before.

The TV was still on the lounge room, some old movie was playing. Denny was asleep on a single seater couch, snoring quietly. Jittering in his sleep. Now I understand what Fiona meant, about her dad and his couch.

I could see inside Fiona's bedroom from the hallway, as she led Blue into his own room. The stuff inside Blue's room looked a lot like shit Cipher would've liked as a kid. Weights, stolen balls, old empty cans as decoration, posters of models.

Fiona's room and Cipher's room were completely different.

From what I could see, Fiona's bed was in the center of the back wall. A window opposite, with old white curtains. Her floor had spots of nail polish stains or some other makeup. She had a desk too with a laptop, and an old light on the floor beside her bed. Her bed sheets were also designed with yellow stripes, and she had an old looking yellow teddy bear laying in her unmade bed. She also had a stack of magazines on the floor by her desk, and posters on the wall behind her bed of One Direction and Justin Bieber.

I caught a glimpse of Fiona tucking Blue in his bed like a baby. I moved to lean against her bedroom door frame so that I could see more of her room without actually walking in. I didn't want to intrude.

Her desk was messy- clutter is what makes a home feel like home, in my opinion. But in the very back corner of her desk was an old stand up photo frame. Inside was a photo of what looked like a young Fiona, wearing a lot more makeup then she does now. And another blonde girl, around the same age.

I wanted to investigate more- see more of her- but I found myself looking back into the room where Blue was sleeping instead. Even after he'd already closed his eyes, Fiona couldn't help but stay around for a little bit longer. Maybe in case he woke up and realized she was no longer there.

The way she guarded him- even in his sleep- reminded me so much of what a mother would do- *should* do. A feeling she felt in that moment- whatever that feeling was- wasn't new to her. A feeling she'd been experiencing for a long time when looking at other people- certain people. The things I'd give to have someone care about me that much.

Fiona Glass

I love the music Link listens to when he drives. It's so refreshing from all the rap and hardcore metal I've grown up around. Back To The Old House by The Smiths- fuck this song is good.

"Have you never heard this song before?" Link asks, peering at the infatuation on my face.

"No, I haven't." I admit.

"That's crazy, you've never heard The Smiths?" Link responds, shocked.

I chuckle at his disbelief as he rolls his window down and turns the music up. The air feels so cool, so peaceful. It feels like nothing could touch us. It feels like heaven on earth.

I roll my own window down, and let my hair fly through the wind as I gaze into the dark distance. The smell of dirt entering my lungs, and the nearing smell of crystal water.

We found ourselves at the waterfalls. Neither of us had been in years, and we were curious to experience the sunrise there again.

To reach this lake you have to drive a few kilometers on a dirt road, finding yourself further surrounded by trees.

At night, it's sort of terrifying if you don't know where you're going- and it's harder to spot kangaroos. But during the day it almost feels magical.

The sun always seems to be bright there- peaking through the tall tree leaves and guiding the way.

The official name is called 'Gray Crystal Lake', but most people just call it the lake or the waterfalls and everyone will know exactly what you're talking about.

The water is clear and green, but during sunset and sunrise, the sun hits the water particles at the perfect angle, and makes the water look like its covered in gray crystals- which is where it gets it's name from.

This lake and its small waterfalls is probably the only beautiful thing in this city. Surrounded by red dirt and sand. Home to kookaburras and spiders, and tiny, tiny fish.

The sandbank is the cleanest sandbank I've ever seen- the only place people will actually pick up after themselves. The only place people can pretend they're living in some kind of magical Sci-Fi book.

Music still playing from his car- Link lights a cigarette as I crouch down by the water to guide my finger tips over the top. It was freezing, but the smell was refreshing.

Link grabbed us both a beer from his back seat, and sat by me- both of us peering into the distance of the water.

I can feel the ponder of Link's mind magnetizing the situation. Somehow knowing he has a thought to share, without saying a thing.

"Can I ask you a question?"

"Sure." I respond hesitantly.

"Who was that girl in the picture on your desk?" he asks. His question echoing and replaying through my mind. "I only ask because I've never seen you hang around someone that looks like her."

I smile- awkward. I don't like having these kinds of conversations.

"Did you ever hear about Skye Sallow?" I ask hesitantly.

Link shakes his head. In that moment, I do the math. I remember that Link is 22 and I'm 18, which means he would've been 18 when I was 14- which means he would've most likely already been in jail the day Skye died. It felt like everyone in the entire city knew about Skye Sallow- and knew me as Skye's best friend, except Link.

"Well, that was her- she was my best friend." I explain hurriedly.

"Was?"

I clear my skinny throat. "Yeah, she.. passed away- when we were 14."

Link nods, pondering whether he questions further or not. The thing is, I don't mind being asked the questions- it doesn't upset me. But I don't know how to talk about topics like Skye or my mum without feeling awkward- or yuck.

"Did she leave a note?" Link asks, surprising me with the unexpected question. No one has ever asked me that.

How did he know she died like that? Is it written on my face?

"Yeah.. she did. But I've never opened it." I admit.

"Why not?"

An answer I truly have to think about. The early sing of birds feeling like whispers to help me decide how to answer that question.

"I don't know- I guess I.. never had the heart to do it. Knowing she was dead was enough- I think."

Silence falls over both of us for a moment- a silence almost.. comforting.

"I've been in that position before- wanting to do that." Link admits.

Those few words, jarring against my heart.

"Courts forced me until I was 18 to see a therapist cause of the shit my dad did- but I never enjoyed that shit- I only did it to make everyone else's lives easier. I let them diagnose me, and medicate me to keep me quiet- but nothing ever dulled the noise of that little voice inside my head. Nothing ever numbed me in the right spots.. to make that feeling go away."

"So why didn't you?" I ask abruptly- my mouth speaking before my brain could stop me- instantly regretting my question.

"Cause I got arrested." Link finally responds. "If it weren't for that, I probably would've by now."

I don't know what to say to him. I feel awful for asking such an absurd question. No one had ever been so open with me- I don't know how to make him feel better about it. I wish I could be perfect and know exactly what to say to people in exactly the right moments.

"I'm glad you didn't." I finally respond. His eyes instantly turning to meet mine.

He smiles. "Me too- otherwise, I never would've met you." he chuckles.

His ability to turn a heavy moment light is truly remarkable- something to admire.

Suddenly, the sound of Knocking On Heavens Door by Guns N' Roses hums from Link's car. We sit in the silence of the songs introduction- feeling every inch of it.

Until quickly, Link stands and holds his hand out to me as the song truly begins.

"What?"

"Come on." he urges, grabbing my hands and pulling me up.

Confused, I stand stiffly, until he pulls me in- almost for a hug- that turns into a drifting rock.

We're slow dancing. My head resting against his chest. One hand holding mine, while his other supports my waist. I feel like I have no rhythm- why am I freaking out so bad right now? He seems so relaxed, and I feel like I'm as stiff as a cutting board.

Suddenly, every ounce of nerve and fear pounding against my mind disappears, as his hand resting on my back, rises up to relax against the back of my head.

Peace, calmness. Such a small change instantly makes me feel undeniably comfortable. I feel so close to him in this moment. Closer then I'd ever felt with anyone before.

We dance slowly until the end of the song- enjoying every last moment. Everybody Wants To Rule The World by Tears For Fears began, and just as quickly as the quiet comfort began- it ended.

Link picked me up swiftly, and I felt myself scream of joy as I gripped onto him- knowing exactly what he was doing. He ran quickly with me against his body as he dove into the lake. Small fish scurrying away from our warm, blood-filled bodies as bubbles pop against our soaked mouths.

The sunrise slowly beginning to hit against the water as we both reappear. I immediately splash him with a great force, and he refuses to stop himself from laughing.

"You think that's funny?" I ask with a smile I couldn't carve from my face if I tried.

"Yeah, I do." Link responds calmly, smiling with his teeth as the water seems to push him closer toward me.

An energy of mutual feelings, and an inability to look away- or to peel the smiles from our mirrored faces.

Our eyes glued to the sight of each other- before I quickly interrupt the moment- splashing as much water as I can into his face. Once more, igniting a war.

Our laughs echoing like a juicy memory of yellow nostalgic childhood as we race to attack each other. A beautiful sunrise I'll never forget.

Link and I started to hang out a lot more following that night. Every Saturday after I finished work, we'd take Blue home and tuck him into bed before venturing on the dirt roads and blasting songs as we drank and sang.

Don't Dream It's Over by Crowded House quickly became my favorite karaoke song- especially on the odd occasion when Maddison and Beau would come for the drives with us.

In those moments- while we shared a blunt around the car- Link driving, Beau queuing songs, and Maddy and I in the back seat. No seat belts, windows down, and singing as loud as we could to every song that played. Our screams drowning to the sound of the wind outside. I felt completely and undeniably invincible. I felt like nothing in the world could hurt me, because I finally found my people.

Cipher and Yana were starting to get on good terms again too. Cipher came over to the house the other day with Alina, while Yana spent the day running errands and getting her nails done. He knew Blue would want to see Alina, and I think deep down Cipher missed seeing dad and I every day. Don't ask me how Cipher manages to get Yana to forgive him everytime. I guess love truly is a drug.

My dads not as talkative as he used to be, even with Nadia. He's kind of just.. there. All we get these days is a grunt, or mere mumble.

I think he's more sad then anything. I truly do feel terrible for my dad- no matter of all the bad he may of done, I could never say he deserves the life he's gotten. I just wish he'd try harder to make himself better again.

Link's been driving me to Yusra(Star)'s house on our days off. She's been teaching me to dance since I got the promotion. As it turns out- dancing on a pole requires a lot more strength then I was expecting.

"You're lucky you're skinny and weigh nothin' more then a kobo." Yusra always tells me. She says the lighter I am the easier it'll be for me to learn.

It's sort of nerve wrecking to think that eventually I'll have to actually perform these routines in front of everyone. The only comforting thing about it all is that they'll all be drunk- but that is also the most stressful part of it all. Because that also means no one will be afraid about voicing their opinions about my quality of dance. No filters.

Maddy always makes fun of me for having Link drive me to Yusra's- but honestly, if he's going to offer, I'm not going to deny.

I think Blue loves the vibe of Yusra's house- I think anyone would. Something about it is incredibly calming and chaotic all at once. She always has music playing- usually something by Frankie Valli or The Supremes.

Kids from the neighborhood are always running around, playing football or drawing with chalk on the pavements outside. I just wish at least one of them went to the same school as Blue. Instead, they all attend the few Catholic schools in the area.

None of these kids seem to judge Blue for the fact he doesn't speak. I love the way they make him feel- makes me wonder why I never came around here beforehand. Their culture is so fascinating.

Yusra invites us over for BBQ's and other gatherings sometimes- says we're basically apart of the family now. They always say prayers before they eat, and the entire neighborhood could dance to classical 80's music all night if they really tried. It's truly something to admire.

Link Jones

I never thought I'd have so much fun at one of Tarn's employees houses.

Star's family extends to the entire neighborhood. To be honest, when I first offered to drive Fiona and Blue to Star's house for dance practices- I didn't think I'd be doing it for this long. But I surprisingly started to enjoy it.

Star's father, Yode, is an older man. Something about him feels so wise. It's not often I'm actually interested in hearing an old person tell stories, but I've grown to enjoy Yode's company while Fiona works away with Star. I've enjoyed getting to know Blue too, he's like a quiet, nicer version of Cipher.

Getting to know Fiona has been good too. She's very different to most of the people I've met. And completely different to all the other girls I've been with. I like hearing her laugh. I like hearing her talk about her past. I like knowing that someone might almost be as fucked up as me. And I like how nonjudgmental she is.

Tonight we spent the night seated in Star's backyard. Music had been playing all night, following a big dinner. Fiona, Blue and myself had never said prayers until we started eating here.

At first, it was sort of funny to us- like a joke. But now, I think we both kind of understand the connection of it.

I mean, I don't believe in God or whatever. But I do fuck with in the closeness it provides when people do believe.

Anyway, Star and her family seem happy- and they make Fiona and Blue pretty happy- so who cares what I think.

I like watching the look on Fiona's face while she's admiring someone. Every time a couple is dancing at Star's, Fiona is always watching. I love the way she smiles as she stalks. She has a pretty smile- beautiful even. Captivating. It definitely keeps me looking, that's for sure.

Fiona Glass

A few days ago Link told me he's never had a home cooked dinner before- and I haven't either. That is why we decided that this week on Tuesday night we'd attempt to cook a chicken roast and vegetables together.

Blue wanted to come too. I said he could on the deal that he would be in bed by 9pm, and he agreed.

I assumed Blue and I would probably sleep on the couch together or something, but Link told me he had a whole other room in his apartment.

"If you had another room, why did you sleep in the lounge room with Cipher? You could've just slept in your own bed." I giggled while asking, genuinely curious to hear his answer.

"I don't know. I wanted to.. look like a gentleman- or something." He responds shortly, chewing on the carrots I'd cut up.

Link and I had gone to the grocery shop earlier today before picking Blue up from school. I used the first recipe I found online to make the chicken.

Blue finds Link hilarious. I think he truly looks up to him, which is probably why he always begs to come along when Link and I are hanging out.

I always wondered if it felt weird to Link, knowing I was bringing my little brother with me everywhere I went. But Link never seemed phased by it. He never said anything that would make me believe he felt a certain way about it, and I kind of liked that about him. I mean, not many guys would enjoy the idea of having to hang out with a kid. I think he'd make a good dad one day.

I never thought about how disgusting it was to cook a chicken. I've decided that I absolutely hate touching raw meat. Allowing Link to know that- though- was my first mistake. Because every chance he got, he taunted me with that damn chicken. Basically chased me around the kitchen with it's wing he accidentally broke off.

We also didn't realize how long it would actually take to roast the chicken and the vegetables, so we had to do something to pass the minutes.

Link went to the same thing he always did when needing to blow off some steam- or time. Music.

He turned on his radio and turned the channel to some number that played the old ass music he enjoyed so much.

Be My Baby by The Ronettes was the first to play. It always felt so embarrassing for me every time Link forced me to dance with him, but he did it so often I eventually started to expect it when music would start to play. I guess it was sort of his thing.

This time, he got a lot more creative with the dance moves. Spinning me around, dipping me, carrying me and swinging me in circles and incorporating our feet into the dance.

The more Blue laughed at my awkwardness and Links incredible rhythm, the more of a show he put on.

The entire time, I knew Blue was smiling- and that fact made me dance more. I'd dance a thousand years if it meant Blue could smile.

By the time the food was ready, it was already 8pm. Finalizing the plates with an even layer of gravy, and a cold drink for each of us was enough to seal the night with perfection.

To the average person, this food would honestly not be that great- but to us, it was the best food we'd ever tasted. So good that we licked our plates clean. I even wrapped up the leftovers to take to Cipher and my dad for them to try. It felt so good knowing I wasn't the only one who fucking loved that damn burnt chicken.

Regardless of our deal, I still had to beg Blue to go to bed. Kids.

I was proud of him though, for being able to fall asleep in a place he wasn't familiar with. That allowed me to know that he was growing- that it wasn't all in my head. That maybe one day he'd be better- maybe.

I felt like I'd be a terrible guest If I didn't at least attempt to help Link clean up his kitchen. I've never much enjoyed doing the dishes, so I more so stood to the side pretending I was helping. My company was enough support- If you ask me.

The apartment was so dark from the night sky barging through the big windows. I used Link's maroon lighter to light the candles I'd bought him from a candle shop I visited on the weekend with Maddy. I fucking love the smell of Christmas cookie candles. The red aroma surrounding the dark room was simply a bonus.

I lifted myself to sit on top of the kitchen counter, and leaned against the fridge as I peered across the room and out to the dark sky. I love the look of stars- so beautiful and quiet.

When Link had finally finished all the dishes, he wiped his hands with a hand towel and turned to lean against the opposite island- looking at me with that damn smile again, of course.

"What?" I giggled.

"Nothing." He smiled, placing down the hand towel and crossing his arms. He actually has really nice biceps for someone who hasn't lifted weights since he left prison.

"It was a good chicken." he praised.

"Of course it was- I'm a great cook." I joke, and he laughs.

Fuck. Me. That damn SMILE. The butterflies in my stomach are definitely on steroids or something catastrophic because the way I am feeling is ridiculous and uncontrollable.

"If I'm being honest- I don't know what I'd be doing If I hadn't asked you out that night." Link admits.

"Asked me out?" oh my god, did I say that out loud?

Link chuckles. "Well, what would you call it?"

"I don't know- a business meeting?" I joke.

He laughs again, while inching ever so close. Fuck, the butterflies are literally going insane right now. Do I look nervous? I probably sound like a fucking idiot. God, why does he make me so nervous?

"Well, I guess I am your boss- In a way."

"Actually, you're just the bosses nephew. So if we were in a book, you would probably be really rude and unbearable."

"So what am I then?"

"What are you?" I ask, as he's stops, standing mere inches from me. His waist basically touching my knees.

"If I'm not rude and unbearable- what am I?"

He asked me a question- but all I can do is focus deeply on his blue eyes. A blue that looks so much better in dark light- so dreamy. Almost like a trance.

"You're.. benevolent, and completely tolerable." I respond in almost a hush or whisper.

His smile increases again as suddenly he starts to drift into me. His warm hand caressing my nervous cheek, pulling me in for our first sweet kiss.

For the first time with him, I don't feel nervous. I feel calm, complete. Something inside me feels together, like this is exactly where I'm supposed to be.

He grips me closer- his smell becoming ever so sensual and comforting.

Link Jones

"What?" she giggled.

"Nothing." I smiled, placing down the hand towel and crossing my arms "It was a good chicken."

"Of course it was- I'm a great cook."

I think I prefer being with her then being alone, and that's never been me. I've always been alone, no matter how many people I'm surrounded by. I've always preferred my time in isolation. But with her, everything feels different. It is a feeling I completely did not expect to ever experience. I didn't even know it existed, until her.

"If I'm being honest- I don't know what I'd be doing If I hadn't asked you out that night." I finally admit. The same words that had replayed through my mind since that night.

I feel like my life would look so different If I'd never found the courage to get closer to Fiona. I always thought she was gorgeous, but I never thought I'd connect with her as much as I did. I truly do think she has changed my life. I've definitely been a lot happier since she's entered it. I don't know whether it's because she's a great distraction- or if she truly brings me happiness. I guess that's something I have to figure out.

"Asked me out?"

Fuck. The way she flirts is so enticing. "Well, what would you call it?" I laugh.

"I don't know- a business meeting?"

The way she looks at me- she has to know what she doing. Nobody has ever had this much control over me. Nobody has ever made me feel so entranced. Something about her eyes- her words. Her body language, or the way she speaks. I don't know. But something about her feels like magnets, and every time I look at her I feel myself being pulled in.

And I have to admit, fighting against these magnets is so fucking exhausting.

"Well, I guess I am your boss- In a way." I tease, curious to hear how she responds.

"Actually, you're just the bosses nephew. So if we were in a book, you would probably be really rude and unbearable." oh, she's good.

"So what am I then?"

"What are you?" she blushes. I know I make her nervous. In some weird way, it makes me feel more like I'm under her control. Like I'm a pig, and she's the carrot.

"If I'm not rude and unbearable- what am I?" Fuck it, I'm taking the bait.

"You're.. benevolent, and completely tolerable." She responds in a hush.

Benevolent? Such a big word- I don't entirely know what it means. But I know, based on the look in her eyes, that it's good. I know that the way she views me is something I'd die to feel- to see myself in her eyes. Perfect and.. benevolent.

In that moment, I couldn't think of anything better to do, but the thing I've wanted to do since the moment I first laid eyes on her. I've never felt so wowed by a kiss before. Her lips- they taste exactly how her lip gloss smells. Strawberry clouds, mixing with a hint of Christmas cookie.

Her cheek is soft, and her hair is thick as it falls against my arm. She pushes her waist further into mine as At Last by Etta James begins. The perfect song to end this blissful, and long awaited moment.

Fiona Glass

It's been years since I've been in a moment like this- but never has it felt so full of rush. Adrenaline piercing through us both as he carried me into his bedroom. His body so strong, and our lips forever feeling stuck together as his bedroom door closes.

He gently lays me on his familiar bed as he takes off his own top, before helping me take off mine. Everything about this moment feels perfect. Nothing like I'd ever felt with any other boys before.

Gently, he lifts me on top of him as he lay flat on his bed. He unclips my bra with ease, kissing every inch of my body, consumed with the moment.

Laying me on my back and helping me take off my shorts and underwear. His head buried between my legs- a feeling so amazing.

Is this what it's supposed to feel like?

It was so hard to stay quiet, but I was honestly so infatuated with him the entire night that all I cared about was being present and with him. I was on top of him again, and the feeling of him going inside me nearly exploded the butterflies from within.

His hands guiding my hips every step of the way- unable to keep us apart. Nobody has ever made me feel so beautiful and sexy all at once.

The entire night was perfect for me- and I think it was perfect for him too. Neither of us could keep away, and I'd never slept as good as I did in his bed, wrapped in his warmth.

Something about the comfort of his arms made me feel secure- protected. I felt like nothing and nobody could hurt me as long as he was around- the kind of feeling I'd fight the death to forever feel. To forever keep.

He invited me to Tarn's cabin off the track to the Crystal Lake a few weeks later. Said he wanted the opportunity to take me away somewhere private. From that I got the hint that he didn't really want Blue to come, which I understood. But I wasn't too sure how Blue would go without me there.

It was really fucking awkward having to explain to Cipher that I needed him to check in on Blue from time to time for two days because I was going away. Because then I had to explain who I was going away with. I chose to have that conversation over text, because then if he got mad, it wouldn't be my problem.

I don't think he was mad though. I guess he was kind of expecting something after I started hanging out with Beau, and working for Tarn. Weirded out, maybe, but nothing could beat him discovering I started working at Queen.

We were leaving Monday and coming back Wednesday morning, which means Blue had school. When I told Blue that I was gonna be going away with Link, and that I'd be back by the time he came home from school on Wednesday, I thought he would be upset. Scared that maybe I'd pull a Merry and not come back. But instead, he smiled. A teasing smile, something you'd expect from a kid his age, I guess. I liked seeing that- something common, a normal persons reaction.

Nadia said she could pack Blue's lunches, and Blue has been fine walking to and from school by himself for a little while now, so everything was sorted for the time being.

On the drive there, I didn't know what to expect. I knew there were cabins off the track to the waterfalls, but I've never been there. Most of them are owned by older couples, never to be used alone by younger folk. Otherwise, I'm sure there would've been some great parties there.

We drove past three other cabins on the way to Tarn's. When I saw it in the distance, Link explained to me how Tarn, his mother, father, Cart, and all their friends used to have parties there all the time. I guess the cabin was originally Tarn's fathers, and that she was given it after he died.

Out the front waved an Aboriginal flag, Link said his father put there. I could smell the mossy lake behind the cabin from the second we stepped out of his ute.

Link led me into the cabin, unlocking it with a rusted key. A squeaky door, opening to what looked like a scene of frozen memories. Empty red cups, old alcohol cans and rotted stains on the big mat in the lounge room. A homemade cassette still sitting in the stereo beneath the TV, labeled 'Carter in 1998'.

"He wanted to be a rapper." Link explains, startling me as I inspected the tape.

"What?"

"Cart. He picks all the music at Queen, because he has always loved music. When he was young, he wanted to be a rapper."

"Not anymore?"

"Probably," we giggle. "But he'd make more money doing what he does now." Link continues, huffing a sigh of relief as he plants himself on the red sturdy couch.

"How come you've never thought to have any parties here?" I ask, sitting beside him.

"That's Tarn's choice- she owns the place."

"Well, why doesn't she want to?"

"I don't know- I guess by now, it's just easier to have it at Beau's."

"I guess so." I agree, inspecting my surroundings further. Feeling Link's glossy blue eyes stilled paved to my cheek. "What?" I ask with a smile, looking back at him.

"What?" he asks stupidly.

"What are you *looking* at?"

I ask, but instead of answering, he gestures to something behind me. I turn around, to see a large green lake. Dancing beneath the lowering sun.

We didn't waste another second before rushing into our swimwear, and running into the water. It was kind of intimidating, how dirty the water was. But I tried not to focus on that. I guess, worst case scenario, a crocodile might eat me. But I don't think the water is deep enough for that.

We stayed in the water for a long time. At some point, Link got out to play Cart's tape. Loud enough we could hear it from outside. Of course, unable to forget to grab himself a beer. He offered me some, but I was at peace the way I was. The golden sky beaming down at the both of us. Coating us in a closing nightfall.

"Do you want to play a game?" I request spontaneously.

"What kind of game?" he smiles.

"One that'll help us get to know each other."

"You don't know enough?" he jokes.

"Oh, come on. Don't you want to know all my deepest, darkest secrets?"

"I doubt you have many."

"What's that supposed to mean?"

"It means, Fiona, that you are exactly who you make yourself out to be. You don't hide anything, because you don't care about what other people think." he professes, the water inching us ever so close.

"So what are you hiding?" I joke, breaking the tension.

"Absolutely nothing. I'm an open book."

"I don't believe you."

"Alright, go on then." he challenges. "Ask me anything."

I think for a moment, deciphering what it is I actually want to know about him.

"Do you want kids?" I say, surprising him with the absurdity of the question.

"Whoa! Bit eager there." he razzes.

"Just answer the question."

"Like.. right now?"

"No, dick- in general."

He finds his mockery hilarious. I think he's deflecting.

"I guess- maybe one day. But only if it's with you."

"Right." I kid.

"Seriously. I think your the only person that could save my kids from my DNA."

"What's wrong with your DNA?"

"No, no, It's my turn now. Remember?"

"Proceed." I say, with a big smile. Curious to what it is he could be interested in asking me.

He contemplates for a moment, sipping his beer as he thinks. "Have you ever had a boyfriend?"

"No." I answer honestly.

"Never?" he asks, surprised.

"No, never."

"Why not?"

"I don't know. I've never really liked anyone enough."

"Fair enough." he responds.

"My turn." I interject. "Do you deal for Tarn- like Beau and Jasper do?" A question I've been wanting to ask since that first night at the waterfalls.

I don't know how I'd feel if he said yes. I guess it would be kind of a buzz kill. I like Link- a lot. But I couldn't do that to Blue. Drug dealers are messy, even if it might not seem that way now.

He hesitates for a moment. His eyes bouncing back and forth from both of mine. "No."

"You sure?" I tease, sort of expecting him to change his answer.

"I used to." he admits. "Before I was arrested. But when I got out, I decided I didn't want to do any of that anymore."

"And Tarn doesn't care?"

"She did, but I think she's getting used to it now. I mean, It's not like they're lost without me." he explains.

I'm happy with his answer. I'm glad he's not involved, otherwise I don't think I'd get involved. And that would be a shame.

"Good." I respond shortly.

"Good?" he snoops.

"Yeah, I'm glad."

"Well.. what would happen if I was?" he speculates.

"I couldn't be apart of that." I admit. "Not with Blue relying on me."

"Always lookin' out for everyone else."

"That's what family is supposed to do."

"You're right." he responds softly.

Looking at him, I see a boy. A boy with hope. I can see the moon, perfectly encapsulated in the blue stones of his eyes. And the stars sparkling against them. Water dripping from his soft skin.

"It's your turn." I say, breaking the peaceful silence. Opening a warming heart.

"Do you like me enough?"

"For what?"

"To be mine?" he asks, cracking a small smile, circling his mouth.

I'd never been asked that question before. I never thought of how I'd react. Even when I write my books, I always hate structuring these scenes. Because I never know what to say. I've never got to experience it. To understand the feelings. The tingle in my toes.

"Yeah." I answer shortly.

His smile rounds a larger dimple against his cheek. Pulling me in, to seal the night with a perfect, perfect kiss.

The remaining time we spent at the cabin was perfect, I didn't want to leave. I loved looking through the few storage boxes we found beneath the floor boards. Old photo albums, bongs, baseball bats, clothes, board games.

I learned a lot about him, a lot about the way he makes me feel. I think he feels the same- I know he does. And that feels amazing.

We came back on Wednesday. I got to hang out with Blue and dad for a few hours before heading to work. I honestly was exhausted by the time we returned, but I couldn't take off this shift, not so close to my starting time.

And even though I only just saw him, I already missed Link. That was the only thing that kept me up through this shift. Counting down the minutes until Link finally showed up. Looking just as warn down and tired as I did.

Link Jones

I came to the club again tonight. Mostly so I could see Fiona. It's Wednesday, so it's not too busy. Fiona had Blue stay home so that he could work on the handwriting homework his psychologist gave him- also because she never lets him come on weeknights.

Beau and Jasper were here too, throwing all their money away. I stayed by the bar all night, talking to Fi. I could sit there forever, just to look at her.

My good moods are always ruined by the sight of Cart and Silas- Aunt Tarn's two big watch dogs. Gesturing me to follow them like a lost child. What could she possibly want from me now?

We enter the guarded doors by the back bar, and they lead me toward the elevators that head down to the private rooms. Aunt Tarn only ever brings me and Beau to a private room when she wants to talk about something nobody else can hear, otherwise she would've just spoken to us in her office.

Room 3 is the only room not occupied, so it is the room that I find Aunt Tarn. Cart and Silas stay inside by the door, almost blocking it so I can't leave.

Aunt Tarn is racking up a thick line of pink cocaine.

"Sit." she orders abruptly, and I listen.

The echoing beats of music from the other rooms and upstairs humming against the square floor.

"What's up?" I ask, as Aunt Tarn snorts one of the lines, before handing me the rolled up $100 note to snort up another.

She watches patiently as I do, not speaking until I'm sitting up again and looking at her.

"I need you to pick up the pace." She explains. "Some of the boys are overworked- I need you to take a few more streets."

"Which ones?"

"Same ones you had before you were arrested. I gave you time- let you settle in, for a while. But I hope you can understand why I need more of you."

My secret. My biggest secret. A secret Fiona might just kill me for keeping.

"Deal?" Aunt Tarn asks with her glass against her mouth.

I nod. Can't hurt to make a little extra money. I just hope Fiona doesn't find out.

"Good." Tarn says with a toothy smile. "You can go now."

7

Chapter Seven- Sapphire

Link Jones

Aunt Tarn set me up in the same streets as I'd done previously. Back alleys, underneath tall buildings where homeless people camp, basketball courts and parks. Places parents tell their kids to stay away from. It felt like a weight on my back with every step I took to get here.

I've done really good so far, at keeping this secret from Fiona. Even though I'm busy a lot more often, most of the time she's at work anyway. I tell her I'm on job interviews, cleaning my house, getting food. She's easy to convince.

I've been working for hours, sold to a few folk. Some people I recognized, some I didn't. Some I was scared to fucking touch. Some I could smell as they approached me. Some lookin' no older then 15. Whatever, it's not my job to play responsible adult. Aunt Tarn would know If I turned away a paying customer for some moral reason, and it wouldn't be something she'd move on from quickly- I promise you that.

It's dark now. The air is cold, and my position will soon be replaced by Cart's cousin, Boisey. Counting down the minutes by watching the stars.

Just as I was about to leave the alleyway to meet up with Boisey, I stop at the sound of faint footsteps approaching behind me.

At first, I wasn't sure if it was the sound of a rat, but the footsteps became too heavy to be anything but a person. And the teeth chattering was something anyone could recognize.

What I didn't expect, was the person I turned around to see. I just about felt my body nearly shit out my heart when I saw who it was. My throat clammed into a tight slam, and his body seemed to react the same way.

Someone I recognized without a hesitation of doubt, though, he looks nothing like I remember him. Wearing clothes hanging off of his skinny body. Neck sores and an itchy arm, and pimples surrounding the left corner of his mouth.

"L-Linkoln?" he mutters, shivering in his stance.

His eye-bags bigger then his actual eyes, and his pupils dilated.

"Joseph?" I say with shock. "What are you doing here?"

He clears his throat, unstable with his ability to talk.

"Long time no see." he tries to joke, but his entire body so uncomfortable with shivers, it almost seemed painful to try and laugh.

Joseph Trader, a familiar face, but not someone I'd consider a friend. And he'd probably think the same.

Back then he had a lot more meat on his bones, and his skin wasn't so similar to the colour of his light blonde hair.

"What the hell happened to you?" I ask.

"Come on, man- can't we skip this part, I'm desperate."

He doesn't want to talk about it, but I do. How did he get so deep?

"After that night, the doctors prescribed me Oxy in the hospital to- ya know- help with the pain. Only, I liked the feeling a little too much." he giggles slightly beneath his shivers. "I started craving it once they discharged me- and you can guess the rest." he explains hastily. "But it's whatever, ya know. Who cares. Shit happens. Life moves on." he rambles.

I did this. I made him this way. If it weren't for me he wouldn't be here. I've never been consumed with so much guilt so quickly. I destroyed his life.

"So.. you buy Oxy from Tarn?" I ask, barely able to get any words out.

"Nah, nah man. I moved on from that shit a long time ago." he sniffles, crossing his arms. "I've moved onto better things."

"Which is?"

"Crank." he laughs, as if I should've assumed.

Meth. He went from Oxy to Meth, because of me. Is this why Tarn wanted me back? To show me what I've done? She wanted me to feel this shame, this guilt?

"So.. you're gonna give it to me?"

I hesitate, I wish I could tell him no. Tell him to find his shit elsewhere, but Tarn would have my head if she knew.

He pays me cash, and I give him his worth. But just as I move to leave with quickness, he stops me once more.

"Hey- what do you say we make a little deal?"

"A deal?"

"Yeah- you know- like a... loan?"

"What?"

"You know- man- I usually get more then this, to last. But some cunt stole my cash and I'm tight."

"Dude-" This cannot be happening.

"Please, man! Please!" He begs- nearly dropping to his knees. "You know- you- you owe me, man." He begs, grabbing my arm and pleading to me.

His words hit me like a million swords. It hurts most because he's right. I do owe him. Surely Tarn wont know, right? She wont notice if a little extra is gone- not if Joseph pays me back.

"You gotta.. pay me back, man." I finally respond, reluctantly.

"I will! I will! On my life, I will!"

Looking at him, his fucked up appearance. I can't stop myself from going through with this deal- the loan. I give him extra, and I make him promise to meet me back here in 8 days.

He doesn't waste much longer before disappearing into the night. It's then that I remember that I have to meet with Boisey before he realizes I'm late. Before Fiona realizes how long I'm taking to buy cigarettes on my way to the club.

The second I walked into Queen, Cart whisked me away toward the VIP area. I hate going up there- seein' a bunch of rich pricks and the way they talk to the girls. Makes me sick.

Cart's never been much of a talker, but he's gotten less chatty with age. Especially at Queen.

When we got upstairs, Tarn greeted me with a big smile. Asked me to sit down, having us face directly toward the aerial spheres.

"I need to ask you a favour." She requests, lighting me a cigarette.

"What kind of favour?"

"It's about Fi." She begins, looking at me. "I need to promote Fiona- but I'm afraid she wont take the offer.. without your support."

"Promote?"

Aunt Tarn nods, sipping her whiskey soaked with cigarette ash. "I've got a client- a well paying client, someone who would be great for business. He came in the other night- said he loved Fiona's show- so much that he wanted to book a private room with her."

"Sex work? You want me to convince Fiona to be a sex worker?" I ask angrily.

"Don't act all high and mighty, kid. You never shit on it back when I ran it through Beau's."

"That was different."

"Was it, Link? There's no room for morals here- so you can throw that shit out the window, right fucking now!"

Fiona will never agree to this. She will never be okay with working the private rooms. I don't know how the fuck I'm supposed to convince her to do something she would never do.

"She loves you Link- I can tell. She'll listen to you, better then she'll listen to me."

"And what If I can't convince her?"

"You will." she asserts.

I don't respond- I can't. I can't agree to this.

"Do you understand?" She asks again.

"Yes" I finally agree.

"Good boy." she says, leaning back into the couch and sipping her ashy drink.

Fiona Glass

It's 9pm on a Sunday, and today I am debuting as a dancer. I've never felt more nervous for something in my entire life- It's all I've thought about for the past year.

To be honest, I'm more nervous about Link seeing me, then anyone else. Luckily Cipher doesn't go to Queen anymore- so I don't have to worry about avoiding him. But I am so terrified in a different kind of way for Link. Everything has been so perfect between us- he's been taking me on real dates. Dinners, drives, and we've been grocery shopping so many times with Blue after school- like our own little family.

We've been doing home cooked meals with Blue every Tuesday night. Blue gets to pick, and find a recipe for me online to collect all the ingredients. I think making homemade pasta was probably the hardest thing I've made so far, but definitely one of the tastiest.

After a year of training with Yusra, I've gotten the hang of a few skills. Yusra told me that I'd only need to know a few routines to entertain on the back bar stage. Luckily tonight I'll be partnered up with Letty(Roxy), so if I really do present a bad job, they could always just turn to watch her.

Tarn told us we had to match our outfits and look coordinated. Yusra told me she got paid a big allowance for helping me train, which I'm happy she did. She deserves it. I hope she uses the extra money for something for herself. Yusra is such a giver- always thinking of others. I hope that she uses that money to do something good for her.

Maybe if I do good enough tonight, I'll start regularly making the money of a dancer. Which, by the way, is way better then the rate of a bartender.

Usually the girls that dance on the back stage wear black or dark blue or purple, as most of the big lights around there are a purple colour so it shows up better. The girls who dance on the four poles surrounding the square center bar are only allowed to wear black, silver or gold, and their hair has to be down. The girls that take in turns dancing on the glowing pole in the upstairs VIP area have to wear sheer clothes- I guess the VIP customers pay more for the nudity show, rather then the view of the open second floor.

And the girls who dance in the two aerial spheres have to wear skin tight outfits, and usually have to wear animal attire like cat ears and tails.

Blue came to work with me again tonight. During the school holidays, Blue still has meetings with Mrs Keen at the school. Mrs Keen spoke to me on Friday about Blue's progress. She said that she's becoming concerned that he's still not showing any willingness to speak. She said in a normal case, she'd probably trial a kid like Blue on anxiety medication, just to see if it might help. But due to Blue's previous history with drug influence, and the trauma that probably comes with it, she's concerned it might do the opposite of what we'd hope.

My dad and I agree. Although, we really have no fucking clue what we're talking about. At the end of the day, we trust whatever Mrs Keen thinks. After all, she's made a lot of progress with him already so far. And I'll take anything over nothing.

I'd been stressing out for weeks about what I'd wear, as I have nothing that is as eye catching as the outfits some of the girls have. Luckily Tarn has enough money that she buys spare outfits from time to time and hangs them up in the pamper room for us to choose from when we are out of options.

Roxy showed me her black one suit with hot pink hearts, and suggested I wear a plain black leather two piece for my first dance. She also lended me her hot pink pumps to ensure we'd match.

I never expected the energy to be so completely different for a dancer, versus a bartender. I mean, stakes are always high and you always have to be doing your best job. But you see a lot more of Tarn when you're a dancer. She walks in and out of her office shouting for girls to hurry up, fixing someones lipstick while simultaneously speaking to the security guards over the ear pieces.

"Are you nervous?" Roxy questioned, while applying her lipstick and I nervously fixed my hair. Tarn rushing around with hurry behind us, bustling the other girls.

"I think nervous is an understatement." I admit.

"Well, trust me, men ain't care that much. As long as you got a pair o' tits and an ass, they ain't lookin' at anything else."

I know her words are supposed to soothe me, but it honestly makes me way more insecure. What if my boobs aren't perky enough? Or what if my ass is too small? I never had to care about my body when I was a bartender. People only talked to me for my face, and my alcohol.

"Is your boyfriend out there?" Roxy teases.

I smile- I think the smile was enough of an answer.

"Well, at least you know you'll always impress someone."

"Or I could completely turn him off of me and ruin my chances of ever feeling sexy ever again."

Roxy laughed- clearly she doesn't understand the true stakes of tonight.

"All I gotta say to that is- if a man cant find the sexy in you, then the rest of us are doomed." Roxy convinces, finally finishing her makeup, and turning to me to help me apply my lipstick. "By the way- if you ever feel super nervous, you could always ask your new boyfriend for something to take the edge off."

"What do you mean?" I ask curiously.

"Girls! Its 8:55, why are we not heading for the stage!?" Tarn shouts- interrupting the conversation- ordering for Roxy and I to get the fuck up.

I give Blue a quick glance before I leave, a nod in return. The club was packed tonight. I searched hard trying to catch a glimpse of Link. He promised me he'd show up, but I couldn't see much beyond the busy crowd.

A security Guard named Nico led Roxy and I with Tarn toward a protected door by the back bar.

I'd never seen behind these doors before. The best way to describe it is a long hallway both to my left and right. Filled with purple velvet walls, purple velvet ceilings, and purple velvet floors. The lights also shined a bright pink.

I assume the hallway to my right leads to the elevators to the private rooms- because instead, Nico led us down the left path. I had no idea the dancers entered the back room stages through this hallway. Until tonight, I always just assumed they'd just step onto the stage and begin. I guess they try and attract more customers by giving the backstage a grander entrance.

I'd never felt my heart beating faster then I did while approaching the black curtains that led to our two separate poles. The bright lights from outside shining through the sheer.

Tarn hurried to ensure both of us looked perfect, before instructing Nico to begin the countdown before we stepped up. Goosebumps igniting throughout my skin.

"Fiona." Tarn spoke softly.

"Yes?"

"You'll do great, okay?"

Her short words- more motivating then anything she'd ever said to me. Honestly, hearing that from her was enough to almost calm me completely- an affect no other person could ever posses.

"3, 2, 1." Nico counts, before rushing us onto our stages.

The second we step out, the lights dimmed, and the music begun to serenade. I have to admit, I'd never heard better hype, dance-style music, then the music I hear at Queen. You know how music can assist in dictating your mood? Well Queen's music always made me feel way more confident. Like I was in a movie or something.

I just kept thinking of Yusra the entire time- face, hips, hands. She said that without those three things, nothing else will matter. I could be doing the worst dance of my life, but as long as my face, hips and hands are seductive, everything else will fall into place.

Face, hips, hands. Face, hips, hands. Face, hips, hands. Face, hips, hands. Face, hips- oh, Link! I see Link!

Link, Beau, Jasper, Dare, Brownie, Archie- they're all here. Quick yelps and lifted drinks from them and suddenly I can conquer the world. The crowd begins to hurry- drunken words and 5 dollar bills start flying our way. Fuck I feel like I'm shaking- do I look like I'm shaking?

Face, hips, hands. Face, hips, hands. Face, hips, h- Link. Fuck, that damn smile again. Beau and the other boys bumping against him and pointing at me like little kids. Fuck I feel so nervous. I feel so determined to impress him and only him. I don't care about anyone else. He makes me feel so damn anxious, while also completely and utterly calming me down. If I just focus on him and the purple light, maybe I can get through this- maybe I can do good.

Eventually I just forgot about the crowd- but their yelps and rainbow money certainly helped in making me feel sexier. Beau even threw a few notes my way.

Crawling across the stage, flipping my hair, spreading my legs and spinning on the pole in every position Yusra taught me, turning the minutes into seconds.

And Link, Link and his damn smile. Link being the only person I could bare making eye contact with the entire time. It truly was the most amazing experience of my entire life- stepping out of my comfort zone. Roxy, Link, Beau, and all the others being there with me every step of the way. I even saw Maxine a few times from the distant front bar- she looked so proud. It made me feel proud of myself too.

Finally I did something for me, and proved to myself that I can do it. Proved to myself that I am good enough, pretty enough. And if I'm being honest, I've never seen so many bills- and they were all for me.

Cipher Glass

I think Yana hates me. I think my kid hates me. Mothers connect with their daughters a lot more then fathers ever could- and I know Alina can sense the hatred Yana has for me.

Ever since that night I spent at Link's, Yana has barely spoken a word to me. I haven't gone out in a year- haven't seen my friends for months. All I do is work, come home, and sleep. Yana barely even lets me read Alina to sleep anymore. I think she thinks I cheated or something. I don't know.

She thinks I'm a drunk- she thinks I have a problem. But honestly, I drink now because I have nothing better to do. It's honestly a blessing when Dare comes over to visit, because then at least I have someone to share a drink with.

I think it would be worse if I just moved back in with my dad, then I'd never get to see Alina. I've tried doing better for Yana, but it's like she wont let me- or doesn't want me to. And if I did that, I'd have to explain to my dad and Fi the truth about Yana and I.

She's been asking to run a lot of errands alone. Having me watch Alina while she goes to the supermarket, or to get her hair and nails done- which is fine. But honestly, I don't think she does it for the independence. I think she does it to get away from me.

It's Sunday night, Alina has her first day of school tomorrow. I think I'm more nervous then she is. I know what kids are like- kids can be assholes. I only know so well, because I was a fucking cunt of a kid. I don't want Alina to meet a kid like me. I want Alina to make friends with the good kids that do well in school, that never cuss or skip class. I want her to enjoy school more then I did.

Yana gave Alina a bath after dinner, and tonight, I wasn't going to let Yana take away my honour of reading Alina a bedtime story. I swept her up and rocketed her into her bed before Yana could say otherwise.

"What book do you wanna read tonight, bub?" I ask her, after tucking her into her yellow unicorn sheets.

"Thumb-ina." Her version of 'Thumbelina'.

Alina has loved that book since the day I told her she was named after Thumbelina.

We almost named her Elina instead of Alina, but when I was writing her name down on the birth certificate, I accidentally spelt it with an A instead of an E.

I could feel Yana standing at the doorway as I read the story to Alina. I could smell her red wine from the bedside.

It didn't take much to get Alina to sleep tonight- she must've put herself to sleep out of excitement for tomorrow.

While I finished kissing Alina to sleep and tucking her in, Yana quietly set out Alina's school uniform on her fluffy desk chair.

I could sense something. Like, you know when someone has something on their mind, but they're just waiting for the right moment to say it?

Yana always does that, especially when she's mad. But usually, she waits for me to say something to piss her off so that she has an excuse to go all out at me.

I needed a shower- I knew I wouldn't have time in the morning. My sister asked me to pick up Blue and take him to school with Alina.

Blue's 13 now, but the schools are all in the same area, and Blue hasn't seen Alina for a few weeks. I don't like having Blue over when Yana and I aren't in a great place. I think It might set him back a few steps if I did. I don't ever want to be the reason he feels uncomfortable with us again.

I'm glad Fiona had more of an understanding with Blue when he first came back. If Fiona had never tried as much as she did with him, I don't think Blue would've ever gotten better- well, better for him. My dad and I aren't good with feelings- and I think I might be the worst.

As I pulled out new boxers from my drawer, Yana came into the room. Setting her glass of wine down with a little more clink then normal.

I debated even saying anything- I knew that's what she wanted. But I was over this energy of walking on eggshells. I know that Alina notices it, and I know it makes everyone else uncomfortable too.

"Are you alright?" I ask calmly, trying not to set off the parade.

"Why wouldn't I be alright?" she asks, closing the door and undressing her clothes. She's definitely mad about something.

You'd think a year would be enough for someone to get over something- but not with Yana.

She does have her days. Sometimes she wakes up at the perfect time to actually be a decent human. But obviously, today wasn't one of those days. It's like some nights she dreams about all the annoying shit I've ever done, and it reminds her that she has to be pissed at me for the entire day again. It's pretty fucking exhausting.

"You seem.. passive aggressive."

With fury, she stops finding bedtime clothes for herself and looks at me with that stare mothers always give their sons when they've done something bad. Fuck, I've done it now.

"Passive aggressive? Really?"

"Fuck, forget I said anything." I say, accidentally slamming the drawer shut.

"Great, wake our daughter up! That'll for sure give her the best first day at school tomorrow."

"I'm not doing this." I say, shaking my head.

"Doing what? Having a conversation with me?"

"This isn't a fucking conversation! This is just an opportunity for you to yell at me!"

She laughs- like a mockery. She knows it'll piss me off, she wants a reaction out of me.

"You think that's funny?"

"No, no. You just sound like a fucking child, Ciph."

"How so?"

"How so?" She laughs again. "It's like your still 16, doing things you think adults do to look cool, but when real shit hits you in the face, you run away like an immature child!"

"What the fuck are you talking about?"

"Right, you don't know. You have no fucking clue because you don't care enough to notice!" she shouts, tearing up as her voice shakes.

"What the fuck are you talking about, Yana!?" I repeat, approaching her furiously.

"I'm fucking pregnant, Cipher!" She admits with a squeal.

Suddenly, silence fulfills the room.

Yana Roche

Three weeks prior, Cipher and I had taken Alina to the mall to purchase her new school uniform from a uniform tailor. It was a good day.

I know Cipher has been trying hard to do better for us. He hasn't gone out in close to a year, and he only really drinks at home. He's been spending a lot more time with Alina on weekends then he used to.

Usually, whenever Dare would call or Brownie, Cipher would drop everything and leave. I hated that- I never knew when he'd come back. He could say he'd be back in a few hours, but not return until the middle of the next day.

I get it, you know. He's young, but he lost the ability to treat me like that from the moment he convinced me it was okay to have our child. He was the reason I went through with it. I would've gotten rid of the problem if he had told me to. But he convinced me it would be okay, convinced me he would always be there- not just for me, but for her too.

Don't get me wrong, I love my daughter. But I feel fucking awful that we couldn't have given her a better life. Now, sometimes when I look at him, I'm reminded of all the times he's left without saying goodbye. All the times he's shouted at me while hungover, or lost his temper with Alina while he's coming down from the drugs he did the night before.

He probably thinks I'm fucking evil, he probably fucking hates me. But he did this. He chose drinking and drugs over us so many times. And he probably thinks I don't know. He probably thinks I'm stupid enough to believe that all he does is drink when he's around those boys. But I'm not stupid. I know everything about Beau and Link Jones- there's not a single person in this city that doesn't know what goes on with that family. Except, maybe Fiona. Because there's absolutely no way she'd be with Link if she knew the truth about him.

For the longest time, I tried to convince myself that I didn't hate Cipher. I do love him- If I didn't love him, I wouldn't be with him. But I also fucking hate him. I hate how selfish he is. I hate how angry he can get. I hate how bad he tried to be different from his dad, but ended up becoming exactly like him. I hate how much I love him. I hate how I love him too much to leave. And I hate what he does to our daughter.

That day at the mall, it was one of our good days. He was making jokes, making Alina laugh at his stupid dad humor. He'd bought me flowers, bought us all ice cream and lunch. He drove us around the city, and he hurried to drop off music CD's for Blue while Alina slept in the back of the car.

But sitting there, in the car, It gave me time to think. I remembered what it was like to be in love with Cipher when we were kids. I'd always had the biggest crush on him. Used to be so jealous of my brothers, because they would always run around the neighborhood, playing football and basketball, and my brothers would never let me come. I would've done anything back then to spend time with Cipher. His curly brown hair and beautiful eyes.

I remember sharing our first kiss when we were 9, under the willow tree behind his house by the creek. I used to love collecting lady bugs, and I'd been out there that afternoon burying the ones Dare killed. Cipher must've seen me and ran down to talk to me. He was the kind of kid to kill every bug he saw, but I would've fucking hated him if he killed one of my ladybugs. And he knew that.

Even at 9, Cipher had game. He was smooth, and he knew exactly how to make me fall right into his arms. The kiss was amazing, the best kiss I'd ever gotten from a boy in my life. It was so innocent, and the way he blushed after made me like him more. He always seemed like such a bad boy, riding a skateboard and a tough shell of resistance. But when he was with me, he was different. He was sweet, kind, gentle. He was romantic, and young.

Once we started High school, he started playing into that stereotype a little more. I don't know why he was like that. I mean, I know his mother was gone, and his little brother. I know his father was an angry man, but I've never understood taking your anger out on other people. I've never understood cussing out teachers, skipping class, and not caring about anything but cigarettes and stealing liquor from your parents.

Brownie made him worse- Brownie made Dare worse too. Eyeball always let them smoke cigarettes, even when they were only 13. Eyeball let them have big parties that you'd be stupid not to attend. Other kids made them feel like they were everything amazing.

I think I was the only person to ever see a different side of Cipher.

I was always so angry at the fact that he could date all these other girls. I never understood how he could be kissing another girl, while still staring at me across the room. I never knew if it was all in my head or not.

Of course, eventually we did start dating- on and off but, dating. Until he cheated on me, and suddenly I understood the concept of trust issues. All of it was so long ago- I know that, but that thought has never left my head.

Were they prettier then me? Were their bodies better? Did they kiss you better? Were they worth more then me? What was it about them that made them good enough to betray me?

I probably would've never spoken to him again after that, but my brother adored him. Even after that, Dare still had Cipher come over all the time.

Dare was never a great brother. He was always so aggressive as a kid, always hitting us and making himself the problem child. Which is why it didn't shock me that he still hung out with Cipher after he cheated on me.

My parents couldn't have done anything either. They were old, and honestly, I think my parents were too scared of setting Dare off. Once something pissed Dare off, you'd never hear the end of it. He breaks things, hits things, screams the roof down, over the smallest of problems. He's always been like that. I've truly never understood how he's had girlfriends and friends all his life.

If it weren't for Dare, I never would've gotten back with Cipher. I would've never fallen for his apologies. I would've never fallen for his gifts, and stares and hugs. He was so fucking convincing- especially when I had to see him every time I went to school or went home.

Now, here we are. Cipher never learns from his mistakes. Every time he does something wrong, he tries to prove for as long as a year that he's a better person now and that he understands that what he did was wrong. But every time I slightly let my guard down, he does something else, and he resets everything I learned to accept about him. It's honestly disappointing, to say the least.

Disappointment for myself, for ever believing he'll change. And disappointment for him, for constantly resisting something better.

Like I said, It was a good day, and we'd been doing good. But sitting there, in the car, I realized it'd been months since Cipher had touched me.

He'd always been so affection in the past, always kissing me, holding my body and seducing me at the worst points of the day. I loved it. But he hadn't touched me in months.

Was he not interested in me anymore? Had he found someone better again? Or has he truly gotten to that point in our relationship, that he hates me too much to touch me.

That was all I could think about all night. During dinner, during Alina's bath time, while Cipher put her to sleep. It was all I could think about.

After his shower, he'd come into our room to find me sitting on the edge of our bed.

I don't know why, but every time something makes me sad, it makes me feel so fucking angry. My sadness always turns into blood boiling rage, every. single. time.

It's something I've always hated about myself. Like I'm just a ticking time bomb. I can never cry without screaming at someone.

"You okay?" He asked. His body dripping from the shower, with only a towel to cover the bottom half.

I don't know what to say. Do I admit how I'm feeling and start another fight, or do I keep quiet and bury my feelings to keep the peace?

He turned to me, looking at me with those empathetic eyes I love.

"What's wrong?" he asks, approaching me.

Tears filling in my eyes as I stand to meet him.

"Do you still love me?" I ask, feeling my chin tensing and my throat burning.

"What?" He exacerbates. Almost shocked at the question.

"Do you still love me?" I ask strongly.

"Is that even a question?" he asks. "Is that a real question?"

"Of course It's a real question, Ciph."

"How could you possibly think I don't love you?"

"Why can't you just answer the question?" I ask, feeling my voice begin to raise.

He stutters. I mock him. Here we go.

"So that's it, that's why you haven't touched me?"

"What the fuck are you talking about?"

He always does this, always tries to make me sound crazy. Anyone who knew us as kids knew that he could never keep his hands off of me. But now? Now he can't even tell me he loves me.

"Just answer the fucking question Cipher!"

"Yes! Of course I fucking love you!" he shouts, using his entire body with emotion. "I have never loved anyone as much as I love you!"

"Then why don't you say it!? Why don't you show it!?"

"I.. do!"

"No you don't!" I wince. "We haven't had sex in months! You barely even look at me anymore, let alone kiss me!"

"You want to know why we haven't had sex in months?- and it has nothing to do with me not loving you!"

"Why, why then!?"

"Because all you do is fucking scream at me! Everything I do is never fucking good enough! I have changed my entire fucking life for you! I moved out of my dads house, left my sister and my brother when they needed me the most, all for you! I stopped seeing my friends so that you could feel more secure in our relationship because you refuse to fucking trust me! Every thing I do you hate me for! Every thing I do you remember, and you keep it stored away in your mind to use against me next time you fucking blow a fuse!"

"So all of this- everything is just my fault!? You convinced me to keep the baby- that is why you moved out of home, Ciph! And don't act like your a noble man- you wanted out of that house the second Blue came back because you couldn't handle someone being more damaged then you! You couldn't handle putting someone else's feelings before your own!'"

"What the fuck-" he sighs, burying his face in his hands.

"Admit it, Blue has always fucking terrified you! You give him CD's and let him stay in your old room so that you can pretend you're a good person, but if you could never see him again, it would be too soon- because you can't handle someone else's feelings! You could never put yourself in someone else's shoes and understand why they are the way that they are- Just like how you couldn't fathom the reason that I cannot trust you, no matter what you do!"

"It was years ago- It was fucking years ago, that I cheated on you Yana! You want to list all of my problems, but you forget to talk about your biggest one- You can never let anything go, not even for your own good!"

"I tried to let that go, Cipher- but then you left me and your daughter to go do drugs at a fucking strip club run by Tarn and her mutant nephews- are you fucking kidding me?!"

"A year ago, Yana! It was a fucking year ago!"

"But how do I know you wont do it again!? And again, and again, and again! You constantly prove to me that you aren't all in this, and you are always trying to prove to me that you are a better person, when you shouldn't have to!"

"So what do you want me to do? You want us to move away, hope that we do better away from this town?"

"I want you.. to try and put yourself in my shoes. Try to understand that you are not the only person who is fucked up in the head, Cipher." I say calmly, begging that he understands me. "I just want you to fucking love me- more then you love someone else," I say, completely feeling myself break down. "More then you love that shit you take."

A shift of solemn paving over Cipher's face, as he watches me welt.

"I do love you." he admits, his voice shaking as his hands caress my face. "I could never imagine loving anyone else- or even myself- more then I love you." he adds, tears rolling down his face and dripping onto mine. "I fucking.. love *you*, okay? I love you."

He repeats, finally pulling me in and exposing me with a passionate kiss. Something my body had been yearning for. Something my mind had been deprived of.

Everything happens almost instantly- one minute we're screaming, and now he's ripping my clothes off. The sex so passionate, and our bodies so starved of lust- I'd never felt anything better. I know he loves me. I know I love him. Maybe after tonight, everything will be different. Maybe everything will finally fall into place, and be as perfect as it always should've been.

Cipher Glass

"I'm fucking pregnant, Cipher!" She admits with a squeal.

Suddenly, silence fulfills the room. Pregnant? It feels like history is repeating itself- DejaVu- but this time, I know how it ends. This time, I know what it feels like to be stuck in this loop. Hatred, regret, despair, never ending fucking fights. I have nothing to say- she wants me to say something, she wants me to hug her, but I cannot. I can feel my heart beating out of my chest. I can feel the result of all my choices falling into this place, and I realize- I did this. I ruined her life, worse then I ruined mine. And now, now I have to ruin the lives of two kids, instead of one.

I'm a terrible dad, a terrible partner, son, brother, person. I can't do this. I can't do this. I can't stand here- I need to leave. Need to leave, need to leave!

Yana Roche

He's... gone. He just.. left...

Link Jones

Thank fuck I made it back just in time, I wouldn't have missed this dance for the world.

I've watched her dance for the past two hours- her set is over now. I've done so many lines with my brother, I could talk my ass off to anyone about now.

I saw her heading toward the front bar- toward the pamper room, only for employees. I followed her over there, eager to hear her voice- eager to look into her eyes. Maybe even kiss her lips too.

"Hey!" I shout, trying to get her attention before she disappears into the pamper room.

She turns around with a smile- her body almost as perfect as her face.

"Yes?" she asks- her voice turning me on immediately.

"What's your name, sweetheart?" I ask, blocking her way and leaning against the bar. Our bodies so close I can smell her hair.

"Sapphire." she smiles.

"Oh yeah? What's your real name?"

"I don't know what your talking about." she teases. "That is my real name."

"Mm, come on, you can trust me." I say, lightly caressing my finger over the strap of her top. Her collarbones begging for me.

"Alright, but If I tell you, it better be worth it."

"I promise it will be." I pledge.

She leans in, her perfume entering my sinuses. "Fiona." She whispers, our noses basically touching.

"You know, now all I'm gonna be thinking about is all the things we're gonna do when you finally clock off."

"Just the way I like it." Fuck, her lips are so fucking magnetizing.

"You better get back to work." I tell her, trying to get her away before I feed into everything that is going through my mind right now.

"Okay, boss." she says with a smirk, brushing herself past me as she walks around me.

So many good feelings, suddenly washed away as I see Tarn peering down at me from the upstairs VIP section. Reminding me of what I have to do. What she's forcing me to do.

Fiona Glass

Blue is asleep. I didn't want him to come tonight- I wanted him to have a good nights rest before school starts again for the new year tomorrow. But he practically begged me, guarded the door so I couldn't leave until I agreed. He's been waking up to nightmares a lot recently, just like our dad. I guess the wires in their brains are transmitting the same images.

I can't wait for this shift to end- teasing Link is only so fun, until it gets to a certain point. Then I actually want to do all the things he's thinking.

My phone is ringing, but finding it under all this makeup and these outfits I tried on in a hurry might be a mission.

Yana? Why is Yana calling me at 2am on a Monday morning?

"Hello?" I answer, barely able to hear her over the club music.

"Hello- Fiona?" she asks with a worried tone.

"Hey Yana, are you okay?"

"Have you seen Cipher?"

"No, I thought he would be home with you."

"He was- but then we got into a fight and he left. But it's been hours- he's not answering his phone." I can hear in her voice, she's been crying.

"Do you want me to try calling him?"

"I guess- could you- can you just let me know if you see him. I have to work in a few hours and there's no one else who can take Alina to her first day of school- and I can't skip this shift."

"Okay, but if I haven't heard from him by then, I can take Alina to school, okay?"

"Okay." she agrees, breaking down.

"I'll call you, okay?"

"Okay, thanks Fi." she says, before hanging up.

Fucking hell. Cipher and Yana will literally be the death of me. Luckily for them I'm about to finish so I have time to try and find my stupid older brother.

Blue must've sensed something wrong- waking up on the couch beside me and looking at me with curiosity on his face.

"Don't worry- It's just Cipher again." I explain, spamming Cipher's phone with messages, asking where he is.

Suddenly, Maxine rushes in from the front bar, and by the look on her face, I can already tell what has her so bothered.

I quickly ask Blue to get his things ready to leave, while I rush out with Maxine to find Cipher trying to push his way past the bouncers at the entrance- stumbling and slurring.

"Cipher, stop!" I shout, trying to stop Cipher from pushing the bouncers.

"I need a fucking drink!" He shouts back.

"Well I'll get you a fucking drink, but not here!" I say, grabbing him and pulling him toward me.

"I can't go back! Please- please don't take me back, Fi. Please don't take me back!" he begs, falling into my arms and crying.

Suddenly, I hear Link rushing out with Blue, carrying all my things.

Behind them stands Tarn with Cart and Silas.

"Come on." Link orders, grabbing Cipher and leading us toward Link's car.

I can feel Tarn watching us- god I hope she's not pissed at me because Cipher can't control his liquor.

As I help Blue into Link's car, I look back to see a glance of Tarn smiling. Slowly waving back at me.

"Lets go." Link orders- wonder what has him pissed off.

We took Blue home first- thought it would be best to take Cipher back to Link's again. He'll disturb less people there. Luckily, my dad was already asleep by the time we walked in. I couldn't imagine explaining Cipher's condition to him right now.

Link was quiet the whole drive- I couldn't tell if he was just tired, or if he was angry about something. He's not usually like this during the drives after work.

Here we are again- laying Cipher's drunk body down on Link's couch while he whimpered and cried.

"Cipher, you should know- Yana called me asking where you were."

"Really?" he asked, surprised. "Was she mad at me?"

"I don't think so- she just sounded.. upset. What happened with you guys? I thought you were doing good.

Cipher hesitates explaining his side of the story. Clearly he fucked up, otherwise he'd be angry-drunk, not sad-drunk. Honestly, it kind of seems like DeJaVu. They were due for an argument that ends with Cipher crying on Link's apartment couch.

"Yana's pregnant."

Fuck me. Again? Really?

"And what- did you.. get into a fight about it?"

"No- not really. I just... left." My brother, the poet.

"Great- okay. Just, get some sleep." I say. Fuck all out of advice at this time of the night.

"Are you gonna tell her I'm here?" He asks.

"Probably- she wont sleep unless she knows you're okay, and she has to work soon."

"Oh- fuck! Alina! I have to take Alina to her first day of school! And- and Blue-"

"It's fine, I'm doing it. Just.. go to sleep." I say, approaching Link and grabbing my phone from his back pocket.

I texted Yana and told her Cipher was with us- she responded immediately. Clearly she's not sleeping tonight. I can't believe she's pregnant again- they can barely handle the child they already have.

"You okay?" Link asks quietly.

"I'm fine- Cipher probably wont be once he sobers up, though."

"Yeah- you're probably right." he responds solemnly. No jokes, no mockery. He feels different- flat.

"What's wrong?" I ask, starting to feel chills as I realize I'm still in my dancing outfit.

"Nothing- are you cold?" he asks, avoiding my question.

"A little- why do you seem sad?"

"I'm not."

"Then what's wrong?"

He hesitates his response, something is definitely wrong.

"Tarn spoke to me right before we left- she.. had some news."

"News?"

"For you." he hesitates again. "She wants to promote you- thought I should be the one to tell you."

I smile- I feel so proud, so excited for myself. I must be doing something right- Tarn must like me in order to promote me again.

But wait- promotion? What does that mean? More money? Will I still be dancing?

"What does that mean- a promotion?"

Link sniffles- cocaine sniffles. Even though he's supposed to be clean- wasn't that his get out of jail resolution?

"You'll still be dancing- but sometimes, you'll be a *different* kind of dancer."

"I'm still confused."

"She wants you to be available to work in the private rooms." He speaks abruptly- almost blurting out the truth.

The private rooms? Oh. I don't want to work in the private rooms. I don't want to have to actually be naked for random men. Oh no. No. No. No.

"Link, I-"

"You'll make more money- a lot more."

"Okay, but- I don't want to do that."

"Do what? It's just dancing."

"It's not just dancing- the other girls, they say you have to have sex with these men- I don't want to have sex with them."

"You really think I'd encourage you to have sex with other men?" Link laughs, grabbing my waist and pulling me closer. "You should know by now that you're mine."

"Do you promise?" I should believe him- but something seems off. I know he's smiling, I know he's pulling me in, I know he's saying all the right words to convince me- but something is off.

He hesitates. "Of course- Of course I promise." he assures, kissing my nose. "You'll do it, wont you?"

I'm still hesitant- I still feel that something is wrong. But maybe it is just nerves. Maybe my stomach is just trying to psych me out of something that could be good. Link wouldn't lie to me- he's never lied to me before.

"Okay- I'll do it."

He smiles- a big smile. He kisses me softly.

'Thank you." he tells me, pulling me in for a tight hug.

Later that morning, I took a shower. Running on zero sleep, getting ready to pick up Blue and Alina. I wondered if Blue had slept enough to be able to get up in time for school. Usually I wouldn't let him come to work on a Sunday, but my dad was having one of his.. bad nights. He's been drinking again- I found out a few months ago that he'd been secretly having Blue hand him beer bottles, and go out and buy more when they were out- just like he did with Cipher and I.

I was furious, at first, until I saw how angry he was when he wasn't drunk. Then I realized it was just easier for everyone to let him drink.

But I also knew that it would be easier for Blue, if I gave him options for space from my dad, whenever he's not doing so great. Even if that means he has to come to work with me more often.

I could hear the bathroom door opening- it's Link. He smiles at me, before taking his clothes off, and joining me in the shower. He stood behind me, running his face through the water while cradling me. I love it when he kisses my neck and ears.

"You're so beautiful." He whispers in my ear.

I smile- he is always making me smile.

"I love you, you know." Link admits. My heart instantly dropping to the pits of my stomach.

He'd never said that to me before. All year I've waited to hear that from him, and finally, I have.

I turn around to face him, water dripping down both of our faces and bodies. My eyes synced with his, our hearts hugging.

"What?" I ask, thinking maybe I heard him wrong.

A moment of silence as our feelings rush toward one another. Suddenly everything I'd ever written about in my book samples were starting to come true. Suddenly I was the main character- getting everything she ever wanted.

"I love you." He repeats.

I wonder if I could write a book- about my life. I wonder if anyone would be interested. I wonder if it would have a happy ending.

"I love you too, Link."

A yearn gravitating against us both, as our lips collide. Everything seems so perfect, so warm. Every amazing emotion rushing through my body, as he picks me up and leans me against the shower wall, kissing every part of me.

Link Jones

I love Fiona. I love the way she makes me feel. I love the way she'd do anything for me. No one has ever cared about me that much.

After taking Blue and Alina to school, Fiona and I literally laid in bed all day.

At some point, Cipher got up, and walked to the closest liquor store- and soon after texted Fiona that he was heading to Beau and Jasper's house. Finally, we were alone.

We felt so tired, after not sleeping all night. But neither of us wanted to sleep- we just wanted to stay awake, and to be with each other.

I knew Fiona had tried cocaine before, but not since she was in school. I'd had some leftover from last night. I didn't want to influence her onto it- but If I had enough to share, I couldn't see why I wouldn't.

When I asked her if she wanted some, she was hesitant at first. Like I said, I didn't want to push her. But we sat on my bed, and as I taught her how to use her license card to carve the perfect lines, I saw a thirst drifting into her eyes. Something everyone experiences at least once in their life.

"You want one?" I ask, after snorting my own line.

She thought about it for a moment. The sun from the outside window burning against her naked body perfectly, as she slowly reached out to grab the rolled up note from my hand.

"Just one." she said, before snorting her first line of the day.

We spent the rest of sunlight lying in bed, snorting lines, and talking about everything we'd never spoken about. Laughing about our childhood memories, reminiscing on the past. It was the perfect day, and I felt honored that she finally let her guard down enough to experiment with me.

We had sex so many times that day- amazing sex. I don't think I could ever get over how perfect her body is. I could stare at her all day if I had nothing else to do. Nothing could beat looking at her.

Fiona told me about that Kash boy- the one that shared that video he secretly took with Fiona and Skye. I've never wanted to punch a kid so bad. Luckily he ain't a kid anymore, so it wouldn't be as bad if I did meet him one day.

"You know, I'd never let anyone treat you like that again."

She smiled- her dimples, almost as perfect as the ones on her back.

"I know." she giggled. I love how giddy she'd always get around me.

"And I'd kill that Kash cunt if he ever stepped foot in the club."

Hearing that, she lifted herself on top of me, and leaned down, gripping my chin with her fingers and smiling into my eyes.

"I love that you'd do that for me."

"I'd do anything for you."

"I know."

I love it when she kisses me- when she pulls me in. Everything she does, I love.

"I never thought about how good it feels to have sex on coke." Fiona laughs.

"You think coke is good?- you should try sex on acid."

"I've never had acid before." she admits, nervously.

"Do you want to?" I ask, reaching for my bedside table, and grabbing out a small baggy with small acid stickers inside.

I could tell she was surprised about my secret stash- but I've always got this shit lying around my apartment from whenever Beau is over. I could also tell she was nervous about taking one.

"What will it do?" she asks.

"It'll just make the world look different."

"Different?" she smiles.

"Yeah- like, wavy and shit. Some colours change too."

"Is it scary?"

"It can be, but not if your here." I say, becoming tempted by my own offer- unable to resist any longer as I place one in my mouth.

"Do I swallow it?" she asks, grabbing one slowly for herself.

"No, just place it in your gums."

I loved watching her put it in her mouth. Having her straddled on top of me- breasts in my hands- watching as she tasted the same thing I was tasting.

I could tell she was nervous- but I kind of found it hot. Like she was a virgin. Virgin to most drugs and experiences- something we could do together, maybe.

And to say the least- and I think she'd agree- sex on acid is in fact the best sex anyone will ever have.

Fiona Glass

It's Wednesday. Tarn hasn't spoken to me much about the promotion, besides thanking me over text and congratulating me. Promising me it'll all be worth it.

The closer we've gotten to today, the more Link has started to act strange. I miss how we were before this promotion.

Maybe it's all in my head- but I just feel like Link isn't 100% okay with me doing these private bookings. But, the thing is, I wouldn't do it if he'd just be honest and tell me he wasn't okay with it.

Tarn pays for all the girls to receive Brazilian waxes regularly, but she inspects our bodies personally, when we're booked in for the private rooms. It felt strange, having her literally feeling my skin with her finger tip to make sure I was clear and smooth.

Tarn also had me try on a few different outfits- red. She said that the client- who's incredibly rich- loves the colour red.

I was confused on why no other girls were trying on red outfits with me. Usually when clients book private rooms, they book it with multiple girls- but it seems that I'm the only girl prepping tonight.

Honestly, I feel so nervous that it makes me feel physically sick. I've had to fight back running to the bathroom since the moment we opened the club. I keep checking the clock, and somehow it's going faster then usual.

I hoped that Link would come and find me before Silas escorted me to the private room, but minutes were passing and there was no sight of him.

"Fiona, are you ready?" Silas asks as he hurriedly walks into the room.

I look up at the clock again, its 8:54. Still no Link.

Yusra looks at me from across the room. Her eyes look pouted- a strange expression. She nods with sympathy.

The way that everyone is acting, is it all in my head? Where is Link?

I thought my heart would beat out of my chest on the walk toward the rooms. That it might rip through my ribs and explode my insides onto the floor. Blood splatter and the smell of organ juice.

Every second of the way, wishing Link would show up. I tried to find him amid the crowd, but nothing. He's no where to be seen.

Fuck. I don't want to do this. How do I back out? I can't do this. I'm scared. I want to go home.

"Come on." Silas says, ushering me into the elevator.

Fuck. Don't cry. Don't cry. Don't cry. Face, hands and hips. Look pretty. Smile. Be confident. Straighten your spine. Numb. Go Numb. Come on! Go numb! Fuck. Fuck. Fuck. I've never regretted a decision so badly before. Where is Link? Why isn't he here? I feel like I can't breathe. Please, don't make me do this!

Link Jones

It's 8:58. She'd be down there already. Fuck.

Maxine is at the bar, she wont even look at me.

"Where's Fi, has she left already?" I ask.

Maxine nods.

Fuck. She's gonna hate me. Fuck. I didn't think this through. I didn't think about the after. She's gonna fucking hate me.

Tarn's office. The door is shut. Tarn wouldn't be in there, not at this time of the night, right?

"Where's my Aunt?"

"I don't know Link, not back here." Maxine shrugs with annoyance.

"You pissed at me or something?"

Maxine is like a mother to Fiona. I know she and just about every other girl in here is pissed at me for convincing Fiona to do this.

They don't understand. They don't know what Tarn is like behind closed doors. Fuck. The office. I'm going in. I need to see it. I need to make sure she's okay.

Thank fuck, no ones in here. I close the door behind me, before quickly rushing to change the computer screen to the cameras in the private room. Skipping through until I get to room 3. There she is.

I can see her, I can see him. The back of him. He looks familiar- super familiar.

Fiona Glass

Room 3. A dark square room with velvet couches, a coffee table with bottles of alcohol, a cocaine plate, and LED pink lights.

Silas closes the door behind me. It's just me.. and him. He's facing away from me on the couch.

"Hello?" I greet, trying to sound polite. Trying to rid myself of my nerves.

Slowly, he stands up. He's tall, super tall. His skin is tanned. His hair is dark and short. He's wearing a business-styled outfit. As if this were a formal meeting.

He turns around. His face is narrow. His eyes, sharp, and a familiar blue. A man so incredibly intimidating- while smiling broad.

"Please, come and sit." he welcomes, grabbing my hand and guiding me to sit on the couch beside him.

Link Jones

Slowly, he stands up. He's tall, super tall. His skin is tanned. Hair is dark and short. He's wearing a business-styled outfit.

"Hello." She greets. She sounds nervous. Fuck.

He turns around. He- he's..

"Please, come and sit." he responds with urge.

Dad?

I've never felt my stomach drop further into the depths of my hollow body.

Without a second for thought- like a scene in a dramatized film- I drop everything and run as fast as I can out of the room. I don't stop running, in fact. Pushing past everyone.

I hear Beau and Brownie call out my name from Eyeball's poker table. Nothing, nothing can stop me. This is not real. My dad? The man I haven't seen since I was 6 years old.

Fiona. Fiona cannot do this. She cannot do this- not with my dad. I have to hurry. I have to stop this before anything happens.

I push past the security at the back doors. It wasn't too difficult, but I hear them saying something into the ear pieces as I disappear into the hallway. The elevator. Hurry up! Hurry up! Fuck!

Fiona Glass

"What's your name, sweetheart?" he asks, pouring me a glass of wine.

"Sapphire." I tell him. He chuckles.

"Your real name." He requests with a sly smirk, sipping from his glass of whiskey.

My throat feels so dry. I think you'd hear my gulp from upstairs.

"Fiona." I admit, even though I'm not supposed to. I just feel so nervous, and I think he can sense that.

"Beautiful name." he compliments, brushing my hair gently behind my ear.

"Thank you." I respond with a whisper.

His eyes following his hand, as it slowly moves from behind my ear, toward the red strap of my outfit, until he reaches my breast.

My eyes- on the other hand, looking toward the ceiling, begging myself not to cry.

"You're beautiful, you know. Someone who possesses such.. unique beauty, is more often found on the cover of magazines."

Magazines. Oh how I wish I was 14 again, admiring Vogue and Playboy covers. Oh, how I wish I was anywhere- but here.

"You look so young- how old are you?"

"I'm nineteen."

"Ah." he smiles, he likes that answer. "You look no older then 16."

I'll be 20 soon- maybe I should've lied. Maybe then he would've let me go.

I feel awkward and uncomfortable, as his hands search my body. When

I'm dancing, I usually feel confident and sexy- but down here, down here I feel trapped- degraded.

I wish I never agreed to this. I wish Link had protected me from this. I never wanted my life to be like this. I just wanted to be a model- on the cover of Vogue. This job was just supposed to get me through the middle.

"I'm Billy- by the way." he finally says, looking at my lips.

"It's nice to meet you." I say, trying to convince myself that everything is perfectly okay, and perfectly normal.

The man grunts, as he slowly places his cup down, and reaches into his pocket and pulls out a small baggy with two pill capsules- blue and white.

"What is that?" I ask.

"Just something to take the edge off- more simply known as angel dust."

"Angel dust?"

"Trust me- you're gonna want it." he entices, holding the pill in his finger tips.

I go to grab it- even if I don't want to- but he stops me.

"Open." He demands with a smirk.

I can't help it- I feel a small tear fall down the side of my face as I open my mouth- staring up at the ceiling again- as he places the pill inside my mouth, and feeds me some of my wine to help me swallow.

Link Jones

"Fiona! Fiona!" I shout, knowing she can't hear me through these walls. "Fiona!" I shout again, trying to push past Cart and Silas as they grab an arm each.

"No! No! Fiona!" I shout more, as they drag me into the room across the hall- kicking and trying to fight out of their grip. "Fiona!" I say, as I disappear into the dark room.

Nothing but an echo of song behind me.

Fiona Glass

He uses his thumb to wipe the tear from my cheek, smiling.

Carefully, he leans back into the couch, and gestures for me to get up. With one hand, pulling me into his lap.

"Dance." he demands, still sipping from his cup.

Face, hips, hands. Face, hips, hands. I wonder If Link is here- I hope Link is here, somewhere. I hope Blue is okay- I miss him.

Wait- he's taking off his belt. Wait. Wait. He's flipping me on my back, laying me on the couch. He could feel me squirming at the sight of his loose belt.

"Shhh." he whispers, as he sits up on his knees, pulling the belt from his jeans.

"I don't think-" I begin, until he interrupts, placing his entire hand over my mouth.

"Don't think." he whispers. "I'm not paying you to think."

Link Jones

"Let me go! Let me go!" I shout, as they force me onto the couch, holding me down. I fight- I fight as hard as I can.

I feel a third person wrap a cord around my arm- everything is happening so fast.

"What are you doing? Let me go!" I shout, as my veins pop out and the third man quickly takes out a syringe and injects me with whatever clear substance is inside.

"What is that!?" I can't feel my feet.

"What did you do to me!?" I shout, as my feeling in my legs and arms disappears.

"Please!" I beg, as I see my Aunt Tarn watching me from across the room- sipping a glass of wine and smoking a cigarette- as I lose feeling in my lower torso.

"Please, Tarn!" I beg again, as Cart and Silas release their hands from my body and take a step back towards the locked door. I'm frozen. All I can do is cry.

"Plea-" I sob, until I can no longer feel my face.

Aunt Tarn sits on the table in front of me. I'd feel her breath on my neck If it weren't for whatever that stuff was.

I want to scream. I want to kick. I want to shout until someone hears me- or cry until someone feels it. But I cannot move. I can't do anything.

"Don't worry, Link. Fiona is in good hands." Aunt Tarn says, with a smirk on her face.

I'd spit in her face if I could. Putting Fiona in a locked room with the man Tarn spent years getting us away from- fuck, I want to kill her.

All I can think about is all the things he'd be doing to her- the same things he did to us. How could she do that to her? How could she do that to me?

"I knew you weren't all in, Link. You never have been- not like Beau." she explains. "I knew it wouldn't take much for you to back out again- and I can't afford behavior like this." she continues, gesturing something at the third man- someone I've never seen around here before.

"Just remember- you made me do this, Link. Your actions- they have consequences. They have *fucking* consequences!" Aunt Tarn continues- veins popping from her forehead as the third man injects something else into the same poke on my arm.

My body is completely frozen, but somehow I know exactly what that is. Even though I can't feel anything- somehow I still feel that.

I feel it in my brain- I taste it on my tongue. I feel it freeze through my nerves, and boil through my blood- Heroin.

"Bring back memories, huh?" Tarn asks with a smug look, standing and sucking on her cigarette. "I realized a while ago that I'd never have you as committed as you used to be- unless I *made* you be that good again. I realized you had everything in you to be that good- but that you were just missing one thing."

I didn't want this- I never wanted this. I knew Tarn would try and get me to lis-

oh.. fuck that feels good.

"Sweet dreams." she smiles, kissing my forehead and leaving the room with her guard dogs.

My eyes are rolling in circl- fuccckkkkkkk.

Fiona Glass

I want Link. I want Blue. I want Cipher- my dad- anyone! Someone please get me out of here. I can feel that pill, it's making me feel weak- powerless. As the big man hunches over me and does what he wants- all I can think is I wish I'd said no. All I can think is- this man better run, because Tarn will kill him for breaking the rules. For... doing this.

I can't stop crying. My entire face is covered in salty water. Please stop.

8

Chapter Eight- Navy

Fiona Glass

I've never felt this much pain before. My entire body, weak. It's been hours since that man left, and I haven't gotten up from this couch. Still naked- still bruised. His semen spread on my back. I'm frozen- drowning in my own tears.

Blue. I need to get to Blue. Link. I need to find Link.

My legs wobbling as I stand to my feet. Grabbing one of the throw blankets and looking in the big mirror to wipe myself clean. I can't go home like this- I can't face my dad like this. He'll know something is wrong, and he'll hate himself more because there's nothing he can do about it. I need to find Tarn. She needs to know what he did.

Putting that outfit back on nearly made me throw up. I've never felt so sick from my own salty waste. My entire body feels raw and rejected. My jaw shaking from that pill. My vision still blurred. I want to sleep. I want to sleep so bad.

Clothes. I need my clothes.

Blue. I need to get to Blue. Fuck. I can see my hands opening the door- but are they my hands? I feel like they're not. Are they my hands?

Am I crying, or is that sweat? Fuck. If I walk out there crying, everyone will be afraid. I can't- can't ruin- I'm so fucking hot. Oh my god, I'm sweating so bad.

I'm in the elevator. Did I press the button? It feels like I'm flying. Am am am I flying? I want to throw up. I feel so sick.

I feel like I'm not walking right. Can anyone see me? The security guards aren't looking at me. Blue. Where is Blue? Am I screaming? Am I saying this out loud?

Ciph- Beau?

"Fiona, are you okay?"

"Blue."

"Blue- Blue's in the pamper room."

"Where's Link?"

"I don't know."

"What?" I can feel my heart beating out of my head. Can he feel that too?

"Is she okay?" Brownie?

"She's alright. I'm gonna get her home."

Beau is taking me to Blue, but where is Link? Why does no one know where Link is? Where is Tarn, I need Tarn.

"Is she alright?" Maxine, hey Maxine. "What is she still doing here?"

"She's fine, can you get Blue- she needs to go home."

Maxine is getting Blue- Okay. Oh, hey Yusra.

"What happened to her?"

"I don't know! I just found her like this."

"Is she drunk? Or drugs?" Yusra sounds worried.

"I don't know- tell Maxine to bring Blue outside. I'm parked out front."

"Okay." Yusra is getting Blue too. Okay.

Beau is on his phone. "Where's Link?"

"I don't know- Come on." His phone is in his pocket. He's carrying me now. I can see his car.

Wait. Where's Blue. Is someone getting Blue?

"Here." He's putting me in his car- in the back seat.

Fuck it's so comfy. I want to go to sleep so bad- Blue. Where's Blue?

"Here you go." It's Yusra, and she's putting Blue in the passenger seat.

"Have either of you seen my brother?" Beau is talking to them.

"Not for a while- I thought he'd left."

"I didn't see him leave." Maxine didn't see Link leave. Where is Link? Is he still inside? Is he okay? What if he's not okay? I can't leave if he's not okay.

"Should I call Cipher?" Yes, Maxine. Call my brother.

"No- don't call Cipher. He's got enough to deal with- just tell my brother I'm looking for him."

Wait. Wait. I want Cipher. Call Cipher. I'm- my eyes wont stay open. It's so comfy. Link- Blue- where's Lin-

………

………

………

………

………

………………………………………………………………………………………………………It's morning. I'm in Link's bed- with Blue. Blue is still sleeping. How the fuck did I get here?

Fuck, my jaw fucking hurts. With my tongue, stroking against the inside of my mouth- I can feel so many sores.

Blue. Sweet little Blue. All the memories of last night flooding in like waterfalls as I watch my baby brother sleep. My poor Blue. I'm so sorry. I'm so so sorry.

Tears falling from my eyes and dropping into his hair that I'd cut- coating him with my sorrows. I wonder what he dreams about. I wonder if he hates me. My poor Blue.

I hear the door open- It's Maddison.

"Hey." she greets sweetly, quietly closing the door and sitting on the edge of the bed. Her face appearing fearful.

"What's wrong?" I ask.

For a moment, instead of responding- she merely shakes her head and cries, quickly moving to wipe the tears away.

"What's *wrong*?" she asks. "You're asking me what's wrong?" she chuckles slightly. "What's wrong with you?"

Me? Oh. Last night- I- Did that really happen to me? That.. man-

"Nothing." I respond simply.

"Nothing? You're telling me you weren't doing drugs last night? Everyone was worried."

"What?" Nothing is making sense. Nothing makes sense.

"Beau found you stumbling around the club two hours after you were supposed to leave. Blue had fallen asleep in the pamper room- Yusra wanted to call Cipher to pick him up- but.."

"But what?"

"Well," Maddy smiles. "I think Cipher might actually turn up dead if he ever stepped foot in Queen again."

We laugh. We laugh- but our laughs quickly turn back to tears.

"What did you take?" Maddy asks with a serious tone.

I want to tell her- I want her to know the truth. But, I don't know what the truth is. What If I'm wrong? I need to talk to Tarn first. Tarn will know what to do.

"Angel dust." I say simply.

"Holy shit- guess that comes with the promotion, right?"

I nod. Wait- "Where's Link?"

Maddy's smile disappears again. "No one knows."

"What?"

"No ones seen him since last night. He showed up to the club around 9- Maxine saw him. But after that- no ones seen him."

"What about Tarn?" I ask.

"Beau's off speaking to her now- said he wanted to handle it alone, so Jasper and Brownie went home. I stayed- just in case you woke up vomiting or something."

Vomiting? Was I really that bad? "That bad, huh?"

"Well- not really. You just kept falling asleep. At first, we just thought you were drunk- but you had the jaw shakes and your eyes were going crazy so.."

"Oh."

"Blue was worried though."

"How worried?"

Maddy sighed sharply. "Just- you know. He was scared."

Fuck. Now I feel awful. What if I just ruined everything? What if I just destroyed every bit of progress Blue has made the past few years?

"I wanted to take him back to your dads, but he refused leaving your side- he wanted to sleep with you."

I feel that hot ball of cheese lodged in my throat. The pit in my stomach growing by the second. I feel so guilty- so ashamed. So embarrassed.

Looking down, I see my little brother. I love him so dearly, and I'd hurt myself before I ever ruined his progress. All I want is good for him- I don't care what it takes. I can't handle the strain of knowing I may have destroyed that.

"He'll be okay though- Fi. As humans, we worry about the people we love. And that is all that he is doing- worrying. Him staying just proves that he loves you- that we all love you."

An explosion in my throat- I still feel so guilty. I can't help but cry.

"What If I ruined him?" I whimper.

"You can't ruin him, Fi. He adores you too much for that to happen."

I sob into Maddy's arms, trying to be quiet- hoping not to wake him.

Beau Jones

Aunt Tarn messaged me last night, letting me know where Link was. That's why I didn't take Fiona to my house. Jasper wouldn't have left Link's if he knew what was happening at home- but I couldn't tell him the truth in front of Maddison. She'd tell Fiona, and then Fiona would want to see him. But if Fiona knew what was happening- she'd be pissed.

Aunt Tarn told me she found Link in the private room he'd rented- a syringe in his arm, passed out and dreaming of glory. Link hasn't done Heroin since we were in High school. He'd been off of it for years- but now..

"Where is he?" I ask Cart as I walk into my house.

"Hold your horses, Beau. He's resting." Aunt Tarn informs, as she exits my bedroom, closing the door.

"I want to see him." I demand.

"Not right now."

"I need to see him, Tarn."

"No you don't- he is fine. He will be fine."

"How do you know that?"

"Because I know people- good people- who can take care of him better then you can."

"But, I need-"

"Do you think I don't want him to get better?"

She always does this- always tries to make it sound like I'm second guessing her.

"No."

"No. Right. So let me do what I'm good at, and you can do what you're good at."

"Which is?" I ask.

"Well, with Link down again- I'll need someone to cover his areas of the city again."

"Are you serious?"

"Just for a few days- until I can get Link up and running again."

"What- you- you want him to start up again? After this?"

"I don't see why not." she responds smugly.

"Are you fucking kidding me?"

"Don't cuss at me!" she shouts, pointing her finger in my face. "I already have to deal with Link and ya mother cussing at me- I shouldn't need to deal with you too!"

Wait. What? "My mum?"

"Right- I would've told you already- except you came in here screaming like a fuckin' hyena."

Without wasting another second, I rush past Aunt Tarn, and move toward the entertainment area- past the kitchen. I knew I could smell weed and roses.

And there she is- my mother. Our mother. She looks exactly the same- skinny, frail, a mess of blonde hair, fake lashes and a wide stare.

"Baby!" she greets with a large smile, rushing to hug me with her bony body.

"When did you get back?" I ask, hugging her back.

"Aw!" she exclaims, grabbing my face and kissing my cheeks. "My bubba- how I wish boo could give me the same welcome."

"When did you get home?" I repeat.

She sighs. "A few hours ago." she responds, sitting back on the couch and lighting a cigarette.

"You've seen Link?"

"I tucked him into bed last night- couldn't bare to see him that way- my little boo." she responds dramatically. "Oh! Sit!" she suddenly shouts with a big grin, patting the seat beside her. "I want you to tell me everything! I want to hear all about your life- my bub!"

I sit down slowly- It feels so strange, seeing my ma. I'm happy she's home- but everything seems so wrong. Link getting back on Heroin, and my mother coming home.

Last I heard, Link was going to jail and my mother had ran off with one of her boyfriends. She seems just as erratic as always- but happier then usual.

"What do you want to know?" I ask.

"Wellllllll… I hear boo boo has a girlyfriend- what about you!?"

I chuckle. "You wanna know If I have a girlfriend?"

"Yes, of course, bubba! I want to know everything- everything I've missed!"

"Well there's not much- my life's been the same since you left."

"Oh! Don't say it like that- you make it sound so bad!" she responds, laughing hysterically at her own words. "Hey- what do you say we have a little get together?"

"What- a party? Where?"

"Well- here of course!"

"What for?"

"So I can meet all of your friends, of course- and boo's friends!"

"Really?"

"Of course! Don't act like you don't love a good party- remember all the parties we used to throw when you's two was kids?"

How could I forget?

"Come on- boo boo will be better by the weekend- it's the perfect time!"

My ma used to throw parties all the time when Link and I were growing up. Every time she and my dad would have a fight- and their fights were never little- she'd lock herself in her room for days.

I'd have to make us sandwiches, or climb the pantry to find the peanut butter. She'd come out eventually- but when she did, people would come with her. So many people. People I don't even remember. I tried my first sip of alcohol at one of these parties. One of the guests let me try a beer- some guy and his friends.

My ma thought it was so funny- watchin' me act like I was drunk. I always loved those parties. Loved getting up on the couches and the TV stands with Link to dance in front of everyone. Loved knowin' I was makin' people laugh.

But I dreaded gettin' tired, because no bed would be free while those people were here.

Most of the time, my ma's parties would go on for three to four days- Link and I would end up sleeping outside in Runt's dog kennel.

The guests would always bring pizza and sometimes burgers. Link and I would always steal the crusts from the bin and feed them to our pup, before falling asleep in the kennel outside with him.

Sometimes when Link is over- at one of my parties or something- and he blows a fuse like he usually does when he mixes- he'll find himself sitting outside by Runt's grave. Sometimes fallin' asleep right next to it.

My ma has always said that Link reminds her a lot of our dad, and that I'm more like her. I think- now that we're older- I agree. Link hates it when she says that though. Neither of us want to be like our dad. But every time he tries to prove that he's nothing like him, he always ends up sounding exactly as he did.

When we were teens, my ma was always scared of Link. I think that's why Aunt Tarn took Link under her wing more then she did me. Link started dealing for her first- I followed about a year after, seein' all the money he was getting from it.

I don't think I'm an angry person- but I know Link is. When he got out of prison, I wasn't sure what kind of Link was gonna come back. The one I knew before my dad left, or the one I knew after.

Turns out, prison changed him for the better- until now. Link is someone that can't handle himself around temptation. Girls, drugs, money. Doesn't matter. I'd never do heroin- can't stand that shit. But Link loves it- just like my dad.

I'll never understand how Link could hate my ma's parties as much as he did- but also be exactly like the people that attended those parties.

"Okay." I agree, igniting an excitement in my mothers eyes.

Cipher Glass

I haven't spoken to Yana since that fight. I'd intended to stay at Beau and Jasper's house- just until I figured shit out- but then Beau's mum came back from wherever the hell she was at, and I decided I don't need to deal with her and everything that comes with her too.

So instead, I've been staying at my dads. Blue didn't come home last night- I assume he went with Fiona to Link's house after she finished work.

Last night I slept in my old bedroom. It felt weird being back there.

In a way, it felt like I was taking a step back in life. But also, at the same time, it felt more comforting then anything I'd felt since I left.

My old bed felt warm, and soft. It made me realize how cold and sharp it felt to sleep next to Yana. I think I still love her- I do. But I can't help but reminisce on how different my life would be If I'd stayed away. If I'd never fought for her forgiveness after that first big fight we had at school. If I'd left her alone. I know for sure her life would be better- simpler.

I *do* love her- I think I just hate myself so much for ruining her life, that space is what I need to figure out if I want to continue to ruin it or not.

I didn't realize how bad my dad had gotten. Fiona should've told me. She should've told me he started drinking again.

When she was a kid, before Skye, Fiona used to tell me everything. It was annoying. She used to chat my ear off about the most random shit- she used to be such a stress head. She hated that I'd buy our dad drinks, and now she lets Blue do the same thing. She used to cry every time dad and I would get into arguments, as if that shit wasn't normal. She was a fucking sook of a kid, but I didn't realize until we got older how useful her big mouth was.

At least back then I was in the loop. At least back then I could control how much our dad was drinking. At least back then- with me in charge- nothing was perfect, but everything was in order.

I thought Fiona could handle it, back when she was working at the bakery. But now that she's working at Queen, and dating Link, clearly all she's been focused on is Link and Blue.

"Fucking dickheads!" he shouts, waking me up with a grumble. Probably yelling about something on the TV again.

He used to do that all the time when we were kids. Except, back then, he could stand and punch holes in the walls. He was only ever angry like that when he was drinking- or when I pissed him off.

He's actually a decent person when he's sober. He's more calm.

I look over and see him on that same couch- the second I walk out, I can smell it. Urine. He's pissed himself.

"Dad-"

"Don't fucking touch me!" he shouts, as I approach him.

"I'm not touching you dad-"

"Go back to your room with that gut rumbling music and fuck off!"

I think its more the embarrassment that's angering him. I wonder how long he's been sitting in this. I wonder how long he's been asleep before he noticed it had happened.

"Where's Nadia?" I ask calmly.

"I fired her a long time ago- don't need some worker telling me what I can and can't do!" See, I bet Fiona doesn't even know Nadia's gone.

"You fired her- what, because she would let you drink?"

"I don't want to hear it." he huffs, exhausted from his own emotions. "Just leave me alone."

"You can't sit in this-" I say, trying to help him stand, but the second I lean forward he starts screaming and shouting for me to walk away. I just know that if he could- he'd of hit me across the face the second I was within arms reach.

"Dad, you fucking stink! You need to shower!"

"You can't make me, boy! You can't make me do shit!"

"Oh, really?" Lets see.

I pick him up- his stiff body, unable to fight against me. Shouting and spitting in my face as I use all my strength to lift him up. I don't know where his fucking wheelchair is. Fuck me.

"Put me down! Put me down! Put me down!" he shouts, over and over again as I drag his body from his shoulders toward the bathroom. "You have no right! You have no right!"

His heavy lump of a body smacking against mine and every surface around us as we barrel into his bedroom, heading toward his ensuit. An overwhelming feeling of aggravation and wanting to prove to him that I am stronger.

I sit him against the bath, and turn on the shower.

"Don't even think about touching me again, boy!" he shouts, huffing with drool. His face as red as a tomato.

"Or what?" I say, kneeling to his level. "What are you gonna do about it, huh?"

"Don't talk to me like that-"

"Or what!?" I shout. "You gonna hit me? Throw me into the wall? Maybe you could- you know- if you'd done the right thing all those years ago and actually tried to fucking get better! Instead you chose to be exactly where you are- pissin' your pants and pushing away the few people left who wanna help!"

He stops me- hacking a giant mucus filled hunk of spit and launching it at my face. Nothing I say will get to him, not while he's like this.

I start taking off his clothes, my hands soaked in his piss while he continues to scream in my face. Lifting him into the bath to sit on the disabled chair while the shower water falls against his back.

"Get me out! Get me out!" he shouts, trying with every might left in his body to get his legs to move, but nothing. "I'll kill you! I'll kill you for what you did to me!"

"For what I did to you!? Are you fucking kidding?" It's so hypocritical, I had to laugh. My laugh confused him, and infuriated him all at the same time.

Looking at his face- looking at his stupid fucked up face- it ignited something inside me I hadn't felt since I was a kid. I left the bathroom, listening to his obliterate shouts as I stormed into the kitchen, and returned with a half-empty bottle of Dark Navy Rum I found in one of the kitchen cabinets. An old rum that'd been sitting there since the days my dad could walk.

I have so many memories with this rum. The amount of times he threw it at my head. Drank it straight from the bottle while pounding down my door.

I walk back in with it- his shouts stopping and his eyes immediately gluing to it- like a dog staring at a chicken. I rip the lid off.

"What I did to you? Yeah- I'll give you something to fucking cry about." I say, sniffling as I pour the entire remainder of the drink over his head.

He shouts, acting as if he was drowning underneath the mixture of water and rum. I almost felt bad- watching him struggle- until I'm reminded of everything this rum represents. Then I realize- maybe, just maybe he deserves it.

"How does that feel, huh? How does that feel!?" I shout as the bottle finishes dripping it's last sip.

It was so strange- after that- watching his screams of anger and resentment, turn into tears of hopelessness and regret. A piercing scream of agony exhaling from his lungs as he starts to quiet down into a humbled sob. Mumbling something about Merry. Dazed and drunk. Pathetic- but also, human.

Maddison Sterling

Ciphers texting Fiona- he's angry. Fiona's texting Link- she's angry too.

I had to drive Blue and Alina to school this morning. I would've taken the day off of work if I wasn't still a student. I think sometimes Fiona forgets that I am training to become a nurse- and I can't just take days off. I do the best that I can to spend time with her and Beau and Jasper when I have nights off- even though it's so rare these days.

I never wanted to be a nurse, but it was my mothers dictatorship that got me here.

When I was a kid- around 8 or 9- I wanted to be a teacher. To do something better then all the fuckass examples I had as a kid. But my mother made me do nursing. It was the only course she'd paid for.

But she doesn't understand the work load. She doesn't understand the abuse I put up with everyday. And I thought dealing with fat hungry people was bad.

When I was 11, my dad- Kallen- died from cystic fibrosis. He was 26. My mother and my dad met in school- classic high school sweethearts. Not once did they ever fight- that I'd seen. I never saw them disagree on anything. They were never petty- always came together to work on everything as a team.

My dad was only a few years off of becoming a qualified cardiologist when he became bed ridden at his own hospital. I remember visiting him all the time while he was working, which then became visiting him all the time when he was sick.

Of course, he'd grown up with his illness. He'd taught me everything I know about it. Let me come to check ups with him, let me hand him his medication after he'd eat.

The last year of his life skyrocketed pretty quickly. He went from feeling a little sick, to coughing up white yolk and choking on his own saliva.

It was strange, seeing a different perspective of the hospital. I've seen it from three different eyes- the eyes of a doctors daughter, the eyes of a dying patients child, and the eyes of a studying nurse.

After my dad died- all I wanted was to be exactly like him. I love the idea of his job, of studying, of saving peoples lives.

I'd have grown up to become a surgeon like him- if it weren't for my mother. Even at the ripe age of 12 she had enough confidence in her bones to tell me that I was not good enough or smart enough to be anything like him. I fucking hated her for that.

Why did he have to die? He was a good person- he *saved* people. All of those years he spent dedicating his life to doing good for the world- all for nothing. All for him to die from something that had been glued to his back his entire life.

Why not just kill him off young? It would've been easier. It would've saved him the trouble, me, my mum, anyone who'd met him. Why didn't his sickness just kill him when he was weak? When he was fragile?

After he died, my mother had some kind of mental breakdown and started dating random men for the fun of it. She's been married 3 times since his death.

Her current husband, Bruce Waterhouse, is probably the wealthiest of the lot. He's a real estate agent, and owns 'Waterhouse Real Estate'. He also makes money through renting out good houses to tenants.

He owns a big boat in a suburb closer to the ocean, and a vacation home in Indonesia.

He's okay, I guess. He'd never had kids of his own, so he always said he was excited to raise me like his real kid.

I don't know. Something about him never felt comfortable. It's like he was just trying to be a replacement for the man we lost. But no one could ever replace my dad.

When I was 16, until I was about 18, I went through a big rebellious stage of calling my mother by her real name- Veronica- after she and Bruce's wedding.

The first guy she married was probably the one I hated the most. Only a year after my dad died and she married the first guy that called her pretty. They didn't last long though. Turns out he was only visiting the city, and actually had a whole other fiance and children in a different state.

The second guy was a creep. Rich, but a creep. My mum married him when I was 14, but she divorced him a year later after she caught him cheating with one of my friends mother's.

She married Bruce when I was 16, and she's been with him ever since. I really didn't think they'd last as long as they have, which I think is why It pissed me off so much- how nice he was.

I called her Veronica Waterhouse every time I addressed her for nearly 3 years because of how angry I was. Angry that she could move on so fast. Angry that she could just fall in love with someone else. My dad had only ever loved her. He died loving her. And he'd be glad he's dead if he knew she could consider loving someone else.

I never really got over that- that feeling. But I guess I grew up a little, and I stopped making my feelings so obvious. I guess, it could be some kind of coping mechanism for losing my dad. Something I could never fully understand. But my mum and I are very different- we always have been.

She's been seeing the same therapist since he died. During those three years where every time we were in the same room, a fight would break out. She tried to force me to see a therapist too, but I refused. I didn't need a therapist, I just needed my dad back.

My mum would always brag about how she gave me a comfy life- one full of money, regardless of dad dying. And I get that, I'm grateful. But I'd choose my dad being alive over money any day of the week. I know it's not her fault, but I can't help but feel guilty for enjoying a life without him.

Fiona and my mother have always gotten along. They like similar things. I think, if she could, Fiona would switch lives if given the choice. I don't know that I could do that, but I wouldn't mind escaping the one I've got for a few hours.

I think that's why I love hanging out with Beau so much. My mother and Bruce were always scared I was seeing him romantically, but it's never been like that with Beau and I. We've never even kissed. I actually met him when

I was 17, dating Jasper's little brother- Jordan.

Jordan was cute- funny, like his brother. But he was also super boring. I mean, he'd party if there were drinks, but he'd never touch anything more then a cigarette. I've always found that so insufferable. If we've been brought on this earth to suffer and die, might as well do it enjoying it's perks every once in a while.

But I guess, Jordan was super into football his entire life, and was super active outside of school. I guess doing drugs on the weekend might ruin his chances of playing in the big leagues one day.

Believe it or not, Jordan actually broke up with me, because he felt I was spending too much time at Beau and Jasper's house.

I loved how free I felt every time I was there. I loved how everyone was happy and enjoying their time. Other parties I'd been to- ones where peer pressure and drunk idiots ruined the night- they were nothing like Beau's parties. And no drugs I've ever tasted, could ever beat the ones that Tarn sold. The day that Beau started selling for her was the best day of my life. Especially because he always gave me a family discount.

I've never really had much to do with Link. He was always just Beau's angry little brother. I mean, he wasn't always super angry- sometimes he was fun. Sometimes, when he had the perfect amount of beer and coke, he'd get everyone up on their feet. Dancing to the kind of music you reminisce about and wish you knew the title to.

He had his moments, and he was always there when a girl was having a bad trip. He always knew how to say the right things- something I think I always envied.

But Link when he's in a good mood, and Link when he's in a bad mood are two completely different people.

Beau was always the same. Everything you see with him is exactly what you get. He never hid anything. He never went out of his way to prove himself to someone. He was always just him. I envy that too- the ability to not give a fuck about what other people think.

I have always thought about what other people think. My mothers voice, squealing in the back of my throat every time I speak.

I've been texting Fiona during my breaks all week, trying to get an update on Link. She's responded a few times, but not with much. Apparently Link's been hiding at Beau's since that night. He must've done something pretty bad to be hiding out for this long.

I have no idea if she's seen him or not, or of what he's done. I don't hear much from her these days, not since she and Link became serious. She seems like one of those girls that lets her boyfriend run her whole life. I mean, It's pretty hard to avoid when your dating someone like Link. He seems like a lot to handle, definitely too much drama for me.

Beau would never talk bad about Link, but I've encountered a few girls in the years I've known the Jonesy boys that used to fuck with Link, and lets just say he has a habit of growing cold feet. I think Fiona is the longest relationship he's probably ever had.

Beau messaged me on Thursday- said he was having a party tonight. I was supposed to work this weekend, but to be honest, something inside me just didn't have the energy to do it. It's like trying to force myself to go to the gym, knowing I hate it. I don't do it anymore, because I'm so much happier when I don't.

I told my bosses that I'd been throwing up all night, and that I might have a virus. Luckily I'm only a student, and It's only really hurting me if I take longer to get my hours done.

I've always been super skinny my whole life- like unhealthily skinny. My mother is a Pilates freak and used to make me to go classes with her on Saturdays when I was like 9. I don't think I've ever seen a single Carb in my house. My mother doesn't even drink alcohol because it's too fattening.

I was a really good ballet dancer when I was a kid- quit when I was 18 to focus on studying. I think ballet was the only thing I ever enjoyed in my life, after my dad died. I enjoyed it because I was good at it. I liked being good at it. I liked being told I was good at it. And I liked other people knowing that I was good at it. If I have any big regrets in my life, it would be quitting ballet to do nursing.

When I was 13- when I was first starting to get boobs- my mother made me got on a diet, because she thought it was too soon for me to start growing out of the same sized leotards I'd been wearing since I was 10. She said she was scared I'd started using food for comfort since my dad died. I don't know how I could do that though, considering the only food we had that I could snack on was carrots, spinach and tofu.

She stopped letting me eat breakfast, and I wasn't allowed to eat before or during practice. Even after I'd lost a bunch of weight, I sort of never got out of the diet.

I eat way more carbs and sugary foods now that I make my own money. But my entire teen hood I constantly had her voice in the back of my head. While my friends were enjoying donuts from the corner store, I was licking the icing and then spitting it into the dirt and washing my mouth out with soap- hoping the calories didn't count.

No matter how skinny I get, I feel I'll always hate what I see looking back at me in the mirror. I don't think I'll ever be as pretty as my mum was when she was my age.

I never look as good in the clothes I own. I never end up wearing the outfits I want to wear- because my boobs are too small, or my stomach isn't flat. I feel like my cheeks look fatter when my hair is up, so I only do it when I work. I always turn to the side when I stand in front of a body sized mirror. Habits I've gathered from being at my mothers Pilates classes. Things I'd seen the other women do every time they entered the room. Envious of how flawless they were- even when they were red and dripping with sweat.

My natural hair is like a strawberry blonde too, but my mother started booking me in to get it bleached to a lighter blonde when I was 15 so that I could match her. The day I cut my long blonde hair was the day my mother nearly had a heart attack. She'd always been obsessed with my long hair. But to be honest, I was just having a really terrible day, so when I came home from school, I cut at it with kitchen scissors until the anger left my skin. The hairdresser had to cut it to my shoulders to make it even. My mother was so upset, but I kind of liked it. I don't think I'd ever let my hair get that long again.

Tonight I'm wearing a tight white singlet and a matching white fabric skirt. I'd wear it just like this if I had a body like Fiona, but I couldn't leave the house without accessorizing with a big blue plaited button up I'd stolen from my dads old boxes a few years after he died. I think the colour makes my eyes pop.

I've always loved a smokey eye on me. I love it because It feels so different. I don't look like someone who would wear dark eye makeup on the average day, which Is why I think it suits me so much.

I don't really wear much else other then some earrings and lip gloss. My hair always looks good with it's natural waves from the damaging bleach.

My mother and Bruce have been on a holiday for the past week on his boat, and they don't return until next Wednesday- which is nice, because I can leave the house without my mother judging the fact that I'm wearing brown knee high boots with a white skirt, or the fact I'm wearing a mans button up to a party.

The party was already alive by the time I'd gotten there. I'd messaged Fiona, asking if she was there, but I didn't get a response before I walked inside.

Though, I didn't feel uncomfortable. It was sort of always the same people that came to Beau's parties.

Jasper was the first person I saw when I walked in- immediately handing me his drink.

"Hey, guess what." he opens suspiciously.

"What?" I ask with curiosity.

"Lydia's back." He reveals.

What the fuck. I have only ever seen Beau and Link's mother a handful of times in the years that I've known them, and that handful comes from the short glances of picture frames hanging from the house walls.

A piece of work she is. Spending every dime on sex and drugs, but somehow still has enough to glue on fake lashes until they rot, and to get her nails done. I think she had a little bit of lip filler done too- they were looking a little migrated in her most recent pictures she's sent to Beau's phone.

"Shut up! No way!" I say, shocked.

"Yeah- that's why Beau threw this party, she practically begged him."

"Wait, why?"

"I don't know- something about celebrating something." Jasper explains, leading me into the kitchen where he grabs another drink for himself.

"Hey! Maddison!" I hear shouting from the entertainment area, It's Beau- accompanied by Archie and Dare.

"Hey Beau!" I greet, as he brings me in for a hug. "Is Fiona here?"

"Oh, yeah, of course. She's out the back."

"What? With Link?"

"Yeah."

"So… Link and her are.. good now?" I ask curiously.

"You know what- I have no fucking clue. I've been too busy dealing with my ma to deal with those two." He explains, grabbing himself a beer from the fridge. Filled with old magnets and postcards, and Primary school photos.

"But guess who else is here." Archie adds.

"Who?"

"Cipher- he's out back too, with Brownie." Fuck, I feel like I haven't seen Cipher in forever.

"Hey-" Beau interjects, approaching me closer to whisper in my ear. "You want a bump?"

"Please." I beg, before he leads me toward the bathroom.

Fiona Glass

First time I'd spoken to Link since that night was when I showed up to this party. He hasn't returned any of my texts or calls. The only reason I found out about this party is because Beau invited me. Best believe when I showed up I did not expect to meet their mother. I wish Cipher could've fucking warned me that she was back, I might've shown up with less of a scowl.

My intentions entering this party was probably to scream my fucking head off at Link for the shit he's put me through the past few days. I'm lucky Frosty was nice enough to cover my shift so that I could do just that. But all my plans came to a quick end when Beau rushed to introduce me to Lydia.

I was sort of hoping Tarn would be here, then maybe I could tell her what happened that night in the private room. She hasn't been answering any of my texts, and I haven't seen her at work since. I guess she's been in whatever hole Link has been hiding in too.

She was sitting in the entertainment area with a bunch of random people I've never seen- around her age- sharing lines of coke and swallowing MDMA pills.

"Ma, this is Fiona- Link's missus." Beau introduced.

Immediately she stood up and welcomed me with a big embrace. She seemed kind- smelt a little strange- but kind. But honestly, my head was elsewhere the entire time she was talking to me.

"I am so happy to finally meet you- I'm Lydia! Beau and Linky's mum!" she exclaimed with a big smile.

"It's nice to meet you too." I responded calmly.

"Beau tells me you're Cipher's little sister- Denny Glass's kid- is that right?"

"You know Cipher?" I ask curiously.

"Of course! Cipher is a wonderful boy- he was such a treat to have around all those years ago." I had no idea Cipher and Lydia knew each other. I didn't think Cipher was ever *that* close with Beau and Link. "Sit! Please! Sit with me!" she begs, basically pulling my arm to sit on the couch beside her.

Beau sat next to me, smoking weed from a shared bong as Lydia rambled in my ear. I've never heard someone talk so fast and about so many things in such a short amount of time in my entire life. I couldn't even repeat half the shit she spoke about. All I could focus on was how shaky she was, and how frozen her lips looked, and how many sores she had covering her arms and legs. Like she'd been sleeping on needles.

I couldn't escape that woman until Jasper showed up with Cipher and Brownie, and the house started to fill with guests.

"Come find me later, okay?" she begged as I stood to greet my angry looking brother.

"I will." I agreed, rushing to Cipher who stood in the kitchen drinking a beer.

"Cipher-" I begin, interrupted by his groan.

"Where have you been?" he asks with a tone.

"What?"

"When were you planning on answering any of my texts or calls?"

"I have been busy, Cipher. I don't know if you've heard but-"

"Yeah, well I don't know if you've heard, but dads off his rockets again." he reveals.

"What are you talking about?" I ask, confused.

"Right- you didn't know."

"Know what?"

"Dad fired Nadia. When I slept there the other night while you and Blue stayed at Links I basically had to force him into the shower kicking and screaming because he'd been marinating in his own piss for god knows how long!"

I knew dad was drinking again, but honestly, this week has been so packed with mountains of shit that I completely forgot to check how he was doing. I just assumed Nadia was there. I never considered he'd get like this again- this angry. Angry enough to fire the only person who *had* to take care of him. This entire week, Blue and I have been living at Link's- waiting and waiting for Link to come home. I had no fucking idea. It just.. didn't cross my mind.

"Cipher-"

"I thought you could handle it, you know? I thought that maybe you weren't that useless kid you were the first time dad was like this. I thought that maybe you'd finally grow up and start thinking of other people before yourself-"

"Are you fucking kidding?" I snap. "All I have been doing since Blue came home is putting other people before myself! I gave up everything to be there for him! And where were you? Oh, right, you were getting drunk and doing drugs with your old High school buddies while your *partner* stayed home raising your child! Such a great dad- you're exactly like the man you tried so fucking hard to get away from!"

"Fuck you!" He shouts, drawing attention from others, before storming away.

"Right, walk away, Cipher! That's what you do best." I call behind him, and as I watch him walk outside, I catch a glimpse of Link sitting in a camping chair by the fire.

I'm already heated, might as well take out more of my anger on someone else that deserves it.

"Link!" I shout, as I step into the backyard. He looks up at me simply, watching as I approach him.

I can't help but laugh in his face. He's shivering, curled up in his own jacket. Shriveled like a fucking shrimp.

"Hey, Fi." He responds simply.

"Hey? Hey!?" I shout. "I have been calling you- texting you- for days! This entire time you've been hiding here like a lost fucking dog, and you couldn't find the respect to even text me back and let me know you're not dead on the corner of the street somewhere!?" I add, drawing attention again.

Link can feel all the eyes circling over him, and I can tell it made him uncomfortable.

He stood up quickly, and begged me to walk somewhere private with him.

"Are you fucking serious!? You really want to talk now? After all of this-" I continue shouting, stopping with a halt as he abruptly grabs my arm and starts dragging me toward the house. "Let me go, Link!" I yell, pulling myself out of his tight grip.

His body instantly rips back, turning toward me. A vein popping out of his forehead as he screams in my face.

"Do you want to fucking talk, or not!?"

"I wanted to talk fucking days ago, Link! I wanted to talk that night, but you weren't there!" I shout, feeling that nuisance of a ball as it grows in my throat.

The memories of that night replaying in my head- every inch of my body reliving it. He doesn't understand- he has no idea what I've been through.

Link Jones

"I wanted to talk fucking days ago, Link! I wanted to talk that night, but you weren't there!" She shouts in my face, igniting a fury inside my brain.

She thinks I wasn't there- but I was. Every second of the past few days I had that memory replaying over and over in my head.

Her, my dad. What I did- what I made her do. She doesn't understand- she has no idea what I've been through.

"Come on-" I try reasoning with her.

"No!" She shouts, pulling away from me again. "Don't fucking touch me!" everyone is looking. Every one is watching. I can't deal with that- everyone knowing it was me, that I was in the wrong.

"We're going home." I demand, walking away- trying with every nerve in my body to contain myself, expecting her to follow behind me.

Maddison Sterling

Link and Fiona are screaming at each other by the back door. Everyone is watching.

"We're going home." Link demands, walking off and Fiona following slowly behind, burying her crying face in her hands. Link appearing stern as he passes me, dragging her toward the front door.

"Fiona-" I say, stopping her as she passes. "Are you okay?"

"No, I'm not fucking okay, Maddy."

"Okay- do you need a ride?"

"No, I haven't been drinking." she responds, sobbing.

"Okay.." I say, trying to thinking of what to say next.

I've never been good with these kinds of situations- confrontation. I've never really been put in this situation, so I haven't had much practice with what to say. "Do you want me to-"

"I have to go, Maddy." She interrupts, storming off to chase after Link. As always.

"Hey, don't worry about it." Jasper says, patting my back. "They'll get over it."

"I'll just never understand that-" I begin, leaning against the kitchen counter. "I'll never understand chasing after a man that clearly doesn't care."

"What makes you think Link doesn't care?"

"The fact that he has been ignoring her for days- not once did he ask if she was okay, or wondered where she was-"

"Yeah, but, you don't know what was going on here." Jasper interrupts, sounding stern.

I never considered that Link could be experiencing some kind of catastrophe here too. I honestly just thought he was ignoring Fiona because he was mad at her for doing the private dance.

"What was going on?" I ask curiously.

Jasper looks around slightly, then whispers "I'm not allowed to talk about it."

"What?" I say, thinking it's a joke, but Jasper doesn't laugh- and it's hard to find Jasper when he's not laughing.

Suddenly, I hear a slam as Cipher storms out of the bathroom, and I watch as he walks into Beau's closed bedroom.

At first thought, I was just going to let him be. I've never been super closer with Cipher, so I don't know what kind of person he is when he's mad, but I also felt some sort of inkling that he was more sad then mad.

Something within the universe pushed me into the room that night. Some sort of gravitational pull.

When I walked in, the room was dark- the only light source coming from the moon peaking through the closed blinds. I'd never realized how empty Beau's bedroom looked until now. Only a double bed, a closet, and some old beer bottles and cigarette butts to fill the quiet room. Music thumping from outside as I close the door.

Sniffles echoing as Cipher looked up at me with tears in his eyes.

"Are you okay?" I ask, feeling slightly awkward, and slightly regretting my decision to come in here.

He doesn't answer my question, he just looks down and buries his eyes in the palms of his hands.

Slowly, I approach him, sitting beside him on the edge of the bed. Surprisingly, he hasn't shouted at me to get out yet.

"Do you want to talk about it?" I ask softly, praying I don't step on a nerve or something.

He looks to me with sniffles again, before looking back down and shaking his head. "I've really fucked up, haven't I?"

"What do you mean?" I ask curiously.

He takes a moment to answer, choking back the tears begging to burst through his shiny eyes.

"Every decision I've ever made seems to be the wrong one. I ruined everyone's lives- Fi, my dad, Yana, my kid, Blue. I fucking destroy everything I touch."

I feel sad, looking at him. I feel an overwhelming abundance of empathy.

"Well, you haven't ruined my life." I say, joking. Surprisingly, making him laugh a little.

He looks at me, still smiling from what I said, until suddenly that smile disappears again and his expression of sorrow returns.

"Give it time." he claims.

"I don't know- I think I'm a little more optimistic." I joke again, making his smirk return ever so slightly.

For a moment, he just looks at me. His eyes scanning my face like a computer. Scanning every flaw, every imperfection, every detail. Until those stares start growing closer, and soon, his lips are against mine- and I can't seem to stop it. I don't *want* to stop it.

In a matter of seconds, we move from talking, to me lying on the bed with him over me as we kiss and our hands are searching.

I haven't been with a boy in a while- my life has been far too busy. I didn't realize until this moment how starved I was. How desperate I was for just an ounce of attention- affection. For someone to look at me as more then just a girl that exists.

Suddenly, everything else disappears. Suddenly, we are the only two people in the entire world, and nothing is stopping us.

Fiona Glass

Blue had stayed in Link's apartment. By now he'd be asleep- thankfully. I just hope he doesn't wake up to the sound of what's to come.

We didn't talk the entire drive home, but the second he closed his apartment door, everything came out.

"Where have you been, Link? Mentally."

"A lot of places."

"I'm going to need more then that!" I beg, feeling crazy as I watch him continue to shake like a frozen child. Scratching at his skin like he's got fleas.

"I don't know what you want me to say!" he shouts, rushing into the kitchen to grab a beer, but the second he takes a sip, it's like his entire body runs a heat rash and he starts to strip his layers.

"I want the truth, Link! I want to know what was so important you had to shut me out!"

"I didn't shut you out, Fi!" He shouts, slamming his beer on the kitchen counter.

"Then what would you call that, huh? What would you call ignoring me for days after making me do something you convinced me to do!" I shout, but the second I mention anything about the private dance, his face winces- like his body wants to throw up. "It's that, isn't it? That's why you've been avoiding me."

He doesn't say anything, he just stares down at his beer.

"Are you mad at me for doing it?" I ask, tears beginning to stream down my face- but I'm not stopping them this time.

"No." he rushes to answer, meeting me around the kitchen counter. "I'm not mad at you for doing that. I couldn't be."

"Then what? What is it that I have done to disgust you so much that you ghosted me!?"

"It's not.. you!" he whimpers, almost breaking down. "It's me." he admits. "It's what I have done!"

"What did you do, Link!?" I shout, but again, nothing. He shakes his head and walks away toward the windows. "No- No! You don't get to walk away, not this time! I want to hear you say it- whatever it is, I want to hear it! Out loud!"

"You don't understand-" he whimpers again, turning to me.

"No, you don't understand!" I sob. "You don't understand the repercussions to your own actions!"

"Fi-" he says calmly.

"You don't understand that the way you view me- the way you think of me- matters! You don't understand that I love you more then I have loved anyone, and that the things you do matters to me!"

"Don't you get it- that is why I can't tell you!" He interjects, approaching me closer. "That is why I can't find the strength to tell you where I've been- because what *you* think of *me* matters!"

"There's nothing you could do to make me think differently of you-" I try to assure, but he laughs in my face and falls into the window, sliding down until he's crunched in a ball on the floor, sobbing into his knees and rocking his body back and forth.

"You have no fucking clue." he adds, laughing beneath his cries.

"So tell me! Tell me the things I don't understand!" I beg, kneeling in front of him. "Please, Link- I'm begging you to let me in! There's nothing I want more then for you to just trust me!"

He sobs more. I can see that something is eating at him. I can see that the memory of something is hurting him.

"You really want to know?" he shakes.

"Please Link." I beg again, gripping his frail hand.

A moment of silence so quiet, you'd hear a rain drop a million cities away. I've never had to beg for a man to love me- I've never felt the need to. Until now. Until him. Until Link.

"Okay." he begins.

9

Chapter Nine- Night

Link Jones

When I was a kid, my dad used to lock me in the washing machine as a punishment.

My parents are Lydia and Billy. Tarn- who's real name is Rose- is my mothers sister. Before my dad got arrested, he'd put up pictures of his dad, George, from when he served in the military.

He kept all of his dads medals and even his gun. The same gun he killed himself with when my dad was a kid.

I know my Grandfather used to throw my dad around a bit. I know it must've been hard for him to see his dad after he was relieved of his duties.

My dad and mum had been dealing drugs for Tarn since before I was born. I have so many memories from when we were kids- when Tarn and my mum would host parties all weekend at the same house Beau and Jasper live in now. These parties would last for days, sometimes people wouldn't leave for weeks. I hated having people in the house all the time. I hated when they'd talk to me, or sleep in my bed. Beau and I used to escape outside.

I have faint memories of Grandma Mabel- my mum's mum- but not enough to form an opinion on her.

When I was 4 and Beau was 6, one my dads friends, Jaxton Ritcher, he brought around a great dane puppy that was mixed with an American pit bull. Said we could keep it to have some company. I think he was Tarn's boyfriend at the time.

Beau and I loved that dog. We named him Runt, and we spent almost every waking second with him when we weren't at school.

Beau and I used to have to meet with people at school all the time. Always asking us questions about home, about our clothes, about our food and all that shit. I didn't know who they were then, but now I do. I guess it was uncommon to find kids wearing clothes too big or too tight and burnt with cigarette ash. But I was a shy kid, I wouldn't of said anything to them. I don't know about Beau, I guess he never said enough to make anything happen.

We didn't have Runt for long. But around that time, I remember whenever those parties would be happening- and Beau and I would find people sleeping in our bedroom- we'd always go outside and sleep with runt in the kennel. Didn't matter if it was raining or cold, we'd rather sleep out there with Runt then in there with those people. I don't know if it was shyness or if it was fear, all I know is it was a refusal.

Beau used to always steal stuff from school, like tennis balls or down balls from other kids. He stole coloured pencils and scissors too. And we used to hide all of it outside in the junk of shit that was in the backyard. You could barely ever see the dirt out there beneath it all. All of my Grandfathers junk was out there and left to rot for years. But Beau and I didn't mind it. We used that shit to make obstacle courses, and used to time ourselves on an old stop watch we found in Grandpas stuff. I always hated losing on that shit.

We trained Runt to do it too. Even as a pup, he was always super smart, and he loved learning with us.

I remember my ma was always drunk, but at least when she was drunk, she was a happy drunk. She used to always make us get up on furniture and dance with us. She showed us off to her friends all the time, making us dance for them. Beau and I didn't mind it. Some of them would give us chocolate or stickers for it. Beau and I would always kill for chocolate. We used to feed it to Runt too. We also fed him raw eggs and our bread crusts, because our dad would always forget to buy him food. The only time Runt ever ate actual dog food is when Jaxton would buy it. I guess we were kind of similar to Runt in that way, because the only time we'd eat is when people would give us food at these parties.

There's a lot of things from my childhood that I remember, but I don't know whats real, and what I made up. I have a very faint memory of my ma dressing Beau and I in princess dresses, and putting makeup on our faces and having us dance to girl songs in front of all these people. I remember the smell of rotting musk and cigarette smoke. I remember it, because I remember the reaction from my dad when he walked into the lounge room and saw us like that- looking like little girls. He slapped my mum right across the face and dragged Beau and I into a room privately, and beat us with a belt while forcing us to take it all off.

After that, he threw us in the freezing cold shower completely naked, and washed all the makeup from our faces. In front of all these guests.

I remember crying, and wondering why no one was asking us if we were okay. I remember everyone staring at us, and at our dad, but no one saying anything. I always wondered about that- the ability to stare but not say anything. The bystander affect.

The first time my dad locked me in the washing machine was when I was 4. I'd wet the bed 3 nights in a row, and I guess he just lost it.

He grabbed me by my arm and dragged me into the laundry, where he threw me in the washing machine and locked it. He left me in there all night. I wasn't let out until Tarn found me the next morning. My dad also forced me to sleep in my piss soaked sheets, while I continued to piss on top of it, until Tarn finally changed them. I started having to wear nappies to bed again, because I was pissing the bed almost every night. Then Beau started doing it too, so Beau started getting the same punishment.

My parents never bought us jocks though. We went from nappies to just shorts or long pants.

My mum never learned. Every time my dad would leave for a few days, she'd always force Beau and I to dress up in girls clothes. We never wanted to, not after the first time when dad caught us. But she promised us it wouldn't happen again. I guess she really wanted daughters.

About a week before my dad was arrested, he and my mum had gotten into a really big fight. I remember they were both drinking- I remember being able to smell beer all through the house, because every time he'd drink he'd get sloppy and spill it everywhere.

That day, the school must've said something to my dad and mum about our appearances, and my dad blamed us. I don't know what my mum said to him- I can't remember- but whatever she did ticked him off more.

My dad burnt us with his cigarette, and yelled at us for crying. He always called us sissy's and fags, and told us we could never be real men. Then he said that only big boys get the privilege of owning a pet. That's a day I see every time I close my eyes.

My dad had grabbed his gun, and Beau instantly knew what he was gonna do. I followed them out. Beau was screaming and pleading with our dad. My mum came out too, but she was useless.

My dad held the gun up at Runt while he whimpered and cowered in front of his kennel. Beau had jumped out, trying to protect Runt from the bullet. The bullet sliced through the corner of Beau's left ear, and hit Runt in the side of his forehead.

I still remember the sound Runt and Beau made at the same time like it was yesterday. I remember my mum screaming, and rushing over to Beau, probably thinking he was dead too.

I remember being frozen in fear, while my dad stood there waiting for Beau to say something back.

The second he did, my dad rolled his eyes and walked back inside. Passed out on the couch. My mum yelled at me to grab her phone and call Tarn, so I did.

I can't remember what they did with Beau's ear. All I know is that, still, to this day his ear is forever marked. I can't really describe the way it looks, but it definitely looks like something fucked up happened to it.

I guess the police got involved once the school noticed the cigarette burns on me and the massive new deformity to Beau's ear, because a week later, they were knocking at our door.

On that day, I think a neighbor had called to complain about shouting- or that's what I was told- because my mum and dad had gotten into a big argument again.

I remember, my dad started flipping the house, searching for a beer he supposedly left somewhere. For some reason he thought my mum had hidden it. I don't know why he thought she would do that. She didn't give a fuck if he drank, but he is also the same man that runs away in the middle of the night because he thinks there's agents surrounding the house, and that aliens are controlling our phones and TVs.

Their fight ended up in the kitchen, and my dad accused her of drinking it. I remember him hitting her so hard across the face, blood spat from her mouth and splattered on the wall as she fell down.

Beau and I then ran over trying to check on mum, but he wouldn't let us. He kicked Beau away, and then he turned his attention to me. And this time, I wasn't just gonna stand there.

I started hitting him, hitting him as hard as my little malnourished fists could. But it was no use. His eyes turned dark and his face red as he knelt down on the floor and tightened his hands around my neck. Pushing me into the floor with such force, that it was nearly enough to take the wind out of me.

I couldn't tell you much about the time between then and when the police broke down the front door. But what they saw when they walked in was a house that reeked of alcohol, cigarette smoke, marijuana. Empty cocaine bags. Broken glass. Furniture everywhere. Holes in walls. A blonde woman who was passed out and bleeding from her mouth, and a grown man who was hunched over a skinny little boy, choking him until his skin turned purple.

The police tackled him off of me, or he stopped, I don't know. What I do know is that an ambulance showed up, and that the police found Beau hiding in one of the kitchen cabinets- so afraid to come out, it took them close to 20 minutes to convince him that they wouldn't hurt him. Beau was 8, and I was 6.

I remember afterwards, we were taken to a small room with a blue couch.

We were given home cooked parmi's with fat chips, and pepsi's from a small fridge. I remember vomiting into a bucket after eating everything, because it hurt my stomach so much.

I remember a woman asking us questions, same sort of questions we'd get asked at school. Asking us about our mum and dad. Asking us about our Grandma, about Aunt Tarn. Asking us about our parents friends, the parties, our clothes, the marks on our bodies. They also asked us about Beau's ear, and the dead dog body in the backyard. I remember Beau sobbing into this ladies arms when she brought up Runt. Seeing him cry made me cry too.

I don't remember much about what happened after that. I do know it took a while for our mum to convince CPS that she wasn't a threat to us. So long that we actually went into Tarn's custody- which was never changed. But our mum was allowed to live with us again eventually.

Tarn did a lot better at keeping the house clean and keeping the fridge full. She also had a lot more money then our parents did, and bought us new clothes and proper beds.

The police also let us come back to the house a few days after the big arrest so that we could bury Runt in the backyard- right by his beloved kennel.

Beau and I didn't have separate bedrooms until we were teenagers. We were too afraid to sleep alone at night. I still have nightmares.

Sometimes even smelling something familiar brings me back to those years. It's like a switch flipping in my brain and making me become a different person.

Beau and I had to regularly see therapists every week after that. Apparently the CPS people suspected we suffered all forms of abuse- sexual, physical, and emotional. Beau would also get diagnosed with Dyslexia when he was 12. But we both got a pretty even amount of diagnoses.

We were both diagnosed with PTSD, and I got diagnosed with ADHD a year after my dad was arrested. I also got diagnosed with IED, and we both started taking a lot of medication.

I didn't get diagnosed with BPD until I was 14, which is when I tried to kill myself for the first time.

Beau and I had started dealing for Tarn by that point. A lot of memories had been coming back to me, like my medication stopped working and wasn't numbing me enough anymore.

I also started drinking everyday and skipping school. I was still hanging out with friends, like Jasper and Beau and Beau's friends, but something inside me felt hopeless.

I started getting flashbacks to things I didn't want to remember. Stuff that made me feel sick. Stuff I'd buried. Things that were worse then watching my dad kill my dog or beat my mum, or stuffing me in a washing machine, and forcing Beau to turn it on when I really ticked him off. Listening to him cry from the outside. Things I didn't want to see.

I'd left school early that day, and luckily for me, no one was home. I'd taken all the pills my therapist had prescribed me and I laid on the bathroom floor waiting for it to kick in- and it did.

Next thing I remember is waking up in a hospital bed with Beau and Tarn next to me. I guess my mother had more important things to tend to- like whatever boyfriend she had at the time.

The second time I tried to kill myself was when I was 16, nearly 17. We were having a big house party and a bunch of people were there. I'd gotten really drunk and had done acid for the first time. I climbed on the roof. I was gonna jump, if it wasn't for Beau climbing up there with me and stopping me. He told me that if I jumped, he'd jumped too. And I couldn't be the reason his life ended.

I'll never forget the way everyone looked at me after that. It just made me feel worse- like I was back in that freezing cold shower.

After that, Tarn introduced me to Heroin. She told me that there was nothing better then a quick high to dull the pain.

At the time, I thought she was helping me. At the time, I didn't think that Heroin was that bad. I didn't think it could control me like it does now. I don't think Beau knew straight away that I was doing Heroin- not until the day he caught me. But what could he do to stop me? He knows I'd never listen. But Beau would never touch that shit- Meth and H. He'd never got that far- not like me.

I remember Beau lost his virginity when he was 13 to a girl the same age- her name was Josie Fletcher. I remember being so jealous that girls looked at him like that.

He dated Josie for a few months, before she found out she was pregnant and her parents forced her to get an abortion and then moved her to a different school. After that, he just started sleeping with whoever.

I think that's the difference between Beau and I. He uses sex as an escape, while I use drugs- hard drugs. Both are addictions, but only one causes destruction.

I didn't lose my virginity until after I started experimenting with drugs- but before H. I barely remember it, but it was at one of those parties.

I remember Cipher had brought Dare's sister to the party that night. Honestly, maybe it wasn't even Yana- I don't fucking know. But I thought it was, and I thought Yana had brought a couple friends with her.

Beau ended up hooking up with a blonde one named Mia- I think. The one I liked had brown hair and hazel eyes. Her name was Grace Galecki, and was only a year younger then me.

I don't remember the lead up, or pretty much anything we did. But I remember waking up the next morning with her in my bed. Both naked, wondering what the fuck happened while a massive headache pierced through my brain.

Sometime after that, Beau and I started dealing for Tarn a lot more seriously, and I fucking loved it. The money was amazing, and I loved the adrenaline too. Not knowing if I might get caught or not.

The parties were the perfect place to do it, before Tarn's strip club really started to blow up. I fucking loved sneaking all my underage friends into that- not that Tarn would care.

I remember the first night I got Cipher, Brownie, Dare and Archie to see a private stripper. Those were some crazy years. It's probably a good thing that I can't remember much of them.

But it wasn't long after my 18th birthday that my life went to shit. Like I said, I can't remember much from back then- and this night was no different.

All I know is that I got into a fight with Joseph Trader, and shit got ugly fast. I know I did some damage- more then him. Enough for him to end up in the hospital, and for me to be charged with Aggravated Assault. If I could take that night back I would, but you can't take back something you don't remember doing.

While I was in prison, going through withdrawals- feeling like every second of everyday might be my last- I made a pact with myself. I wanted to do better, be better. I didn't want to be like my father, and I was scared shitless I might see the old cunt in prison with me. Luckily I never did, but the fear was enough for me to power through.

I got clean, started straitening up. I was working out every chance I got, and trying to earn money on the inside. I got a tattoo on my back and one on my arm to honour Beau and Runt. I was doing better, feeling better. No medications, no drugs, no outside influence.

Honestly, I liked jail more then I ever liked being on the outside. It felt more like home then any other house I'd ever stepped in.

The only thing I hated was not getting to see my family. I honestly thought more people would visit me more often. I only ever really heard from Beau and Cipher. Jasper visited me a few times with Jordan, like on my birthday. Tarn came in maybe once every few months. But if it weren't for Beau and Cipher, I'd have been completely alone.

Leading up to my release, I was excited. I wanted to get out. I was ready. I thought, with all this progress I'd made, I could do better. I was gonna get a job, something I could really focus my mind on. I was gonna stay away from the drug life- no dealing, no receiving. I didn't want to be one of Tarn's puppets anymore, It wasn't worth it.

For the first time in my life, it felt like I was worth living. It felt like maybe I was wrong, maybe I'm nothing like my father. Maybe I am a good person, without the bad influence. Maybe I was stronger then I always thought I was.

It was a good feeling- great in fact. But you know what they say, all good things must come to an end.. eventually.

I just wish I had a better understanding of my childhood, or my parents. I wish I remembered more then I do. When I'm sober, I can't remember anything. Nothing about my life. Not until someone flicks a switch- a sound, a smell, a familiar vibe or person. Then suddenly I'm flooded with memories. I think that's why I do drugs and drink. Because at least then, during those moments of memories, I wont remember remembering.

I should be honest with Fiona, about dealing. But after everything, after laying out the few memories I have of why I am the way I am on a silver platter- can't that just be enough?

Fiona Glass

Hearing it- everything. His story, the real him. I broke down. So many horrible things, to such innocent children. I couldn't stand knowing someone did that to them- those two beautiful little boys.

"I'm sorry." I say, apologizing.

"For what?" he asks, still shaking from his own story.

"Everything- all of it." I admit, placing both my hands on his cheeks. "You didn't deserve any of it."

"Neither did you." he responds softly.

I kiss him, a sweet, sweet kiss. "We can do it Link, together."

"It's- not easy, Fi."

"I never said it was easy. If it was easy, everyone would do it."

"You don't get it, Fi." he sobs with a whimper.

"Get what?" what else could there possibly be for me to understand?

Silence. A deafening, life threatening, ear-aching silence. A silence, soon broken up by the sound of Link's boiled tears.

"Link-" I pause, fearful of my own question. "Have you started dealing again?"

He hesitates for a moment, his jaw shaking. "No." he finally responds.

A sigh of utter relief exhaling my body.

"F-Fi." he speaks, grabbing my face gently with his cold hands. "I- I need something."

"What?"

"I c-can't do this on my own, Fi."

"You don't have to, Link. I'm here. I promise, I'm here."

He's shaking profusely. His entire body absolutely freezing.

"I need you to get me something."

"What is it?"

He hesitates again. Now fearful of *his* question.

"There's a package.. beneath our bed. I- I need it." he pleads.

A package?

"What kind of package?"

"The kind of package that can.. h-help me. Please, Fi." he begs. His lips turning dry and purple.

"Okay." I say, standing up slowly.

I entered our bedroom, and looked beneath the dark bed. Spotless, beside a singular square box wrapped in children's birthday paper. A blue backdrop with swans and pink polka dots. A yellow ribbon tying it all together.

Holding it in my hands, I see nothing out of the ordinary.

Link basically ripped it from my hands the second I sat beside him. His entire body writhing for whatever is hidden beneath the innocent paper.

Grabbing the yellow ribbon, he unties the bow and with it, falls the wrapping paper. Like a magical mechanism. Revealing a square case inside.

He flicks it open- a small baggy with white powder, a silver spoon, a red lighter, and a syringe.

"Link-" I say, interrupted by his frantic focus.

"Please- Fi. I- I promise it'll be the last time-"

"Link-"

"I promise! I promise, Fi! Please!" he begs. Like a child begging their mother for a cookie off the shelf.

I don't respond. Instead, I simply watch as he empties a small amount of the white substance onto the silver spoon. Placing the red lighter beneath it, boiling it from the bottom up. The entire time, our eyes never make contact.

I should stop him. I know that. But I also know that no matter what I do, nothing I say will change the way he feels right now. Not while he's like this.

He uses the syringe to suck up the thick liquid substance he'd cooked, before searching his inner elbow for a vein. A singular tear dripping from my sunken eye as he jabs himself. His eyes rolling to the back of his head as it enters his system.

I kept waiting for him to see me, to notice me. Awaiting the second he'd see the water streaming down my cheeks, and hug me. The longer I waited, the less I understood hope.

Finally he did. He looked at me, a small smile in his eyes. I'd never seen someone look so peaceful, so satisfied. Regardless of how I was feeling.

He leaned in, kissing me. I should've pulled away, forced him to address my blatant distress. But I didn't. I don't know why.

Lying on the floor, kissing the man I love. Taking off our clothes, and feeling our skin entering each others atoms.

I wonder what it felt like for him. I wonder if he felt good, because I know I didn't.

We woke up the next morning naked on the floor. I was laying with my head against his chest. I'd been awake for a while, but I kept my eyes closed because I knew he was awake. And opening my eyes meant that I'd have to face the music. Pretend like last night never happened, or start another fight.

When I did open my eyes, I was nearly blinded by the bright daylight of the windows beaming from outside.

Link had been playing with my hair for a while now. I looked up slowly, and before I could say anything, he kissed me.

"How'd you sleep?" he asks, a smile almost as bright as the beaming sky.

"Okay. You?" I ask.

"Perfect."

Perfect. Okay. Does that mean it's over? Does that mean we can move on?

Is he proud of me for giving him what he wanted? Did it make him love me more, knowing he could trust me?

"Can I ask you a question?"

"Ask away." he responds happily.

"If you were in a room full of people, who would you choose?"

"I'd choose you." he responds quickly, as if it were obvious.

"But what if I wasn't in the room? Then who would you choose?" I further ask.

He looks at me softly. That damn smile peering back at me. His eyes fixated on mine as he brushed my dark hair behind my ear with his hand, and rests it against my warm cheek.

"I'd still choose you." he finally responds.

Perfect, perfect answer. Perfect. Perfect.

I sit up swiftly, looking out to the radiant sun. The blanket covering us both slowly falling from my body.

"What's wrong?" he pries, still smiling up at me.

I debate it, for a moment. Do I dare ask more questions, to dig deeper, if it means ruining his perfect morning?

I should be happy, I should be satisfied. He gave me what I want, everything I've been asking for. He let me in. But still, there's something missing. There's still something I yearn for. Something I know is there, something he can't yet say out loud. Something I need.

"Can I ask you something else?"

"Yeah." he responds kindly, sitting up to meet my eyes.

A delay of my inconsistent thinking. Shall I lead on with a regretful conscience?

"Were you honest last night, about everything?" I ask, trying to ensure my voice sounds calm with exact.

"What?" he asks, his face dropping.

"I mean- I believe you, and everything you told me. But you told me everything, right? Nothing you forgot, or left out?"

His face dropping further. His glazed blue eyes bouncing across my face as his mouth aligns with his thoughts, before blurting them out loud furiously.

"Are you fucking serious, Fi?"

"Link, I-"

"Do you seriously still not trust me? After everything we've been through- I gave you what you wanted last night." he continues with a sharp tone.

"I know, I'm-" I begin, but he stands abruptly, shaking his head while hurrying to put his loose shorts on.

I want to stand too- and rush to fix the mess I created, but I can't. I can't move. Frozen and naked and shivering on the floor as he towers above me with fury.

"You know-" he ejects, still shaking his head with annoyance. "Have you ever thought that.. maybe the problem isn't with me?"

"What do you mean?" I ask softly.

"Maybe- Maybe this distrust you have for me- maybe it comes from some kind of fucked up wire in *your* brain, not mine!" he conspires cruelly, pointing his stern finger hard against my forehead. "You know, you're- you're not perfect, Fi!"

"I know."

"So- So why- why do you always assume that I am to blame? Why am *I* always having to explain myself to you?"

"I just-"

"What!?" he shouts, inching closer to my fragile presence.

My chin quivers. "I just want this to be... perfect."

He nods. "It was- It was, until you decided that you still weren't happy with the shit I've told you."

He's getting worked up, pacing and mumbling to himself. I'm trying to stop him, trying to apologise. Trying to fix myself and correct my mistakes. But he's not listening. He's not listening to my sorry's, because I've upset him.

"Link, I'm sorry-"

"There's probably still a little voice in your head that thinks that everyone is just gonna leave you- just like your mother! Or maybe you think I'm gonna disappear- still be here, but disappear- just like your dad and your brother-"

"No, no, I don't think that-"

"But I'm not them! I'm not a clone of your junkie mother, or your fucked up father!"

"I know-"

"- And that's not my fault, Fi. It's not my fault, that your parents fucked you up inside! Okay! It's not my fault that you refuse to trust me!"

"Link, It's not like that. Please!" I say, trying to hold myself together. Trying to get him to understand.

"So what Is It like, then? Huh?" he begs, his voice shaking. "Because I'm not a bad person, Fi."

"I know!"

"And I don't mean to do the wrong thing, or say the wrong things-"

"I know, Link! I promise, I know!" I plead. Begging for his forgiveness. Begging to forget and move on. "I trust you, I do!"

"I've never cared about anyone like this, Fi. I've never shared as much as I have- I've never loved anyone like you!"

"Link, It's okay- It's okay, I swear. Let's just forget it."

"You'll never be happy, Fi. Not with me. Not with me-"

"That's not true! That's not true, Link! I am happy with you. I am!" I say, finally standing from my fetal position and rushing to hug him tightly. Hoping he hears me when I say it.

I felt so awful, accusing him like I did. I knew I shouldn't have said anything. I should've trusted my gut when I thought it. I should've listened to myself when I said to keep my mouth shut.

I never meant to hurt him. I never mean to hurt anyone, but I always seem to. Always saying the wrong things. Maybe Link is right, maybe I am the problem. Maybe I am fucked up inside from my mother leaving. Maybe I am fucked up from watching my father slowly disintegrate during my childhood. Maybe I am fucked up from having to raise the kid my mother built. Maybe it is me, maybe I am the problem.

10

Chapter Ten- Midnight

Fiona Glass

It's been 2 days since the night of Beau's party, and it feels like everything has changed. Even if everything looks the same, it all feels so incredibly different.

That night, we made a pact. We agreed that Link would free himself, with my help. And Link promised me that I'd never have to work the private rooms again. I wasn't sure how he'd convince Tarn to go against her own decision, but so far it's worked.

Like I said, everything has felt different since. Sometimes I wake up, believing I've done it too, and thinking to myself how easy it would be if I did just do it. Maybe it would rid me of the everlasting jarred state my heart has been in since that night.

I've been trying to get Link a job, but everything I suggest he says no to. He thinks no one will ever hire him again because of his time served.

I don't know where he's been getting all of his money from. I guess he and Tarn have some kind of deal for him to pay it all back- but I don't know how he'll ever do that if he refuses to look at the jobs I pick for him.

Putting Blue to bed was hard tonight, I don't know why. I felt sorry every time I looked at him. Link thinks its strange that I still tuck Blue into his bed, considering he's a teenager now. But he doesn't get it. He should, considering his mother was never there to do it when he was young, just like Blue never received that affection either.

Before my mother left, she was good at the little things. When we were alone, she was calm, almost like a child stuck in an adults body. She never read me bedtime stories, but she never failed to kiss me goodnight.

I couldn't tell you what it was that made her snap, the thing that made her leave and become the person she is today. But before any of that had happened, I could understand why my dad had fallen in love with her. She was always fucking crazy, and she knew how to get under peoples skin, but she was human.

"Have you been doing okay? How's school?" I ask Blue, knowing I wont get a response.

"What about Mrs Keen, has her work been helping?" I ask, receiving a small smile.

You don't realize how important words are, until that ability is taken away from someone. I wish I knew who Blue's friends were at school. Who his favourite teacher is. What his favourite colour is. But I'll never know that, not unless one day he randomly decides to start speaking.

The longer the years become, it's starting to feel like he may never reach that point. I don't want to lose hope, for him. But at some point, I guess, I have to be realistic. Maybe Blue will never be completely normal.

I needed a drink tonight. Tomorrow I have work at the club, and I needed a drink to get me through the night. Just a small glass of whiskey to carry me through. But a strange revaluation hit my body as I took my first sip. A flash of fire from the fireplace, and suddenly, a small figure was knelt down and embracing it's warmth.

"Hello?" I ask, unsure of who it could be. Dirty blonde hair, body of a child.

I slowly approach, waiting for some kind of response.

"Hello?" I ask again, as I kneel down behind the child.

The second my knee hits the ground, she turns around, and I immediately recognize who she is. It's Skye Sallow.

"Skye?" I say, almost out of breath.

"Hey Fi Fi." she smiles softly.

In shock, I have no other words. Skye Sallow is dead, but somehow, Skye Sallow is sitting before me, feeling the same warmth of fire that I feel against my skin. Real skin.

"What are you-" I begin to ask, interrupted by her childlike tone.

"Don't be so shocked- You couldn't forget about me, even if you tried."

"I don't think I ever would." I respond, unsteady with my words. "Why are you here?"

She sighs, turning her body more to face me. I see the bracelet we shared on her wrist.

"You're not wearing yours?" she asks.

Clearing my throat- "No. I gave it to my little brother- he needed it more then me."

She smiles. "So he came back- I guess that's a wish come true, right?"

I smile awkwardly. I don't know if this is exactly what I wished for.

"What is it?" she asks.

"Nothing." I respond, and she giggles.

"I guess you've gotta be careful what you wish for."

I smile. "Skye?" I begin to ask.

"Yeah?"

"Is this real?" feeling tears forming in my left eye.

Slowly, Skye reaches for my hand, holding it. I can feel it. Her skin on mine. It's real. I can feel the blood beneath her layers. I can feel the bones in each of her fingers. It's real, she's real.

I look back up, connecting my eyes with hers- but I'm distracted by the bruising circulating her neck, bruising that wasn't there before. Bruising from a tight rope.

"Of course it's real." she responds, almost offended. Becoming even more upset by my reaction to her wound. "What?" she asks, touching it with her other hand. "Do you think it's ugly?" she continues, beginning to cry.

Her cries, turning into a dry sob.

My heart beating faster with every tear she sheds. Her sobs becoming louder, and louder, and louder, until suddenly.. I'm awake.

I fell asleep, by the fire. My hand- close enough that I rip it away in pain.

Beside me, an empty bottle of whiskey and a spilled glass. Clenching my raw hand, I sit up. A pounding headache ripping through my brain as I take in my surroundings. My eyes feeling droopy and filled with toxins. Feeling every bone in my body rubbing against my joints as I turn to see Link, asleep on the couch in his boxers. Scratch marks on his neck.

Was I dreaming?

Suddenly, Blue walks out from the bathroom, passing me and heading toward the kitchen. He grabs out a loaf of bread from the pantry and places two pieces inside the toaster.

I stand, wobbling as I walk closer to my little brother.

"Did you have a good sleep?" I ask, cuddling my body tighter in my bedtime robe as I shiver.

With hesitation, Blue turns around, giving me a small smile.

"That's good." I respond.

Thinking to myself about what day it is. It must be a school day, because Blue is wearing his uniform.

How long was I asleep for? The ulcers in my mouth feel as if they're ripping as I yawn a loud yawn.

My eyes drift to see the time on the microwave. It's 8:05am.

Suddenly, a vibrating ring grabs our attention. My phone is on the floor by the empty bottle. It felt like I was walking across a mountain just to reach it. It's Cipher.

"Hello?" I answer.

"You need to come to dads." he demands angrily. Loud screams from my father in the background.

"What?" I say, still not fully awake.

"I've been dealing with him all week- it's your turn."

"I need to take Blue to school-"

"I'll take him- just get here!" he demands, hanging up the phone.

Fuck me, he needs a nap.

I turn to Blue, who's buttering his toast. "Cipher's gonna take you to school- okay?"

Blue nods.

For some reason, I feel like he's upset with me. What did I do now?

"Hey, are you okay?" I ask, approaching him again. "Only a few months before your birthday- how about you make me a presents list during your lunch break today, okay?" I request, placing my hand on his shoulder.

Finally, a real smile.

I didn't bother waking Link before Blue and I left. Honestly I'd been avoiding any kind of real interaction with him for a while.

Driving felt like I was still in a dream. Like, you know when your dreaming and you're trying to hit someone, but for some reason you're not hitting hard enough. It was kind of like that, but with driving.

Life has felt so different since that night. It's like I'm watching my life from above- no control, no say. No dreams, no wishes. I wonder If I'll ever get to explain that feeling. Knowing that all roads are slowly closing ahead. I wonder If I'll ever get to outlive it.

I believe it is our childhoods that depict whether this earth is worth our love or not. Not the earth itself, but the beating heart it provides.

Cipher was already outside when Blue and I approached in my car. He didn't waste a second before rushing up to greet Blue, with a scowl in my direction.

"Don't look at me like that." I demand quietly, as he pats Blue's shoulder.

"Like what?" he asks with stupidity. As if he's oblivious to the off-putting look he's giving me.

"Like you hate me." I respond, crossing my arms and watching as Blue drifts off- heading to check if there's anything in dads mailbox.

"I don't hate you." he responds quickly. "But I hate your father." he adds.

"*Our* father." I answer. Acknowledged with a snarl.

In the corner of my eye, I see Blue find something interesting hidden beneath the stack of whatever organizations my dad had been ignoring.

"What's that Blue?" I ask kindly.

Slowly, Blue approaches to where Cipher and I stand, his eyes remaining glued to the blue envelope he has gripped between his finger tips. As he steps closer, I lean over to read who the envelope is addressed to.

'Baby Blue Glass' is scribbled on the front in red ink, with no postal address.

Cipher and I share a concerned look as Blue hastily rips the back of the envelope open. Revealing a letter inside. The same red ink and scribbled writing, but I couldn't see exactly what was written.

"What is it? Who's it from?" I ask, trying to get a better look, but Blue snaps the letter away and shoves it quickly into his school backpack.

His suspicious response making me second guess whether I should've let him open it- especially before he has to go to school.

"Go wait in my car." Cipher instructs, waiting for Blue to enter the passenger seat and close the door before he turns back to me with almost an angered whisper. "Dad didn't sleep last night, but he's been drowning his morning in booze since 4am, so it shouldn't be much longer."

"What about his mood?" I ask. "Should I have brought my armour?" I joke dryly.

"Honestly, probably wouldn't have hurt." Cipher says, turning to approach his car.

"Wait." I say, stopping him. "Have you spoken to Yana?" I ask with slight hesitation.

"Why?"

"Just curious- don't you miss Alina?" I question. Though, clearly it was the wrong choice of wording, because Cipher's expression quickly hardens to his scowl.

Approaching his ute with a slam, before driving away.

Great. Good chat.

Link Jones

Fiona's been at her dads all morning.

The first cigarette of the morning is always the best, better then after a feed. It dulls my headache for a bit- nothing like a joint. But nothing could compare to the dull of a needle.

I always fucking hated needles as a kid. I still hate them. Hate putting them in my skin. But the feeling after is worth a million of them. All of my fears are suddenly whisked away, all my pain. Nothing can dull that thought. The crave.

I barely had the chance to enjoy my morning cigarette, before a loud ring burst between my eardrums. My phone was ringing. It was Beau.

"Hello?" I greet, with a groan.

My eyes sensitive to the window light.

"Link?" he responds, sounding disoriented.

"Beau?"

"Where are you?" he asks sternly.

"Home, why-"

"Did you hear?"

"H- Hear what?" I hiccup.

"Trader's dead."

Everything is frozen. My breath, my heart. My mind, my body, my soul. Time, space. All of it, frozen in place.

Can you feel that? Can you feel it? It.. it's like I'm burning. I'm on fire. I... I can't see. Fuck, I dropped my phone. Can can you, can you feel it?

Beau is repeating my name, I can hear it. Like a whistle in the distance. But I can't react, because everything is frozen. I need- I need something. I can feel everything. I can feel everything. I can feel everything. I need something. I need something!

My entire body is on fire. I'm sweating profusely. Ripping off my shirt, I rush into my bedroom, searching for that box. I can't breathe. My heart- it's on my chest. I can feel it. I can feel everything.

Where is it? Where is it? Where is it? Where is it?

I found it! I found it beneath my bed. Fuck, I can't breathe beneath the sweat. I can't breathe at all. I need it. I need it.

I open it. Fuck. Fuck. Fuck. Fuck. Fuck. Fuck. Fuck. FUCK.

It- it's empty. There's nothing left. Nothing. Nothing. Nothing. Nothing. Nothing. Nothing. NOTHING!

I'm hurting myself. I can feel it. Everything. It's all my fault. It's all my fault!

I- I- I'm.. I'm at Beau's. I walked here, I- I think.

Walking into that house, seeing ma, it's like living with a ghost. She's there, she's breathing, she's talking to me, but she ain't real. She ain't the ma I know. She ain't the ma I grew up with. Some kind of clone or demon that's infested her body, waiting for the perfect moment to attack. But I ain't gonna be there when that happens.

Beau Jones

I called Link. The second I found out that Joseph Trader was dead, I called him. He deserved to know.

Now he's here, basically breaking down the front door as he barrels in. No shirt, one sock and no shoes. His entire body sweating. Was he drunk? Had he relapsed again? What the fuck is happening?

Cart and Silas and all their boys are here, sitting in the lounge room drinking with Jasper. All standing the second Link walks through the front door.

My ma and I heard the commotion from the entertainment area, we heard his voice.

"Link?" Jasper greets, approaching Link cautiously as he stumbles.

"Link!" I interject sternly, directing his attention to myself.

"Where is Tarn!?" he demands, slurring his words.

"Hey- hey," I say calmly. "How about we go talk somewhere, privately?" I offer, carefully placing my hand on his shoulder.

He pushes me away. Pushes me hard.

"Don't fucking touch me!" he shouts, and Tarn sprints into the room.

She'd been having a smoke beneath the fresh air of the backyard. Cart rushes over too, ready to contain Link.

"What the hell is goin' on!?" Tarn demands as she assesses the situation.

"Boo-boo.." my ma comforts, attempting to bring Link in for a hug, but he refuses. shoving her too.

"Hey!" I shout, as ma's exterior begins to crumble.

Aunt Tarn gently pushes me back, as she steps forward.

"Link, talk to me!" she demands.

"I- I need something." he sniffles.

"You need what, baby?"

"I- I.." he stutters. "I- I need- I need a little.. courage."

"Courage?"

"Link- Link!" I interject. "Is this about Joey- Is that what the fuck is happening?"

Tarn turns to me, appearing enraged. "You told him about Trader?"

"Of course I fucking did- he deserved to know!" I protest.

"You shouldn't have done that-"

"What you- you don't think I can handle it?" Link chortles. "You don't think I deserve to know that I killed someone!?"

"What?" Tarn exasperates.

"You didn't want me to know the truth- You didn't want me to know.. that I'm a fucking murderer!?" he repeats. His voice cracking as his anger turns to somber.

"Boo Boo, please-" Ma pleads, attempting to touch him again.

"Don't fucking touch me!" he shouts, getting in her fragile face. "Don't ever fucking touch me again!"

"Linkoln!" Tarn shouts, attempting to pull Link away, but instead he pushes closer.

"What the *fuck* are you crying about!? Huh, what the fuck are you crying about!" he continues, Cart attempting to gently pull him away, as Ma is backed into a wall. "I know what you are- I know what you did! What you let him do! You- You-" he shouts illiterately, barely forming sentences.

"Boo Boo-" she weeps.

"You did this! You did this, ma! But you still love me, don't ya ma? Don't you!?"

"Yes!" she shouts beneath her drowning tears, covering her face with her hands.

"Yeah, you love me. You love me- you fucking love me!? You love the thing you created? Th-The thing I have to live with!?" he continues, pointing at his forehead. "Do you get it too?" he adds, now ripping Ma's hands away to point at her forehead.

"Alright-" Cart announces, before more aggressively pulling Link away from Ma, as he continues to scream in her face.

"Link! Link, look at me! Look at me!" Tarn shouts, pulling Link's face. Forcing him to look at her.

While I slip into the shadows of a corner.

"What do you want, huh? Speed? Dope?" Aunt Tarn begs with desperation. Cracking between the shell of her hard exterior, and the scared little girl within.

My Ma, falling to the floor and sobbing into her knees. Unable to look at Link. Unable to look at the boy she raised.

Suddenly, Link stops fighting against Cart's restraints. His chin quivering as he breaks down. His entire body falling limp, as he plummets to his knees. His face hidden in the floor.

A sob I didn't recognize, as he looks back up at Tarn, pleading for his courage. She obliges. Trying to contain her shakes as she gestures for Cart to grab him a package from one of the kitchen cabinets. A zip lock bag, full of Heroin.

A shared look between Cart and Tarn, one without words. Both hesitant to whether they should do it or not. Cart, clearly not wanting to. He's known us all our lives, watched us grow up. He was there in the room when we were both born. Now? Now he stands before Link, as he pleads on his hands and knees for the one thing our dad also fought so hard to obtain.

With reluctance, he hands it to Link. And Link, slowly rises. His tears coming to a quick halt as he looks at Cart. Cart's eyes filled with an oppressed stream. Before looking at Tarn, with a neck so tense she can't even breathe.

"I-I'm sorry. I'm sorry." Link sniffles, before turning around, and walking back out the front door.

Fear, silence. I'm frozen.

Mrs Rachel Keen

The first time I met Blue Glass was 6 years ago. Back then he was only a kid, now hes a teenager. Regardless of the fact he now goes to High School, we still schedule appointments around his classes. Crossing the road to meet me in the same spot as always. My office.

When Emma Zane, Blue's social worker, first handed me his file I just about gave it back. A file like his, is something you don't often see within my profession. A whole lot of unanswered questions, and statements with large question marks at the end of them. No facts or certainties. No one knew who Blue Glass was. No one knew anything about him besides his name and birthday. Nothing. Not a clue.

The police had already established that Blue had suffered years of physical and sexual abuse due to the results of his medical evaluation. And based on his blood tests, his body had normalised the effects of secondhand drug exposure, so much so that it altered his brain permanently.

The biggest question I had to solve once I was assigned Blue's case, was whether I believed he chose to not speak, or if he was born without the ability. Based on the very limited information I had on Blue, at first glance, most people would assume that Blue was never taught to speak- or that he didn't understand how.

It wasn't until I met with Blue for the first time, that I started to think otherwise. The way he responded to Fiona, on his first day of school. The assurance and comfort he sought from her, even though, by that point, he had no idea who she was. Possibly, because Fiona was the first person he'd ever met that allowed him to feel any kind of emotion besides fear.

If you think about it, how is a child supposed to recognise and identify specific feelings, like happiness, sadness, anger, hunger, exhaustion, when they have not been taught to process it.

From the first few months of his life, immediately taught that a single sound from his little mouth might result in the violent impact of screams from another person, or even physical harm. Having never been taught to communicate hunger or tiredness through a vocal cry, resulting in the inability to express as much with actual words.

He'd become accustom to the sensation of physical harm, as much as the average person becomes accustom to the sensation of happiness. While most toddlers cry for food, and are often rewarded with such, he learned to dispose himself of the grumble of hunger. And doing so from such a young age, makes it near impossible for his body to grow to understand that a grumbling stomach means that you are hungry.

While most parents battle to have their child's first word be either 'mum' or 'dad', he was surrounded by people who battled against his influence to speak or do anything at all.

That first day, after Fiona and her family left, Blue sat in my office fiddling with that bracelet she gave him. That allowed me to understand that he took that bracelet from Fiona, because he understood that she was offering it to him. He understood why she offered it to him as well. Meaning that unlike a toddler, who simply would've taken the bracelet to feel it in their palms, before disposing of it once they realized it didn't make sounds or cause a sensation of happiness. Blue understood that his sister was giving it to him to offer a feeling other then fear. He probably didn't understand which feeling that would be, but he was eager to experiment.

Information like that, assisted in my diagnosis as well. Because Blue did not suffer from a Neurodevelopmental Disability, such as Autism, or ADHD. He did not suffer Receptive Language Disorder, and I'd later discover through his quick learning improvement, that he also did not suffer from a Developmental Language Disorder. There was a possibility of Childhood Apraxia of Speech, but never once did Blue attempt to form a singular word or sentence. And he did not suffer from Aphasia, because to everyone's doubt, Blue did not suffer any form of physical brain damage.

Blue had great receptive language abilities, he was just simply never given the courtesy of expression. Which is why I diagnosed him with Selective Mutism, PTSD, and Anxiety Disorder- due to Childhood Trauma. I believe Blue knows how to speak, he just chooses not to. Because for more years of his life then not, Blue was taught that speaking is not okay for him. He was forbidden from it. And ultimately, it may be one of the only things I can not fix. Not unless Blue chooses to fix it.

Most of our appointments consist of cognitive learning. I had the tough job of bringing him up to speed with other children his age- when it came to his age-expected development of learning. Luckily for the both of us, Blue was eager to learn, once he understood that he could trust me.

I realised early on that Blue was extremely receptive to a reward system. So with every piece of homework I send him off with, he receives stickers- no matter how well he did. When we're together, I use affirmative language, as well as positive body language. Blue also learns best when he is physically shown how to do something, he prefers to be a mimic.

For the first week after meeting Blue, I spent a lengthy course of days creating cue cards for him. Cue cards of his family, animals, structures, objects, colours. And I would allow Blue to decide what it is he wanted to learn for the next two weeks. Because Blue deserved the options of choice, as that had been taken away from him for so long.

He was hesitant at first, in picking. He displayed great fear for a long time. Constantly worried that I was tricking him, and that I'd suddenly change my mind and take away the kindness I'd displayed. But I was patient, because that was all he needed.

The first word he chose to work on, was 'Fiona'. He picked out her school photo with her name on the front, and decided that she would be his first assignment. We started off with understanding our emotions.

I have a wall of emotions in my office, and after explaining all of them to him, I gave him the opportunity to point at the emotion he feels when he thinks of Fiona. I expected him to pick 'safe' or 'happy', but instead, he picked 'love'.

For the next two weeks we'd learn how to write and spell Fiona's name. Studying each individual letter, and putting them together. I tried to get him to read her name out loud, but he refused. But that was okay, I was happy with the progress.

I could tell early on that he was a child that was eager to understand. Some children love learning, some children hate it. Blue loves it. And regardless of his terrible upbringing, he was incredibly intelligent.

The next word he chose was 'Dad'. A picture of his father that I'd asked Cipher to print for me. We worked on both 'Dad' and 'Denny', and I took the opportunity to explain to him the concept of nicknames. Denny is short for Denis, and how the word 'Dad' is reserved for only Blue, Cipher and Fiona, when in reference to Denny. When picking the emotion he feels for Denny, he also picked 'love'.

Next, of course, he picked Cipher. I was intrigued by the fact he chose to start off with three people. I was also interested in his choice of picking 'love' for each of them, when describing the way they make him feel. As I did not yet believe that Blue understood the concept of love. I think he knew what it meant, and he knew that you're supposed to love the people you are related to, but I don't think he understood that feeling. I didn't think he had the ability to identify when he feels love for someone. He just knows that it is expected.

Next he wanted to work on colours, and to my surprise, he didn't start with blue. But instead, he started with yellow. Working on the spelling, the exact way that they are written. Also identifying objects that are yellow, such as the sun, or a duck, through some colour prints I made.

He adamantly avoided any 'Mother' related topics. And I noticed that when he would draw pictures in class, he would always draw Fiona, Cipher, Denny and himself. Never would he include his Mother in family pictures. Maybe because he'd never seen a real photograph with the five of them together. But often, when colouring in picture stencils I'd give him, he would always make the women in the pictures have brown hair and blue eyes. Fiona has brown eyes, so I knew he wasn't drawing her. He was drawing his mother.

I also discovered through our focus on colours, that he fears the colour purple. I don't know why, but it makes him uncomfortable. I sacrificed the colour, knowing that one day we would have to tackle it, but not while he is still developing his trust.

When we started diving deeper into emotions and identifying them, Blue chose to start with 'sad'. I explained that sometimes when we are sad, we cry. I explained that I feel sad when people are unkind to me. I asked Blue what makes him feel sad sometimes, and he searched through my cue cards until he found the one of his mother.

When we started discussing 'fear', I asked him to find things that make him feel scared. He found the cue cards that displayed 'fire', 'waist belt', 'straw', 'spoon', 'shoe lace', 'purple', and the 'angry' emotion.

Every time we dive into these emotions, I always give him the opportunity to explain to me why these things make him feel that way. But never has he taken it.

Regardless of how much he's grown, I do believe that Blue fears one day all of this may come to an end. Fearful that one day his mother will return and force him back into that state where food is not a courtesy. Where talking, crying, or pleading, results in physical punishment. And where freedom does not exist.

Today I met with Blue again, like we always do. He chooses to see me during his lunch breaks sometimes, usually when he's finished some of the homework I'd given him. On this particular day, Blue seemed off. He seemed sad.

I tried talking to him, asking how he was feeling. To my surprise, he pointed to the 'fear' emotion on my wall. I tried asking him what he was scared of. Whether it was a person, a thing. He searched through my cue cards until he found the one, 'Mother'.

"Why are you scared, did something happen?" I ask, to which I received no response.

His face was different. It was like he was trying so hard to smile, that his face looked dull. He'd never mastered the skill of faking it.

I tried giving him some words of advice, about things he could do whenever he feels scared. I tried reminding him that he was safe, and that his mother would never have the opportunity to take him away again. He nodded, though I don't think he was truly listening.

Cipher Glass

In all honesty, I've been trying to reach Yana since she told me she was pregnant. Ever since I moved back into dads, it's brought me back to a place I haven't been since school. The way he drinks, the temptation everywhere, it's unbearable to ignore. It's easier to drown my sorrows, and getting plastered is the only way I have enough confidence to call Yana.

Only problem is, every time I've tried calling her, she's never responded. Not to my calls, my voicemails, or my texts. She probably knows I'm drinking again, maybe that's why. Or maybe she's still pissed at me for walking out.

What she doesn't understand is that I just needed time to think. Another baby comes with a lot of fucking problems and I just needed a second to think without having to deal with her disappointed eye peering at me from every corner of the house.

I fucking miss Alina. I miss her smile, her laugh, her little voice. I miss when Yana used to let me pick her outfits, or when I'd let her pick movies to watch every Friday night. I miss being around them, and it's taking everything inside me to not just show up to the house uninvited.

I was planning on asking Blue about that envelope during the car ride to school, but I sort of got side tracked in my own head and by the time I remembered to ask, we were already at school.

I promised Blue when I dropped him off that I'd pick him up later, maybe take him to see Alina, and he sort of looked happier at that promise.

All day at work, all I could think about was my kid, and the kids I'd soon have. I was trying to think of all the ways I could say sorry without Yana slamming the door in my face. I know I've done her wrong a lot of times, but I'm only human.

Around lunchtime, I got a call from Blue's school asking me to pick him up. Apparently Blue got into some fight with these other dickheads at school. The principle wouldn't tell me much else- reckons he preferred to talk to me in person.

I called Fiona on the way to the school, but she was too busy with whatever shit dad was doing to meet me there. All I was hoping is Blue's teachers wouldn't notice I'd been drinking.

When his principle told me Blue threw the first punch, I couldn't believe it. Blue wouldn't hurt a fly. Then he made some sly remark about how they only knew the other kids' side of the story, because Blue doesn't speak. That shit nearly left that old cunt with a black eye. He's lucky Blue was sitting a few feet away.

Anyway, they suspended him for the rest of the week. I'm sure Fiona will be back up here once I tell her that.

I didn't really know how to handle the situation once we got back to the car. I obviously couldn't ask Blue what happened, and I'm not really good at reading how people are feeling. I think Fiona would probably be better at handling this then me.

As we closed the doors and sat inside my car, my phone chimed as I received a message. I thought maybe it would be Fiona, after giving herself time to process what I actually told her on the way there, but it wasn't Fi. It was Maddy.

I haven't spoken to her since that party at Beau and Jasper's. Didn't think I had to. I only have her number because she put it in my phone after that night, told me to call if I ever needed to talk again.

And honestly, maybe I do.

Fiona Glass

My dad finally fell asleep. He mumbles in his sleep. He talks a lot about Ronny and mum. He talks about Blue too, sometimes. Sometimes he cries in his sleep too. Jitters and jolts.

I'd been texting Link all day, wondering how he was. It sort of made me nervous, the fact he hadn't been answering. Maybe he was mad at me for leaving without saying anything. Or maybe something bad happened.

Regardless, I couldn't do anything until Cipher came home. He called me, saying Blue got into a fight at school. Left work early to pick him up. I couldn't believe it, what he was saying. Automatically assumed that other kids had been picking on him. Made me fucking furious to think about, because I don't care how old they are. If they're old enough to make someone else feel miserable, then they're old enough to deal with the consequences. I couldn't wait for Cipher to get home so that I could hear the full story.

Of course, that was until I got a text from Beau, asking if I'd spoken to

Link today. Now I'm worried. No one has heard from him, and it's caused enough of a panic for Beau to text me. Beau never texts me about Link.

When Cipher and Blue walked through the front door, I told Cipher I needed to go. He was confused, didn't understand why I needed to leave in such a hurry. But he'd never let me go if he knew it was about Link, so I didn't leave much room for explanation.

Blue avoided me at all costs, rushing directly into Cipher's bedroom. Like any other teenager would after getting in big trouble at school. I'll deal with that later- he probably needs the space anyway.

I promised Cipher I would come back as soon as I could. He might've protested it, If I'd given him time. But I've never ran out that door as quickly as I did.

The entire drive there I was worried. Stressing and twirling my hair tighter, the closer I got. All of the bad scenarios running through my mind. All of them.

Walking up the stairs was a blur, but the second I entered the apartment, I could feel every sense on my body heightened and utterly aware.

He was laying down on the couch, topless, with his head hanging over the edge. The cord still wrapped around his arm.

"What the hell, Link!?" the sound of my furious voice clearly ruining his high as his head snaps toward me.

He looked caught.

"What-" he responds, slowly sitting up with a hunch in his posture.

"Is this what you're doing when your not answering my texts!?" I shout, approaching where he's sat.

"I, I- I have a headache-" he responds, rubbing his forehead.

"And I don't? I have migraines every fucking day, but not because of drugs- but because of the shit you put me through!"

"I-I didn't..." He responds sluggishly, avoiding eye contact. "Wait-" he speaks, standing abruptly and looking directly at me. "Beau."

Watching the expression on his face change as I remain silent. Inspecting him, and the way he's looking at me- almost making me take a step back.

"No- No, not Beau! Not Beau!" He mumbles, but at the floor- strangely.

"How do you-"

"You- you have no right. You had no right!" He shouts. His hands shaking.

"Link, what the fuck are you talking about?-"

"D,D,D- Don't talk to me like that!" He demands aggressively, placing his hand tightly on my shoulder. "Don't!" he repeats, pointing his finger in my face.

I can't explain the look in his eyes. It's something I've never seen on a person before. But those eyes are looking less and less like the ones I fell in love with by the second.

I flick my shoulder, pushing his hand off of me, and I walk away to the other side of the couch, but he follows me.

"Why would you do that?"

"Why would I do what?" I snap, turning toward him.

"You don't ever do that again! D,D- Don't ever- Don't ever again!" he snarls with an unsteady sob, gripping his chin with his hand.

"Link-"

Abruptly, Link turns around, shaking his head and burying his face in his hands. Fighting the urge of something bulldozing inside his head.

"Link- I thought we made a pact! I thought you were trying to be better!" I question, feeling that burn scalding inside my throat.

Overwhelmed, he snaps.

He turns around abruptly, giving me a fright as he backs me into a wall shouting.

"You don't get to treat me like this anymore!" he sobs. "I- I'm not a kid anymore! Don't-" He adds, shattering his knuckles as he punches the wall beside me as hard as he can. "- EVER FUCKING TALK TO ME LIKE THAT AGAIN." he continues, his spit dripping from my terrified face.

"I will fucking kill you!" he shouts, punching the wall again.

I - Punch.

WILL - Punch.

FUCKING - Punch.

KILL - Punch.

YOU - Punch.

"STOP!" I whimper with a beg, attempting to shield my face with my own hands, but he rips them away and backs me so far into the wall with fury I physically feel my lungs stop.

"OVER AND OVER AND OVER AGAIN IT PLAYS IN MY FUCKING HEAD! I see it all the time!"

"What are you talking about?" I cry, gripping the wall behind me and watching Link shake with the secret his body is bursting to expose.

"You don't know what I've done! YOU DON'T KNOW WHAT I'VE DONE!"

He's looking at me- those deep eyes of black. Everything about him suddenly changes.

"So tell me, Link!" I weep.

"I- I..."

Link Jones

The world is spinning. I can- can't even remember how I got home. This is the best hit I've ever taken.

I think I'm laying on my couch, but the entire world is spinning. I can feel my eyes drifting to the back of my skull. I can see everything. The blood and bones.

Fuck it feels so good.

Fuck it feels so free.

Spinning. Spinning. Spinning. Spinning beneath my dark ceiling. Spinning. Spinning. Spinning.

I'm still spinning, but I'm somewhere different.

I'm spinning. Swinging. Swinging on a flat swing, hanging from a tree. I'm outside a house, I can feel it. I can smell trees. Grass.

My eyes are closed. I can see the backs of my eyelids. The sun and shadows are shining against them.

Do it. Close your eyes, and listen to the light. Follow the colours, and everything will be alright.

Swinging. Swinging. The colours are mixing. The colours are swinging.

Blue. Pink. Green. Yellow. Orange. So many colours written on the back of my eyelids. So peaceful, so calm. I want to stay here forever. I want to fall asleep beneath the colour and warmth.

F.. Fuck, I'm freezing. The colours are dull, cold. But now my eyes are open.

I'm at home. I'm in my old bedroom, but this time, I'm alone.

Wet. I feel wet. Wait, who is that? Who is that at my door?

Fear. I feel scared. Why are you yelling at me? Why are you yelling at me? I was just sleeping. Why are you yelling at me?

I, I- I have a headache.

He's yelling at me. That man. He's taking off

his belt again. No. PLEASE. NO NO NO NO NO.

He's mad that I wet the bed.

Why- why- why did YOU wet the bed. He is yelling at me.

I-I didn't... I didn't do it.

DON'T LIE TO ME BOY!

Was it me, or was it Beau? Who did it? Who did it? He wants to know.

Don't hurt Beau. Please don't hurt Beau.

Beau.

He won't let me speak. He won't let me explain. He's looking for Beau, but Beau is hiding.

No. No it was me! It was me! Don't hurt Beau. No- No, not Beau! Not Beau! **You- you have no right. You had no right!**

GET THE HELL OFF ME

He's yelling at me, because I'm trying to stop him. I know Beau is hiding. Please! PLEASE STOP!

D,D,D- Don't talk to me like that! Don't!

He hits me. He hits me hard. A belt buckle across the face. Hard enough to launch me deep into the floor.

Why would you do that? I'm shouting. Blood dripping.

You don't ever do that again! D,D- Don't ever- Don't ever again!

You don't get to treat me like this anymore! I- I'm not a kid anymore! Don't-

He grabbed me. I pissed him off. He's kneeling over me, punching the floor. I'm scared.

DON'T EVER FUCKING TALK TO ME LIKE THAT AGAIN

He's screaming at me. I'm crying. I'm scared. Where is my ma? Somebody stop him please!

I WILL FUCKING KILL YOU

Somebody help me!!!

I - Punch.

WILL - Punch.

FUCKING - Punch.

KILL - Punch.

YOU - Punch.

Over and over again I see it. Over and over again It replays in my head over and over and over and over again.

Every time I close my eyes I see it. Every time I follow the colours I see it. It makes me want to fucking die.

I can hear her. I can see her. I thought it was my mother, maybe an angel. But it's her. Fiona. She's screaming for me. She's screaming at me. Why is she yelling at me? I am scared and she is yelling at me.

"You don't know what I've done! YOU DON'T KNOW WHAT I'VE DONE!" I admit.

She hates me. I know she hates me now.

"So tell me, Link!"

Tell her.. tell her…

"I- I…" I hesitate. "It- It wasn't Joey."

"What?" she asks, confused.

"I-it wasn't Joey, it was me."

Suddenly, I'm whisked into a memory. A memory? Maybe. Maybe my imagination. How to tell the difference?

"So.. you're gonna give it to me?" Joseph inquires.

I'm back there, in that alleyway.

I hesitate, I wish I could tell him no. Tell him to find his shit elsewhere, but Tarn would have my head if she knew.

He pays me cash, and I give him his worth.

I wait, and wait. And wait. And wait. Waiting for him to turn around. Waiting for him to strike a deal. Waiting for me to give him that extra dose- the one that kills him.

But nothing. Nothing but darkness. Nothing but my full pockets. Nothing but an overwhelming feeling of despair and spinning horror.

I did that to him. I destroyed his life. I ruined him. It's all my fault. Everything is all my fault. I fucking did it. **It was me.**

I was late that night. I was supposed to see Fiona before she went into the private room. I.. I was late.

I went home, after seeing Joey. I went into my bathroom. Looking at myself in the mirror. Looking at my stupid face. Fuck I wanted to kill it, that thing looking back at me. That thing. That demon. Fuck I can't take it. I can't take it!

I took the drugs, not Joey. I took the drugs. I took the drugs. It was me. It was me.

It wasn't Joey.

I'm there again. It's 8:58. She's down there. I'm late.

Maxine is at the bar, she wont even look at me. She wont look at me. She fucking hates me too. She knows what I did. She knows I'm a terrible person.

Tarn's office. I need the office. The cameras. I need to see.

Room 3. I see her, I see him. Him. My father.

I'm running. I'm running. Running. Running.

"Fiona! Fiona!" I shout, she can't hear me. "Fiona!" I shout again.

I'm here. I'm here! Hello! I'm here!

Room 3. I'm here, standing in front of the closed door. Something is wrong. Something isn't right. Cart and Silas- where are they? They.. they're supposed to take me. Shove me into a room kicking and screaming. WHERE ARE THEY?

My hand touches the door nob, but I freeze. My breath deep. Heavy. I can't. I can't open it. It feels locked, even though I know it isn't. I can't. I c-can't. I'm falling, falling into the opposite room, falling onto the couch.

Let me go. Please, God, let me go. I'm sobbing. Weak and crying.

No need for a cord, no need for drugs. The feeling is still there, bubbling to the surface.

What is that? That feeling of nauseating shallow.

What did I do to me? What did I do?

Please. Please. Let me go. Just let me drift into the forever unknown. Let me feel peace, even if I don't deserve it. Let me go.

Frozen. I feel stiff. My eyes drifting toward a far away land.

Plea-

I feel it in my brain. I taste it on my tongue. I feel it freeze through my nerves, and boil through my blood. Regret.

Memories. Such terrible memories, suddenly, whisked away into the darkness. Separated from my conscience.

I didn't want this. I never wanted this.

oh.. fuck that feels good.

Sweet dreams, daffodil. Forever hold your peace, for the reckoning within shall tear the heart apart.

Never cry, never weep. Never sell your soul, to the everlasting sleep.

Colours of wind, time turns, and never shall you part. For I, as one, will live on within my art.

The climb to reach the light, of the eternal midnight.

The eyes remain dark, with time of endless mark.

Fiona Glass

He feels my heart skip a beat, as I try and process this information in a scramble. He turns around quickly, suddenly overbearing with sincerity.

He's rambling, I can hear him rambling. He's trying to defend his actions. Trying to convince me that he's not in the wrong and that I should forgive him and move on, but I can't. I can't just move on. His dad? His dad did that to me- and he knew about it?

"Wait." I interrupt with a huff, out of breath from my own exhaust.

Suddenly, the rage has returned. It's returned twice as hot, and powerful enough to overrule any other feeling I'm experiencing in this terrible moment. A burning sensation in my chest fueling me as I lock eyes with the man I love- the man I'm supposed to trust.

"You didn't keep it from me because you cared about me, Link. You kept it from me because you didn't want me to know the truth! Because you didn't want anyone to know the truth! You didn't want anyone to know how fucking selfish you are, Link, because you do things without thinking and you destroy people's lives in the process! You are a terrible, terrible person!"

And there they are- eyes of black.

Regret, overwhelming regret.

Link Jones

"You didn't keep it from me because you cared about me, Link. You-you kept it from me because you didn't want me to know the truth! Because you didn't want anyone to know the truth! You didn't want anyone to know how fucking selfish you are, Link, because you do things without thinking and you destroy people's lives in the process! You are a terrible, terrible person!"

With every sentence, my mind deteriorating more and more. I see my dad. I see the things he did to me, to my brother, to my ma. I see a girl standing in front of me who hates me because of a mistake I made. I see a girl blaming me because of something someone else did. This isn't my fault. I tried! I tried to stop it. Fuck. I'm sweating. I c-can't think. I can't hear. Everything is blurry. I feel sweat dripping down my spine. I can't see. I'm blind. I'm stuck in a memory of deep waste and horror. Childhood screams and blood curdling nightmares. How do I get out? How do I get out?

Fiona Glass

In this moment, I thought back to my favourite book as a kid. Little Woman.

I don't know if Amy was right. I don't think we choose who we love, because if we could, I'd choose someone who was perfect- and simple.

I fall deep into those black blank eyes as his palms grow tight around my neck. I can feel his fingernails digging into my skin as my feet are lifted from the floor beneath me.

It isn't much the pain that is bothering me, but the feeling of old oxygen stuck inside my body. Unable to let anything escape, or to welcome new air through.

I feel myself clawing at his arms. Looking to him with wonder. That is not the boy I fell in love with. His caring smile is gone. His ocean blue eyes have evaporated. His sweat is entering my pores, as he watches the life get sucked out of me.

Please, why me? I thought he loved me. If he loved me, why would he do this to me? How could he be okay, seeing me in despair? Is this a dream? A painful everlasting nightmare?

Does he even see me? Is he thinking about me?

If this is it for me, I wonder if Linkoln will regret his actions today. I wonder if he will still love me, even after this.

Just as I start to accept my fate- feeling my eyes close as my entire body falls limp and numb- suddenly, a burst of electricity pulsates through my body like a wave, as I hit the floor.

Accompanied, by the blurred vision of Beau leaping through the front door.

Choking and gasping for air as I grip the floor for some kind of support, but half of my body still feels numb.

I can feel Link standing above me. I wonder what he thinks as he looks down at me. I wonder if he has any regret yet.

It feels like my jugular is stuck between my collarbones. Nothing feels right. Nothing feels real. That did not just happen. I just imagined that. Is this truly all a dream? When will I wake up? I'd like to wake up now, please?

"Link!" Beau shouts, charging at his little brother and shoving him against the window. "What the fuck!?" he shouts. He's crying.

He rushes over to me. Still gargling acidic air as I try to stand up. He helps me.

"Are you okay? Are you okay?"

I can't respond, I can't look back. I need to leave. I need to leave. Run. Run!

I don't even remember driving. I don't remember much, beside the vision of rushing toward my dads front door. That old chipped blueberry door. Bursting through it, still gripping my throat.

What is time, in a moment like this? What is presence? What is reality?

Cipher.

He's standing in the kitchen. Cipher must've moved dad into his room. He's looking at me. He looks concerned. He looks terrified.

Help. Help! Help me! Help me! Please!

I can't breathe. I can't breathe. I can't breathe!

Everything is closing. Everything is catching up and surrounding me. Pushing me in. Trapping me. Wrapping around me like a cord. A zip tie. A rope.

My face feels blue. Thick. I can't, I can't breathe! My chest is on fire, as I fall to the floor. Cipher rushing toward me. I can see that he's speaking, but I can't hear him.

I can't hear anything. I can't see anything. Help! Help!

Nothing, nothing but the subtle drift- as I fade into ebony.

11

Chapter Eleven- Ebony

Fiona Glass

Fumes filling the air. A station of needles and burnt spoons by the big windows. The lights dimmed and stains puncturing the walls.

Only his underwear, looking pale and covered with red scratch marks. Loud music blaring. He looks at me with his red eyes, tears streaming and mixing with the blood dripping from his nose.

I could see his jaw clench, and I felt his entire body turn cold. I knew it meant something. I knew everything had a reason and a purpose and I knew this truth could help me understand everything. I was desperate, I needed to know.

I could feel a nauseating squeeze pulsating through my body. I felt my hands immediately detach as my skin clammed. I was shaking, shaking so much. Shaking so undeniable that he could almost feel it.

"Fi-" he speaks, but the second I hear his mumbled tone, I lost control. My body reacted before my mind could. I slapped him. Hard.

A silence echoed through both of us. It felt like we were stuck there, unable to move. Unable to know what comes next.

Then so suddenly, everything looked different. Suddenly I could see myself, staring at the man I love. But it wasn't love painted on my face, nor anger, but fear. The utmost amount of purple fear.

I watch, as his eyes turn black, and suddenly his bruised right fist is connecting with my cheek, and knocking me flat against the floor. A ringing bouncing between my eardrums, like a large bell on a cat collar. A tense pull leaching from behind my eyes as a blur lifts my head to see the room around me. I'm on my stomach, trying to crawl, but everything seems so slow, so unattainable.

Suddenly, I feel Link kneel down and ripping my left leg. Pulling me on to my back. I can see his sweaty face above mine. Veins popping from his forehead as he fights against my clawing hands. I scream and beg him to stop, while unable to even hear myself scream.

He's stronger then me, and he pushes my wrist so hard it hurt. And quickly his anger turns to frustration, and he immediately pulls that same fist back and plummets it against my chest, hitting me so hard I couldn't breathe for a moment.

A sharp pain wrapping around my lungs like string, and my lower back pulsating from my heart.

I gasp. I couldn't think of anything else but to claw him as much as I could with my nails. Clawing at his neck and face while he lifts me from my armpits tightly until we're both standing.

"Let me go!" I shout with a croak, finally able to find the strength to speak.

Unsure if my eyes are becoming puffy from the tears or the booming blow.

There was nothing, nothing in his mind. Nothing behind those eyes I fell in love with as he pushes me so hard against the kitchen counter I feel the corner jabbing into my hip, causing a jerk reaction for me to knee him as hard as I could between his legs.

Finally, I breathe and the sound comes back as we both drop to the floor. He's writhing in pain. Moaning and groaning on the floor, and watching me slip as I try to run away.

It felt like I was being chased by a wild animal. Too afraid to turn around, but I could feel that he was only inches away from grabbing a hold of me as I sprinted away with terror and screams.

My mind couldn't think quick enough, and all I could do was follow the direction of my sight. The bathroom was directly ahead of me, so I ran toward it.

I don't know how I did it, but I ran in and slammed that door shut with a lock as I felt his entire body bang into it on the other side.

If there were a word to describe something more intense then fury then I'd use it. His voice sounded so different as he punched and kicked that door trying to bring it down while I pressed my back against it on the other side. Fearful of what he'd do to me if he got in.

I feel all the years of trapped tears as they start pouring from my heavy eyes, and every aching point on my body releasing as I loose my footing and fall to the floor. His angry words echoing behind me like a headache. Feeling like the sounds will never end.

His insults, calling me a whore, a slut, telling me I'm ungrateful. He doesn't love me. That I don't love him. That I'm not pretty enough. Not good enough. That I'm an immature child. That I need to grow up. That I have always hated him. That I've always thought I was better then him. He just kept on going and going until I couldn't take it anymore.

I felt my hands travel to shield my ears while a scream erupted from the deepest depths of my stomach. Gurgling out of me and piercing through the walls so loud you'd hear it from Antarctica.

For a moment my scream drowned out his noise. For a moment I couldn't hear anything but myself- still feeling the pounding of his body against the door.

But for a moment I was alone. For a moment nothing could hurt me but a sore throat.

Until, my throat ran so dry and damaged that my loud shriek turned into a whimpered whisper of ringing, drowned in tears.

Ringing. Ringing. And suddenly. GASP.

I'm awake. Terrified. Hugging at my clammed throat. Gasping for air as I realise where I am. I'm home, in my bed. It's daytime, and the sun outside is bright. I'm here, and I'm safe.

Ringing. Ringing. A phone is ringing, until it isn't. I always sleep with my bedroom door shut, but it's open. I hear Cipher answer his phone. Quiet mumbles and hushed tones. Not a mere grunt from my father. Am I still dreaming?

It is then, while trying to listen to Cipher's phone call, that I realise Blue is asleep next to me. He's waking up. I lay back down, facing toward my little brother. Inspecting his young face as his eyes slowly open. Those honey-light eyes.

Rather then the two blue circles they usually are, they're instead, a droop of sorrow. His eye line overflowing with imprisoned liquid.

"Morning." I greet with a dry voice. Both of us still lying down, looking at one another.

I watch his eyes as they inspect my face too. My neck. Suddenly I'm reminded of what it looks like, and the way it aches.

It feels like 2020. Cipher sleeping in his bedroom, dad on the couch, and Blue and I cuddled in my old bed. A home that had been frozen in place.

Everything looks the same, but everything feels so incredibly different. We're all older, but we all act the same- just in different shades.

"What do you say we do something fun later? Maybe.. we could get dinner, at a nice restaurant?" I offer, hopeful that maybe a dinner could fix everything.

I don't know how much Blue knows, but I know he's not stupid. I can't remember where he was, when I came home last night. I can't remember much from that point. But I know at some point, he decided that he'd prefer to sleep in bed with me, then to leave me on my own. I know he knows that something is wrong.

Finally, he smiles. A genuine smile. I don't think Blue has ever been to a restaurant before.

Suddenly, we're both distracted at the sight of Cipher standing at my bedroom door, quickly sitting up. I can tell by the look on his face that something is wrong.

He clears his throat. "Blue, what do you think about coming to the garage with me for a few hours?"

I look to Blue, curious about his reaction.

"Go on," Cipher continues. "Go take a shower." He adds, gently.

Blue listens. Standing up from my bed and leaving the room to do as Cipher says.

Not long after does Cipher walk into my room, speaking in a hushed tone.

"What is it?" I ask, trying my best to not sound so strangled.

He hesitates, but only for a short moment. "I just got a call.. from Maddy."

"Maddy?" I ask curiously, as Cipher sits on the edge of my bed.

He nods. "We didn't talk for long, but she told me that it was either we hear it from her, or the police."

"Hear what?"

He hesitates again. Leaning his body to make sure Blue isn't somehow standing outside the door listening.

"Mum's dead."

I don't know whether I'd exhausted all my tears, or If I simply had none spare to shed for her, but I didn't cry. I felt sad, but not for myself.

I felt sad for Blue and my dad, because I know they'd care more. I know they'd be devastated.

Cipher and I decided not to tell them yet, we thought it'd be best to do it when dads a little less.. dazed. And due to the recent events, maybe giving Blue a break might be beneficial.

I'd texted Frosty and asked If she could cover my shifts at the club for the rest of the week. I knew I'd need the time if it meant I had to break the news to everyone.

Cipher took Blue to the garage to see Justin. I think maybe he was hoping that Yana and Alina might be there too, not that they ever hang out there on the regular. Maybe he was grasping at straws.

Beau has been texting me nonstop. Asking if I'm okay, or if I wanted to meet for a chat.

It makes it so hard for me, to ignore him. I've spent so long relying on Link and his family, just for it to feel wrong to do so in the exact moment I should. It kills me not being able to even tell him that my mother is dead. I fucking miss him, while also hating him. There must be something fucked up in my brain to miss a man like that, but I can't stop thinking about who

I know he is. If it weren't for Tarn and the drugs, he's a good boy. A good person, with bad influences and in a shitty situation.

I needed something to distract my mind. All morning all I could think about was Link, and when I wasn't thinking about him, I was thinking about the dreadful conversation Cipher and I would be having with Blue and dad.

I checked on my dad before I left. He didn't want to get out of bed, but I basically forced him onto the couch. Putting on a movie for him because he refused to pick something.

I went to the grocery store to fill up his fridge. It hasn't looked that bare since before Nadia. I really want to call her and get her back, but I don't want to doom anyone with the responsibility of my father, especially after he finds out my mother is dead.

I'd filled my trolly halfway with groceries when I entered the chocolate isle, searching for something to clench the iron taste in my saliva, when suddenly I was stopped by the sound of someone familiar behind me.

"Fiona?" I hear, turning around to see who it was.

It's Yana, with Alina sitting in the front of a trolly full of groceries. Alina was eating a fruit bar, and I watched as Yana's face shifted from curiosity to horror as her eyes locked in with the sight of my bruised neck. I tried hard to cover it with makeup, but makeup can't cover the puffiness.

"Oh my god, what happened?" she asks sentimentally.

"Oh-" I stop, hurrying to think of an excuse that's better then the truth. "I injured myself at work- I'm out for a couple of days."

She definitely didn't believe me, but Yana has never been one to pry in my business, even if she really wanted to.

"How've you been?" I ask, trying to change the conversation.

"Okay." she responds shortly. "How's Cipher?" she asks curiously, inspecting me- possibly to see if I knew about the baby.

"Hurt.." I say shortly, receiving a smile as Yana cuffs her small bump beneath her baggy top. She knows I know.

"I guess I'm not surprised- he's not too excited about it."

"He'll come around, he's just— stupid." I say, making Yana giggle.

"How've you been, Fi? I haven't heard from you for a while." she asks kindly.

I clear my throat, debating whether I should be truthful or not. But to be honest, keeping this secret from everyone might just kill me too.

"Uh.. our mother died, so-"

"Oh my god." Yana responds, shocked. "What happened?"

"She overdosed- apparently the police found her beneath the city bridge. Probably heroin, maybe meth- I don't know."

"Are you going to host a funeral?"

"I don't know- uh, maybe, If dad and Blue want one."

"And what do they think, are they okay?"

"They don't know yet- Cipher and I decided we should tell them together tonight."

"Oh.." Yana responds, looking hopeless for an appropriate response. "Is Cipher okay?"

"I think so." I nod. "Ciph and I.. we.. have a different perspective on our mum, I guess."

"Yeah, but you know- It's okay to be sad, even if you didn't particularly like her." Yana explains, her words cutting through my shrinking heart.

I just nod- it's not about not liking her, it's about not knowing her. "I should get going, dads waiting for me." I finally say, rushing to walk away.

"Sure- but Fi." Yana adds, stopping me. "You know, even when Ciph and I are having.. problems, you're still welcome to talk to me about *anything*. Alina's been missing her favourite Aunt and Uncle." she smiles sweetly.

I nod, "Sure, I'll- I'll call you." I say, before continuing to walk away.

I couldn't get out of that supermarket quick enough, crying the second I sat in the drivers seat, looking at myself in the mirror with pity and hatred. It took forever for me to leave that car park and drive back to my dads house. So long the milk was probably stale.

As I unloaded the groceries into the fridge, I felt an uneven shift in the nature between us.

Denny Glass

It's Fiona behind me, unpacking groceries. I can always tell the difference between each of my kids and the way they sound when they walk. Fiona's steps felt upset today. I could hear the grumble through the floorboards.

"Fi." I croak, reminding myself of a frail old man. "Fi" I say a bit louder, calling her over.

She'd been avoiding me for a while now, but I needed to see her- my little girl.

She stepped in front of me with a huff, and my face instantly dropped at the sight of her. The precious little face I'd crafted myself, destroyed at the hands of someone else. I didn't need to hear her version of events to know the truth- with a short glimpse of her bruised neck, I know enough.

I straiten myself with a stern face. "You need to get rid of that boy- you're too good for him." I say, but my words fall on rolled eyes as she huffs back into the kitchen.

"Fiona-" I say, but I'm interrupted by her moody words.

"Sorry, dad, but right now, I do not need a lecture from you."

"It's not a lecture."

"Right." she snarls, continuing to unpack groceries.

"I'm telling you right now, you need to move on."

"I'm 19 years old, father. You don't get to tell me what to do anymore."

"I'm still your dad- doesn't that count to something?"

"You lost that privileged a long time ago." she says, her words digging a knife through my chest.

"So what, now I can never show concern for my little girl again?"

"I'm not a little girl anymore." she responds, becoming more rough with her unpacking.

"No, but you'll always be my little girl." I say, finally snapping the straw.

I hear her march over toward me, stomping her feet as she boils with rage at me.

"Really? All of a sudden you want to move on and pretend like the last 5 years never happened? Like your the same man you were when I was a baby?"

"That's not what I'm saying-"

"Then what!? What could you possibly want from me!?" she shouts, wide-eyed.

"I-" I stutter, struggling to find the words quick enough. "I just want to care about you-"

"Really? Where have you been!?" she snaps, her raised voice turning to sobs as she lets for all the built up anger toward me finally unleash. "For years you've drowned yourself in your own guilt and shame, burying yourself in the past while the rest of us moved on with our lives! And now- what? You can't lift your forearm high enough to feed yourself beer through a straw, so suddenly you have to involve yourself in our lives to keep from being forgotten!?"

I could feel a ball of sadness filling my throat, making it difficult to breathe, and impossible to speak the way I want to. I just want her to hear me- I want her to understand that I'm here, that I've always been here.

"Right- silence. Well that's lifetimes better then the responses I usually get from you." she adds. "Ran out of insults to throw my way?"

"I'm sorry, Fi." I say, fighting against my own body to get it out.

For the past few years I've felt like I've been wrapped in a tight blanket and chained to this chair, unable to free my hands far enough to find the key.

"I'm sorry.. about everything. But even I can see that he is not good for you- even I can see that he does more harm then good-"

"And what about you? Whats the difference between you and him? Who would you consider a better person in this equation?"

"Please- just don't.. waste your life on someone, just because you're angry at me-"

"Oh, that's rich coming from you! You wasted your whole life away because of a woman! What you did is the exact same as what she did!"

"Don't say that. At least I'm here! At least I was there!"

"When? When were you there!? You were never here! Your body was here, stuck to this couch like a fucking lump- but *you* were not here! *You* haven't been here since the day she left and In my books being mentally gone is the same as actually being gone!"

I feel tears dropping from my drooped eyes. "Fi-"

"If that's not true then tell me one single thing about our lives that you would know and she wouldn't!"

I feel frazzled. I think of the way Fiona scrunches her nose when she laughs. And the way Cipher licks his teeth when he smiles. Or the way you know Blue is truly happy, when both of his dimples show up on his face, instead of just the deeper right one. I think of all these things, but under the pressure of failure I crack, and I'm unable to respond out loud quick enough.

"Right, you can't answer. You don't know- anything! You don't know anything because you don't care! You don't know that Cipher and Yana broke up because Cipher was never taught how to put others before himself- even when he's scared! You don't know that Blue got suspended from school for fighting- probably because other kids were picking on him because of whatever fucked up shit happened to him when the love of your life took off with him and then dropped him back one day when she realized he was too fucked up to play with! You don't know anything- you don't even know about mum!—"

She stops, abruptly. Her face shifting from anger to an expression of.. feeling caught.

"What about m-mum?" I stutter, fearful of the truth.

She tightens her chest, and takes a deep breath. "She's dead."

Those words hitting me harder then the crash that destroyed me. Suddenly I feel everything. I feel every inch of my stiff body. As if the chains and blanket are gone, and replaced with a thousand swords.

Fiona Glass

He lets out a yearnful shriek, similar to the one I'm familiar with.

A scream so loud, his entire body levitates, and I watch as his stiff self plummets to the floor in a puddle of tears. Wishing with every might that he could run outside and scream into the wind, but instead, tasting his own salty tears as he sobs against the floor.

Suddenly Cipher, Blue and Maddy run inside, startled by the sound. I felt frozen, like I was the one paralysed. Unable to move as Cipher rushed to tend to our father.

I was so consumed by everything that I didn't even have time to question why Maddy was arriving at my house at the same time as Cipher.

"What the hell happened!?" Cipher shouts at me, as he rushes to try and help our dad to his chair, but its as if my father refuses to return. Refuses to be stuck in those chains again.

It took hours for Cipher to settle him, doing so by offering him a warm bubbly bath. It didn't take long before Cipher realized what I did. I thought he'd be pissed, but he wasn't. Honestly, I think he was just glad he didn't have to be the one to do it.

Blue had fallen asleep again in my bed, he sleeps a lot these days. I think maybe it's his escape. He doesn't have as many nightmares as he used to, maybe his brain has finally started to create new memories to replace the old ones. Even if they aren't particularly great, they're better then the shit our mother put him through. I know that.

Maddy took her time to find the courage to walk into my bedroom. I guess she knew I'd have questions about why she was even here.

"Hey." she says, slowly approaching me.

"Hey." I respond, sniffling. Sitting beside Blue on my bed.

Maddy sits herself opposite me, on my desk chair.

"Are you okay?" she asks.

I shrug my shoulders. "Why are you here, Maddy?" I finally ask.

Silence. I'm patient.

"Fi-"

"Please?" I beg softly. "Please just- just tell me the truth."

She hesitates for a while. After some time, you start to replace the silence with your own thoughts. Questions running around in your brain, wondering what could be so difficult for her to admit out loud.

"Um.." she finally says, bracing herself. "Ciph and I-"

"Ciph and you?" I repeat.

"Yeah." she responds, smiling awkwardly.

"When?" I ask sternly, understanding exactly what she's trying to tell me.

"At Beau and Jasper's last house party- we were both super upset and just.. one thing led to another-"

"You and Cipher… you fucked my brother?"

She nods, fearful of my expression. I stand.

"You- you know Yana is pregnant, Maddy. That's why he was upset at that party, that's why she and him haven't been talking- because he walked out on her."

She looks shocked, she obviously didn't know. She stands too.

"Maddy- he has a girlfriend! He already has a child, and you're supposed to be *my* friend."

"I know-"

"You can leave." I demand abruptly.

"Fi-"

"What? Your life wasn't dirty enough- you had to go and sleep with my brother?"

"What?-"

"Miss Private school with ya' rich parents, hanging out at the Jonesy house and sleeping with a Glass to prove you're different, is that it?"

"No- I-"

"Maddy, get out." I order. Feeling myself crumble again. I'm so fucking sick of crying.

She looks choked up, I feel bad. But then I think about Yana, the girl who we've grown up with. The girl who already mothers my niece, and is pregnant again. Cipher cannot be that cruel.

She rushes out of my room, grabbing her jacket and keys by the front door and slipping out the front door with a slight slam. Suddenly, as I struggle beneath my exhausted breath, something catches my eye. Blue's journal, sitting on my bedside table. A blue envelope sticking out of it.

It's wrong, to snoop. I shouldn't do it, not without asking first. But an overwhelming sense of protection hits me violently, and I feel like nothing can stop it.

I pull it out gently, hoping I don't wake the sleeping Blue beside me. I can see where Blue aimlessly ripped the envelope open. Uneven.

I take the letter out from inside, seeing that familiar red scribble.

```
to my baby blue

i couldn't tell you how long i've spent missing you. sometimes I
wondered where you went. i wondered if you still missed me too.
im sorry i left, but i knew i wasn't good for you. and i knew
that your daddy missed you, and fi and ciph. i hope you had fun
with them my angel boy.
im writing this letter to let you know that im coming back for
your birthday. i would never miss mamas boys birthday. i think
we should go and see a movie too, i think that would be fun.
tell your daddy that im coming around, and that i might need to
stay at his for a few days before i can find my own place.
i want to be there for you, and for your brother and sister. i
miss everyone so much. I miss yous more then anything.
ill see you soon my baby boy. i love you.

mama
```

I couldn't believe it. I can't believe she would do that to him. I hope he didn't believe it. I hope he knew it couldn't be true.

I could feel Blue jolting in his sleep, so I hurriedly placed the letter back in the envelope, and back inside his journal.

I cooked dinner that night, just some homemade pizzas. I let Blue put all the toppings on each of them, while I rolled out the dough and spread the sauce. All I could think about was that letter, and how I'm supposed to convince him that she's now dead.

By that point, Cipher had placed dad in his bed. I guess he didn't want to be there when we told Blue either.

"Hey champ!" Cipher greets, masking himself behind a false smile as he enters the kitchen.

Blue smiles back, continuing to add pineapples to his own pizza.

"Is he asleep?" I ask.

"Yeah." Cipher nods, suddenly his smile disappearing as he looks at me.

It's interesting to think; when you're a child, everyone is masked with smiles and support during tough moments. But the second you grow up, the second you can form your own opinions; that is when you're faced with the facade. That is when smiles turn to frowns, and people expect realness and maturity. I miss being a kid. I miss being careless.

I wonder if Maddy told him I sent her out. I wonder if he knows I know.

He watches me quietly for a moment, as I place dads pizza in the top shelf of the oven, and Blue's in the bottom, while Blue gets started on decorating mine and Cipher's.

I turn back around, and Cipher quickly approaches me with a hush.

"Do you know why Maddy left?" he asks.

He doesn't know I know. "Yes." I respond, clearing my throat.

"Why?"

"What I want to know is why you were with her in the first place?- you two have never been friends." I ask, baiting him. I want to know if he'll tell me the truth.

He's silent. With his eyes he inspects my face, reading my expression and trying hard to enter into my mind. Then suddenly, it clicks.

"She told you?"

"She didn't have to." I shrug.

He huffs, leaning back against the kitchen counter, shaking his head with frustration.

"Are you mad at her?" I ask.

"No- not for telling you." he responds.

"Then what?" I question, but it takes him a moment to finally answer.

"I'm not mad at her- I'm mad at myself."

"Because of Yana?"

He looks at me again, nodding.

"I saw her today, at the supermarket."

"You saw her? Was Alina with her?"

"Yes, she was." I explain. A moment of silence falling over us again. "I don't get it, Cipher. Why destroy everything you have with someone as good as Yana, just to bring more chaos?"

He buries his face in his hands, and he immediately starts to cry. No matter how many times I hear it, that sound will forever be unfamiliar to me. Even when we were kids, he never cried.

I don't know what to do, how to react. I don't know how to show affection for someone like him, or if I should.

I like it better when he's drunk and crying.

"Fuck- I feel like no matter what I do… I just keep fucking everything up." He finally admits. "I don't know whats wrong with me- I must be some kind of fucked up to treat people the way I do."

"Hey-" I say, placing my hand on his shoulder. "You and I- we're more alike then you think. You can't forget, we were raised by the same man, and we share the same DNA- so if you're fucked up, then I am too."

"You're better then me, Fi. You care about people- I don't think I do."

"You care, Ciph."

"Really? Because I've been replaying my whole life over and over in my head the past few weeks and I can't pinpoint a single moment in my life where I thought about someone else before myself." He sniffles, becoming furious with himself. "And the worst part is I know all of this- I know that I'm a shitty person- but for some reason I can't change it, or wont."

"You're not a shitty person Cipher- you just make shitty decisions. There's a difference. And there's always time to try and fix it."

"How? Yana will never forgive me when she finds out."

"Maybe not, but it's better she hears it from you."

He wipes his eyes harshly, before looking back at me. His eyes dancing back and forth from mine and my bruised neck.

"I should've protected you more- looked out for you more. I'm sorry."

A moment of complete understanding, interrupted by a knock at the front door. I go to answer, but Cipher shoots past me. Wiping his eyes in a hurry.

"Stay here." I tell Blue, hoping he listens.

Cipher and I approach the door, and I watch as he nearly slams it shut, as the person behind it is revealed. Tarn and Lydia.

"Wait!" Lydia begs, placing her hand firmly against the door.

"You're not wanted." Cipher responds sternly.

Tarn looks to me over his broad shoulder. "Please, Fi. Please. We just want to talk."

"You want to talk?" I question, rushing out the door. "Then we talk out here." I demand.

"That's fine." she agrees.

Silence.

"Talk." I demand, and Lydia immediately begins to cry.

She tries to compose herself by grabbing a hold of my arms, restricting herself from collapsing.

"I- I'm sorry." she stutters. "I'm sorry for what he did, Fi- I," she hesitates beneath her sobbing breath. "I know he must seem terrible.. but- but Linky is a good boy. He's a good boy- but he makes bad- awful, decisions!"

I don't say anything, neither does Cipher. We just listen, and watch. Watch as she tries so hard to defend the son she created.

"I'm sorry!" Lydia pleads.

"Look, Fi. We know it may be impossible for you to forgive him- we understand, but we need something, desperately." Tarn proposes.

"What is it?" I say, trying my hardest to fight against the boiled ball of heartache toasting inside my throat.

"Link-" Tarn stops, hesitating. "He- he's just a little.. misguided. He just needs support.. to get him back on track. And right now, he wont listen to anyone- but you."

"No- No!" Cipher shouts, trying to come in between Tarn and I.

Blue is now standing at the front door, and suddenly Cart steps out of their black car as Cipher poses as a bigger threat beneath his heated execution.

"Over my dead body will I ever let her talk to him again!" Cipher demands, as Cart approaches.

"It's not your decision, Ciph!" Tarn fires back.

"Stop." I say, muffled beneath the sound of arguments.

"It's not our responsibility to fix him!"

"He's your friend too, Cipher!" Tarn responds, shocked at Cipher's lack of empathy.

"*Was*!" Cipher responds, as Cart attempts to push him back, creating a bigger space between Tarn and Cipher's bodies.

"Step back, Cipher." he orders gently.

"Don't fucking touch me!"

"I wouldn't have to if you'd just step back!"

"We're not looking for a fight, please!" Lydia begs, but her voice is muffled out too.

"You're on our property- fighting for a cunt that hurt my sister! Have you got no fucking sympathy!" Cipher fights, his voice cracking.

"There's no right or wrong here." Tarn argues back. "Link needs people who care about him-"

"I'm not gonna tell you again, step the fuck back!" Cart demands, becoming more aggressive.

Suddenly, Cipher's fist reaches up to connect with Cart's face. Cart isn't phased, he goes to attack back, but something stops him. A 13 year old boy, overwhelmed by memories and a crippling fear of yelling. Blue rushes out, speeding toward Cart. Appearing half the size of him. He fights back. Getting between the two grown men and punching Cart in his abdomen over and over again as hard as his teen fists could.

Cart doesn't fight back, he doesn't do anything. Everyone falls silent, simply watching as Blue breaks down while attempting to defend his older brother.

"Blue-" Cipher interjects softly, attempting to pull Blue back. But he doesn't listen.

As if he's stuck in a position where he has to choose between fight or flight. He chose fight.

"Blue, come on." Cipher repeats, physically pulling Blue away. Cradling him from behind as Blue washes over the group in tears. Possibly fearful of retaliation.

But nothing. No one hurts him. No one yells at him. Cipher merely grips against him, hugging him until that fear exudes from his body.

"Fiona-" Lydia interrupts. "Please- he needs you." she begs, still crying.

A rage. Rage that I'd never experienced before. Watching Blue, seeing him be forced to use physical violence to resolve conflict so much recently. Watching him crumble beneath the eye of onlookers.

Seeing three grown ups, who have come to my house to plead for me to do what they should've done many years ago. It is not my responsibility. I do not owe them anything. I am not in the wrong. I deserve freedom.

"He doesn't need me." I begin, approaching Lydia with a disgusted look on my face. "What he needs- what he has always needed- is his mother! You!" I shout, and everything falls quiet. "He needed his mother his whole life, and you were never there. You created that person, not me!"

She begins to sob. Her frail body unable to handle accountability. I turn to Tarn, who's looking at me with those same piercing eyes.

"And you-" I begin. "You walk around looking at everyone else as dirt on the bottom of your shoe, thinking you saved those boys all those years ago- but you didn't save anyone! The blood is on your hands! You control people, and force people to do bad things to benefit no one but yourself!"

Her face is frozen, like she's not even there. Nothing behind her eyes.

"You used my love for Link against me once before- and it nearly killed us both!" I shout, breaking down as my voice perishes beneath the boil. "I will never get that night out of my head, and that is your fault! Just like Link will never be a good person, because you failed him- not me!"

Finally, a crack within her ice cold exterior, as a singular tear plummets down her face. Nearly sizzling against her skin.

I wipe the fallen tears from my swollen eyes. "Get the hell off my property, all of you!" I demand, reaching over to grab Blue's hand and leading my brothers back inside.

I just about fall into another panic attack as we walk back into the house. Cipher rushes to turn off the oven as the pizzas are beginning to burn. Blue turns to me, still holding one of my hands. His big eyes almost as swollen as mine.

Without a second thought, he brings me in for a tight embrace. A beautiful hug, filled with blue rain drops and yellow love.

"Fiona." I hear mumbling from another room.

Cipher turns around the corner, looking at me. Both of us curious about the sudden voice.

"Fiona." we hear again.

Blue and Cipher follow me as I walk past the kitchen, and toward the bedroom door to the left of the lounge room. The door is open, and my dad is lying on his back in his bed. Peering toward the door.

"Dad?" I say, surprised to see him still awake.

"Come- come sit." he requests, trying to tap against his bed with his hand.

Slowly, I approach. Sitting down gently beside him. He has watery eyes, with big bags beneath them. Looking to me with such hopeful misery. I feel tension- a wish. A wish to place his hand on my cheek, or to hug me like any father would. But he cannot.

His chin is tensing, and his brows for the first time in many years, are not a stern frown.

"Are you okay?" he finally chokes out.

I nod, because I cannot speak. If I speak, I will cry. I wonder if this is how Blue feels.

"I-" he hesitates. "I'm sorry, about everything."

I shake my head, trying so hard to say something to comfort him. But I begin to hyperventilate like a little kid. A little kid, who's been hurt for the first time, crying to her dad. Unable to catch my rapid breath as my face is flooded.

"I'm sorry I wasn't there- I should've been." he begins to sob. Seeing me hurt, hurts him too. "I'm sorry I can't... fix this. I want to make it right. I want to... rid my baby of that pain." he continues, sinking beneath the heavy pressure, hyperventilating too. "I'm- I'm sorry. I'm so, so, so sorry."

I can't take it anymore. I fall into my father and bring him in for a tight cuddle. I haven't hugged my dad since I can remember. It felt unfamiliar, and incredibly overdue. I miss him. I miss my dad. I miss his ability to be the man he wishes to be. I miss his heart.

The three of us decided to tell Blue about mum after that. We thought it'd be best if all of us were there to support him.

He took it well. He cried, but he took it better then I was expecting.

The past week has been a blur. Days filled with invites, planning, decisions, and heavy eyes. I haven't slept since I found out my mum was dead.

My mother's parents paid for her entire funeral and headstone, but they let us pick the design.

Meredith 'Merry' Goldie Mitchell
May 26, 1986 - April 1, 2026
Mother to Cipher, Fiona and Blue
Sister to Charlotte and Hannah
Daughter to Rupert and Uma
'In shades of darkness, there will always be light.
In times of darkness, there will always be hope'

25 days before my birthday she decided to die. Today is the 11th of April, and my birthday is 15 days away. In the letter she said she'd be back for Blue's birthday. I guess I wouldn't put it past her to mix them up.

My grandparents, Rupert and Uma, wanted to host her funeral in a church. I guess they hoped that if she was honored in death via the Gods eye, she might be sent to Heaven instead of Hell.

I don't know if I believe any of that. What I do know is that someone who was as terrible of a person as my mother, should never be gifted with the afterlife of heaven. Not after what she put Blue through. People like that don't get second chances.

Charlotte and Hannah's husbands, as well as Charlotte's eldest son, Easton, and Hannah's sons, Daine and Tommy, assisted Rupert, Cipher and Blue in carrying her casket into the church for the ceremony.

Surprisingly, a lot of people showed up. I guess she had a lot of childhood friends. Or maybe people were bored.

Uma insisted on hosting an open funeral- I guess she knows her daughter better then anyone else.

Uma also deigned a slideshow, to the song Angels by Robbie Williams. She said in her speech that my mother used to love that song when she and her sisters were kids. I don't know how true that is.

I didn't realize how differently she and Rupert saw Merry compared to us. They saw a different side of her. They saw her before she became the person she is today. They could barely look at Blue during the entire planning process. I guess they knew what she did must've been awful- so awful they could never admit it was true. I guess they underestimated just how bad her addiction was.

Uma and Rupert spoke together, followed by Charlotte and Hannah. My dad was supposed to speak next, but he chickened out at the last second. Looking to me with eyes of hopelessness, and handing me his sheet. I'd never force my dad to get up in a moment like that. Not without dignity.

So alas, it was time for myself, Cipher and Blue to go up. Cipher wanted to go first, said he wanted to get it over with.

"I didn't know my mam for long. The most I remembered from her were stories other people told me. I guess she wasn't always the person I grew to know. I guess life changes people like that. I understand leaving. Sometimes I wish I could just run away- rid everyone of the thought of me too. But I could never do that- not to my family. Not to my daughter. I wish my mum could've met my little girl- I think she would've made her stay. She certainly makes me stay. My mum didn't teach me much, but she did teach me one thing- and that's to never let regret consume me. To never prove the inner voice right. I wish she would've given herself a chance- or at least, given herself the opportunity to explain to us why she did what she did. I hope life seems clearer now- and I hope that somewhere up there she gets to see us, and guide us to live a better life then she did."

I could almost hear Grandma Uma's sobs from the stand. I knew it hurt her to hear Cipher's truth.

Next was my turn, but I thought I'd read my dads first.

As I opened his sheet, and cleared my throat- trying to shake away the jitters from every set of eyes peering over at me- Cipher stopped me with a tap.

He gestured over, and there he was. My father, being pushed in his wheelchair up the ramp by Eyeball, who'd sat in the row behind him.

He changed his mind. I've never seen my dad so broken- so filled with hopelessness. It was only then that I thought about crying. Truly crying. Crying because I hated my mother for destroying him. Hated her for creating the man he is now. But also crying because I'm so fucking proud of him for coming up in front of all these people, and telling his truth.

The funeral coordinator handed him a separate cordless microphone, and I handed him his sheet. Eyeball and I shared a look, one that allowed him to stay, and support my dad through his speech.

He choked up into his hand as he glances over his own words. Choked up with the memories of her.

"I- I met Merry a long time ago. Our relationship was silly from the start. From the outside looking in, I know it looked.. hopeless. But we really did love each other. Merry used to always pick me flower bouquets from her parents' garden. I'd never received flowers like that before- usually it's the other way around." He smiles kindly. "But Merry was obsessed with flowers. Her favourites were orchids, and marigolds. She used to fantasize about our wedding- hosted in a garden full of colour. A little ring barer, a flower girl. Surrounded by nothing but love." he pauses for a moment. Choking on his own tears as they repeatedly fell. "I wish my kids could've met the Merry I knew. I wish they could've heard how beautiful of a singer she was. I wish she could've been around to see how.. how wonderfully they've grown." he grumbles, failing at suppressing him emotions as his old frail body trembles with utter sadness. "-Because I know.. the real Merry, my Merry- she'd be just as proud as I am."

It almost seemed like the crowd wanted to applaud, before remembering funeral etiquette.

"Merry didn't care about what other people thought. She didn't care about standards and regulations. She'd be the first to stand up and cheer for someone she loved- because she always loved loudly."

Eyeball rested his hand on my dads shoulder. His chin quivering as he looks my way. I pressed my lips together to stop the shake. Debating whether I should just give up, forfeit my right to speak.

But alas, with a heavy gulp, I proceeded;

"It took me three days to write this speech- though, I feel like I'd been preparing it for years. I don't know if my mothers death was an accident, or suicide- but I do know that no matter her faults, no matter her past, she was still my mother. Pieces of her are stuck inside me forever, and inside my brothers. She's like a memory of confetti- you remember the beauty, and the smile you had when you saw it. But you don't remember touching it, or the way you felt when you looked at it. I wish she'd have been different- I wish she would've chose us. But I came toward forgiveness a long time ago, because it is exhausting to hate someone you didn't know. I hope now our family can live in peace, knowing she is. I hope now the darkness may pass."

The second I spoke my final word, I felt my heart drop as I peered over the crowd. It was Link, right at the back. Standing beside Beau, Tarn, Lydia and Cart.

Link.. my Link. Why is he here? I can't deal with him right now- but oh, how badly I wish to run across this room and hug him. Hug him like a lost child.

I'd had Blue working with Mrs Keen the past week to work on something to say, so I distractedly looked down at Blue to see if he wanted me to read anything- but he just shook his head. I get it, not wanting to say anything. I mean, no one actually knows what happened to Blue all those years, but I was sort of hoping he would let me. To finally be inside the mind of Blue. To understand him a little better. Reading words he wrote.

I knelt down to meet his level, gripping his small hand inside mine. A frown in his brows as his childlike eyes look to mine.

"It may help." I say quietly, hoping he understands me. Hoping he listens.

Patiently, I wait, as Blue slowly grabs out a scrunched piece of paper from his back pant pocket. It took a lot inside him to actually hand it over. But I thanked him with a sigh-filled smile, before standing up, to proceed with the service.

One last time, I looked back down at Blue. Giving him one last chance to change his mind. But instead, he reaches that same little hand out to hold mine. An act that brought comfort to not only him, but me as well.

"This is something that my little brother has written." I say, suddenly spotting Mrs Keen in the crowd.

Her hands are together, holding her chin from falling apart. She looks proud.

I flatten the piece of paper out on the wooden pedestal in front of me, and heavily prepare myself for the speech ahead.

His hand writing was a little difficult to read, and a lot of the words were spelled wrong, but I understand. I understand.

"Not long ago, my mum took me to a place.. away from everyone. I felt very sad and alone. Sometimes, when my mum was sad too, she would sing us songs, and she would hug me very tight." I choke. Fuck. I'm fucking crying. Sobbing, in fact. "I thought my mum was playing hide and seek. I thought that maybe she was winning. Sometimes we would play hide and seek too, and she would always win." I cover my mouth, barely able to continue. But I have to, for Blue. "I wished my mum wouldn't leave me, but after a while I was glad she did. I was glad.. because I got to see my sister and my brother and my dad again, and I got to play different games with them. Games that didn't make me sad, or scared." I stop again. I hear the sound of Cipher snorting back his tears and it nearly makes me break. But I can't. I have to stay strong. "I do love my mum, but I am too scared to miss her. I hope she is happy now, because I don't like it when she feels sad, because It makes me feel sad too."

Once the speech was finally over, I immediately dropped to my knees to embrace my little brother- who'd cowered behind my knees to sob quietly.

I told him it was okay. I told him that it was good to be sad. I told him that he did great.

Cipher rubbed his back, and helped us both back to our seats while Eyeball helped dad, who's completely buried his face in his drenched hands.

The church paraded Oceans by Hillsong UNITED as all the boys helped to bring her casket back out to the funeral limo.

I saw Link in the distance as people walked down toward the cemetery grounds, following the limo like an army.

It's hard to believe so many people knew her. It's hard to believe that none of these people tried to save her.

Watching all of these people place Orchids and Merigolds on top her casket as its lowered, I wonder to myself if it's true what everyone else said in their speeches. That there was a real person in there. That she wasn't just a figment of my memory- never to be truly seen or discovered. Never to be fully understood.

I don't think anyone really understood her more then my father. He saw the good and the bad, and still somehow loved her. Though, I do now think he loved us more- I don't think he ever truly despised her. I don't think he could.

After the ceremony, some people stuck around. Blue felt frozen by her lowered casket, unable to move. Mrs Keen stayed with him for a while, and I gave them space to talk.

After she left, I decided it would be kind to give him a moment, so I sat myself on a bench with a cigarette and a flask that I'd stashed in my purse.

I saw Cipher talking to Yana and Alina. I saw Maddy too. She didn't speak to me, but I could read her like an open book. It hurt her to know Cipher chose Yana. It hurt me to know she was hurt.

"Hey." I hear abruptly, turning my head to see him.

Linkoln. He's smiling, that soft smile I fell in love with.

He sits down beside me, and looks into the distance- avoiding eye contact.

"Are you okay?" he asks, looking back at me.

I couldn't speak. Part of me was terrified, another part wanted to fall into his arms, and the other part was furious he had the nerve to show up- let alone speak to me.

"Fiona I- I'm sorry, for lying.. for the fight." he shakes his head, looking down in shame. "Beau- he can barely even look at me anymore." he explains, his voice full of shame. "I don't expect you to forgive me, but I just wanted you to hear me say it."

I couldn't find the words, speechless would be the perfect description.

"I think I know what I have to do.. to fix this. But I didn't want you to feel like I'd forgotten you, or like I didn't care." He continues, keeping his blue eyes planted on mine. "If you're willing to hear me out, I'd love to cook you dinner tonight- and Blue. I just want to be there for you both, even if it might be the last time."

Without me saying anything, he places his finger on my cheek to wipe the fallen water, before leaning in to kiss my forehead. He pauses there for a while.

"I love you, you know." his tone shaky as he pulls away. "I love you more then anything." he adds quickly, kissing my forehead one last time.

He then stands and disappears into the distance without a second to look back.

My heavy breath pants as I start to feel my chest tighten, and just when I thought my moment of concern was over, I'm greeted again, but by a different voice.

"Are you gonna go?" she asks, as she walks around to sit beside me.

It's Maddy. I thought she might've left.

"I don't know." I say slowly, swallowing my tears. My breath slowly recovering.

And eery silence falls over us for a small moment.

"Fi.. can I ask you something?"

"Sure." I respond, feeling all my bottled emotions rising at the sound of her voice.

"Do you still love him?" she asks softly.

I should walk away. I shouldn't let her ask me such absurd questions, but I don't want to. I don't want to walk away from her. I think my silence was enough of an answer.

She bows her head for a moment, before returning to look at our surroundings.

"Fiona, you've always been someone to put everyone else's needs before your own. It's one of the reasons I love you." she explains, choking up at her own words of wisdom. "But you're too sacred to let a man like that destroy you. You're too… good-" she continues, suddenly bursting into tears. "-to think you don't deserve real love, because you deserve everything and anything that is… wonderful."

I feel myself crying too. The kind of cry you experience when you're a kid, when you get hurt by the act of someone else for the first time.

"Because if anyone deserves a happy ending.. it's you." she bows her head again, wiping her tears. "I'm sorry for what I did." she admits quickly, before standing.

With a rush, I grab her hand to stop her from walking away. She looks down at me with eyes of solemn regret.

"I forgive you." I say, because I know it is what she needed to hear in that moment.

She sits back down slowly, and I wrap my arm around her as she leans her head against my shoulder.

I don't know if Yana and Cipher are going to get back together, but I do know that I don't want to lose one of the only friends I have left.

When I returned to Blue, he was crying. Our dad was in his wheelchair beside him, while Eyeball and Brownie were getting the car ready.

"Are you guys okay?" I ask. They both lift their heads to look at me. Their faces appear like a spitting image.

Eyeball then walks over. "You ready to go, Den?" he asks.

"How are you two getting home?" my dad asks.

"I drove here- but I think I owe Blue a dinner, so we might be a bit late home tonight. And Cipher is hitching a ride with Yana and her parents."

My dad nods, looking back down at the open grave. Eyeball quickly pulls me to the side, to ask me something in private.

"Hey, is it okay if Cooper and I stay the night? You know, just to help out."

"Of course you can, you know you never have to ask."

Eyeball smiles, attempting to continue with his assistance with my dad, but something stops him. He inspects me- every inch of my face.

"Fiona-" he begins. "You want me to deal with it?" he asks politely.

"What?" I say, genuinely confused.

With his eyes, he points to my neck. The neck I tries so hard to cover with makeup. Looking to me with the same look my dad did when he saw the damage for the first time.

"Oh." I say simply.

"You know it kills him- your dad- to not have the ability to do it himself."

"I can handle it."

"I know you can." Eyeball admits, as his light blue eyes slowly fill with a puddle of tears. "But you don't have to." he adds.

Such a beautiful soul. Tough exterior, but the heart of a true parent.

I place my hand on his arm. "I'm okay." I assure. Our feelings of disparity mutual.

He nods hesitantly, before returning to assist my dad to the car.

Blue and I stayed at the cemetery for an extra hour after everyone else left. I sat on the grass beside him the entire time, just waiting. Watching as all the funeral workers packed up all the event chairs and other resources. Giving us the time we needed.

The entire time, all I could think about was that letter she gave him. At some point, he sat down beside me, his eyes still fixated on the lowered coffin. Beside him, was his journal. With the blue envelope still sticking out of it.

"Blue, can I ask you something?" I say, my mouth speaking faster then my brain.

Finally, he looks at me.

"Why didn't you tell me?" I ask gently, pointing at the letter.

He appears uncomfortable, quickly looking away. I remain calm, patient.

"Is it-" I begin, stopping myself to think of the perfect execution to my question. "Did it make you feel sad.. or happy- reading that letter?"

I give him a moment, allowing the time needed to answer my heavy question.

Suddenly, with his finger, he points to himself. I didn't understand at first, what it meant by pointing at himself. Until I remembered some of the school work he used to bring to the cafe all the time. The colour work. Identifying emotions through colour. The colour blue, associated with sadness. Blue is sadness. He feels sad.

"Did you want her to come back?" I further question.

He shakes his head slowly. He didn't want her to come back.

"Are you sad that she's gone?" I ask, and he looks at me again. His mouth hidden behind a deep frown, as he again shakes his head.

I can tell it hurts him to admit that. I get it. It doesn't feel great to admit that your happy someone is dead. But I understand why he feels that way, I do too.

I can see his chin quivering, and I rush to compliment the way he feels.

"I feel that way too." I respond, and his expression immediately changes. He's softer now. "Now, I don't have to worry. Now, I don't have to be afraid. I can rest, knowing that she's at peace." I continue, looking down at her casket. "It's okay to feel that way."

I look back up at Blue, he's still looking at me. Acceptance. A mutual understanding. Something we both can feel, together.

While I was driving, I wondered to myself about Link's offer. Wondered If I should do it- just drive to Links and forget about everything. But when I looked at Blue, and I saw his face- I couldn't do that. I didn't want to.

Instead I took him to a restaurant. An Italian place in the city. He mightn't have lightened up as much as I'd hoped, but I got to see him smile. Smiling because it was his first time eating at a fancy restaurant. Smiling because he loved having a competition over who could colour in the kids stencils on the tables the best while we waited for our food. Smiling because he'd never tasted expensive cheese, or tried lava cake before. I finally felt like I did something right. Like I did something pure and correct.

I thought everyone would be asleep by the time we returned home, but I was mistaken.

Eyeball, Brownie, Archie, Dare, Cipher, Yana, Alina, Yana's parents, and my dad were out the back, listening to music and singing drunkenly to songs.

Blue and I walked out to a big greeting and laughter. Laughter this house hasn't heard for years.

It'd been a long time since I'd seen Eyeball and my dad together, and it was like he never left.

It'd been years since I saw my dad smile- and I didn't realize until now how similar he, Blue and Cipher looked when they were happy.

None of us realized how late it was until Alina finally fell asleep in Cipher's arms.

I left Blue outside- listening to Eyeball tell the same rancid stories about him and our dad from when they kids- while I followed Cipher into his old bedroom where he placed Alina beneath the sheets to sleep.

Leaning against the door frame, Cipher looked up at me, following a bedtime kiss for Alina.

Slowly, he approached me, leaning against the other side of the frame, and gesturing toward a joint in his pocket.

The two of us snuck out the front of the house to sit on the double rocking chair upon the veranda. The dark night illuminating as we shared that beloved joint. An overbearing weight, dulling the conversation.

"Fiona." he says subtly, looking to me with a familiar expression.

"Yes?" I say curiously.

"What happened with Link?" he questions sternly.

The brotherly stare of his eyes forcing me into a corner. A corner I'd spent years trying to claw my way out of.

In that moment, I didn't see my angry older brother. Instead, I saw the brother that gave me a journal for my birthday. I saw the brother that used to let me hang out with him and his friends in school because he knew I didn't have any of my own. I saw the brother that came with me to Skye Sallow's house for many dinners following her death.

A moment that controlled me, and ultimately forced me into truth.

A sob unleashed from my weakened body as my head collapsed into my hands. Cipher's arm eagerly wrapping around me. A ball of fury blocking his airways.

"I thought he loved me." I wept. Unable to contain my truest despair.

"Shhh." he hummed softly as he tightened his hug and soothed me.

"I thought I could make him better… but I couldn't."

"Hey, hey, hey-" he pleads with a hurry, forcing me to listen to him. "You shouldn't have to prove anything to a guy to make him love you."

"I just wanted it to work- I wanted him to want to love me."

"Fi- If he doesn't love you already, then clearly there's something seriously fucked up goin' on in his head." Cipher objects. "Don't ever lessen yourself in hopes a guy like him will ever understand. Some things as great are clearly out of his reach."

I sit up slowly, burying my fingers into my puffy eyes in attempt to stop the free flow. Cipher's heavy hand continuously rubbing my back in comfort.

"I just don't get it." I say.

"Get what?"

"I don't get what it is about me that makes it so hard for people to love me."

"What are you talking about?" Cipher asks, shocked at my statement.

"No matter what I do, everyone always ends up leaving me." I explains, buried beneath my sobs. "Mum, Skye, Link- no matter how much time I spend loving someone, it never seems to be enough."

"You can't compare yourself to people who aren't on your level, Fi. If you've never been shown love, how are you supposed to accept it from others- even when it's right in front of you."

Cipher's calming words of wisdom, so strong it even speaks to himself.

"You should be grateful you know what love is- then you'll know it's true when it does come." He continues, still holding me tightly.

I finally wipe my eyes clean and look to my older brother with such amazing respect and peace.

"I know I never say it, but you know I love you, Ciph." I admit. My words immediately strangling his heart.

He pulls me in quickly. Hugging me tight enough to express his gratitude without words. Clearly, a conversation we both needed to have. Faint rain patter beginning to fall.

Cipher Glass

I drove Yana, Alina, and Yana's parents home that night. I wasn't expecting to stay, I was just happy with the day we'd had together. Even if it was at my mother's funeral.

It's raining. It feels muggy from the hot day. My skin felt sticky beneath my shirt, even before I stepped out beneath the water.

We ran through the front garden, over to the veranda, and barreled through the chipped sage door.

Melody and Justin went to bed pretty quickly. Dare left- probably headed for Queen.

I nearly cried putting Alina to bed that night. I still finished reading the story, even though she fell back asleep after only the first page. It felt like a privilege to finally be back in her bedroom.

I felt my heart shrink as Yana stood at the door. Smiling.

"Hey."

"Hey." I respond, still holding the book.

I know I just need to do it. Rip off the band-aid. She deserves the truth.

I put the book back in Alina's bookshelf, before walking through the main area of the house with Yana. Neither of us saying a word, but both of us hidden behind our childlike smiles.

As we approach the front door, I feel my time running out. I need to do it. I need to.

Behind me, the fly screen is closed, but the main door is open. The heavy rain nearly flooding our conversation.

"I-" I begin, but I feel my emotions choke me back, my entire body filling with an instinct to run. But I can't. I can't be that person anymore. "Thank you, for letting me tuck her in."

Yana just looks at me, no response.

I shake my head, clawing through my brain for the words to say.

"I- I'm sorry, for everything. You always deserved a better person then me." I admit, her eyes falling with sympathy. "I want to change- I want to be there for you, for Alina, and the baby."

She smiles. "Really?"

I nod.

"How do I know you wont change your mind?" she interrogates.

"You don't- I guess. But I do. I know it- it's what I want. I want to be a family."

She smiles again. At the end of the day, she's just a woman. Once upon a time she was a girl, dreaming of her knight in shining armour. A Prince, to come and sweep her off her feet.

For a moment, I debated pulling her into me and forgetting the rest of the conversion. Grabbing all of our things and running away with Alina to start a new uncomplicated life somewhere else. But I knew I couldn't. I knew I couldn't live a lie like that. I couldn't do that to her. I needed to give her a choice. I owed her that.

I think she can sense it, my pull.

"What's wrong?" she asks kindly.

I hesitate, suddenly flooded with the karma of my wrongdoings. Flooded with the feeling of knowing that I fucked up, big time. Knowing that what I say next could destroy her. How do I know that, and still follow through with it? How could I tell her something, knowing it'll hurt her?

"There's.. something else." I admit.

"What is it?" she asks without hesitation.

I pause again, drowning in fear. Drowning in resentment for myself. Gripping her closer, knowing it may be the last time I get to do so.

"I- I did something.. bad." I admit. She pulls away slightly.

"Go on." she says sternly.

This is it. This is the moment I might lose her. "I... I slept with someone else."

She pulls away completely. She looks confused, hurt. She looks betrayed.

"Who?" she asks, barely able to stand on her own two feet.

"Yana I-"

"Who, Cipher?" she demands to know. Looking at me with those disappointed eyes.

I want to deflect. I want to get on my hands and knees and beg for her forgiveness. But I know she doesn't want that- not right now.

"Maddison Sterling."

She gasps angrily, pacing as she tries to come to terms with what I've done to her. Rushing out the front door, probably to avoid waking everyone. I follow her. Both of us, immediately becoming soaked by the heavy winds.

"That rich junkie? Are you fucking kidding me?"

"Yana, I'm sorry-" I say, trying to hold her hands, but she rips them away from me.

"Don't! Don't.. touch me!" she says with disgust.

"Yana, I'm sorry. I'm sorry, I'm sorry! I'll live the rest of my life sorry-with regret, regret for everything I've done to you-"

"Did you even think of Alina in that moment!?"

I stutter, I couldn't answer. But she was right, right to feel that way. Right to question me the way she was. Right to look at me like that.

"Maddy- she's- does Fiona know?" she asks, confused.

"Yes."

"So she just *forgot* to tell me?" she asks, feeling betrayed.

"She wanted me to do it- she wanted me to take the fall!" I plead, hoping she hears me. Hoping she doesn't blame anyone but me. "Fiona hates me for it almost as much as you do."

My words cutting through her like knives. She buries her face in her hands and breathes heavily. Maybe she's having a panic attack. Panicking because she doesn't know what to say- how to react. I feel terrible for making her feel this way. For putting her in this situation. I wish I could do everything all over. If I could, I'd do so many things differently.

"You know- the worst part, Is that I *don't* hate you. I *should*! But there's some sick little voice in the back of my mind telling me that I love you and I fucking hate that little voice!" she explains, tearing up as she looks at me.

"I don't expect you to know what to do now- I just wanted to give you the choice that you deserve."

"Choice for what?"

"To decide if you still want to be with me. To decide if you still want me in your life."

"We have a kid together, C! I don't get to make these choices when there's other people involved!"

"I know, I know. But I want you to know that if there's ever a choice, I pick you. I pick you because It's always been you!" I plead, holding her hands and forcing her to listen to my confession. "I have loved you since the day I met you- since we were kids, sneaking away from our siblings to go and kiss by the willow tree. I have loved you- I was born to love you!" I begin to tear up, feeling emotional with the energy. "Fuck- I'd kill myself everyday if it proved to you that I'd do anything to get you to forgive me."

"And if I chose you- If I chose to forgive you, what does that say about me? What does that teach our kids about relationships?"

"It- it'd teach our kids that... that love is powerful. That love should be cherished."

She drops her head, penalizing herself as her forehead leans against my chest. Fighting my every urge to kiss her again.

The rain patter around us beating against our dying hearts.

After a moment, she finally looks up at me again. At some point our hands had joined together- though we couldn't remember when. Her eyes search mine and I search hers. Those big green eyes I've had the privilege of looking at my entire life.

"I- I need time.. to think." she finally admits.

My heart feels heavy with her decision, but I understand. Anything is better then a no.

"Okay." I finally say. "Okay, Yana. I can give you that."

It felt like magnets begging to pull us closer. Begging us to kiss and forget everything. But she's stronger then me. Strong enough to pull away and turn her back to me. Walking toward the sage door, glancing over her shoulder, before disappearing into that house.

I felt my entire body break down. I walked over to Alina's window with her closed yellow princess blinds, and sobbed quietly into the glass. Hoping the sound of the rain storm dulled my whimpers.

My beautiful little girl, I'm so sorry. I'm sorry for all the mistakes daddy has made. But I'll be better, for you. I promise.

12

Chapter Twelve- Blue

Fiona Glass

The next few months felt different, like a weight had been lifted off of everyone's shoulders.

The most shocking of the days was when I'd heard a knock at the door, and was greeted by Nadia. My dad had called her.

Cipher and Yana aren't together still, but I think they are trying to be friends- for Alina, and the new baby. A girl, by the way.

And Cipher has been trying to get a new house, because he knows that he needs to act in order to prove to Yana that he is all in. I hope he means it, I hope he proves himself right. They know it'll never be easy, but it will get easier.

Blue and I spent an entire month cleaning up dads house. Grandpa Rupert had shown up, sweating and appearing dazed. He was kind, for the first time actually speaking to Blue like he was a real human. He was distracted by the sight of the house. A mess of wall holes, chipped paint, dead gardens, and tobacco stains. I guess he remembers what it looked like, back when my mother fixed it up.

I'd never before seen that man without his tie on. I'd never even really had a proper conversation with him. But he and dad clearly used to be good friends, picking jokes at each other. Grandpa Rupert making fun of my dad for the fact he needs a wheelchair, and my dad making fun of Grandpa Rupert's bad knees. And it was fun working with him to clean the house, to make it something new.

Cipher even offered to help Blue redesign his old bedroom to make it more him.

We spent the entire month repainting walls, fixing the holes, buying new furniture to replace the old broken furniture. Finally getting my dad a new couch, as the old one started to reek of piss and body odor. Melody also came around too, helping to teach me about gardening, and how to keep up with it. Justin, Yana, Alina and Dare came over too, helping us fix the wooden panels outside, and to remaster the exterior of the house with vibrant colours.

Grandpa Rupert even surprised Blue with a brand new pet. My dad is very slightly allergic to cats. Nothing deadly, it just gives him a really runny nose when he's around them. So to pester him, Grandpa Rupert gave Blue a brand new kitten. The look on my dads face was worth a million kittens when Grandpa Rupert walked in. Nadia's laugh was undeniably hilarious.

A little brown kitten Grandma Uma had found beneath their house a few days prior. Alone and desperate for a home. The kitten was a girl, and had the most beautiful blue eyes.

When I asked Blue what he wanted to name it, with a massive toothy smile on his face, he looked to our dad.

With a subtle snarl, my dad finally gave in. Naming the little kitten 'Goldie'.

Everything seemed better, different. Filling the house with photographs of us definitely made it feel more cozy.

I quit Queen shortly after my mum's funeral, and I've been working as a florist in the city. A little boutique called 'Mother Orchid'. Melody's sister, Harmony, owns it. Apparently, gardening runs in the family.

I'd never met Harmony before, until the interview. But she's exactly like Melody. They're twins, so they look identical. Very soft spoken. The only way I tell them apart, is that Harmony's hair is graying slightly more then Melody's.

Harmony has kids too. She's had two Husbands in her life. With the first she had 3 kids, and 5 Grandchildren. With the second she has 4 kids, and 8 grandchildren. She's a lovely lady.

Her boutique is right next to a candle shop too, so I always bring home bouquets and candles to coat the house with homely smells.

I still see Maddy. She and Cipher avoid each other at all costs, which kind of makes it awkward. She still talks to Beau, and last I heard, Beau and Link don't talk anymore.

Blue's 14 now, and he's been a lot more excited about going to school recently. Mrs Keen told me it might have something to do with a new student, named Amber.

On this particular day, he did not have school. For his birthday, Cipher gave him a new dirt bike, and showed him some of the tracks he, Brownie and Dare made behind the house. He's out there right now, practicing while he waited for Cipher and Brownie to finish work so that they could join him.

I was inside, loading the dishwasher, when I heard a subtle knock on the door. I thought maybe it was my dad and Nadia, maybe they forgot to grab the house key when they left to do the grocery shopping.

I looked at the key hooks on the wall on my way to the door, and saw that only my keys were there. Hmm.

I approached the door, opening it. Immediately startled by the people standing in front of me. Beau Jones, and Jasper Krike. Both holding two big boxes.

"Hey Fi." Beau greets, with a sunken smile.

Speechless, I close the door behind me, as I step outside to greet them both.

"What are you guys doing here?" I ask softly. Hoping there's no one else hiding around a corner to convince me to do something I don't want to do.

Beau looks down at the boxes they're both carrying, before they place them down in front of me. They both seem quiet. Numb.

"They're from Link's." Beau explains. "Thought it'd be best if we brought it over here."

"What is it?" I ask curiously.

"Stuff you left there- clothes, some of Blue's school books." Beau explains, barely looking me in the eye.

"Oh.." I respond, trying to think of what I'm supposed to say.

"Are you okay?" Jasper asks, abruptly.

"I think so." I say slowly.

"I'm sorry." Blue interjects.

"For what?"

"I- I know it's not an excuse, but.. our parents fucked us up bad. It makes it hard to function like a normal person, when you were never shown how." Beau explains, choking back his sobs.

"You're pretty good at pretending." I compliment, dryly.

"Yeah-" he chortles. "Yeah, I- Unlike my brother, I don't hate the world. I don't have room for hate. I know who's fault it was, and I don't want to give anyone a reason to say I deserved it."

"You didn't deserve it-" I object. "Neither of you. You were kids."

Beau nods, quickly wiping his eyes before allowing a singular ounce of emotion to crack through his exterior.

"Beau-" I say, waiting for him to look at me. "You didn't deserve it- any of it."

He nods again, unable to fight against his emotions. I pull him in, hugging him tightly. I felt, it is exactly what he needed in that moment.

"Do you hate me, Fi?" he pleads, as he cries deeply into my shoulder.

"Of course not." I say, looking up at Jasper, who's just as heartbroken. "I could never hate you, Beau."

He sobs, he sobs loud. I've never heard someone sob so much into my ear. I feel awful. Awful that someone as good and pure as Beau, is cursed with the memory of his last name. Of the opinions it provides.

It takes a while for him to pull back, to look at me. Jasper patting our shoulders.

"Can we still be friends?" Beau asks, removing every bit of shame and ego. Reminding me of what it feels like to be in a Primary School playground. Begging everyone to be your best friend.

"Of course." I laugh, looking at both Beau and Jasper. "I still love you both."

"Me too." Jasper responds vaguely, buried beneath his tight throat.

They didn't stick around for long, but we spoke, over text. I didn't want to ice Jasper and Beau out, after all, they are not the fault for someone else's wrongdoings. They know that what Link did to me was wrong, and I'm honestly surprised they had enough courage to tell me that.

I carried the box's into my bedroom, placing them on the floor. I used my tweezers in my vanity to rip open the tape to see what was inside.

When I looked, I saw it was filled with mine and Blue's things. A few pieces of clothing, our spare toothbrushes, some old candles, and some of Blue's school things. All stuff we left at Link's apartment.

Stuff I expected, except for one particular thing. A letter, addressed to me, in the second box. My world froze in place when I saw the handwriting inside. Handwriting I could never forget.

Dear Fiona,
I'm sorry for everything. I'm sorry I couldn't be the man you needed me to be, or the man you deserved. Never doubt my love for you, because no matter what, I always loved you. I have never and will never love anyone like I love you. You always saw the good in me, even when there might not have been any.
I told you at the funeral that I knew what I had to do to fix this, and I'm going to keep my word. I have to disappear before I cause you anymore destruction. I have to leave, knowing that you will be okay while I'm gone.
I don't know If I'll ever come back, If not I know it'll be because I'm still not good enough to be with you.
As much as It kills me to say, I hope you meet someone who compares to how perfect you are. I hope someone cherishes you, and treats you better then I ever did. I hope you get to have a big family of your own like you always dreamed of, and I hope one day you forgive yourself for all the things you couldn't fix. You don't deserve to live a life in regret, you deserve everything that is great. You deserve to make all of your dreams and wishes come true.

```
You're a good person, the best person I will ever meet. I know
the universe has already given me too much by giving me you,
even if it was for only a short while.
So now I will repay my honour by letting you go. Even if it
hurts.
I love you so much, and please trust that you will never be
forgotten. Trust that I will always be there, even if you can't
see me. You will always have someone in your corner.
Love you Fi, never forget that.
```

I couldn't stop myself from crying uncontrollably. My little Link. It can't be true. I can't accept it. I want to run out the front door and run all the way to his apartment and beg him to stay.

I'd say the sudden sight of Blue at my door may have been what stopped me. Sweaty and covered in dirt.

He rushes to sit beside me, looking to me with concern. I hand him the letter.

"Link is gone."

He takes a moment, skimming the words, reading the things he wrote. Understanding me- understanding me exactly. Better then anyone else ever could.

My heart shattering into billions of pieces. Replaying the last moments we had together. Wishing I kissed him one last time. Wishing I could forgive him for everything.

Blue instantly grabs my hand, as I sob into the air, unable to refrain my sound or overflow of tears.

"God, I love him, Blue. I love him and I know I shouldn't." I explain beneath my whimpers. "And I'm so fucking scared that no one will ever love me again- even if our love wasn't real. To me, it was still love."

Silence befalls over Blue's calculated expression as he struggles to know what to do.

"I love you." Blue finally whispers with a sweet and sorrowful hush.

The world stopping in real life at the sound of his beautiful voice. His sweet, young, innocent, and real- so fucking real- voice.

My breath is heavy, unable to compile a true response. I instantly pull him in, my baby brother, hugging him tighter then I've ever hugged anyone. Sobbing so hard I feel like we're floating in the clouds. Peace, purity.

"I love you too- I love you so much!" I compile. He hugs me tighter.

Suddenly, he pulls away, standing up and walking over to my vanity, grabbing his journal.

He sits back down in front of my wide eyes, and holds it out to me. His journal, his words, his thoughts. All collected and organized like poetry. Touching it felt like reaching for glory.

I could never explain the feeling- feeling of true understanding. The feeling of utter acceptance. Utter passion. Utter and unconditional love.

It was real, he was real. He's here with me. He loves me. He trusts me.

I feel the urge of flying as I open the first page, and inside is the old goodbye letter left to me by Skye when she died. Here it is. I'm holding all the answers to every question I've ever had, all in my own two hands.

I'd forgotten what it felt like, to feel inspired. I hadn't been writing for a long time. Life just got so busy that I forgot to do the things I enjoy.

Later that evening, Nadia was cooking dinner while dad watched TV, squeezing his ball. Cipher and Brownie were carving the dirt tracks with Blue, and I was sitting in my bedroom. At the desk I hadn't sat in for a long time. With the laptop I hadn't opened for months.

Seeing my background, a picture of Link and I. I quickly changed it, finding a picture of myself, Cipher, Blue, Alina and Yana the night of my mothers funeral. My dad had taken it, he took so many photos that night. My dad has always loved taking photos, especially of us. I think that is something he had forgotten to enjoy. I forgot my writing, and he forgot his photos.

I've always wanted to be a famous author, and for the longest time, I thought my first book would be some kind of romance novel. That I'd make all my money through the relationship of a boy and a girl. I thought that It'd be inspired by Link, my first love. Of our love. But now I know that it can't be. I can't fabricate a lie through the blood of trauma.

I want my story to be real, I want to be heard. I want people to feel heard too.

I thought back to a conversation I had a long time ago with Skye. One of the first afternoons we'd spent together out of school, smoking a cigarette for the first time. She asked me what I wanted to be, and I said an author. She told me to include her, to write a book about her. I never even considered it at the time. I just wish she could be here to tell her side of the story.

I stayed up so late that night, just writing. Writing down ideas, plots, characters. Backstories, personalities, highlights. I spent so long writing that I forgot what time it was. I was so consumed in this story that it felt real. And to be honest, it was.

I realised that my story should be something inspiration, and what is more inspiration, then the story of my baby brother. Or the story of Skye. Or the story of Beau Jones.

So many people, with so many devastating stories. All three of them with completely different endings. Three different outcomes, among a billion.

I spent an entire year writing that book. Draft after draft. Editing over and over again. Making sure that every aspect was perfect. Zero regrets.

I named it 'Life In Blue' by Fiona Glass. It took a long time for me to pick the perfect title. I hoped that Blue would read it, and understand that his name does not represent sadness. But instead, it represents the colours of life. It represents the shades we need to survive.

Sadness, Happiness, Anger, Regret, Hope, all of these colours are important in their own ways. Blue understands more then anyone that life is worthless when it is only allowed one singular feeling- fear. That you do not experience life to it's fullest, unless you have experienced everything. All of the colours.

Can you imagine how dull the world would be, if it was forever green? We spend our entire life, trying so hard to understand ourselves, not knowing that it isn't us that we need to understand- but the world.

I know that now. I know that everything happens for a reason, I just need to find it. Because living with regret, that is worse then living in blue.

Yana gave birth to their second daughter a few months before I finished my book. Her name is Willow.

It made me realise how badly I want that- to be a mother. I know how easy it would be to fall back into my past. To forgive Link and live a life forever painted in misery, but easy.

But I know I will never get that. To experience true and utter love. Love for my family, for my friends. Love for my child.

I think that what he wanted, was a mother. While I wanted a lover. And that will never work, no matter how hard we try.

We both wanted love, but in different shades. We both wanted love, but with different standards. We both wanted love, but with different outcomes.

I understand that now. And I know I should hate him, but I don't want to live a life full of red. I don't want to live a life, drowned in orange regret.

The world is forever mine. My little shades of Blue.

No matter the truth, I will not allow the **red** destruction.
No matter my youth, I shan't threat the **orange** of regret.
To my child self. Forever tinted in the **yellow** of nostalgia and innocence.
Never to be destroyed.
Forever protected, in a bubble of **green**.
However the threat of **blue** rain, never to be captured in chains.
For **purple** fear, shall never destroy the sphere.
And **pink** desire, will never harm the choir.
Eternally painted in the **colours** of life.

Epilogue

Blue Glass- The Journal
('A Glimpse' from 2021-2026)

It is Fiona's bday teday. I think I am better at writin. My teecher say my spellin is getin beter.

I am tryin to write beter becuse school is hard and I want to mack frends. Most of the tim I jus draw picters or practus with leters, but I want to do good at school.

Fiona has ben workin at her new job. I like comin to work with her becaus the girls are realy nice and they help me with my home work. I don like goin home some times becaus I don like seein dad be sad. Some times when I cant sleep I look at my baby book. My dad said I can look at it whenever I want. I like seein pichurs of my self becaus I never got to see them befor. Some times dad watches sad movees on the teevee and it makes him sad. I don like seein him sad becaus it makes me sad too. I don like when he drinks becaus he gets loud and mum use to drink all the time and I did not like it.

Emma com to school and see me all the time. I like Emma becaus she is nice and she is frend with Mrs Keen. Emma help me som time in my class to help me lern.

Fiona wen to work after diner and I stayd home becaus Fiona wanted me to sleep eerly tonight. I was sittin in Ciphers room and I was lookin at his music stuff. I like Ciphers cds. I don like when music is lowd but I like lisening to some songs. I herd my dad talkin to the teevee so I walked out and ased him what was rong. He sade that the movie made him up set becaus the animals in the movie were bein sad. I think It was a movie about a baby deer and a bunny. My dad ased me to sit down with him and wach the movie. My dad ased me If I like school. I don have any frends yet, but I like my classes and Mrs Keen. Mrs Keen helps me with my writin and she told me that she wants me to write in my journal if I'm sad or mad. My dad told me that when he was in school he wasn't very smart. He sade that he had to go to speshal classes when he was my year. He sade that Ronny was relly smart and that he loved school. Dad sade that I am like him becaus we both are not very smart. I liked that he sade that to me. It made me feel happy becaus now we can help eech other.

I wan to tell my dad he make me feel better but I can not. I wan to tell my dad that I do not like school but I can not. Maybe he can reed my jornal but my writin is not very good yet. Maybe he can reed it when my writin is beter.

Cipher is allwas sad. Cipher comes to Fionas work and he crys a lot. Cipher has a kid her name is Alina. I love Alina becaus she likes to play weth toys and she does not relly talk. Cipher allwas drinks and it makes him sad. I do not want to drink EVER becaus drinkin allwas makes you sad. My mum allwas was sad when she drink stinky drinks and I hate it.

I like wen Cipher comes over. I like when Cipher and Fiona and dad are at home becaus I miss them. When I'm at school I miss them and I want to go home. I do not now why but I still do not have frends. I try to play with the kids but I get shy. Some time the boys put blue tack in my hair. Some time peeple ask me why my name is Blue. Some time peeple laugh at me becaus my name is Blue. I think my name is weerd. It is a colour. I do not now why my name is a colour.

Yusra sade I look sad at Fionas work. She sade that I can talk to her If I want but I can not. I don like talkin. Talkin is scary and I mite get in trobble. She sade I can talk abat school to her if I wan but I do not wan to talk. It makes me feel sad to talk. But Yusra made me feel better. Yusra sade that some time peeple can be mean to her at school. She sade that peeple laugh at her name too. She sade that some time she calls her name Star becaus some time it is fun to lie. She sade that I should not be frends with meen peeple.

I had a bad dreem abat mum las nite. I do not wan my mum to com back. I do not wan to leeve Fiona. I like Link too. Link is funny. Link has a brother like me and Link told me that his brother can not write very good words. Link said that his brother went to speshal class too like my dad becaus he can not write or reed very good. It is good that maybe I can leern and maybe 1 day I can be beter.

I like it when Fiona cuts my hair like Cipher. She dos it all the time becaus we are brothers and we look the same. Cipher sade dad use to do the same hair cut too befor he lost his hair. I hope I do not lose my hair.

I hav ben takin drinks from Fionas work for my dad becaus my dad miss them. My dad was sad when Fiona was away with Link and sade he wants a drink. I try to giv him water but he say no. He ask me to get drink from the cabinet. It was one of the bad drinks. I start takin bad drinks from Fionas work from the big boxs and put them in my school bag so that my dad can drink them. I hope Fiona dose not find out. I hope Fiona dose not get mad at me. I just want my dad to be happy. He has been crying a lot becaus my mum makes him sad like she makes me sad and when I feel sad I like to listen to music. When my dad feel sad he drink so I get him drinks to make him feel happy again.

I was scard that Fiona mite die. Fiona was workin and then Max told me that Fiona was waitin for me in Beaus car. Max and Yusra weer there and Fiona was lyin down in the back seat. Yusra and Beau were yellin. I could not see Link and it made me scard. I could not see Cipher becaus I did not know where he was. Fiona keep fallin sleep in the back seat and Beau was drivin relly fast to Links house. Beau also calld Maddy and told her to come becaus Beau wantd to find Link. I wantd to cry in the car becaus every one was scard. I do not know why Fiona was fallin asleep and why every one was scared, but I did not like to see her like that. Fiona was vomiting on the floor and Jasper had to help Beau get Fiona in to the bath room. I wantd to give Fiona a bath but I could not tell Beau and Jasper. Baths make me feel better all the time with soap and bubbls. It scard me becaus Jasper and Beau did not know what to do becaus Fiona kept vomitin and kept askin where Link and my big brother weer on Beaus phone. Beau and Jasper wantd to put Fiona in the cold shower so when Jasper turnd the cold water on I turnd it off becaus the cold will make Fiona more sad. I know becaus I have feel it before. When Maddy came to Links house she asked me if I wantd to go home but I did not want to. I wantd to sleep in bed with Fiona becaus if I was sick Fiona wood sleep with me too. Fiona was cryin in the bath room in Beaus lap and he was hugin her. Fiona was cryin becaus she wantd me and dad and Cipher and Link. Fiona told Beau and Jasper not to leev her becaus she is scard. I sat with Fiona and Beau and hold Fionas hand to try and make her happy. Beau try to ask Fiona what happen and Fiona was sayin that some 1 hurt her and that he made her sad. When Maddy got Fiona in bed Beau and Jasper left to go ask Tarn who was with Fiona at work to make her sad. They also want to find Cipher and Link. I am sleepin with Fiona so that when she waks up she will not be scard becaus I am here. Good night journal.

My reedin is gettin better so I reed some of Fionas journal words. I know It is bad but I want to know who hurt her at work. I want to ask Fiona but I can not and it maks me sad. Fiona had a best frend namd Skye who die. Fiona and Skye had a lot of boy frends and 1 of the boy frends hurt Fiona and Skyes feelins and Skye die. Skye rite Fiona a note like a journal when Skye die but Fiona did not reed it. It makes Fiona very sad that Skye die and she was too sad to reed her note. I think Fiona will reed it and she will feel happy agan. Fiona is my best frend and I do not like her bein sad.

My dad giv me some shirts today. Fiona was with Link becaus they are fitin so I stay at home with my dad. I have not seen Nadia for a bit and I miss her. She makes relly good orange jooce and she is relly nice. Some tims she brings me pensils and books to help me reed and lern new words. My dad was happy today and he told me to go to his bed room and find a big box in his closet. My dads room is very cleen but his closet is very dirty. I foun the box on the floor in the closet and I bring it to my dad by the teevee. My dad told me to open the box and insid was shirts. My dad told me that befor I left with mum my dads brother die. My dad told me that it makes him sad becaus he loves his brother like I love Cipher. My dad told me that when he was small his mum put dad and his brother in the same shirts. My dad told me to look at the pichurs in the box and told me that the boy on the left was always my dads brother and his name is Ronny. My dad is always on the rite in pichurs. My dad and his brother look the same becaus they are twins and that meens they have bdays on the same day. My dad and his brother had light hair colour when they were smaller. In the box there was a lot of pichurs and shirts from the pichurs. My dad sade that I can have the shirts. I think that is relly cool becaus I never got presents befor but now that I am with my dad I get presents all the time. I love my bday becaus I get presents and cake but some times my dad and Cipher give me presents when its not my bday and that is relly cool.

Mrs Keen is my best teecher. Mrs Keen sade that makin frends is hard some times and that soon I will hav lots of frends. Mrs Keen some times ask me why I do not talk but I am too scard. Some times she ask me to rite words on paper to tell her how I feel and I always feel scard. Mrs Keen ask me why I feel scard but I do not want to say. Mrs Keen sade that no one can hurt me but that is not rite. I am scard becaus I do not want to be hurt and I am scard becaus I do not want to make some one sad. Some times when I talk to Mrs Keen I want to cry becaus Mrs Keen is relly nice and I want to talk but I can not. I feel like she is sad that I do not talk. Mrs Keen always ask me if I am scard of mum or of some one else. She ask me if some one ever hurt me and I nod my hed. I do not like to talk about it.

Mrs Keen told me to spend more time with my dad becaus it will make us both happy. My dad gets angry some times when he drinks and he braks glass so I cleend it up. My dad always is very quiet when he sees me when he is drinkin.

Fiona and Link have been fitin a lot. Fiona and Link have been yellin at eech other and I do not like it. I have to hide when they are mad becaus I do not like it. When they yell it makes me feel like I am scard. I do not like to dream about my mum and when they yell it makes me dream about mum. Link has been not happy and he keeps on yellin at Fiona and makin her mad. I am scard that some thing bad will happen.

Fiona and Link were yellin and then they were relly quiet. I am scard that they are not okay but I do not want to look. I am hidin in my closet.

I hope Fiona and Link are happy again soon becaus I miss when they were happy.

My mum send me a note to my dads house and I reed it. It made me relly sad and when I was at school I was too sad. A boy named Blake keep slamin my locker shut when I open it and it made me relly angry. He do it all the time but today I was sad becaus my mum sent me a note and so when he shut my locker again I got relly angry. I wantd to yell but I did not. I push him and so he push me back and then we had a fite. His frends hurt me too and then Mrs Keen and Mr Rokan stop us. My teecher sade I am sespented and I can not go back to school for a few days but I do not want to. I do not ever want to go back ever agan becaus Blake make me sad and I can not make frends. I want to have frends like Mrs Keen say but no one likes me and no one wants to be my frend. When Cipher pick me up I ran away becaus I was scard he wood be mad at me for fitin and I ran to Links house becaus I wantd Link to be there. Link did not like school so I wantd to see him but I could not find him. I made my self a jam sanwitch and wated for Link. I wated for a long time and I start to cry becaus I saw mums note. I cry until I fall asleep. I woke up when Fiona and Link were fitin again. They were yellin relly loud and I hide in my closet again. I cover my eers so I do not heer it and I try to close my eyes so I can sleep again but it did not work. I hate it when they fite.

Fiona told me she wood take me to dinner if I went back to school so I did. Mrs Keen try to talk to me about the fite but I did not want to. All I was thinkin about was dinner but Fiona did not pick me up becaus Cipher did and he take me to dads. I wantd to ask where Fiona was but I could not. I hope she comes later and we can go to dinner.

My mum is ded. She sade she was comin back for my bday but she is not becaus she die. Cipher and I were lisenin to a new CD called white pony by deftones. I relly like the songs but I was destractd. Fiona had a broose on her face and I know it was from Link. My mum would always have brooses on her face and it would make her relly sad and now Fiona is too. Cipher said he had to tell me a secret and I think it was abot Fiona but it was abot mum. He sade that mum has die and he was very quiet. He said that he is shure mum loves me and that she did not meen to leeve but some times things happen that we can not explane. It made me sad but also happy. I was sad becaus my mum die and I did not say good bye. But it make me happy becaus now she can not be sad or hurt any more. I cry while Cipher hug me but I cry with happy teers.

Fiona told me to work with Mrs Keen on some thin to say at my mums funeral. I do not want to talk but Fiona sade she can reed it to every one. Mrs Keen told me I shold rite abot things that make me happy but the only thing that make me happy is that she is ded. My mum is in heven and Im glad that she is. Mrs Keen ask me if she ever did any thing to make me smile or gave me any thing to make me smile but she did not. Mrs Keen ask me if I loved my mum and I do wich is why I am happy she is ded.

My mum had a funeral today and it was very sad. My mums parents spoke a lot abot when she was small and I did not under stand. I did not think my mum had a mum and dad becaus I did not see them. I did not know my mum had two sisters becaus I did not see them. My mum did not talk abot them to me becaus she only spoke about my dad some times. My mum told me that Fiona and Cipher love me and that they miss me and she talk to me abot my dad all the time when she was sad. I did not think my mum was ever small like me. It was relly hard for me to see her for ever box becaus I did not want her to sleep in the dirt. I wood not like to sleep in the dirt and she wood not. Fiona sat on the grass with me becaus I could not leev becaus I was watin to see if my mum would open the for ever box and come out. I was scard she wood try to open the for ever box after I left but I stay for a long time and she did not.

When I went to dinner with Fiona I thort Link mite come and I did not want him to becaus he hurt Fiona but he did not come. Fiona was relly happy at dinner and it made me feel better to see Fiona happy. When we came home there was a lot of peeple at my dads house. I like eyeball becaus he has a speshal name like Yusra and like me. Brownie also has a speshal name and I like it. I like heering every one be happy and every one larfin out side. I like seein Alina again and Yana becaus they are my frends. I like seein my dad and Cipher and Fiona happy too. I hope Fiona does not be frends with Link agan.

Link is gone. He gave Fiona a note where he said good bye and gave us our stuff back. Fiona was sad becaus she missd him but he was not good for her. I am glad that Link is gone. I thort Link was my frend but then he hurt Fiona and I did not like that. I knew that Fiona wood not feel better unless I talk so I did. I told her I love her becaus I do and I wan her to know it so that she does not go back to Link. I think Fiona will be okay becaus she has me. Fiona has done a lot to make me happy so now I need to do some thing to make her happy too. I think then we will be okay.

It is my birth day today and I went to school. Fiona told me that we would selebrat after school. I was sittin in my favourite class and my teecher Mrs Nework showed us a new student. Her name is Amber Wood. Amber has long dark hair and she wore pink glasses. Mrs Nework told Amber to sit next to me becaus it was the only chair. When Amber sat down I saw that she had yellow nails. I like Ambers name becaus it is a colour like my name. Mrs Nework told us to work with the person next to us and practise spellin words together. Amber askd me what my name was and I point to my name tag on my table and she smild. Amber told me that she likd my name too. Amber and I sat at the picnic bench out side the English rooms together during lunch. Today Fiona gave me a vegemite sandwitch an apple and an orange flavor juise box. Amber had leftover spag and a chocolate bar. Amber ask if I want some of her chocolate and I nod. Amber ask me why I do not talk but I did not want to speak. Amber gave me some of her chocolate and ask me if I want to be frends and I sade yes. After lunch I talk to Mrs Keen and I write on a paper that Amber wants to be my frend. Mrs Keen was relly happy for me. Mrs Keen told me that I should tell Fiona and Cipher and my dad when I go home becaus they will be happy for me too. I am so exited to finaly have a frend. I am so so very happy now.

www.ingramcontent.com/pod-product-compliance
Lightning Source LLC
LaVergne TN
LVHW050930080826
845145LV00001B/289

* 9 7 8 1 7 6 4 5 8 3 4 0 4 *